A KILLER PLOT

A KILLER PLOT

E. C. NEVIN

ZAFFRE

First published in the UK in 2026 by
ZAFFRE
An imprint of Bonnier Books UK
5th Floor, HYLO, 105 Bunhill Row,
London, EC1Y 8LZ

A CIP catalogue record for this book is
available from the British Library.

Hardback ISBN: 978-1-78530-611-2
Trade Paperback ISBN: 978-1-78530-610-5

Also available as an ebook and an audiobook

1 3 5 7 9 10 8 6 4 2

Typeset by IDSUK (Data Connection) Ltd
Printed and bound by CPI Group (UK) Ltd, Croydon CR0 4YY

Every reasonable effort has been made to trace copyright holders of
material reproduced in this book, but if any have been inadvertently
overlooked the publishers would be glad to hear from them.

The authorised representative in the EEA is
Bonnier Books UK (Ireland) Limited.
Registered office address: Block B, The Crescent Building
Northwood, Santry Dublin 9, D09 C6X8 Ireland
compliance@bonnierbooks.ie
www.bonnierbooks.co.uk

For Rob

Chapter One

Thursday, 5.45 p.m.

The book world is full of social butterflies, but Jane Hepburn is not one of them.

Though a butterfly would surely be crushed to dust at this event, Jane thinks to herself as she squeezes through a crowd of chattering young women. *So maybe it is for the best.*

Cecil Court, an ancient London side street lined with independent bookshops, troves of antiques and intriguing map dealers, is heaving. The crowd radiates from one shop in particular, but Jane is failing miserably to get closer. The early-September evening light bathes everyone in a golden haze, adding a Gatsby-like air to the clinking glasses, braying laughter and overly effusive greetings.

It's a little like being in a glamorous movie. Or a lot like being in a rugby match, Jane thinks as she is shoved roughly to one side.

Hopelessly, she peers over the crowd towards the shop at the beating heart of the event: Willow Tree Books. The name is regally painted in gold against the pitch black of the old-fashioned sign, the curlicue W weaving with the T. The perfect bookshop. If it wasn't for all the people, that is.

Jane can just about see the window display, the glass expanse crowded with special editions of one particularly beautiful hardback book. At the sight of it, her heart expands a little against the crowd. Her good friend Natasha Martez is here somewhere, shaking hands with those wishing to congratulate her on the publication of *One Dark Minute*, a 'whip-smart debut thriller which will astound, shock, and mesmerise'.

Jane is happy for her. Really. Jealous? No, no, not at *all*. Well, maybe a tiny bit. One can't help that. Especially if one's own crime-writing career feels about as promising as the government's climate-change plan.

Despite her impressive height of six foot, Jane can't yet see Natasha and even the broad shoulders she loathes aren't helping her with crowd control. A particularly nasty boy at school once compared Jane to the Michelin Man. Her friend Daniel Thurston, who should also be here somewhere, says Wonder Woman.

This isn't the first publishing event Jane Hepburn has been to. Just a few months ago, she attended the Killer Lines Crime Fiction festival, which took place over the course of four days in the Cumbrian village of Hoslewit. Though it was *slightly* marred by someone sticking a knife through the heart of Jane's literary agent on the very first evening, the upside was that Jane came away with the first friends she's made since acne gave way to greying hair.

It's with relief that she finds herself squeezed through the crowd like toothpaste from a tube to burst into an air bubble of space. She feels the cool bricks of a wall against her skin and presses herself back against it, tugging at the hem of her favourite red dress with a deep, steadying breath.

Her dear late mother, fond of an aphorism, may frequently have said *Seek and ye shall find,* but she had also been keen on that one about a needle in a haystack. So this needle is staying here until someone jolly well stands on her.

'Ow!'

Which doesn't take long at all.

Sadly, it isn't Natasha or Daniel, but a tiny woman in black who has stamped heartily on Jane's foot.

'Oh, no, I'm sorry!' She removes the heel of her patent Mary Jane from Jane's now-smarting big toe. The attacker only reaches Jane's chin but looks up with an apologetic smile. A sleek dark bob dances around her jawline, a bright purple streak running through it like a slice out of an apple.

Perfect pearls dot her earlobes, matching both the string of them around her throat and the milky pallor of her skin, and a silver moon studs one nostril. She is clutching to her chest a tote bag decorated with a dragon, her glossy black nails glinting in the afternoon sun.

'Don't worry,' says Jane with a smile. 'It's impossible not to stand on people in this.' She tries to gesture at the crowd, but her arm is pinned to her side by a large, round man standing next to her, so she wiggles her eyebrows instead. 'I feel like a tinned peach.'

The small woman looks grateful, and in her demeanour Jane recognises a fellow misfit.

She scans the crowd again – still no sign of her friends. As well as supporting Natasha, Jane's other plan for the evening was 'networking'. She's never quite managed to network in the past and is a little unsure of what it entails, but all good books start with a cautious first sentence.

'I'm Jane,' she says with as much confidence as she can muster. 'Jane Hepburn.'

'Lucy Tallow, nice to meet you.'

I'm great at this, Jane congratulates herself. *Already on a first-name basis.*

'I'm an editorial assistant at Eagle's Wing,' Lucy continues with a slight wince.

'Oh! I was published by Eagle's Wing!'

'You're an author then? Who are you writing for now? I assume you moved on to a bigger and better place.' There is a trace of bitterness in Lucy's voice, and Jane suspects that she, too, would rather move on to somewhere bigger and better than the small, perpetually cash-strapped Eagle's Wing Press. The editor is looking at her expectantly, and Jane realises she has been asked a question.

Ah, she thinks. *I forgot about the actual chit-chat involved in this networking business.*

She hesitates, scanning the crowd as though it will contain answers. The truth is, she *is* an author, but in this buzzy crowd of successful publishing people she can hardly bring herself to say it.

Jane Hepburn's PI Sandra Baker series consists of eight books, the last of which is yet to appear. All were produced by tiny independent Eagle's Wing with minimal fanfare, minimal readership, minimal financial compensation.

Jane had found a fair part of the process distinctly torturous. Waterboarding is one thing, but have you ever refreshed your empty email inbox so many times you get a blister on your index finger?

Change of pasture makes for fat calves, her mother would have said, which sounded bad to Jane but is apparently a good thing. So, in the final book of her series, the protagonist is shot while apprehending a gunman, and on the final page her heart stops beating at the base of the Angel of the North.

And now? Her editor has left the company, her agent is dead, her contract has ended – Jane is in the netherworld. A few literary agents showed vague interest – Jane had enjoyed a burst of internet fame after apprehending a murderer – but they'd all, fairly, asked to read some of the exciting new project she is supposedly working hard on. The new start. The other side of the new leaf.

However – and even her friends don't know the full truth of this – Jane Hepburn hasn't written a word. She is suffering, and never has the word *suffering* felt more apt, from writer's block.

Lucy Tallow is looking up at her expectantly like a baby bird in the nest, but words are sticking in Jane's throat. How to tell her that she *is* an author, but one without a publisher, without an agent, and without a single good idea? Is she even still an author at all?

Is Jane Hepburn . . . just a nobody?

'It's complicated,' she says with a pained smile.

Lucy puts a pale hand on her arm, squeezing gently. Jane notices that on one fingernail, she has painted a tiny dagger. 'Not everyone's path runs smoothly,' she says softly. 'Sometimes it's bumpy, or winding. Sometimes you even double back on yourself or turn the wrong way. But we'll get there, eventually.'

All very well and good, thinks Jane, *but can you direct me to the highway?*

It's been months since she has written anything – other than terminally boring emails about white-goods insurance for her day job at Baxter's Insurance. Night after night, she sits down at the desk in her one-bedroom flat and opens her laptop, only to be confronted with a blank page. She clicks around on the desktop a lot. She stares out of the window. She keeps a tally of how often her upstairs neighbour flushes the toilet. She eats a lot of cheese, cut into very small slices.

The furthest she has got is writing a thousand words of an underwater crime series, but that proved difficult due to the paucity of possible dialogue, and the issue of evidence immediately drifting away in the ocean. If only she had an *idea*. Something to start her off. Part of her hoped that this trip to London, the heart of the country's book scene, would be just that.

'If in doubt,' Lucy continues, 'you could consult a tarot reader? I've always found great comfort in the wisdom of the occult. Last time I checked, it said I'll be back on my planned career track in the next year or so.'

Oh, good, Jane thinks, edging a millimetre to the left. *I'm networking with a devil worshipper.*

Through the crowd, she thinks she catches a glimpse of the person she is here to see – Natasha Martez. The woman of the moment. But then she's gone again, probably swept up into a crowd of admirers, or pulled away by her editor – the famous Hugo Strauss.

She pushes herself up onto the tips of her toes, peering over the heads of the crowd. Near the shop door, she catches sight of her ex-editor and some authors she recognises from publicity photo shoots, but Natasha has vanished.

At her side, Lucy Tallow squeezes her arm again, and Jane doesn't know if it's the slightly patronising air, the mention of the occult, or something else entirely, but it sends a shudder down her spine.

She pushes back her shoulders and forces a smile to her face. This *will* be the start of something. Something, she hopes, very good indeed.

Chapter Two

Thursday, 5.50 p.m.

The party in Cecil Court puts Hugo Strauss in mind of the summer his ginger cat Roger died. Hugo had been thirteen, made to attend his mother's fortieth birthday party to be poked and prodded and cooed over for what felt like eternity. When they had got home that night, it was to find Roger dead on the road just outside the front gate, his tiny skull crushed by a car that had fled the scene. This was almost as bad. But at least at *this* party he hasn't been forced to wear a bow tie.

It's not just the constant clamour of those trying to get his attention – literary agents wooing his favour for their clients, junior editors hoping to climb the professional ladder, authors he has worked with in the past or who hope to work with him in the future. It's also the looming sense of dread that something bad is happening, all while having to smile and preen for people he couldn't care less about if they were the maggots in his food waste bin last August.

But despite the unease in his soul that has been worsening for the past six months, Hugo is here, because it's his job to be here. And he really is proud of this book. His author, Natasha Martez, is an extraordinary young talent originally hailing from Portugal, and he knows she will be a roaring success. Far more so than his last acquisition – a non-fiction book about the British sewerage system which he found fascinating, but reviewers found 'distasteful'. Edward Carter at the *Daily News* wrote that it put him right off sausage sandwiches, which was just childish.

Natasha though, thinks Hugo, *is different. This will be big.* It's the moments when you know you have discovered someone who will cause a million sleepless nights that make this job worthwhile. Soon, readers the world over will be lying in bed muttering 'just another chapter' to their annoyed spouses, simply unable to put down *One Dark Minute.* Hugo's been in this business for nearly forty years, but that thought still gives him a thrill.

Doesn't mean he likes the parties though.

By his right ear, a woman cackles at a pitch that could make dogs cry and bats shudder, and Hugo shuffles over as far to the left as he can. The noise reminds him of his wife, or ex-wife now he supposes, and the way she used to meet in the kitchen with her friends on a Saturday night. They would shriek with laughter like *Macbeth*'s witches over a cauldron of wine, and when he'd enter the room they'd all fall silent. He'd never understood why Jessie was friends with those women. My God, he misses her.

'Hey, Hugo!' One of the shriekers has spotted him. 'Come join us!'

Hugo grimaces and points to his throat, trying to signal that he has lost his voice while edging further and further to the left until he is out of sight. Always a good manoeuvre for these events.

He doesn't have time for nattering with tipsy publishers. He has work to do. It's almost time for him to make his speech, and he has serious business to conduct before that. Business that will require a little privacy, which isn't going to be easy with so many people around.

Cecil Court, in the centre of today's Theatreland, has been host to artists of every stripe for centuries. It is where Mozart lived while he composed his first symphony. At the turn of the nineteenth century, it was the beating heart of the film industry, known then as 'Flicker Alley', and now as London's 'Booksellers'

Row'. T. S. Eliot lived here, Foyles Bookshop started off over at number 16, and everyone from Graham Greene to Lawrence of Arabia has frequented these cobbles. This place has seen murder, it's seen romance, and it's seen many, many stories.

The fact that it's still lined with bookshops seems to Hugo a sign that the world is still in balance. That everything is solvable. Everything forgivable. Even the things *he* has done.

Across the crowd, a tall woman bashes into a group of guffawing men, who in turn bang into Hugo. Prosecco slops from his glass over his wrist.

'Sorry, mate!' one man says with a cheerful grin, not looking sorry at all. Since Hugo stopped drinking, this sort of party has become far less fun for him. Maybe it's just his age.

Despite never drinking, he always carries a glass of whatever is on offer. It avoids having to explain himself over and over again when progressively drunker people start insisting *Go on* while waving a bottle in his face. The now-half-empty prosecco glass in his hand is warm, the liquid already flat. Still, he clasps it in front of him like a shield.

Once he has conducted his business and delivered the speech, Hugo will quietly slip down the lane and round the corner, jumping on the tube at Leicester Square. Though maybe he'll walk the other way to avoid even more crowds, through to Covent Garden or Charing Cross. Maybe drop into the Ivy Club to grab a coffee in peace. Yes, that's the ticket. Then back to his Canonbury townhouse. His cat Roger VIII will be pleased to see him.

Chapter Three

Thursday, 6.30 p.m.

'Jane!'

Spinning around when she hears her name, the sight of a familiar crop of floppy brown hair fills Jane Hepburn with warm relief. Daniel Thurston's broad, toothy grin is a sight for sore eyes, and the boundless energy he seemingly always has surges towards her like electricity between conductors, or fleas between dogs.

'There you are! Come with me.' He grabs her by the arm and pulls her through the crowd. With a popping sensation in her ears, Jane bursts into the vacuum of an empty doorway. Well, almost empty – star of the event Natasha Martez is standing there smiling at her, eyes shining and cheeks glowing.

Jane hugs both of her friends and accepts some warm prosecco from Natasha. Cheers-ing their glasses with a clink, she feels a grin spread across her own face, as if it is infectious. All of a sudden, the evening seems full of promise rather than awkwardness.

Though they'd stayed in touch via phone, it's been months since she's seen her two friends, not since the exciting murd— sorry, *dreadful* murder in Hoslewit. But standing opposite Daniel, with his bright blue eyes and chiselled cheekbones, and Natasha, with her charming, sticky-out ears and naturally coiling ringlets pushed back in a ponytail, it might have been mere hours.

'I'm so glad you could come,' says Natasha. 'It means a lot to have my friends here tonight. My mum couldn't get over from Portugal – she can't leave Granddad.'

"/>

'How are you feeling?' Jane asks. 'Big moment, your first publication day!'

As Natasha tells her, pink-cheeked, about visiting bookstores to see her novel on the shelves, a fabulous lunch with her editor, Hugo Strauss, at an upscale restaurant, and then preparations for the launch party, Jane tries hard to remain excited for her. Even so, she can't suppress that little pang of jealousy from creeping in. Not in a *bad* way. Just like when someone you love gets the bigger slice of cake. You are happy for them, sure, but part of you still wants to swap plates.

Don't let the green-eyed monster eat you up, Jane hears her late mother say in her head. Quite right. Jane gives her friend another hug.

'And now,' Natasha concludes, 'I'm just waiting to get my speech out of the way, and then I can relax. I'm *terrified* about that part. There are so many people here.'

'You'll be great,' says Daniel, shaking back his floppy hair with an expert flick of the head. Whenever he does this Jane is reminded of a spaniel excited for its walk. 'We're proud of you, Nat.'

Natasha's face glows with happiness, dimples deepening in her chubby cheeks and her prominent ears turning red. As they chat, Jane can't help peering through the crowd to catch a glimpse of Lucy Tallow and feels oddly as though she'd imagined her in a time of need, just as she'd imagined her best friend in primary school – Gary the Canadian Mountie and his horse Jackson.

She does spot Edward Carter, a tall and bookishly handsome newspaper reviewer who had once asked her on a date – before she wrongly accused him of murder that is. She catches his eye and he raises his hand in an awkward wave before being pulled back into conversation.

Jane has exchanged a text here and there with him since their last meeting. She'd plucked up all her courage to call him once, but he didn't return it. They live in different counties and so a relationship is impractical, but still, his dismissal of her stings.

'Enough about me,' Natasha says, placing a hand on Jane's shoulder to get her attention. 'How is *your* writing going?'

Luckily, just as Jane opens her mouth to try and form an answer, the heart-shaped face of a young woman appears at Daniel's shoulder. She's startlingly beautiful, smartly dressed in a cream linen jacket, with pale-blonde hair curling across one shoulder with an artful elegance Jane can only dream of. A large gold ring flashes on her pinkie finger and her eyes, the colour of the sea in a holiday brochure, invite the viewer to dive right in.

'I'll be taking that, Daisy,' Daniel says with a triumphant laugh, plucking the prosecco bottle from her hand. Her perfect cupid's bow mouth forms a round 'O' in shock, before she breaks into a grin.

'Daniel Thurston, you rogue,' she says with a laugh, swatting him on the arm and pulling the bottle back. 'I *need* that,' she says, recapturing the prosecco. 'My ex-boyfriend is here. Don't be surprised if I bolt off early – and if I do, I'm taking this with me.' Rolling her eyes, she pats Daniel on the arm and slips away.

'Daisy Olsson,' he explains to them. 'She's Hugo's assistant. I don't know her well but she's super friendly. Started at Polar Bear not long before I did.'

'I've had a few emails from her,' Natasha says with a chuckle. 'She keeps calling me Natasha *Martin* and my book *One Dark Mitten*.'

Mercifully, the others seem to have caught on to Jane's reluctance to talk about herself, so instead, in high spirits they discuss Daniel's new job as a publicity assistant at Polar Bear Publishing and the publicity for Natasha's book.

Eventually, the tolling of church bells in the distance interrupts Daniel's story about how he choked on his lunch on his first day at work and Jane glances at her watch.

'Seven o'clock. When are the speeches happening, Nat?'

Natasha frowns. 'Now, supposedly. Hugo was supposed to come get me twenty minutes ago.'

'Maybe you shouldn't be skulking in this doorway with us then?' Daniel says with a laugh.

'I'm not skulking,' she protests. 'I'm just . . . existing. In a doorway. Anyway, I told him I'd stay near this antique shop.'

'We'd better find him,' Jane says. 'He should be calling for everyone's attention.'

Natasha looks worried, searching the crowd the best she can on her tiptoes. 'He said he had to speak to a few people. Maybe something important came up?'

'What about your agent?' Daniel is saying. '*She* could do the speech instead.'

But Marabella Rhodes is eating croissants in the South of France with her new boyfriend, and Natasha explains that she isn't due back for another few days yet.

'You stay here,' Jane says. 'We'll find him.'

'Has anyone seen Hugo Strauss recently?' Jane and Daniel are pushing through the groups of people clustered in the alley-way. If it weren't for the disappearance of Natasha's editor, this book launch would have been deemed a roaring success. Everyone who's anyone in the UK book industry – and Jane Hepburn – is in attendance.

Daniel pulls out his phone and they huddle around it to look at a photo of Natasha's editor. Roman nose jutting proudly between high cheekbones, thick eyebrows raised in challenge. A white beard covers his lower face, artfully concealing a weak chin. The collar of his tweed jacket is just visible in the head-shot, adding to the overall impression that he is a relic from another age, a Harvard history professor . . . or a Basil Brush impersonator.

'Hey,' Daniel says to a passing group of women. 'Has anyone seen this man?'

One of them turns, a curvy blonde in a plunging jumpsuit.

'Hugo?' she says, glancing quickly at the screen.

Her voice has a surprising Yorkshire twang that makes Jane long for home, even though this woman's accent is dwindling after presumably years of working among upper-middle-class Southerners. 'No, sorry,' she says brightly. 'Not seen him all night. Maybe he's snuck away with someone!' She raises her eyebrows suggestively before dissolving into giggles, and her friend pulls her away.

What was that *about*? Jane thinks, but Daniel is already holding the phone up to a young man in an alarming baby-blue tracksuit and leopard-print cap, shoulder-length curly blond hair protruding from under it. Maybe he writes experimental poetry. No luck with him either.

'Has anybody seen this man?' Jane shouts at random.

She's considering lifting Daniel up onto her shoulders for a better vantage point when a response makes her spin round.

'Hugo Strauss? I've seen him.'

Jane finds herself face-to-face with Edward Carter. The blush staining her cheeks feels hot and bright as glowing coals.

'Miss Hepburn,' Edward says, with that familiar diffident smile of his making a reappearance. 'Delightful to see you again.'

Edward Carter has a long, thin frame, as though he had a go on the torture rack as a boy. His grey eyes are kind but sad behind thick-lensed glasses, his peppery-blond hair neatly combed. 'Sorry I haven't called, it's been a . . . busy few months.'

'Edward! Lovely to see you too.'

Jane pastes her brightest smile onto her face, cheeks straining. Edward is a good man, and she feels the renewed fluttering of butterflies in her stomach as she meets his kind eyes. But he lives in London, she in Cumbria, and she has no desire to spend much time in crowds like this.

Quite apart from that, Edward is a coward. He'd shied away from helping the police when it came to his friend's murder at Killer Lines, despite having relevant information. He'd run when accused of committing the crime himself. And, she's realised now, he is too scared to risk gambling with his heart.

Yes, attractive as he is, Edward is a coward. Jane knows, after everything that has happened to her over the past few months, that she needs someone who will match her for courage. The realisation brings a burst of pride, and to her surprise, her fake smile morphs into a real one.

'I would love to catch up,' she says hurriedly. 'But we really *must* find Hugo. When did you see him?'

'He was here at the start. I last saw him talking quite intensely with Lambert Graves,' Edward says, using his six foot four inches to peer over the heads of the surrounding crowd, eyes narrowed behind his glasses. 'Can't see him now though. Have you looked inside? Hugo sometimes likes to find a moment's peace at parties.'

Jane peers doubtfully over at the window of Willow Tree Books, which, if possible, looks even more densely packed than earlier.

'Thanks, Edward,' she says with genuine warmth. 'Speak soon.'

'Come on,' Daniel says, with a look of steely determination taking over his face. 'We're going in.' He grabs Jane's arm and marches forward. 'Excuse me! Important author coming through! Get out of our way!'

Somehow, Daniel gets them to the doorway of the shop, where people are pushing in with empty glasses and out with full ones. Copies of *One Dark Minute* fill the window. The shop's special edition features wisps of smoke sprayed on the edges of the pages, and the name 'Natasha Martez' is picked out in twinkling silver foil.

Daniel surges forward, clearly angering a handsome man with a golden-blond quiff of hair whom Jane vaguely recognises. As they become jammed in the doorway together, an incongruous scowl mars the man's perfect features, but it disappears almost as quickly as it appears. As a hand reaches from the crowd to grab him by the shoulder, his face transforms itself into a picture of delight. Pushing out of the shop, he smooths back his hair, rings glinting on his fingers, and flashes a bright smile before stepping out of view.

Daniel tugs on Jane's arm and they burst onto the shop floor.

Having a slight phobia of London, what with its baffling transport system and overpriced sandwiches and rats the size of dogs, Jane has never been inside this famous place. Even in the midst of their urgent task, she stops for a second to take it in. Shelves stretch up to the ceiling, featuring row after row of glorious books. Signed copies are boasted about with stickers, special editions proudly displayed, and rare first impressions protected behind glass. All of these words in one space; it gives Jane a buzz of pleasure.

'Jane! Come *on*.' Daniel is gesturing to her from behind a group of women refilling their glasses at the counter-cum-bar area, spilling fizzing liquid onto a book she hopes isn't expensive. He is standing next to a pale-faced Natasha, chewing on her bottom lip and wringing her hands.

'Is there a back room, Nat? Somewhere Hugo may have gone to escape the crowds?'

'There's the stock room in the basement.' Natasha nods at the door behind the counter. 'I signed my books in there the other week. I can't imagine he would be down there though . . . '

Jane has one hand on the doorknob when a high-pitched voice pipes up a challenge.

'Employees only. Read the sign.' A stressed-looking young woman with curly red hair is at the shop counter, topping up fresh glasses and handing out slices of a huge Victoria sponge cake.

'I'm with Natasha?' Jane says. The sales assistant narrows her eyes and Jane straightens her spine, trying to embody a confident haughtiness that no one would dare argue with. 'And . . . and she, *the author,* has told me I *need* to check something in the stock room *at once.*'

The red-haired girl rolls her eyes and returns to the overflowing glasses.

'Whatever,' she mutters to herself. 'People aren't supposed to be down there, but you can't say I didn't try.'

Jane turns the handle, steps through the doorway, and closes the door behind her with a click.

She finds herself in darkness, the noise of the party not quite cut off but dulled to a muffled background buzz that feels far away. The sudden sensory deprivation is both immediately calming and slightly spooky.

Jane steps forward, one hand groping on the wall for a light switch.

'Mr Strauss?' she calls in a rasping whisper. 'Hugo? Are you in here?'

Though she hears no response, she continues searching for the switch, finally alighting on a swinging piece of string when it hits her on the nose. A sharp tug and a dull overhead light clicks on, filling the room with a low buzzing sound.

Jane edges down the concrete stairs into the stock room, ducking to avoid scraping her head on the low ceiling. The sound of the party dwindles with each step down she takes, and when she alights from the final stair it is into silence.

The room is a mess, but not devoid of any sense of organisation – a contradiction that many a writer understands perfectly. Cardboard boxes fill the floor, most with titles scribbled on the side in black marker pen.

As well as the boxes, piles and piles of books fill the room, some stacked almost to the ceiling. Even more so than the shop floor above, the space gives Jane an extraordinary thrill. Seeing behind the scenes of this famous shop makes her feel like she is truly part of something.

Though virtually all of life seems to be contained in the books in this room, one absence is glaringly obvious. That of Hugo Strauss. Jane knows she should go straight back upstairs to continue the hunt, but something stops her. Much like the missing Mr Strauss, she isn't one for parties. The solace in this quiet room full of books feels like a balm on her buzzing skin.

One minute more, then she must get out of here. Jane runs a hand down a stack of boxes, each labelled with titles, half of which she recognises. In some places the dust is thick; the boxes in corners look like they haven't been moved for years. She has turned to leave when her back gently knocks against something. With a sickening sense of dread, she squeezes her eyes shut as though this may stop time. A tottering pile of books sways undecidedly next to her. When she spins around to try and steady the entire stack in her outstretched arms, she simply precipitates the inevitable. She whacks it sharply with one elbow and forty books crash to the floor simultaneously.

Her eyes flick towards the door – still closed. The noise above has hopefully drowned out the clatter of the landslide she has caused. She gets on her hands and knees and begins to pile the books back on top of one another frantically, with no regard for their original order. What was she thinking, poking around down here? She needs to be upstairs, helping her friend.

But, reaching for a chunky poetry anthology, she stops. Because suddenly, the tumbled stack of books no longer seems important.

Just visible behind some nearby boxes, Jane can see one shiny black shoe.

On her hands and knees, she crawls towards it, sending the newly stacked books back to the floor as she edges past them. Inch by inch, more of the shoe comes into view, followed by a long leg, a linen-jacketed torso, and a white, wide-eyed face with cherry-red cheeks.

It seems remarkable all of a sudden that she hadn't detected the tang in the air, lingering beneath the scent of new books and old dust. It fills her nostrils now, fills her throat, fills her eyes. The familiar smell of death.

Jane crawls towards the body in disbelief.

And still, under her shock, a question resurfaces with new urgency.

'Where,' whispers Jane in the silent basement, '*where* is Hugo Strauss?'

The dead body of Daisy Olsson doesn't answer.

Chapter Four

Thursday, 11.45 p.m.

Jane tries to look at her watch subtly by stretching her arms, but the watch is small and her arms long, so it doesn't work. Instead, she coughs into the back of her left hand, but this time the watch face is too close to her eyes, and the overhead light bounces off the glass.

'It's 11.45, Miss Hepburn,' says Detective Inspector Hawberry.

'Oh, is it?' Jane stifles a yawn.

'Look, I know it's late. It's past your bedtime, I get it. But there has been a murder, and *you* were found with the body.'

DI Hawberry doesn't strike Jane as the warmest of women. A scowl was etched onto her face when Jane first met her at Willow Tree Books, just after all hell broke loose, and it's still there five hours later. Her greying hair is pulled back into a severe ponytail that tugs at her skin, angry red eczema marks the back of one hand, and her cheap suit jacket is a little too tight across the shoulders. Everything about her screams discomfort.

'Many people would consider finding a dead body rather traumatic,' Jane says with a kindly smile, to try and soften her up. 'But I've found one before, so you'll find me hardier than most. I'm here to help.' You never know why someone's built up a wall of aggression. Maybe she thinks Jane herself is the killer. Or, worse, a generally unpleasant person.

'Um, right.' The detective looks momentarily thrown but still doesn't crack a smile. 'Well, that's something we'll probably have to get to later. *This* murder is what we are talking about today.'

'It was then – a murder? You're sure?'

Jane had immediately suspected as much, but there hadn't been any blood on Daisy's body, no visible wounds. She could have dropped dead of a sudden heart attack, a brain aneurysm, any number of things. But no, the angry expression on Hawberry's face tells Jane clearly that this is murder. Even if the inspector doesn't want to dignify the question with an answer.

Despite having written eight detective novels, Jane has never been inside a police station. Well, she went in once to report the theft of her handbag, but never past the front desk. The police weren't that interested in the handbag theft, which turned out to be for the best when Jane got home to discover she'd left it on the sofa.

She certainly hasn't had the luck to get inside a *real interview room* before. Of course, she's seen them on the telly, but that's just not the same, is it? Despite her tiredness, she can't stop her eyes from darting over the room, taking in the bland nothingness of the space and filing it all away in her writer's brain.

Sadly, it wouldn't make for a particularly rich description in a book. Grey lino flooring. Uncomfortable grey chairs. Walls that, although painted white, give the depressing impression of greyness nonetheless.

There isn't even a two-way mirror, which is a shame because Jane has always wanted to look into one of those and raise an eyebrow knowingly. She contents herself by doing it at the CCTV camera in the corner instead.

The world-weary chatter of the investigating officer she had dealt with when Carrie Marks was killed, Detective Inspector Ramos, had been a lot less intimidating than this woman's ferocious stare. However, Jane is becoming concerned that the London Met might be even less amenable to hearing her ideas than Ramos was. And she always has *plenty* of ideas.

'If you don't mind my saying, Detective Inspector,' Jane begins, 'I've had some thoughts about the crime scene. You see, when I—'

'I *do* mind. Now, tell me why you were in that basement? It was clearly labelled as being for staff only. You, unless I am mistaken, are *not* employed there. You are . . . ' Detective Inspector Hawberry checks her notes '. . . some sort of *author*?'

She says the word with disdain, leaning back on her uncomfortable chair and folding her arms. The stiff plastic bends dangerously and Jane wants to reach out and pull the woman up straight. It's not going to help anybody if Hawberry cracks her head open, and it wouldn't make Jane look good at all.

'I was looking for Hugo Strauss,' she says, opening her hands in a show of honesty she'd learnt from *The Mind of a Murderer*. What if Hawberry has watched the same episode and realises what she is doing? Jane closes her hands into tight fists. Hawberry looks a little alarmed. 'Hugo was supposed to be giving a speech about Natasha's book – do you know Natasha Martez? It was her launch party. It's a great book.'

'Right. I don't really read. Tell me more about this Hugo Strauss.'

'You don't read? But there are so many detective stories, I bet you could learn a l—'

'Tell me about Strauss.'

Hawberry is proving to be more of a disappointment by the second. Jane thinks back to her fictional Private Investigator, Sandra Baker, and how she ploughed on with the disagreeable Detective Fields in book two, *Murder at Dawn*, until he broke down and agreed to share a bottle of wine with her. Perseverance, that's the ticket.

Despite the fact that she is starting to feel so tired she could topple off her chair, Jane pushes back her shoulders and puts an Extra-Strong mint in her mouth to keep herself alert. She wishes someone would offer her a cup of tea. That is protocol in this sort of situation, isn't it? People can't be expected to answer questions without *tea*? This isn't *France*.

'Mr Strauss is an editor,' she says patiently, the icy blast of the mint pushing back exhaustion. 'He was due to give a speech but had gone missing and I decided to check the stock room.'

Detective Hawberry frowns and scribbles something in her notebook. She has dark grey circles under her eyes, and her skin is dull and dry. Jane wonders if she is drinking enough water, getting enough sleep. Those things do wonders for the skin. She'd learnt that from a particularly glamorous American editor, though Jane suspects Botox may have played a part in her regime too.

'And that is where you found Ms Olsson?'

'Exactly.' Jane closes her eyes and pictures the scene. She shudders in the chill of the interview room. 'She – Daisy – was sitting in a chair. Just sitting there, like butter wouldn't melt. Sort of hidden behind boxes of books. But her head was slumped to one side like this,' Jane flops her head down onto her shoulder, 'and her eyes were open.' She widens her own. 'Cheeks all pink. I'd only just seen her when the sales assistant came down, saw us and screamed.'

It had indeed only been a moment, but one that Jane suspects will be seared into her mind until her own dying day. It won't be easy to forget those staring eyes, the open mouth, the glint of gold from the ring on one finger in the flickering light, the champagne glass lying smashed at her feet.

'Rather convenient, don't you think? That you happened to search for someone in the exact place – a room where you were not supposed to be – that the body was left?'

Jane remembers DI Ramos walking with her around the lawn in Hoslewit. *Are you a lucky person, Miss Hepburn? Because this is the second body you have stumbled upon this weekend.* Why these police officers seem to think she relishes finding corpses when she is simply trying to have a good time, she does not know.

'On the contrary, I didn't find discovering Daisy's body convenient at all. Have you secured the crime scene?'

'You call her Daisy, I notice,' snaps Hawberry. 'Rather familiar of you. Did you know the victim?'

'No, not really. She is – was – the colleague of a friend of mine. She spoke to him at the party. Does Daisy have any known enemies?'

'And y— what? Just answer my questions. You didn't touch the body, you say. Did you touch *anything at all*?' Hawberry fires the question at her like an accusation. Jane can picture her as a rabid little squirrel, snarling down from a branch. That's probably the lack of sleep too.

'Just some books. I knocked them over by accident.'

Hawberry sighs very deeply and makes another note. 'Of course you did.'

On her way out of the station, Jane has her fingerprints taken – sadly, on a little screen rather than with a pad filled with ink, like in the films. Even so, it is all rather thrilling. She tries to take a photo on her phone to show Daniel and Natasha, but the desk sergeant says she isn't allowed. Killjoy.

Name, address, fingerprints, phone number all given, Jane is finally pushed out into the night. It's dark now, or as dark as it ever gets in London. Charing Cross Police Station is on a back road, but even that is lit by tall streetlamps at either end.

Jane isn't well versed in London life. She has only been here once before, to meet with her editor and agent when her very first PI Sandra Baker book was sold to Eagle's Wing Press. And now she is on a quiet street, alone, in the middle of the night, with a dead phone battery. There are no taxis in sight, and she's not sure if the Underground – an unwieldy and confusing beast for the uninitiated – is even running at this hour, never mind where the nearest station is.

She had been planning on going straight back to Cumbria tonight in time for work in the morning, but that ship has now sailed. Or that train has now left the station, if she wants to be literal about it. All Jane wants in the world is to be transported to her bed in her little flat, a cup of herbal tea on her bedside table, a good book in front of her. The party had been wearing, the murder horrifying, the interactions with Detective Hawberry draining, and she is *exhausted*. She is just starting to feel a heavy sense of hopelessness steal over her when she catches sight of a two-headed silhouette under the streetlight. Sitting on the pavement, swigging from a bottle of wine, huddled together for warmth, the unexpected appearance of these two people fills her with a giddying sense of relief.

'Daniel! Natasha!'

The figures look up, and soon they are enveloping her in a bone-breaking hug.

'We were so worried!' says Natasha, pulling back to look at her friend's face. 'What happened? Why were you in there so long?'

'Were they grilling you?' says Daniel, white-faced. 'Trying to frame you? Did they *throw the book at you*?'

'No, no, nothing like that. You watch too much television.' Jane grins at her young friends, the loneliness of the past few hours vanishing like a packet of biscuits on a Sunday evening. 'I was waiting for *hours*. Then the detective just wanted to know why I was in the basement. She wasn't really interested in what I thought or anything like that.'

'Well, let's get out of here and you can tell us everything you told the detective,' says Natasha, shivering in the night air. These might be the dog days of late summer, but it was still the middle of a British night and Natasha had dressed for a party that ended at a reasonable hour.

'Let's get out of here,' agrees Jane, 'and in the morning, I'll tell you quite a bit *more* than I told the detective.'

Chapter Five

Friday, 10.00 a.m.

'*Je voudrais un plane*, now. *Un ami est trez . . . mort.*'

Marabella Rhodes is at the EasyJet desk in Nice Airport, try-ing and failing to get an earlier flight home. It's a shame really, she thinks as the girl behind the desk shrugs; she likes everything about France apart from the French.

'*Mort!*' she says again, louder this time in case that helps with the translation. She sometimes finds flapping her hands about works too, so she tries that. '*TREZ MORT?*'

Interminable tapping of computer keys and clicking of the mouse follows, some more back and forth in approximations of various languages, and, eventually, Marabella agrees to purchase a new ticket for the flight leaving in a few hours' time. It's heart-less and unfair, but at the end of the day, it's also only £12.99.

Sitting in Bar la Plage while she waits for her gate to be announced, Marabella taps out a text to her new boyfriend Eric to let him know what's happening. She is supposed to be in her St Tropez house for another three days, and she is most put out by having to leave early. It's Friday, and the local bistro has a special happy hour then that allows her to drink six glasses of Côtes du Rhône for just €18.

It also means she'll miss Saturday, and Saturdays in St Trop are possibly her favourite thing in the world. She planned to get up at 8 a.m., walk to the local boulangerie to order *deux croissants* and *deux cafés au lait* for their *petit déjeuner*, and then enjoy them on the terrace with Eric, reading books in companionable silence. She wanted to take a walk on the beach, or if the weather remained good, a hike in the hills. The afternoon was to be spent searching for old books in local markets and shops, then relaxing at home, an audiobook on the Bluetooth speaker, a bottle of wine open on the sideboard. Bliss.

Instead? She's left Eric tucked up in bed and hailed a taxi to the airport without even the most *petit* of *déjeuners*.

But Marabella isn't one of London's top literary agents purely due to her impeccable sense of style, though that does help. No, she takes her job seriously, and when one of her shiny new authors has their book launch disturbed by a grisly murder, she is going to hotfoot it back to smooth things over. She'll just have to return to France very soon. Not great for the old carbon footprint, but if she has a vegetarian lunch today that will probably make up for it.

With a sigh, she puts her phone down on the table, the screen flashing up a large 11.38 above a photograph of the sun setting over Lisbon, taken from a high viewpoint. What she wouldn't give to be sitting back at the top of that hill, or, even better, be transported back in time to when she was last there.

Her glass of wine arrives on the table, and she gives the waitress a weak smile. An announcement in French sounds over the Tannoy: '*Air France vol AF66Y pour Barcelone est maintenant en cours d'embarquement, porte douze.*'

A family runs past, pulling suitcases on wheels. The father is yelling at one of the children who is refusing to hurry. Airports always remind Marabella of that film *Love Actually*, which uses Heathrow as an example to show that love is (actually!) all around. In the Nice check-in queue, she'd seen a woman dump her boyfriend because he'd left her new sunhat at their hotel, so isn't sure she quite agrees with Richard Curtis on that life lesson.

Despite being over a thousand kilometres away from the scene of the crime, Marabella was one of the first to know about the death of Daisy Olsson. It's often said that she is the 'best-connected woman in the publishing industry', and that was proved true last night.

Within minutes of Daisy's body being discovered, she'd received texts from the bookstore assistant manager, her new junior agent Abi Ellis, plus multiple other minions and spies she has scattered around the literary world. There was also a tearful voice note from her debut author, Natasha Martez. The whole affair was extremely unexpected, and Marabella simply can't be absent from the country when such a lot is going on. It's like the time she went to the loo during the scene in *The Sixth Sense* where Bruce Willis finds out he is a ghost.

But it's not just fear of missing out, or even loyalty to her upset author, that is bringing her flying back to town as early as possible.

Marabella has the perfect life. A lovely new boyfriend, two grown-up children flown the nest, one house in London and another in the South of France, a thriving business and respect within her industry.

She'd left Abi in charge in her absence, but now she needs to be back in London to make sure this perfect life doesn't become a perfect mess.

Because something Marabella knows to be true, is that murder tends to bring secrets out in the wash.

Chapter Six

Friday, 10.15 a.m.

The thing about murder is, it does tend to cause a bit of a fuss. Jane Hepburn should be back in Cumbria right now, in a meeting discussing the excess options on Baxter's Insurance new dishwasher policy. Instead, she finds herself blinking awake in a London hotel room at – she checks her watch – 10.15 a.m.!

Sitting up, she sees a human-sized pile of coats and blankets on a beautiful sofa. A loud snore erupts from under it. Daniel.

The whizz and click of the electronic hotel keycard precedes Natasha, pushing backwards into the room with a newspaper stuffed under her arm and holding, to Jane's relief, three Starbucks cups in a cardboard holder.

'*Bom dia,*' she says, putting everything down on the desk and bringing a flat white over to Jane. 'Here, you must need it.' She gratefully takes a sip before finding her phone under the pillow. She taps out a text to her boss claiming food poisoning and apologising for the late notification. She blames being up all night in the bathroom, with just enough detail hopefully to forestall any further enquiries. Deborah Templeton, head of the White Goods Department at Baxter's Insurance, texts back right away.

Interesting, Ms Hepburn, because you've been tagged on social media attending a party in London.

Jane's heart sinks to her stomach.

> Be in on Monday at 8.30 for a meeting with me. This is serious
> breach of conduct, and you're already flagged as 'on warning'
> about absence.

When Jane's mother was dying there *had* been a few days when she'd had to put her before work, but she had believed a dying relative to be a special case. More fool her. Trying to remain calm, Jane sends an apology and confirmation of the meeting. She'll think of an explanation before then.

As it was her first book launch, Natasha had decided to splash out on a room in the Savoy Hotel, which was luckily big enough to accommodate the two friends she had successfully snuck past the concierge.

Jane's work obligations having been taken care of, she props pillows behind her head and takes up her coffee again. This is the first, and will almost certainly be the *last,* time she has stayed in a luxury hotel. With one hand she strokes the blinding white duvet cover, marvelling at the softness against her skin. At home, it's Asda's finest bedding, £18.99 for a full set. The frothy coffee warms her chest, and the richness of the aroma makes her smile as she sinks further into the full, fluffy pillows which all smell so . . . *expensive.*

'Anything about . . . what happened last night?' Jane calls to Natasha, now flicking through *The Times.*

'Nothing. It will probably be in here tomorrow.'

Jane is wearing one of her friend's t-shirts, which ends just above her navel, and her pants. She slides out of the giant bed and into the bathroom, reappearing in a long white robe and complimentary slippers. This room is almost as big as Jane's whole flat. Elegantly patterned pale pink paper covers the walls, and her feet are cushioned by the lush carpeting. A chandelier hangs from the centre of the ceiling, and the window is surrounded by curtains that look heavy enough to sink a ship.

'Nice room, Nat,' she whispers in awe. It had been too late the night before to appreciate their accommodation; Jane was so tired she would have slept in a bin or even, God forbid, a party hostel.

'They upgraded me to this suite,' Natasha answers from the armchair, not looking up. 'Check out the balcony.'

Jane steps to the window and throws back the curtains, prompting Daniel to wail like a vampire and hide his eyes.

Outside, Jane shivers, the morning air chill against her bare legs, but the view takes her breath away. Sunlight bounces off the Thames and glints from the windows of the Shard. To her right, she can see the slow revolution of the London Eye and imagines all the happy tourists in the capsules; she's always wanted a go on it. Last night she may have felt as though she was in a crime drama, but this morning is pure rom-com.

Had poor Daisy Olsson ever been on that revolving wheel? Had she ever stayed in a hotel like this? She'll never get the chance now. With a sigh, Jane pulls her dressing gown tighter, feeling depression wash over her. She should get going. She needs to check the train times. She might even make it back in time for a few hours' scintillating work at Baxter's Insurance.

'Wow, it's nice out here!' Daniel says, poking his head out of the French window. 'A far cry from my place.' He lives, Jane knows, in an eight-person house-share in zone four, which he has described as 'ugly', 'smelly', 'crowded', and, once, 'dangerously filthy'. 'What you thinking about?'

'Daisy,' says Jane, looking back over the river. 'And the trains. I should get on my way soon.'

'Not so fast,' says Natasha, squeezing in next to Daniel and fixing Jane with an expectant glare.

'Aren't you supposed to be at work, Daniel?' Jane says, turning back to the view with a smile. The night before, she'd refused to give details of her police interview as she could barely keep her eyes open. But now it is morning, and they have questions.

'Took the day off. I knew it would be a late one. I just thought it would be because we'd be hanging around a pub, not a police station. Besides . . . I don't know who will be working today, not after last night.'

Jane looks back at her friend, noticing for the first time that he appears wretched. Of course, Daisy had been his colleague. She can imagine the news travelling around the office: whispers by the coffee machine and tears in the toilets, perhaps an announcement over email. Who will write it? How will they convey the sadness of that loss of life in black-and-white, the brutality of death in a few short, corporate paragraphs?

'I'll call down for some eggs,' says Natasha, and Jane's stomach growls at the thought. 'And then we want details.'

'So the police told you *nothing*?' Daniel looks furious as he flops down on the sofa, his expressive face unable to conceal any emotion. It hadn't taken long for Jane to relate the story of her chat with DI Hawberry.

'Not *nothing*,' Jane says, pacing the room while draining the dregs of her cold coffee. 'She did confirm it was *murder*, though I'm pretty sure she let that slip by accident. I told you, she mostly wanted to know what I'd seen and why I was there.'

'Tell us again. It was all such a muddle last night,' Daniel says, sitting up.

Though Jane has happily told them both about the unsatisfying discussion she'd had in the bleak interview room, she has so far shied away from what she'd seen in the stock room. She didn't want to upset Daniel by describing the body of his colleague in too much detail. But seeing him now with such a determined expression on his face, she knows that time has come.

'I was looking for Hugo, as you know.' She crawls back into bed, pulling the covers around her as though a feather quilt could protect her from harm. 'The stock room seemed like one of the places where someone might find privacy during the party.'

It seems odd to be discussing murder in such a beautiful setting. The sunshine fanning through the window, the soft white bedding enclosing Jane like a cloud.

'So I opened the door.'

At that moment, a sharp rat-tat-tat sounds on their own door, and they all jump.

'Room service?'

Natasha jumps up and lets in a uniformed waitress, who wheels behind her a trolley holding three silver domes. She removes them one by one. 'Scrambled eggs with smoked salmon,' she says in a bored monotone. 'Full English, Eggs Benedict, and a pot of English Breakfast tea. Can I get you anything else?'

What must she think of me? Jane muses. *Lying in bed in a world-class hotel at 11.30 in the morning, having eggs delivered to my lap.*

When the woman has closed the door behind her, Daniel spears one of his sausages on his silver fork, bites the end off, and turns to Jane. 'Go on!'

She'd forgotten his eating habits, and momentarily stares at the little piece of semi-chewed sausage now lying on the sheets.

'Yes, yes, where was I?' She prods gingerly at her Eggs Benedict. She's never had these before, the pink ham poking out from beneath a fat poached egg under a layer of perfectly yellow hollandaise sauce. 'So, I went down into the stock room. It was very odd. Daisy was sitting up in a chair, leaning against a wall. Her eyes were open. Her cheeks were cherry red, and her mouth ajar.' She shudders at the memory.

'You were in there for some time,' says Natasha, carefully slicing up her salmon. 'Not that I'm *accusing* you of anything, of course.' Jane nods her understanding while putting the first forkful in her mouth. The richness of the sauce goes perfectly with the saltiness of the ham. The bright yellow of the yolk is now staining her plate and flooding her taste buds. 'Were you inspecting the crime scene?'

'Not really,' Jane admits. 'I was . . . momentarily distracted. By the books. There's *everything* in there. Signed copies from big-name authors – including you, of course Natasha! Books that aren't even published yet! Old, rare ones too. There was even a stack—'

'Jane,' says Daniel, clicking his fingers and dropping some baked beans on the bed. 'Focus.'

'Yes, sorry. Well, I was looking at the books. Daisy was hidden, you see, behind a stack of boxes and it wasn't until I knocked over a pile of books that I saw her. Then that sales assistant came down.'

'Anything else? Any weapons? Blood?' Natasha is sitting forward in her chair, breakfast forgotten.

'No, nothing like that. No marks on her at all. It was just her, sitting on the chair.'

Jane closes her eyes to bring the image of Daisy Olsson back into the foreground. She'd seen a shoe first of all, a shiny black pump resting at an odd angle. Daisy's legs had been bare – long, slim and tanned. The sort of legs that brought to mind youthful drunken holidays in Croatia with girlfriends, short shorts. Her body had been slumped on that plastic chair, pushed up against a wall, in a short black dress and linen jacket. Her head had rested against one shoulder, sea-green eyes and Cupid's bow mouth open. One hand had been hanging down by her side, the other resting in her lap, gold ring glinting against skin flushed pink. What else?

'There was a smell in the air – of dust, and something sweet . . . alcohol, and . . . something else. I'm not sure.'

'What else, Jane?' says Daniel. '*Think*.'

'There was a broken glass on the floor, and some liquid. She must have dropped her drink. And . . . and something else. But I don't know what it was.'

'What did it look like?' Natasha sounds calm, but there is urgency in her tone.

'Silver?' says Jane, uncertain, opening her eyes. 'Maybe a tube of lipstick? Honestly, it was all a bit of a shock. And then the sales assistant screamed, and it was chaos.'

'That's a shame,' Natasha says, shaking her head and returning to her breakfast. 'We'd thought maybe you'd been down there gathering clues, you know.'

'Sketching the scene,' Daniel picks up, mouth full of black pudding. 'Finding rogue hairs or partial footprints. That sort of thing.'

'Why ever would I be doing that!' Jane stares back at her friends with a cold feeling in her chest.

'So we can solve the murder?' Natasha says, as though it's obvious. 'Tea, Daniel?'

'Oh, yes, please. Adore the silver teapot.'

'Hang on,' says Jane. 'Solve the murder? But the police . . . '

Daniel rolls his eyes at Natasha. 'Come on, Jane. The three of us, a body? I think you know that it's time to get the gang back together. Time for the Meddling Kids to solve a new case.'

'You were at the crime scene,' says Natasha. 'And the police won't listen, you said it yourself. It's just like last time. Tea?'

'I – well . . . ' Jane splutters, and at a loss for what else to say, eats more of her Eggs Benedict while Natasha fills her cup.

'Look, Jane,' says Daniel kindly. 'You're involved now, whether you like it or not. *We're* involved. You've really no choice. Besides, Nat's got this room all weekend.'

'But I need to— '

'And don't use writing as an excuse. I know you've not written a word in months. Who knows, this might unstick you?'

'But the police!' Jane protests, ignoring her friend's astute observation. 'They have *experience* of this sort of thing!'

Surely they didn't expect to outsmart the entire Metropolitan Police? Jane doesn't have the foggiest where she would even *begin* in a place like London.

'So do we,' Natasha says, in customary calmness. 'Are you not *curious*, Jane?'

Of course I am of course I am of course I am, Jane thinks. But this is above her pay grade. She isn't even a crime *writer* anymore, never mind a detective. She is a nobody, in a city that scares her. How is she to solve the mystery of an unmarked body in an empty basement?

And besides, she imagines her mother saying, *didn't curiosity kill the cat?*

'Someone needs to get justice for Daisy,' Daniel says with urgency. 'Just give it the weekend. That's all.'

But if Jane listens closely to her mother's voice in her mind, she isn't really saying that about the cat. She closes her eyes and pictures her dear old mother at their kitchen table, frowning at her over her cup of lemon and ginger tea. *Jane Hepburn, are you a man or a mouse? You know, a bold heart is half the battle.*

'Daisy was a *good person*, Jane,' Daniel continues, eyes starting to glint as tears threaten to spill. 'Funny and charming and full of life. And I don't believe for one second that that detective is going to look into every last detail of what happened to her. Remember last time.'

'And I need to know,' Natasha says in a small, sad voice, 'if Hugo is involved in this. I can't work with a man I don't trust. Who might even be . . .' She trails off, looking down at the bed.

'But Detective Inspector Hawberry,' Jane says in a quiet voice, a last charge in a war she knows she has already lost, 'was adamant about me leaving *everything* to her. This isn't Hoslewit. This is *London*.'

'We know that, Jane,' says Natasha sweetly, gesturing out of the window at the Thames below, the iconic skyline looking like a still from a film. 'But do you *really* think the police are *any* less useless here?'

Chapter Seven

Friday, 11.20 a.m.

Lucy Tallow pulls the little comb out of her pocket and runs it through her black bob. A bob is a dangerous hairstyle. Too neat and you look like a playmobile figurine. Not neat enough and you look as though you are trying to be cool. Lucy is neither. Though she is quite small.

Thoughtfully, she rolls a pearl on her necklace between her fingers while inspecting herself in the mirror. Offices always have such horrible lighting. The strobe strip above the sink makes her look washed out, bringing out any blemish or dark circle no matter how much make-up she is wearing.

Lucy straightens the pussy bow at her neck, adjusts the silver crescent moon stud in her nostril, sharpens the purple line around her lips. The bathroom is empty, so she winks at herself to show she has a fun side. Not that a fun side is appropriate in the office, of course. Especially today, when she needs to focus on acting normally.

It's Friday, and at Eagle's Wing Press, this means most of her colleagues are 'working from home'. Strange how no one seems able to answer emails when they are doing this. Or their phones. Lucy knows that working from home is for slackers, which is why you'd never find her doing such a thing. She believes in showing up on the premises, good old-fashioned hard work, and consulting the stars to help her get to the top. Fantasy publishing is a serious business.

Marching back onto the office floor, she makes a beeline for her desk. The place might be half-empty, but she doesn't want people thinking she's been taking too long in the bathroom. Like Regina Farnham in Sales, whose movements Lucy once kept a spread sheet on. Forty-eight minutes spent in the bathroom over the course of one Thursday! Lucy never heard back from HR about it, but hopefully Regina was given a talking to.

'That's not how to fill out an acquisition costing correctly, Marcus,' she calls as she walks past a row of desks. The man in question rounds his shoulders in annoyance, but really! He's been here six years. If he is cutting corners, or just plain stupid, she is going to call it out.

'*Thanks*, Lucy,' he mutters.

'That's quite alright,' she says as she finds her desk, though she isn't deaf to the sarcasm. 'You'll find a tutorial in the help section of that program if you need a refresher. It's important to be accurate with these things. What you were doing there, which looked like *estimating* certain printing parameters, can have a huge effect on our bottom line.' Marcus turns in his seat to stare at her and she gives him a sweet smile. 'Good luck!'

What would people do without her? She knows that sometimes they find her a bit much, she isn't stupid. Jealousy can be a dreadful thing, really corrosive to team spirit. But it's not *her* fault if others are envious of how well she handles her job after only a few months. Hopefully, people will soon realise how brilliant she is and how little she deserves to be in this lowly position at the country's worst publishing house. After all, the tarot had said she would soon get her career back on track.

People underestimate Lucy. They see a baby-faced woman with a charmingly polished gothic aesthetic and a deep love for romantic books about dragons . . . and don't expect her also to be as efficient as a bullet train and as precise as a cat on a windowsill.

However, even *she* can't be completely perfect. Guiltily, she opens her web browser and types 'willow tree books murder' into Google.

The results that pop up are uninteresting and vague. Only a few are about last night and offer no information; the rest are about parties at Willow Tree for books that *feature* murder.

Lucy has never been a fan of crime fiction. Morbid, she thinks. She worked on it in her last job – beggars can't be choosers – but the very slight upside of moving from the prestigious Polar Bear Publishing to Eagle's Wing, is that she is working on their fantasy list, Star Gazer.

Exiting the browser, she glances at the time. Less than a minute wasted. Maybe ten minutes in total if she adds up the time spent checking on the story throughout the day, and she can work a bit late to make up for that.

The police had taken far too long to reach the alleyway yesterday. Staffing cuts, she'd heard. With that sales assistant screaming bloody murder – though she supposes if there ever is an appropriate time to scream bloody murder, it is straight after a bloody murder – most people had got out of there by the time the flashing blue lights flooded the street.

Lucy hadn't been going anywhere, not after hearing people desperately searching for Hugo Strauss just before the screaming began. She'd secreted herself in a doorway and watched the pandemonium as partygoers tried to ascertain if the victim was anyone they cared about. It was, in a way, amusing. Word wasn't yet out about who was dead. But Lucy knew.

Did she feel guilty? She isn't sure yet. She feels unnerved. She feels . . . *powerful.*

After a quick look around to see if anyone is looking at her screen, Lucy pulls up TheQuestersHeart.com. Just a few more minutes, then she'll get back to work.

Of all the role-playing games she has been sucked into over the years, The Quester's Heart is her favourite. Her character, a purple witch called Moonshade987, has even reached level six. A fun mix of magic, battle, puzzles and interaction – who needs reality when you have highspeed internet?

She is currently head-to-head with a German player called RedRuin66 in a strategy mini-game within the Quester's universe, started just this morning. After checking on the dragon eggs due to hatch – not quite ready yet – she opens it and moves a piece forward one square.

Hello :)

The message pops up in the corner of her screen. RedRuin66 is online. Lucy smiles – all morning they've been missing each other, leaving moves for the other to find when they next log on, like dog poo on the doorstep. Lucy prefers playing with people in real time though. It's almost like having a friend.

His Dragon Rider jumps forward to kill one of her elves, *and* she notices her Warden is within striking distance.

Hi RedRuin. Nice move.

Thanks :).

On the screen, she moves her own Dragon Rider forward, simultaneously taking out his Warlock and protecting her Warden.

Not nice enough though ;).

Slow and steady Moonshade. I wouldn't get too cocky if I were you.

His next move is a blunder, leaving one of his own pieces wide open.

'Yesss,' Lucy mutters to herself.

'Um, Lucy?' Frantically she clicks out of TheQuestersHeart.com and spins on her wheeled chair to find Marcus standing behind her, arms folded and eyebrows raised. 'Working hard, I see.'

Her face burns. How *dare* he?

'Actually, Marcus,' she spits, 'I'm double-checking the details of the game mentioned in the new Raven Blackwater novel. *Not* that's it any of your business.'

Marcus puts his hands up as though to stem a flurry of bullets. 'Woah! Chill out, I was only joking. I just wanted to hear about last night?'

Lucy spins back to her screen, cheeks still flushed, and opens up a blank email. She starts typing out a publication update that she sent two days ago.

'What about last night?'

'Well, someone died at that book launch. I thought you went to it?'

'I did go. Yes, someone died.'

'And,' says Marcus, hesitating, 'they're saying . . . they're saying it's murder?'

'I believe that is what "they" are saying, yes,' Lucy replies, still mindlessly typing.

Your book will be stocked by numerous independent bookshops, though sadly the supermarkets didn't have space this time around.

'Did you know them? The victim?'

Oh, did she ever. She'd had plenty of contact with the 'victim'.

'Not really.'

The marketing team have an exciting roster of social media posts that will be shared around publication, making sure to point any potential fans to your beautifully designed Amazon page.

'Poor girl,' Marcus says softly.

Girl? Lucy spins around in her chair, a question mark written all over her face. *What did he mean, girl?*

'Who on earth would have killed Daisy Olsson?' Marcus continues, shaking his head. 'I only met her once, but she seemed so nice. Lucy . . . are you okay?'

'Yes, yes. Sorry, just tired. I really need to get on now, Marcus.'

He walks back to his desk via the kitchen, presumably trying to find someone else around to gossip with. Lucy sits, slack-faced, staring at the computer screen, the half-written email glaring at her.

Yes, she thinks, *Daisy Olsson. A shock indeed.*

Chapter Eight

Friday, 12.15 p.m.

A trickle of excitement is buzzing through Jane's body as she steps out of the Savoy Hotel with her friends by her side. The sky is clear, bright blue, and around them the city is bustling with life.

Having decided it wasn't worth getting back for a few hours' work and with the weekend looming, Jane has agreed that there is no harm in doing a *little* bit of digging around. As long she is home on Sunday, ready to go and apologise to her boss on Monday morning.

There is no better place to start any investigation, Jane wisely tells her friends, than the crime scene. At least, that's where PI Baker always starts. In consequence, the trio are marching towards Willow Tree Books, sharing thoughts and theories as they go.

Despite her reservations, the thrill she experienced when unmasking the killer in Hoslewit is returning to Jane, as is the joy of working on something side by side with friends and the satisfaction of untangling a puzzle worthy of Sherlock Holmes himself.

'Something I don't get,' Natasha says when they stop to buy three takeaway coffees from the sullen barista in Pret à Manger, 'is how exactly Daisy was murdered in that stock room, but when Jane went down there moments later there was no one else around.'

'Well . . .' Daniel starts, fumbling for change in his pockets, pulling out crumpled receipts, 67 pence and a button. 'They must have already scarpered. Unless they were still in there and hiding?'

'The sales assistant was right outside the door, remember?' Jane says. 'Even if the killer had been hiding down there for hours, she would have seen whoever it was coming back *out*.'

The thought that she may have been in the basement with the murderer sends a shiver down Jane's spine. But she remembers the silence, the stillness.

'And I'm *sure* there was no one else in that room.'

With a deep inhalation, Jane lets the mystery flood her mind, lets her brain absorb all the questions, clues, contradictions.

How was Daisy murdered alone in a room behind a guarded door? *Who* would choose to murder a lovable editorial assistant at a book launch? *Where* did the missing Hugo Strauss disappear to? And who knows . . . perhaps what Natasha says is true? Perhaps this *will* unstick Jane's writer's block.

Jane isn't sure if she is imagining the hush when they enter Cecil Court, as though the very stones know it's now a place of death. It's shaded and cool after the heat of Covent Garden Market.

'Oh, poor Daisy,' Daniel whispers. 'Poor Daisy.'

Without the crowds of celebrating, or panicking, publishing folk, Jane can appreciate the attraction of this place. Painted wooden signs above neat shopfronts, gold lettering reading Sullivan's Antiques, Lipman & Sons, Bryars & Bryars.

Outside Stafford's Gallery sits a folder of vintage posters and a display of wooden mouldings used for picture-framing – dragged gilt, ornately carved dark wood, elegant mahogany. Jane peers in the window of Bryars & Bryars at a display of maps – from Victorian etchings of the city streets to outdated depictions of Europe and vintage maps of her enemy, the London Underground.

Finally, near the end of the street, they reach Willow Tree Books.

To look at it, you'd never suspect a murder had taken place here less than 24 hours ago. A woman exits the shop, paper bag in hand stamped with the Willow Tree logo, and the door swings shut. Natasha's books are still piled high in the window, their beautiful sprayed edges drawing the attention of some students who are pointing and talking loudly in a language she doesn't understand.

Jane glances at Natasha, who looks pale and a little sad. She isn't one to complain, but this whole mess has rather overshadowed her big moment.

With a deep breath in, she pushes open the door. A small bell tinkles, announcing their arrival. As she steps over the threshold, yesterday's trip down to the Willow Tree's basement and all she found there come vividly back to mind. She'll have to add that memory, along with finding the dead body of her literary agent and the time she wet herself during PE in Year Four, to the list 'Things That Will Always Haunt Me'.

A woman is slowly sweeping the shop floor, curly red hair hanging limply down to hide her face. She moves the broom over the floorboards, so slowly and with such lack of intent that it's more like tickling the wood than removing dirt.

Glancing around, Jane can see remnants of both the party and recent police presence. Books are in disarray, and she spots two abandoned prosecco glasses hiding in a corner like lovers. There is one other customer present – a man frowning at a copy of *How to Win Friends and Influence People*.

A door swings open and a deliveryman in a yellow tabard enters backwards, wheeling a stack of boxes on a trolley. Jane reminds herself she is looking for clues, not her next must-read, but still finds herself drawn to a shelf of repackaged Christie novels. Next to her, Natasha is pretending to inspect the poetry section, but her eyes are busily scrutinising the room.

The tinkle of the bell makes Jane turn. The deliveryman has left, and the red-haired bookseller is unpacking the boxes. She pulls out a stack of books and deposits them on the counter with a *thump*. Moving towards the window, she scoops up the copies of Natasha's novel on display and drops them into the now-empty box.

Natasha lets out an involuntary squeak and the woman looks up. On spotting them she double-takes, sunlight flashing from the lenses of her round glasses. She flicks open the copy of Natasha's book she's holding to look at the photograph inside the jacket, then back up at them with an awkward grin. With her flaming hair, pouting lips and watery eyes, she reminds Jane of a red snapper she once saw in the fishmonger's.

'Natasha, hello. Please do come in.' She replaces the book she was removing from the window and approaches the counter. 'I'm Lizzie – Lizzie Yardley. Assistant manager here. Sorry the shop's a mess.'

She scoops up some books from the counter, moving back towards the window. 'I've only just got the police out of here about twenty minutes ago. And . . . well . . . I'd say sorry about last night, but I could hardly have predicted what would happen. Still, it's a real pity.' She stands a chunky new book on a display platform.

The man browsing the self-help section pulls out a hardback and flips it open to read the blurb, making a performative sound of interest that causes them all to look over at him. Lizzie rolls her eyes before returning to her work. The group watch her stack the new books in the place Natasha's stood moments before. 'What a mess,' she mutters as she does so. 'And I barely slept a wink after . . . what happened.' Her voice is heavy with sadness.

In fact, up close, *everything* about Lizzie Yardley is sad. Her face is drawn, eyes teary and with remnants of mascara lurking on the skin underneath, almost disguised against dark circles that make her look like she's been in a pub brawl. Her hair is lank, bottom lip red and bitten, painted nails ragged. Even her clothes are wrinkled, as if they have curled up in a ball to cry.

Natasha is staring, transfixed, as her window display is dismantled piece by piece. As she seems to be lost for words, Jane steps forward.

'Miss Yardley?'

Lizzie frowns at Jane, her hand stilling mid-stack when recognition registers.

'I'm Jane Hepburn,' she continues, before adding rather pointlessly, 'I'm an author.'

'You're . . . you're the one who . . . '

'Found the body, yes.' Jane tries to give her the sort of smile that speaks of Werther's Originals and soft jumpers.

Lizzie gives a disgusted-sounding snort, putting the last book in place in the window and carrying the box of *One Dark Minute* to the counter where she slots it out of view.

'*The body*. Like Daisy wasn't a person.' She opens another new box to reveal brightly jacketed children's books. 'Look,' she says, turning to Natasha, 'I'm sorry your launch party was spoilt by what happened, but there is nothing I can do about that. Now, I'm tired and I need to get back to work.' She gestures to the box.

'We'll help,' Daniel says decisively, picking it up before Lizzie can argue. 'Through here, I imagine?' The women follow him as he marches under an archway and into the eye-catching children's section of the shop, adorned with cardboard cutouts of witches, princesses and large, friendly dogs. It reminds Jane of how she felt as a young girl in a good bookshop – as though anything was possible. As though she belonged.

Dropping the box on the floor, Daniel pulls out a copy of *The Very Hungry Caterpillar*.

'Nice! I used to love this one!' he says, looking around for the book's home.

Lizzie hesitates for a moment before giving in and collapsing onto a bean bag.

Daniel hands a stack of books to Natasha and they get to work while Jane crouches down with Lizzie, her knees feeling as ancient and unstable as the leaning tower of Pisa.

'I know it's distressing,' she says. 'Give yourself a break. Last night was awful, wasn't it?'

Lizzie nods, swiping at fresh tears.

'Did you know Daisy?' Jane enquires.

'Not really,' Lizzie whispers. 'That one goes in Middle Grade,' she calls to Daniel, pointing to a shelf. 'It looks like it's for toddlers, but apparently cutesy animals are very *in* right now.'

Daniel nods and runs his finger along the shelf, searching for the correct alphabetical spot. Jane spies a second bean bag, pulls it towards her and hesitantly collapses into it next to Lizzie.

'But you'd spoken to her?' Jane asks. She feels absurd, almost lying on the floor, and shifts around trying to regain some dignity.

'Mr Strauss liked to throw his launch parties here, so she'd been in touch a few times about planning them. Daisy usually came to help set up and we always chatted a lot. It's not like we were *friends* or anything, but we sort of . . . clicked. You know when that happens?'

Jane thinks of a night a few months back, spent sharing a bottle of wine in a bathroom with Daniel and Natasha the first time she met them. 'Yes,' she says kindly. 'Yes, I do.

'Did you . . . ' Jane ponders how to phrase the next question without it sounding accusatory. 'You were standing just here by the door, weren't you, last night? Did you know Daisy was down there?'

Lizzie sniffs. 'She said she needed a vape break and some peace. Needed to get away from her boss for a few minutes, I think. So I suggested the stock room.' Lizzie's eyes start to fill again. 'I *told* her to go down there.'

Jane remembers the cylinder at Daisy's feet. Of course, it was a *vape*. 'It's not your fault Lizzie. It is only the fault of the person who killed her, no one else's. Okay?'

Lizzie nods but doesn't look convinced. Daniel bends down to pull more books from the boxes by her feet.

'I knew Daisy too,' he says, and Lizzie looks up in surprise. 'Not well, but we worked in the same office.'

Lizzie smiles properly for the first time and looks him up and down. 'You're lucky you aren't her type, or she would have been all over you.'

'Hey!' Daniel says, hand to his breastbone in mock offence. 'I'm *everyone's* type.'

'She liked them scruffier. You're too –' she gestures at his floppy brown hair, sharp cheekbones and startling blue eyes '– clean-cut.' Lizzie laughs softly, a tinge of colour returning to her skin.

'Daisy didn't have a boyfriend then?' asks Natasha, pretending to flick through the pre-school age books in her pile like the question was of no importance.

Lizzie moves her head from side-to-side in a so-so motion. Eventually, she says, 'No. Not a *boyfriend.*'

'Someone she had just started seeing then?'

'Daisy looked like a *supermodel.* I'm sure she had a lot of men after her. She was messaging some guy on a dating app last night. Said he was keen, she wasn't.' Lizzie shrugs and then hiccups. 'Don't know why. He was gorgeous, six foot two, worked in finance *and* played guitar. What more could you want? Though apparently he had a computer game habit, so maybe that put her off. And she mentioned an ex. Scott, I think he was called. He was still in love with her, but she said she didn't have space in her life for a real boyfriend.'

With a start, Jane remembers their brief interaction with Daisy at the party. *My ex-boyfriend is here,'* she'd said. *Don't be surprised if I bolt off early.*

'Do you know Scott's surname?' Natasha says lightly, as though someone's second name is simply an interesting conversational fact rather than a potentially vital clue. She is pretending to read the jacket copy of *The Tiger Who Came to Tea* but her eyes aren't moving.

'Umm, something with a W? I can't remember. He works in IT though, at one of the publishers.'

'Excuse me?' a male voice calls through from the main body of the shop. The man who'd been browsing appears in the archway. 'Can you help me?'

Lizzie struggles to her feet, a smile suddenly pasted to her face, and moves over to him.

Jane tries to get up too but is stuck in the bean bag. She wobbles frantically trying to get purchase, until Daniel grabs her by the hand and heaves her upwards.

'An ex-boyfriend, eh?' he whispers to her.

Lizzie is nodding at the man. 'So it's a blue cover . . . okaaay. And someone dies in it, right? I'm going to need a bit more than that . . . '

'And he was here,' Jane hisses.

'I see,' Lizzie is saying to the customer. 'I see. Well, I don't see, but let's go and have a look.'

'Lizzie,' Jane says, reaching out to grab her sleeve. 'Sorry, just one more thing.' The assistant manager frowns down at the hand on her arm, suspicion starting to creep into her eyes. Jane knows this is her last shot at questioning her before she clams up completely.

'You were right by the door,' she says in a quick, low voice that she hopes doesn't carry to the waiting customer. 'Did you see anyone else go into the basement? Either before or after Daisy?'

Lizzie shakes her head, shifting her weight between her feet, eager to bring this conversation to a close. Her eyes flick up to the wall clock shaped like Elmer the Elephant. 'No. No one. I told the same thing to that horrible DI Hawberry. I'd brought stock up from there at the start of the event. Then I stood at the counter until the party was over, to sell books and pour drinks. I didn't move all evening. No one went into that room apart from Daisy.'

Jane lets out her breath in disappointment. How can it be possible that someone was murdered in an empty room with a guard at the door?

'And,' Lizzie continues in a suddenly wary tone, 'there was *you*, of course. Why exactly *are* you asking all these questions? And why were you looking for Daisy in the first place?'

Jane stops breathing, the room stills.

'Excuse me?!' The voice of the waiting customer makes everyone jump. 'I have places to be, you know?' With a last look at Jane, Lizzie turns back to him.

'Sorry, sir. Now, a *blue* book, you said?'

Jane, Natasha and Daniel slide out of the door and into the street as a group of students comes in.

'Well, what do you think of that then?' says Daniel. 'Sounds like there is definitely no way someone else could have got into that room without Lizzie seeing.'

'But then *how*', Natasha says, stamping one foot in frustration, 'could Daisy have been *murdered* down there?'

'Dunno,' says Daniel, looking around at the surrounding restaurants filling with hungry tourists. 'But I do know two things. One, that comment about the ex-boyfriend is worth looking into. And two, I'm starving.'

'There is a lot to digest,' Jane says. She ignores Daniel's muttering about what he'd *rather* be digesting. 'But one other thing stood out to me. Lizzie said that Daisy went into the basement to get away from her boss. When she died, Daisy was *hiding* from Hugo Strauss. Natasha, it's high time we tracked down that elusive editor of yours.'

Chapter Nine

Friday, 1.30 p.m.

Jane Hepburn is eating pie and chips. They aren't as good as the pie and chips in Cumbria, but they are probably better than the ones in, say, Portugal.

'Natasha? Would you say this pie and chips is better than any you've had at home?'

'I don't think I've ever had pie and chips in Portugal.'

'What do people eat then?' Daniel says, spraying the table with crumbs.

'Oh, you know. Fresh octopus. *Arroz de marisco* – that's rice with lots of fresh seafood. Roast chicken with piri-piri sauce. Salt cod. Grilled sardines with new potatoes. That sort of thing.'

Jane isn't sure she likes the sound of all of that, but it would be impolite to say so. She fills her mouth with pie, and nods instead. Yes, even if it's not a Northern pie, she'd choose it over . . . what was it? *Octopus?*

Jane has only ever travelled through the pages of books. She's wandered Paris with George Orwell, dug her toes into Thailand's white sand beaches with Alex Garland, grown up in Naples with Elena Ferrante. But even though the thought of eating *octopus* is rather unappealing, there is still a pang of regret in her at the mention of Natasha's home, for lands not seen and food not tasted.

The past year has shown her the fear and joy of new experiences, and Jane feels a brief, surprising pang of desire to spread her wings. She pushes it from her mind, heaping another mound of steak and ale pie onto her fork – travel, glamour, exotic food, they're not for a person like Jane. Though she used to think London wasn't either. Or friends.

They are sitting in the red-leather-covered booth of a pub round the corner from Natasha's hotel called, fittingly, the Sherlock Holmes. Daniel pours a glass of red wine for them all as he polishes off his burger in uncharacteristic silence. Jane is grateful for the wine – something about murder brings out a real thirst.

It's also a welcome distraction. She can't get Lizzie's suspicious expression out of her mind.

Jane pulls out her phone to check the news for the hundredth time that day. There is a brief mention of Daisy's death on the BBC now, but the details are sparse. She opens Instagram next and types in Daisy's name.

The search results spring up and Jane double-takes. The first is Daisy's profile – the beautiful blonde holding an extravagant bunch of flowers. It's set to private. But below that, the next result is a picture of *Natasha's* face.

The caption reads, 'The missing link?'

Confused, Jane swipes across, and is brought up short by an unexpected image of her ex-literary agent Carrie Marks.

Natasha's launch party was overshadowed by Daisy's murder. But why should someone now be trying to connect this with Carrie's death at Killer Lines a few months ago?

Concern must be written all over her face because Natasha puts a hand on her arm and Jane turns the phone away so that her friend doesn't see the screen.

'Listen,' Natasha says, 'I hope you aren't worrying about what Lizzie said. Because if you were under any suspicion, you would be in a cell right now. The police *know* you had nothing to do with Daisy's death, okay?'

Jane nods, but she has to swallow past a lump in her throat as she does. What was it Detective Inspector Hawberry had said about her finding Daisy's body? *Rather convenient, don't you think?* She remembers how they had taken her fingerprints, carefully noted down her phone number. Just in case. She tries to swallow again. It reminds her of the time she got a gobstopper caught in her throat when she was eight. She'd eventually turned blue and coughed it out with the force of a speeding train, causing a black eye for the birthday girl and a lifetime ban from her parties for Jane.

Suddenly, Daniel puts down his knife and fork and raises his glass.

'To Daisy,' he says, with a catch in his voice. 'A lovely person. She'd only been working at Polar Bear Publishing for six months, and I've been there for just two, so I didn't know her well. But I . . . I liked her.' He blinks back tears, and the three of them clink their glasses in solemn silence.

When they have all taken a sip, Jane gently pats Daniel's hand in solidarity and turns to Natasha.

'Did you ever meet her? Seeing as she was your editor's assistant?'

'I didn't. We communicated by email, but I only met Strauss himself a few times. Daisy was never there. What was she like, Dan?'

After a loud sniff, Daniel smiles, and Jane marvels at the way he always manages to summon up joy from somewhere. 'She was . . . fun. Naturally happy. She showed me how to use the photocopier. Sort of.' He chuckles and shakes his head. '*Dreadful* at her job.'

Natasha laughs too. 'I got that impression over email.'

'Yeah,' says Daniel, leaning back on his chair and diving into the reminiscence. 'She was *always* late. And always with a story to tell. I sit with the publicity team, so I didn't always hear every detail, but I got the gist. She was the sort of person that other people describe as "the life and soul".'

'But why would someone kill her then? She sounds delightful,' Jane muses, stacking their empty plates in one corner of the table.

Daniel's expression turns grim again as he slumps forward and leans on the table.

'That's just it, Jane. What's the motive here? *That's* the question we need to answer first. Because this makes no sense. Daisy was sweet. She wasn't important, not in the grand scheme of things. I don't see how she could have an enemy, or certainly not one who would do something like this.' Floppy brown hair falls in front of his face as he moves, but Jane can still see the determined gleam in his eyes.

Natasha pulls out her notebook. 'Let's debrief.'

Jane tries to focus on the conversation, pushing the accusing glare of Lizzie Yardley to the back of her mind, along with the sneer on DI Hawberry's face, the demands of her boss at Baxter's, the blank pages of her new novel, the dead body of Daisy Olsson.

The pertinent details of Lizzie's 'interview' are discussed and written down in Natasha's notebook. Then the reason for Daisy's presence in the basement – vaping but also, interestingly, to hide from the missing Hugo. Her ex-boyfriend and use of the dating apps.

'This man she was speaking to on there,' Jane ponders. 'She might even have invited him to the party. Or maybe she'd tried to break things off and he didn't take it well? Lizzie said he was keen, but Daisy wasn't.'

'It's a real possibility. And you never know *who* you are speaking to on the internet,' Daniel says with a grave nod. 'Once I thought I was speaking to Britney Spears on MSN Messenger, but I twigged when she asked me to send her £200.'

'Why,' Jane says, 'did you think Britney Spears—'

'It's not important,' Natasha snaps. 'What else was said about this mystery man? We need to write it down before we forget.'

The barman, large in all directions, stomps over to their table, expertly carrying three desserts. 'Almond cake for the gentleman,' he announces in a booming voice. 'And a couple of tarts,' he winks at Natasha, 'for the . . . lovely ladies.' He chuckles at the innuendo, and it turns Jane's stomach. Was Daisy's death a flirtation gone wrong?

Daisy had seemed bubbly and kind – why on earth would she be killed? And *how*? Jane had seen the body herself. There were no marks, no obvious weapon in sight, no blood. Daisy had been alive in that alleyway just *minutes* earlier. Then, dead, alone behind a closed and guarded door. Jane remembers the scene perfectly.

In body, she is sitting right next to her friends in the pub, but in spirit she is back in that basement with Daisy Olsson. Once again, Daisy is sitting on that chair, two hectic circles of pink staining her cheeks. Jane smells something sweet in the air mingling with the dust from the books – it must have been strawberry from the vape, but there was something else too. Something she can't quite put her finger on . . .

Natasha shakes her arm. 'Earth to Jane? I was asking what you thought about finding Scott. The ex-boyfriend?'

'Can I have a bit of your chocolate tart?' Daniel says, lunging forward and littering the table with crumbs of almond cake.

Maybe it's the progress they've made, but something in this room is making the image of Daisy's body ever-present in Jane's mind. It's as though she is actually there, knocking to be let in. As if she is saying something to Jane, willing her to understand, to catch the person who did this.

'Wanna bit?' Daniel says, pushing his own mangled piece of cake towards Jane as he digs into her dessert. 'It's great.'

'No, thank you,' she mumbles, still feeling oddly distant as she pictures that basement. Her on hands and knees, Daisy sitting upright in the plastic chair.

'Go on, try a bit!' He nudges the plate closer. Daisy knocks. Jane's mother whispers. *Sometimes what you're looking for is right under your nose.*

'I've got it!' Jane's on her feet now, clutching her hands to her head.

'Got what?'

'Of course,' she mutters. Closing her eyes, she puts herself back at the scene of the crime so easily. Sees Daisy's body in the chair. The champagne glass smashed at her feet. 'Of *course*. How could I have been so *blind*? Or,' she chuckles, 'more like *nose* blind.'

'Um, Jane?' says Natasha, looking at her with something like concern. 'Want to elaborate?'

'I know how Daisy died. I know how she was murdered, even though she was completely alone in that basement.'

Jane sits back down, her whole body buzzing with excitement, the sensation of victory. She can still hear Daisy in her mind, but fading now. Though, of course, she hadn't really been there at all. Jane had just been remembering her so strongly because of . . .

'Daniel's cake.'

Daniel looks a little alarmed. 'My . . . cake?'

'*Almond cake*. I've remembered what the other smell was, in that stock room. Remember, I said that it smelt of dust and damp, but that there was something else I couldn't put my finger on? *Almonds*. And you know what the scent of almonds at a crime scene indicates?'

Natasha gasps, though Daniel still looks non-plussed.

'Haven't you read *any* Agatha Christie?' Natasha says, clutching his shoulder. 'Whenever there is a lingering smell of almonds, it can only mean one thing.'

Jane gives a grim nod of confirmation.

'*Cyanide.*'

Chapter Ten

Friday, 3.10 p.m.

Scott Wallace hates books. They are dull. The plots are often stupid – wizards and dragon slayers, true love and solvable mysteries. They are bulky and old-fashioned, taking up an absurd amount of space in a room or a bag. But most of all, he hates the world attached to them. Daisy's world.

She had been Scott's girlfriend for four months before she broke his heart. Not long to some people, but to Scott? A lifetime.

The rusty chains of the swing creak as Scott drifts backwards and forwards, his legs dangling uselessly. He is supposed to be in the office today rather than drinking Tango in a children's playground, but it is understandable that he hasn't shown up. He can barely bring himself to care about the mind-numbing toil of IT support as it is, no matter on a day like today.

Yes, Daisy was part of that world of books. Sort of. Him too in a way. But neither of them liked it. Neither of them understood the evangelical draw of stories the way their colleagues at Polar Bear did. Scott answered their emails about being locked out of the cataloguing system, printer woes and wi-fi issues. Daisy arranged meetings for her boss, pretended to read things and went to pretentious parties. Whenever they could, they would share a can of cheap cider in the post room, laughing about the things people upstairs had said.

Digging the heels of his trainers into the grass, Scott brings his swing to a halt and jumps off. The park is blissfully empty, but he knows in around 15 minutes it will be flooded with little brats from the local primary school, mothers dressed in clothes from John Lewis and Whistles tapping away on their phones while their children risk their lives and waste their youth on the monkey bars. Time to head home and crack open a beer, watch some rubbish on YouTube, speak to someone online.

Beautiful Daisy. Magical Daisy. Scott was astounded that he'd managed to pull a bird like that. Long legs, naturally sun-blonde hair, full lips and wide blue eyes. She could be on a magazine cover. There was something dark about her though, something . . . *wild* that he'd liked. He'd presumed that was the bit of her that liked him too.

It was his fault they'd broken up. He should have *accepted her boundaries,* she'd said. Now they would never crack open an Old Rosie behind the Jiffy bags again. Never sneak off early to sunbathe on the grass. Never spend a weekend smoking weed and eating biscuits she'd stolen from her aunt's cupboard.

Scott tips the can of Tango into the air, shaking the final drops into his mouth as he walks towards the park gate. In the distance, he can hear the screeching and shouting of children leaving school.

The break-up had devastated him, but Daisy moving on so quickly was even worse. It was an insult. A purposeful slap in the face. He'd felt used, and disrespected, and *livid.*

He crunches the empty can into a twisted, angry shape and throws it into the bin, spilling Tango residue onto his neon blue tracksuit.

No, Daisy won't be doing *anything* this weekend, not now. Not with him, not with anyone else.

And maybe, he thinks with a momentary jolt of pleasure, it serves her right.

Chapter Eleven

Friday, 3.15 p.m.

Tired of London, tired of life, as the saying goes. But there is more to life than cars and roads and angry people tutting at tourists for getting stuck in the ticket barrier on the Underground. Jane isn't tired of *other* things life has to offer – say, rolling hills and birdsong, hot baths on cold nights, good books and greasy food. But London? Oh, yes, she is quite sure she will tire of this extremely quickly.

Right now, for example, she is rather tired of being stuck between a grubby man's armpit and the constant dinging coming from someone's phone as they play Candy Crush. *Aren't we crushed enough?* she thinks. *Maybe it helps to crush something else in retaliation?*

Jane needs, at the very least, some new underwear and another set of clothes if she is staying for the weekend. However, after getting lost on the Underground for what feels like an eternity followed by a humiliating experience in a shop called Louis Vuitton, she gives up. She heads back to the Savoy on foot, hoping to find an M&S on the way.

With her black coat done up to hide last night's stained dress, Jane is starting to sweat. The crowds are making her paranoid. She could swear she feels a prickling sensation at the back of her neck: someone watching her. Whenever she spins around, though, it's only to see hordes of faceless people filling the pavement. Huge adverts for West End musicals fly like flags along the roads – *The Lion King, Les Misérables, Wicked*. At street level, tourist shops sell overpriced umbrellas and mugs featuring the

King's wrinkled face. Jane looks down at the map on her phone again. Shaftesbury Avenue.

It's with relief that she sees a familiar sight on the far side of Piccadilly Circus – a huge Waterstones bookstore, like a mirage in a desert, or a reasonably priced glass of Pinot on an extortionate wine list. She quickens her step, eager to leave the London streets behind and bask in the oasis of peace the shop represents. Hopefully, there won't be a corpse among the pages this time.

Waterstones Piccadilly is the largest bookshop in London and even claims to be the biggest in Europe – but so do quite a few others, so someone somewhere is lying. It's extravagantly large – six storeys of stories, eight miles of pages stacked along its shelves. Jane has *always* wanted to visit. This trip to London may not have been quite what she expected when she boarded the train yesterday, but at *least* she is seeing some good bookshops.

Huge curved Art Deco windows feature extravagant displays of the latest top releases, Natasha's novel proudly centre-stage. Real tree branches surround a pyramid of hardback copies of *One Dark Minute,* framing it and luring the onlooker forward as though stepping into a deep, dark wood. As Jane gazes into the window, she feels those eyes on her again and sees the hazy reflection of someone standing still across the road, observing her. But when she turns, there is no one there. She needs to get out of this heat.

Two booksellers are standing just inside the door, discussing something in hurried whispers. Periodically, they glance over towards the back of Natasha's window display. Jane can only see the face of one of them, a young man with pink cheeks, a double chin and sparse hair, who looks shockingly similar to a baby if that baby was six foot tall. He leans over to frown at something on his colleague's phone, jerking upright at the sight of Jane's interest.

'Can I help you?'

'Oh . . . oh, no. Sorry. I'll just . . . ' She points at random towards a display and marches over to it, ears turning red. Unsure what else to do, she decides to head for the first floor: Crime Fiction.

She is making her way towards the stairs, strolling through the tables stacked high with success and allowing herself to dream of seeing her name among them one day, when a face catches her eye.

A black-and-white photo of a man is staring out at her from a framed poster balanced atop a display of hardbacks. She recognises him immediately – the immaculate quiff pushed back from a handsome face, a charming grin displaying pearly teeth that stand perfectly straight like soldiers called to attention. A line of studs punctuates the curve of his left ear and a chunky ring adorns the finger brought up to press into his dimpled chin: Lambert Graves.

He'd been in Cecil Court on the night of Daisy's murder. Edward had even mentioned that he'd seen Lambert speaking to Hugo.

Jane has read some of his novels – sprawling, beautiful, literary works which straddle the often-unbridgeable gap between critically acclaimed and commercially successful. He had been writing for well over twenty years.

Lambert looks more like a film star than an author, and had indeed graced the silver screen in his youth before turning to the written word. Jane remembers his performance as Hamlet in a film adaptation many years ago. He was dreadful, but his bewitching smile almost made up for it. Jane picks up a large, shiny hardback of *A Magpie's Lament* and continues up the stairs.

She didn't mean to do it. When she walked into the biggest bookshop in the country (possibly the continent), it wasn't with the thought in her mind that her own books might be stocked there and she should check. It was almost subconsciously that she felt her feet taking her past Classics – Dickens,

Austen, Bulgakov – past Horror – King, Jackson, Poe – and over to the section flagged Detective Fiction. It was quite without conscious intent that she kept moving through the aisles before stopping at H. It was almost magnetic, the way her eyes travelled along the shelves, to where her own name should be. But all the same, it still hurt when it wasn't. Not a single book by Jane Hepburn visible.

'Do you need any help?'

Jane looks up to see the baby-man from earlier smiling at her, a trolley stacked with titles to restock next to him. *Brave the storm, Jane,* she fancies her mother whispering.

'Well,' she begins, already regretting it, 'I'm looking for an author? But it doesn't seem like you stock her?' Jane clears her throat; she hates the way each sentence comes out as a question when she's nervous. 'Jane Hepburn? She writes a series about a private investigator called Sandra Baker? They are really *very* good.'

The baby-man smooths down his thinning hair, thinking as his eyes scan the shelves. 'Jane Hepburn . . . hmmm. Can't say I've ever heard of her.' He pulls out his phone and taps in her name. 'Oh, she had a moment on TikTok a few months back? When she whacked that murderer round the head with a book? We got a few in then, but pretty sure we didn't restock.' He scrolls down the Amazon page and spots the small, blurry photograph of Jane's face. He glances up at her with a questioning expression and she hurriedly thanks him, heading determinedly back to the shelves with her cheeks turning pink.

The six-foot baby waddles off and Jane pretends to browse, telling herself that she doesn't care. After all, she already owns multiple copies of her own novels. It's just that not many other people do.

She settles herself in the café on the fifth floor with her newly purchased copy of *A Magpie's Lament* by Lambert Graves alongside a cup of English Breakfast tea. Again, she studies his photograph – the artfully pushed-back hair, the twinkling eyes. What was he doing at Natasha's party anyway? Flicking to the book's Acknowledgements, she finds her answer. Among the thank yous to his wife, his deceased parents and his adoring fans, Mr Graves thanks his literary agent, Marabella Rhodes, and his new editor, Hugo Strauss. The very same team as Natasha's.

Sipping her tea, Jane returns to the first page and begins to read. The ease with which Mr Graves weaves words into seductive images immediately engrosses her, and for the next ten minutes she even forgets to be jealous of someone with such talent.

'Is it . . . Jane? What are the chances!'

She looks up from her book in surprise to see the small, pale woman from Natasha's book launch sliding into the seat opposite her. Pearls still ring her throat and dot her earlobes, a silver crescent moon stud adorns one nostril while the purple streak stands out from her black bob.

'Oh! Er, Lucy, wasn't it?'

'That's me!' The woman smiles with lips painted a dark purple shade that Jane would never dare try. 'My boss sent me to buy some competitor books for comparison reading.' She holds up a bulging Waterstones bag, and grimaces as she continues, 'Not that our marketing budgets are anything like the Big Five's, so I don't know why she's bothering. Anyway, funny to bump into you!'

Jane inspects the woman opposite her. She is, Jane decides, in her mid-twenties, her face line-free and eyes bright with youth. She taps one black-painted fingernail nervously on the tabletop as she waits for Jane to reply.

'I was going to get a slice of cake,' Jane says. 'Would you like to join me?'

Lucy grins in apparent relief, nodding earnestly. Whatever she says, Jane isn't sure she believes that story about happening to bump into her.

She returns to the table with fresh tea and two slices of carrot sponge. Lucy sits back in her chair, bringing her cup to her lips gratefully.

'Dreadful business last night,' she says. The cup looks huge against her small face. 'I felt sorry for your friend Natasha. I'm sure it wasn't how she expected her party to go.'

Jane agrees, cutting into her cake with a ludicrously small fork.

'I heard . . . well, I heard that you found . . . her?' Lucy says, voice rather breathless. Her eyes are round, imploring. 'What . . . What was that like?'

'I did,' Jane says, carefully not meeting Lucy's eye as she places her cup back on the saucer. 'In the stock room. It was . . . unpleasant.'

Lucy swallows, and Jane can see the string of pearls bounce against her throat. It puts her in mind of a snake devouring its prey, gulping a life down whole. But this innocent-looking young woman isn't a *snake*. Is she?

'Do you know if there are any suspects?' Lucy asks, looking down at her nails, the tiny dagger painted on one of them stabbing at the table.

'I don't. But then, why would I? I'm just an author.'

'Poor Daisy.' Lucy breathes out with a pitying shake of her head.

'Did you know her?'

The young woman pauses, her face averted, before looking back up at Jane.

'I was aware of her,' she says eventually. 'Her boss, Hugo Strauss? He is . . . well known in the industry.'

'Oh! You know Strauss?' Jane pushes aside her plate and leans forward in her chair. 'Did you speak to him last night?'

Colour comes to Lucy's pale face, presenting itself in two perfectly round, red circles on the apples of her cheeks. 'I did not, no.' She pulls her cake towards her and starts to pick at it. Her eyes dart around, latching on to the copy of *A Magpie's Lament*. 'I saw Lambert Graves speaking to him though.' She nods at the book. 'He's one of Hugo's star authors now, moved over from Magic Box last year. Hugely successful these days.'

Jane notes the change of subject. Lucy is keeping something back, but she knows not to push it. People have secrets, and they aren't *always* related to murder. Although sometimes they are.

And what of Lambert Graves speaking to Hugo? If they're editor and author, it's not a huge surprise. *Someone* must have spoken to Hugo Strauss last night after all. But still, Jane logs it in the back of her brain.

'Yes, I felt like I was seeing a real celebrity,' she says, and Lucy exhales, relieved perhaps at Jane accepting her conversational steer. 'Very striking, isn't he? That hair, the jewellery.'

'He used to be a movie star, I heard,' Lucy says with a smile. 'And his wife makes the jewellery. She obviously doesn't need a job, what with *his* money, so she makes these rings and things.' She picks at her slice of cake with the tiny fork. 'Though I've heard on the grapevine that she left him, so I don't know why he still wears it.'

'Maybe he wants to win her back?' Jane says with a shrug, studying the young woman in front of her. She remembers her the night before, standing quietly against the wall. Watching. This is the sort of person who knows things. Who *notices* things. 'Lucy,' Jane says, leaning forward and lowering her voice to a conspiratorial tone, 'you didn't see anything out of the ordinary at the party, did you?'

'What do you mean by that?' She says it quickly, startled by the question.

'You know, just anything . . . odd. Did you see Daisy at all?'

Lucy's eyes rake Jane's face shrewdly. Jane waits.

'Nothing suspicious,' Lucy finally says, putting down her fork, not meeting Jane's eye. 'And the only time I saw Daisy Olsson was when she was talking to this man in a baby-blue tracksuit. Didn't really look like he belonged there, to be honest with you.'

Jane thinks back to the night before, remembering a scruffy-looking man leaning moodily against a wall, dressed in blue. He *had* stood out.

'Did you hear what they were saying?' Jane says, pushing aside her empty plate. Lucy brings a hand up to her necklace and starts to spin one of the pearls on the string.

'I was too far away, but it looked a little tense. Do you think it's important?'

'I'm not sure,' Jane says, almost to herself. 'But it's certainly interesting.'

'And she was with Hugo for a while. But he is her boss, so that's hardly a surprise, right?' Lucy looks up at the large clock over the stairs and gets to her feet, heaving a dragon-branded tote bag onto her shoulder. 'I have to be at my meeting in ten minutes. I'm going to have to run. Thank you for the tea and cake. It was lovely to meet you again, Jane Hepburn.'

There is still something about this woman Jane can't put her finger on. The purple streak in her otherwise classic bob, her pearl necklace contrasting so acutely with the rest of her clothing. It's like she doesn't know quite who she is.

Lucy raises a hand in farewell before disappearing down the stairs and out of sight.

She has given Jane a useful lead though – the man in the blue tracksuit. There is no real reason to distrust her. And after all, what possible harm could this tiny woman do?

When Jane finally gets back to the hotel, she is proud of her new M&S clothing. She hadn't been beaten by the city after all.

Daniel, who'd had to return home to collect his own belongings, arrives just as she steps out of the shower, relieved to have washed the dirt and stress and very London-ness of her day from her skin. Happily, he has picked up a handful of chocolate bars en route.

'So, any news, Nat?' Daniel asks, passing out Twixes. 'Hugo didn't turn up to work today apparently. I made enquiries.'

Natasha shakes her head sadly. 'I've been calling him all afternoon. No answer.'

Jane is starting to think that, if Hugo Strauss isn't already in police custody, he is on the run. This whole investigation may be over before it's even really begun.

'Jane met someone interesting though,' Natasha says. 'She was just telling me before you got here.'

Wrapped in a fluffy white dressing gown, Jane sits cross-legged on the bed while she tells Daniel about bumping into Lucy Tallow – something that Daniel thinks extremely odd given the city's size.

Jane concentrates on unwrapping the golden foil of her chocolate bar. 'Anyway, never mind that.' She tells him about the sighting of Daisy speaking to the man in blue. As she describes what she remembers of him, a frown appears on Daniel's face. He pulls out his phone (*a little rude*, thinks Jane) and starts to tap.

'You don't mean,' he says, holding up the screen, '*this* guy?'

Jane peers at a photograph of a young man with scruffy blond curls, dressed in a pink-and-yellow striped tracksuit.

'Yes! Yes, that's the one!'

'Say hello,' says Daniel with a grim smile, 'to Scott Wallace. I was searching for Scotts in publishing IT departments on LinkedIn earlier and found a few. But if this guy was seen arguing with Daisy last night, I'm going to guess he's the ex-boyfriend we've been after.'

Jane perches on the edge of the bed and chews thoughtfully on her Twix. He must have come to try and win Daisy back. And when she said no? Suddenly Hugo's guilt isn't looking as slam dunk.

'IT whizz,' Daniel says, tapping away on his phone again. 'I bet he can find a way to get anything on the dark web. Even cyanide. And – yes!' He grins up at Jane as though he is about to hand over an extravagant gift, and he does. 'I have his address.'

Scott Wallace, it transpires, has a sideline coding business registered with Companies House. At what looks to be his home address in Peckham.

With a look of determination, Natasha stands up from the sofa and comes over to the bed, her notebook and pen in hand. She kneels, placing it on the bright white duvet cover.

'I think it's time we discussed our top suspects,' she says solemnly.

And after some discussion, names are written in the centre of the page.

DATING APP MAN

SCOTT WALLACE

'And,' says Natasha with a deep sigh, 'let's face it – our number one suspect is my editor, the suspiciously missing HUGO STRAUSS.'

It's in a grim mood that Jane crawls into bed, Natasha lying silent next to her. She remembers Lizzie Yardley clearing the window display. Remembers the whispering salespeople in Waterstones. The Instagram post throwing suspicion where it wasn't warranted.

If they don't find the answers soon, Natasha's glittering career as an author will have tanked before it's even really begun. Everything her friend has ever wanted could be ruined.

You're making mountains out of molehills, Jane's mother whispers in her mind. And she's right. It'll blow over soon.

Jane is absolutely certain that this isn't going to start to spiral wildly out of control. Not a chance.

Chapter Twelve

Saturday, 3.28 a.m.

It's 3.28 a.m., which is Natasha Martez's least-favourite time of day. There is no good reason to be awake at 3.28 a.m. Not one. That very much includes the one keeping her up right now.

Jane isn't the most discreet person, God love her. Her emotions flit across her face as subtly as the Red Arrows trailing smoking flares. Natasha had seen the furrowed brow as she scrolled Instagram in the pub earlier, had noticed the way she pulled her phone closer to her face, widening her eyes in horror. She'd see the darting pupils and swiping finger as she quickly took in the information. And Natasha had also seen the guilty start when she'd said Jane's name, the way she'd put her phone face down on the table. The pitying look had been the final clue Natasha had needed. It was something bad, and it was about *her*.

The room is dark now, Jane breathing steadily, body slowly rising and falling on her side of the huge bed. Daniel is snoring softly on the sofa. Natasha has waited patiently until she is sure the others are asleep before investigating what alarmed her friend.

It hasn't taken much research. Tapping in her own name on her phone search engine had produced plenty of publishing news and marketing for her new book, along with some photos taken at the launch the night before. But the most recent entries she's been tagged in are more troubling.

Beneath a photo of her face is the caption, 'The missing link?' She flicks on to the next picture.

Carrie Marks, literary agent to Natasha Martez, was found dead in April at the Killer Lines Crime Fiction festival.

Natasha swipes again, a picture of Daisy Olsson appearing now.

Daisy Olsson, found dead at the book launch of *One Dark Minute*, the debut novel of the same Natasha Martez.

She swipes to the third picture. Another photograph of her, this time holding a copy of her novel and smiling awkwardly for the camera.

Natasha Martez: The missing link? Is she involved, unlucky, or even cursed?

Scrolling down, Natasha checks the Comments section. There aren't many of them, and the ones that are there are a mixture of excitement and dismissal. She spots one from their influencer friend Laura Lane:

What utter nonsense.

At first, she feels a rush of relief, but it's followed by apprehension. How has Laura even *seen* the post? Is it spreading already?

So far, Natasha has only found four other Instagram posts mentioning the theory that she is linked to the murders. But social media is a wild beast. You never know when something will spiral or sink.

With a sigh, she exits the app, puts down her phone and closes her eyes. The steady sounds of her friends' breathing is a comfort. She won't be left alone to face whatever storm is coming, if indeed there is one.

What is worrying her isn't necessarily people speculating that she murdered Daisy. She knows she did not, and as she wasn't alone for even a second all evening it wouldn't take much effort to prove she is innocent. What is worrying her is the damage that will be done to the book she spent years of her life writing. Will her reputation be smeared beyond redemption by crazy internet sleuths?

Like a drug, she reaches for her phone again. There is her own face, grinning stupidly at the camera, clutching a copy of her debut novel. Her sticky-out ears like handles on a mug, her awkward smile, embarrassed yet proud.

In the silence of the room, the phone suddenly dings loudly in her hand, a WhatsApp notification bursting to life at the top of the screen. The noise startles her, and she drops the phone painfully onto her own face.

'Ow!'

'Natasha?'

'Wassgoinon?'

'Sorry!'

A groan comes from across the room and Natasha sees the silhouette of Daniel sitting up on the sofa.

'Sorry,' she says again in a stage whisper. 'I must have turned my phone on loud by accident.'

'Who is texting you at this hour?' Jane asks, sitting up too and checking the time on her own phone. 'It's 3.45 in the morning!'

Natasha scrambles around on the floor to where her phone has fallen after bouncing off her smarting nose. Finally, her hand finds the smooth, slim rectangle. She opens it with her pin code and taps the WhatsApp icon.

'Who is it, Nat?' calls Daniel, wide awake now.

She doesn't answer right away. Natasha has to read the message a few times to take it in, even though it's just one word.

Sorry

'It's . . . it's from Hugo Strauss.'

Chapter Thirteen

Saturday, 11.00 a.m.

In the village where Jane lives, there is one bus. It leaves from outside the post office and drives to the nearest town 35 minutes away, then comes back. It runs four times a day. On Sundays, it runs twice.

The thing with only having one bus that runs to one location four times a day (or twice on Sundays), is that you know exactly where you are with it all. Sure, sometimes it's annoying if Jane wants to visit Marks & Spencer but can't find her house keys and so misses the bus by four minutes, as happened last weekend. In that case, you have to give up and go home, or sit in the Sunshine Café for two hours until the next bus. But you still know, in two hours, that bus will come, and it will take you to Marks & Spencer.

In London, Jane is finding things to be quite the opposite. If you arrive on the platform to see a train departing, the other travellers huff and groan as though they have missed the last safe passage out of hell. This is confusing, because there always seems to be another one arriving in around three minutes. On top of this, the trains go *everywhere*. The overground map is a complex web of colours covering miles and miles of the city. That's before you even *look* at the buses – there is definitely more than one.

However, with Natasha and Daniel at her side, Jane is finding being herded through London slightly less traumatic. Even though, when they have to change train line, she grips onto Daniel's arm to avoid being left behind and ending up in Essex.

'Nothing new from Strauss?' he asks for the tenth time that morning.

Their journey to Peckham has been loud and crowded, and it's only now, on the last leg that they have found seats in a relatively empty carriage. Natasha shakes her head glumly.

'Why send that text and then refuse to answer your phone?' he says, also for the tenth time. 'I can't think of any way to get his address. It must be on the HR computer system in the office, but how on *earth* would I break into that?'

'Well, we can think about Hugo later,' Jane says, already sick of the circular discussion. 'We have *three* suspects, remember? What is our tactic with Scott?'

They don't have long to plan their interrogation of Scott Wallace, because at that point a mariachi band enters the carriage and plays at full volume until they reach their stop.

Peckham Rye is not at all like the Strand, Piccadilly, or anywhere else Jane has been so far in the city. She trails after Natasha and Daniel staring wide-eyed at nail bars, betting shops and pawn brokers. Trestle tables outside the shops display bowls of brightly coloured vegetables, brown paper bags of red and green peppers, and heaps of strawberries.

A bar advertises 'jam jar cocktails' on a chalkboard (does this mean the drinks are made with jam? Or come in jars?) as well as 'various small plates' (why are plates being small something to boast of?). Next door in a butcher's shop, naked chickens hang in the window like baubles. Posters are stuck on every outdoor surface advertising a 'car park rave' and musical acts with names like DJ Blender, Arsewipe, and Sad.

It is all, she reflects, very confusing. But also, sort of incredible.

Eventually, Daniel turns down a side road and comes to a stop in front of a tall block of flats. 'This is it. Number 68 Cassandra Towers. Scott Wallace's home.'

Natasha presses the buzzer.

They wait for 30 seconds, a minute, longer. Jane is starting to fear that Scott isn't home when the speaker crackles into life.

'Yeah?'

'Um, is that Scott?' says Natasha.

'Yeah?' the speaker repeats. 'Who wants to know?'

'We . . . we're here about Daisy Olsson.'

The speaker falls silent. Natasha chews on her bottom lip and Daniel shifts from foot to foot. Eventually, a crackle indicates Scott has pressed the lock-release. 'Come up.'

A low buzz announces the heavy front door is open and Jane pushes it, stepping into a dingy hallway. Four bikes and a buggy are entangled outside a lift labelled 'Out of Order'. A steep staircase stretches up in front of them.

When they arrive on the tenth floor, Jane is sweating and red-faced. Natasha is wheezing. Daniel looks exactly the same as always. They come to a halt outside a door with a rusty number 68 sign screwed into the wood, and knock.

Today, Scott's tracksuit is a jolly lime green that seems inappropriate in the face of death. His expression, however, tells a different story.

Much like Lizzie Yardley's, Scott's face hints at sleepless nights. His stubble looks longer than in his photo, less as though it could light a match and more like cat's fur. His curly blond hair is tangled, his eyes red. He reminds Jane of the long-haired guinea pig her teacher bought for the class when she was six. Though Scott wouldn't fit so neatly down the boys' toilet, even if David Brody *did* attempt to push him down with a stick.

'Yeah?' Scott says once again. Honestly, Jane thinks, the vocabulary of some young people. They should read more.

'May we come in?' she asks, sensing Daniel and Natasha shrinking from Scott's hostility. In contrast to his avant-garde style, they look small and bookish.

'Yeah. I guess.' Scott leaves the door open for them when he walks back into his kitchen-living room, collapsing onto a pleather sofa, which gives a loud squeak. The flat feels small, cramped, and dirty. Numerous cups, glasses and cans litter the coffee table, as well as a small stack of dirty plates.

Jane moves a pile of junk mail and a PlayStation controller from the seat of an armchair opposite Scott and tentatively lowers herself into it. Daniel perches on the arm, and Natasha sits next to Scott on the sofa. They all wait for someone else to begin.

Eventually, Jane decides to take the plunge.

'We understand that you and Daisy Olsson used to date?'

Scott flinches, though Jane can't be sure if it's at Daisy's name, or the words 'used to' that causes it.

'Yeah, we dated. She dumped me.' He closes his eyes, leans his head back.

'And you were there on the night she . . . died?'

'Yeah, I was there.' He looks over at Jane, angry and suddenly alert. 'You here to pin this on me, huh? Who even are you? You don't look like police.'

'We aren't,' says Jane. 'But we are working with them.' Is this properly speaking a lie? She isn't sure. She *did* say she would call DI Hawberry if anything else occurred to her. 'Can you tell us about your relationship with Daisy?'

Scott glares at Jane, eyes narrowing in distaste. His hands are balled into fists, resting on his knees, and he clenches and unclenches them in a way that she suspects is to help him contain a bubbling fury. He opens his mouth to speak but can't find the words. And then suddenly, unexpectedly, he starts to cry,

'Oh, Scott!' Jane heaves herself out of the chair and moves to the sofa, putting her arm awkwardly around the sobbing young man. 'Come on now . . .' She squeezes his shoulders, but he just cries even harder. On his other side, Natasha pats his arm gingerly.

Daniel is on his feet, looking alarmed, but Jane catches his eye and gently shakes her head. When her mother died, she cried for weeks. Someone would ask her what the time was, and she'd cry. She'd run out of milk, and she'd cry. She'd stub her toe, and she'd cry. (Though that last one might still bring on tears if it was hard enough.) Grief is confusing, it's unstable, and she knows that all you can do is wait for it to fade.

After a good ten minutes, Scott's sobs start to slow, and he sniffs in deeply between choked breaths. Jane reaches into her handbag, to pull out a packet of Extra-Strong mints. He takes one without speaking.

Finally, his shaking shoulders fall still.

'Daisy and me, we were good together,' he says, finally looking up at Jane. 'I know she *looked* like a pop star, but really, she loved staying in playing *Mario Kart*, eating pizza, goofing around. She was chill. People might say otherwise, but we were good together for a time.'

'Why did it end?

He shrugs, not meeting her eye. 'Something stupid. She would have got over it though.'

'I've heard you had trouble . . . letting her go?'

'She was shoving my face in it!' Scott chokes on another sob. He flops back against the sofa cushions, looking at the ceiling, his blond curls landing on Natasha's shoulder, resting there like snakes in the sun. 'Daisy wasn't an angel. She looked like one, I'll give you that, but she wasn't one.'

'What do you mean?' says Natasha gently.

'She was speaking to other men. Straight after we'd ended. Maybe even before, who knows! I *loved* her, and she just went on to the next.'

'How do you know that?' Jane asks. Scott sits up again, his mouth twisted with unhappiness. 'Saw it, didn't I? On her phone.' He looks away like he regrets his words. 'We met for a drink and . . . I saw the messages come up on the screen.'

'Do you know the name of anyone she was speaking to recently?' Jane asks.

He shakes his head tersely.

'You spoke to Daisy on the night she died?' Jane continues. When she shifts on the sofa, it creaks and squeaks. Her thighs feel stuck to it. She has a sudden unwelcome image of a mouse on a glue trap. 'Why were you at the party?'

'Just had to talk to her. Wanted her to see sense.' He sighs again and gets to his feet with an ungodly squelching sound from the sofa as he peels himself free. Crossing into the kitchen, separated from the living area by a dining table piled with junk, Scott removes a can of Tango from the fridge. The crack of it opening reverberates around the room, and his prominent Adam's apple bobs up and down as he gulps.

The fizzy drink seems to revive him. He is not the type of man Jane would gravitate towards, even if she was ten years younger, but when he smiles she can see his appeal. 'Sorry, but who *are* you guys? Why are you here?'

Jane can sense that they don't have much longer left before they are evicted from the flat. Unless she plays her cards right.

'Look, Scott,' she begins, eyes darting towards Natasha who gives her a small nod of agreement. What are they agreeing to? Can Natasha read her thoughts, or feel them on the air? 'We are trying to find out what happened to Daisy. We aren't the police, but it's not the first time we've done this. You don't resent us *trying*, do you?'

He brings the can to his lips and takes another long swig.

'No. I don't resent that. I'd help, but I don't have anything to tell you.'

'You work in IT, yes?' Daniel says from the arm of the chair, speaking for the first time since they'd entered the flat.

'Yeah, what of it?' Scott bristles on being addressed by another man.

'You're a computer whizz then. Bet you can get anything online.' Daniel looks at Jane meaningfully.

'Whatever. It's time you went. If I could help find who did this to Daisy, I would, but I can't. And I want to be left alone now.'

There is a moment of silence while Jane racks her brains for an argument against this, but there is none. She can't even think of anything else to ask him. *Did you kill Daisy Olsson? Did you slip cyanide into her drink? Was rejection by her just too much for you to bear?* They were foolish to come here, barging in on a grieving, perhaps dangerous man with nothing but a vague hope of . . . what? A bottle labelled *Cyanide* left on the kitchen counter? She gets to her feet.

'Thank you, Scott. You've been helpful.' Natasha and Daniel rise too, following a shame-faced Jane to the door. 'If you remember anything else, we're staying at the Savoy this evening.' She feels too big in the crowded flat, and as far from PI Baker as can be. However, when she and Daniel step out of the front door, Natasha lingers behind.

'Scott,' she says, 'maybe you *can* help.'

He gives her a sceptical look, so she goes on.

'It's just . . . I bet you *can* get anything online.'

Scepticism turns to anger, his face darkening and top lip pulling up in a snarl.

'Look, I've had enough, alright? I didn't bloody kill Daisy if that's what you're getting at. I *loved* Daisy.'

'No, no, no. That's not what I'm saying.' Natasha looks over at Jane, asking for permission to proceed in the same way Jane had done of her. Jane nods. She doesn't know what Natasha is doing, but she doesn't need to. She understands now that their look means, *Do you trust me?* And she does.

'What I'm saying, Scott,' continues Natasha, 'is – can you get into the Polar Bear computer system and find someone's home address?'

Chapter Fourteen

Saturday, 12.30 p.m.

Marabella Rhodes doesn't like to work on a Saturday, but there you go. Daisy Olsson probably didn't like being cut off in the prime of life, and Natasha Martez presumably didn't like having her book launch ruined because of it. We can't all have what we want, all of the time. Though Marabella does at least get *most* of it, *most* of the time.

Alone in her apartment, she paces the living room, thinking. Everything has continued to be extremely . . . unexpected.

She is just off the phone with Natasha. Having flown back from France partly for her sake, she is put out by how little her client seems to need her. She hadn't seemed too upset at all about her book launch being ruined, and by a *murder* at that. In fact, she'd said she didn't really have time to speak because she was doing something in Peckham, of all places! You wouldn't catch Marabella dead in Peckham. They'd arranged to meet at her office on Monday morning.

Her office. That's the main thing that's shaken Marabella. She'd popped in first thing this morning to collect her mail, only to find the door ajar and her papers disturbed, though nothing appeared to have been taken. She can't tell the police, of course, but she needs to do something about it.

Marabella flicks her long, sleek grey hair over her shoulder and wanders into the kitchen. She puts a compostable coffee pod into her Nespresso machine, placing a chunky coffee cup next to it to catch the dark, bitter espresso.

Natasha had faltered at the mention of the growing online buzz though, her upbeat tone cracking as she confirmed having seen it. She must know, deep down, that this could spell the end of her writing career. That should make the meeting with Polar Bear easier on Monday. It marks how serious it is that the Managing Director had called on a weekend to arrange it. Poor girl.

Marabella adds a dash of organic semi-skimmed to her coffee, walks back through to the living room and stands by the sash window, looking onto the garden. In a minute, she'll try calling Hugo again, though she doesn't have much hope of him answering. It's gone straight to voicemail the last eleven times she has tried.

It's part of her nature that she is not a panicker. She wouldn't be as successful and revered as she is if she panicked at every little issue. But this . . . this is starting to make her nerves twinge, just a little. There is no good reason Hugo wouldn't answer his phone to her. Unless he has been arrested.

If he has been, then the police will be looking into his life, overturning every stone to see what scuttles out. Will a particularly juicy spider lead them to her? Will they start overturning her stones?

Pulling her iPhone from her back pocket, she tries Hugo one more time, once again going through to voicemail. She fires off a text to Eric, still relaxing in France, reminding him to water the plants before he leaves.

Then, she calls her assistant.

'Yup?' Abi's voice is too loud and yet far away, like someone shouting across the room on speakerphone.

'Hello . . . Abi?'

The sound of clanking pans comes down the line followed by water running from a tap.

'Marabella? Hold on.' More crashing, a slam, and the voice returns, closer now, subservient. '*Sorry,* Marabella, I didn't know it was you. I was just cooking.'

'Sure. Well, sorry to call you on a weekend. It won't take long.'

Abi Ellis has worked for Marabella for the past few months. Technically, she is a junior agent, which in reality means that she can find her own clients if she has time after doing Marabella's admin, but as the admin is never-ending, it's a moot point. She is abrasive and often rude but has a tenacity that Marabella can't help but admire. The young woman is ambitious and, Marabella has soon realised, without much of a moral compass. An extremely valuable combination.

'I'm testing out the new copper pans I bought with the bonus you gave me,' Abi prattles on. 'They are *incredible*.'

Marabella half-listens to her go on about the pans as she watches a squirrel in the garden, darting down the trunk of the cherry tree and across the lawn. When she has heard about the baking tray (so heavy, you can really tell the quality) and the saucepan (gets super-hot, you wouldn't *believe*), she decides to come to the point.

'Abi, look, were you in the office yesterday?' Silence falls at the other end of the line. It's only been a few months, but this girl is astute. She is already starting to understand what the subtle changes in Marabella's tone mean. Knows when something is light, just a joke. Knows, perhaps, when something could be life or death.

Of course, she is closer than Marabella would like her to be. It wasn't exactly her *choice* to let her in so far – Abi stumbled across things she shouldn't have. Dug her own way into Marabella's hole and now is trapped there with her, in the darkness.

'No,' Abi says quietly. The scrape of a chair against tiles, lowering of her voice. 'You said I could work from home after, you know, Thursday night . . .'

'Right, yes. Of course.' Outside, the squirrel pauses, twitching its bushy tail. 'It's just, someone's been in there. Someone *broke in*.'

Silence radiates down the line for a beat.

'You don't think – it's nothing to do with—?'

'I don't know. Have you . . . heard from anyone? About anything important?'

'Nothing,' Abi says, her tone dropping even lower. 'Is there anything you need me to do?'

Outside, next door's cat is stalking along the top of the fence, one paw placed in front of the other with such care, such skill. Its eyes, Marabella realises, are trained on the squirrel.

'No,' she says slowly. 'I've got a meeting with Natasha Martez on Monday now, let's talk in the morning. Before that.'

'You've got Lambert Graves at 10.30, remember.'

'Oh, damn. Yes, fine. First thing then.' Outside, the cat slips down the fence and onto the lawn. It crouches low as it stalks.

'Right-ho,' Abi is saying. 'See you Monday.'

'One more thing.' It comes to her in that moment. It's not perfect, but it'll have to do for now. After all, they are in this together. 'With the office being compromised, there are a few things that . . . shouldn't be there. I think you should take them back to *your* place. Just in case.'

The silence only lasts a beat before Abi agrees. No questions follow other than about logistics, and after a few more instructions Marabella hangs up with relief flooding her veins. remaining by the window while she mulls over everything that's happened in the last few days. In the last few months.

On the lawn, the cat takes its chance. It springs up, running full pelt at the squirrel. Its prey leaps forward, and both animals disappear from Marabella's view. Did the squirrel escape? Did the cat get what it wanted? She'll never know. She turns back to her living room. The expensive coffee table. The beautiful cream sofa. The awards on the shelf. She always gets what she wants. It's who she is.

There is no reason for that to stop now. Not unless someone, somewhere, gets in the way.

Chapter Fifteen

Saturday, 2.00 p.m.

By the time they find themselves in Canonbury, the 3 a.m. theorising is catching up with Jane and she's flagging. Natasha gives her a jab in the ribs.

'Look alert, Baker,' Daniel says. The affectionate use of her fictional Private Investigator's name works on Jane like a tonic. They have a job to do.

Scott Wallace, it turns out, is an incredibly useful man to know professionally speaking. Once he understood what Natasha was asking, he had ushered them back into his flat and pulled out a grubby-looking laptop.

He'd never liked Hugo, he told them, tapping away.

'Why's that?' Natasha had asked, a slightly defensive note in her voice. He is her editor after all.

'Oh, Daisy used to complain about him,' he said, waving her question away. 'I barely spoke to the man. Got a few emails from him about the printer, that's it.'

'What did she complain about?' Daniel asked, by this stage drinking a can of Tango and eating a slice of cold pizza Scott unearthed for him.

'Nothing specific,' he said with a shrug, eyes still locked on the screen. 'Just used to say he was a twat. To be fair to the bloke, I don't know how good an assistant Daisy was.' He smiled sadly, eyes still trained on the screen. 'Was late for everything except her own death. Hot people can do that, can't they? Turn up when they want, not try, get away with it. And, wow, was Daisy hot.'

Jane hadn't known what to say to this, so she'd just put another mint in her mouth and continued washing the dishes.

It hadn't taken Scott long to find Hugo Strauss's home address on the Polar Bear Publishing HR database. He lived in a townhouse on Compton Road in Canonbury, which is apparently about 45 minutes away from Scott's flat and yet feels to Jane like it is on another planet. The road is wide and clean, each house an imposing Georgian semi-detached built of pale orange brick.

As exciting as she'd found Peckham, it was also overwhelming. But *this* London, Jane decides, watching a man lovingly wash his Porsche with a bucket of soapy water, she could do.

'He's at number 42,' says Daniel, peering at the house number of Mr Porsche. 'This one isn't far enough along. Let's move.'

They trudge past beautiful townhouse after beautiful townhouse: some with wisteria climbing up the front and hanging in heavy purple clouds over the bay windows, some with shiny cars and children's bikes sitting outside, some with perfectly kept front gardens boasting fragrant lavender bushes and late-blossoming roses. Jane is falling deeper and deeper in love with this setting. Perhaps she could base the new novel here? And the protagonist falls in love with someone who lives in Scott's block of flats, and then . . . what?

'Number 38,' Daniel is muttering, '40 . . . and here we are!'

Number 42 stands near the end of the street, imposing black door firmly shut. They stand and stare at it from across the road, not knowing how to proceed. Then Jane sees something.

'Someone's in there.'

A shadow moves across the living-room window, followed by another. Finally, they are about to get some answers.

'Looks like a woman?' Natasha whispers, even though they are far enough away from the house not to be audible. 'And a man too, but I don't think it's Hugo.'

'They're coming out!' Daniel says as the front door opens. 'Quick.'

He pulls them into the front garden of number 41, behind a thick green hedge. Jane whacks her shin on a tricycle and tries hard to focus her pain into biting her lower lip, hard.

Daniel is peering through the foliage. 'Three of them,' he says in a breath. 'Two uniform branch and a woman in plain clothes.'

Jane gently moves a branch aside until she can see across the street. Recognition is instant. 'That's Detective Inspector Hawberry.'

They fall silent, watching one of the uniforms pull the door closed and lock it.

'What a waste of time,' Hawberry snaps. 'Where *is* this man?'

The uniform constable at the door shrugs, a vacant expression on his face. He opens his mouth to speak but Hawberry gets in first.

'Oh, shut up, Johnson. Where did the ex-wife tell us to put the key back?'

'Under the blue pot, ma'am,' the female uniform says, taking the key from her gormless colleague. 'I'll do it.'

Hawberry taps her foot with impatience, a familiar scowl on her face. When her colleague returns, the police officers walk down the garden path and Hawberry unlocks a grubby Volvo nearby.

'We're parked around the corner, ma'am,' the uniformed woman says as the DI climbs into the car.

'Didn't ask, don't care,' Hawberry says, before shutting the driver's door, turning the ignition and pulling away.

'What a cow,' the woman left on the pavement mutters. 'Come on, Johnson. Let's get back to the station. I want to be in the Red Lion with a pint of Sauvignon by six.'

Jane, Daniel and Natasha remain frozen and silent behind the hedge, hearts beating wildly. She doubts Detective Inspector

Hawberry would have taken kindly to her turning up at Hugo Strauss's house.

'Well,' Natasha says eventually, pulling some leaves from her hair, 'I guess this was a bit of a waste of time for us too.'

'What do you mean?' says Jane, dusting herself down and removing a spider that has made itself at home on her cardigan.

'You heard them. Hugo isn't in. *They* don't know where he is either!'

'They also said,' Daniel pipes up as he steps back out onto the pavement, 'that the spare key is kept under the blue flowerpot.'

Whereas Natasha has formidable intelligence and a quiet determination, Daniel has heaps of a different quality that also makes for an excellent investigator: a total disregard for rules.

Natasha plays lookout while he retrieves the key and Jane walks up the steps on shaky legs to slot it into the lock. It requires a few tries, with deep steadying breaths to keep her calm before she finds the 'trick' – lean on the door a little and turn slowly. When the shiny black front door finally clicks open, she hears Daniel repeating her own sigh of relief.

The door closes softly behind them and they stand in silence, breathing in the stillness of the house. Natasha tentatively calls out Hugo's name, but the only response is the slight echo bouncing off the black-and-white tiles of the hall floor.

Jane has never been in a house like this. The ceiling is twice as high as the one in her flat. The walls are panelled and painted a tasteful grey to waist-height, where they then give way to brilliant white, punctuated with elaborate artworks. A staircase sweeps up directly in front of them, its beautiful mahogany banister rail curling at the bottom, like a crooked finger tempting them forward.

Daniel finds a switch and a small chandelier comes to life overhead, light bouncing off the gilt-framed mirror positioned above a narrow sideboard. The only thing that looks odd is that the towering vase that sits atop it is empty of flowers.

'So,' Daniel finally says in a hushed outbreath, 'what are we looking for?'

'Well, we have no idea when Hugo will return,' Natasha replies, her voice an octave higher than usual. 'So let's take a *quick* look around then get out of here.'

Worse even than that, the police could come back at any moment, and then they'd be in real trouble.

Screw your courage to the sticking place, my girl. That's what Jane's mother had said when she hadn't wanted to go back to work after her love affair with her scoundrel of a boss backfired. *Put on a brave face and walk in like you own the place.* 'Daniel,' Jane says determinedly, 'you check the kitchen. Natasha, you've got the office. I'll search the bedroom. As for what we are looking for – we don't know yet. But anything that links him to Daisy Olsson or any clue as to where he has gone would be a good start.'

She senses rather than sees her friends nod their heads behind her, and they move off in different directions. Daniel opens the door to their right, finding the kitchen on his first try, whereas Natasha continues down the corridor. Jane reaches towards the mahogany rail and begins to climb.

The bathroom is decorated in a matt forest green. More panelling coats the walls, more tiles – this time, black eight-pointed stars set in white squares – cover the floor. A bathtub with claw feet sits against one wall, a waterfall shower against another. Even the toilet looks sophisticated. The room smells just as Jane suspects a luxury spa may smell.

As she steps into the room, she allows herself a moment to inhabit an imagined life. She's come home from an important literary event. Maybe debating the pros and cons of the Oxford comma or generously handing out prizes and cash grants. Helping those on a lower rung than herself was rewarding, but exhausting, so she'd called ahead to her housekeeper to make sure the bath was filled in readiness. Expensive products laid out in a line, a towel warming on the heated rail . . .

When she catches sight of her own face in the mirror it's a disappointment. In her vision, she'd glowed, and it stings to be confronted with her reality. Just Plain Jane.

The bathroom cabinet is strangely empty. It feels sad, somehow. A tube of toothpaste lies next to an electric toothbrush on to charge. Some shaving foam and a razor. A full bottle of shower gel, waiting to be called up. Six packets of ibuprofen, all with a few pills missing. Jane doesn't know why she expects more; it's not like a collection of toiletries adds up to a full life. Perhaps it's the solitary, meagre nature of the belongings in contrast to the style and abundance of the house.

In the master bedroom, lush paper covers every wall in a pattern she vaguely recognises; olive green leaves against a cream background. A large unmade bed sits centrally on the back wall, light shining through the sash windows picking up the gleaming, polished wood of the frame. In contrast, a heap of clothes lies on the floor, old socks mixed with discarded boxers and crumpled shirts. Jane looks away; she may be happy to break into his house and go through his bathroom cabinet, but it feels indecent to look at a man's worn undergarments.

A bare dressing table sits in the corner, and she pulls open drawers that rattle with lone products and old receipts. She inspects bits of crumpled paper: zero percent beer at Co-op, a muffin at Victory Coffee, some washing-up liquid and biscuits at Londis. Notes on an everyday life. Nothing that suggests murder or Hugo's immediate flight.

Behind the doors of one side of the double wardrobe hangs a row of smart jackets on wooden hangers, trousers slung over their centre bars. Shoes lie in a haphazard pile. Ties loll like tongues.

She opens the other side of the wardrobe and, finally, understanding dawns. It's empty. But not empty in the way that it's always been empty and is hopeful of being filled. Empty in the way that a belt has been forgotten on the floor, in the way that only the worst hangers – the plastic ones acquired free from shops – have been left behind.

Jane thinks of her own tiny flat, crammed full of her things in every corner. A world built for one.

'Anything?' Daniel's face has appeared around the door. 'Nothing much in the kitchen, I'm afraid. Or, at least, nothing that makes me think "murder". Plenty of things that make me think "money", you know?'

He comes in and perches on the bed as Jane closes the wardrobe door and moves to the bedside tables.

'His wife left him,' she says. 'I'd say long enough ago that she is absolutely certain she isn't coming back, but not long enough ago that he's over it.'

Daniel, always one to make himself comfortable, lies flat on the bed.

'Hmm. Because he was sleeping with his assistant perhaps? That age-old tale?'

'Could be.'

The right bedside table is empty, but the other is clearly Hugo's. A pile of books sits next to an old-fashioned alarm clock and some discarded reading glasses. In the top drawer, she finds more books, tissues, various cables, cough sweets. In the next two, a collection of clean underwear and socks.

'What is odd,' Jane says, straightening up, 'is that there are no signs of him planning to take off somewhere. Even for a few days. Look,' she points to the plug socket by the bed, 'he's left his phone charger. And his toothbrush is still in the bathroom.'

'Let's find Natasha,' Daniel says, sitting up. 'I bet *she's* got something.'

In fact, Natasha has yet even to find the study. Jane and Daniel meet her in the corridor, coming out of the bathroom and shaking her head.

A man who lives in a house like this, who wears tweed, panels his walls, works with famous names, *surely* has a study? A desk at least? Even Jane has a desk. It's crammed into the space between living room and kitchen, piled high with books and scraps of paper scrawled with ideas.

They make their way to the kitchen, exchanging theories. In contrast to their initial whispers and tentative footsteps, everyone appears to have settled in very nicely. Daniel even puts the kettle on while he talks.

'You never do know,' he says, pulling out three mugs like he's lived here for years and placing them on the white marble countertop. 'Some people put on a fancy show, but in reality they are the type to work from bed and eat Pot Noodles with a dirty spoon.' He inspects a box of tea bags, raising an eyebrow, impressed, before dropping one into each cup. 'But you *would* think, in a house this size, he'd have his own workspace. I mean, it has four bedrooms! Four! Just for him! My house has six bedrooms and eight residents. Andy sleeps in a cupboard.'

The kettle wails and he pours water into the mugs. Jane notices an empty cat bowl by the back door. It seems that *everyone* has deserted this place.

'The milk is still in date,' Daniel says, as though this is their biggest worry. 'Thank God.'

'Four bedrooms,' Natasha mutters.

'I know!' Daniel hands around the tea and pulls out a chair with a screech from the parquet floor.

'No, *four bedrooms*!' Natasha says, looking urgent. 'Jane, notebook.'

Jane fishes the notebook and pen from her bag, and Natasha starts to sketch on a fresh page. As it comes together, she realises she is drawing a floor plan.

'*That* is what doesn't make sense!' Natasha says, writing the name of each room in the individual boxes like a Cluedo board. *Was it Hugo in the study with the cyanide?* 'Look.' She spins the paper around so everyone can see.

'Downstairs, we've got the living room, kitchen and dining room. Upstairs, there are four bedrooms and two bathrooms. Even allowing for the fact that the kitchen is huge, the upstairs is *bigger* than the downstairs.'

'So,' Jane says, pulling the drawing towards her with a frown, 'we are missing a room?'

Natasha jumps to her feet, tea slopping over the table. 'And I know exactly where it is!'

Chapter Sixteen

Saturday, 2.55 p.m.

The tap tap tap of the intruders' feet echoes on the hallway tiles as Natasha leads them down the corridor. She pushes open a heavy wooden door and Jane gasps, taken aback by her first sight of yet another beautiful space.

The walls of the plush living room are painted in a dark grey-blue, and heavy, patterned curtains hang from floor to ceiling either side of the huge window. A wrought-iron fireplace sits empty and judgementally clean, as though it's above the filthy job of burning fuel. It makes Jane think of the shiny Land Rover she'd seen parked outside on the street.

A half-full cat litter tray sits in one corner, potentially explaining the funny smell she'd become aware of when entering the room. Two sofas – one a rich orange velvet and one a weathered tan leather – are perfectly puffed up, both longing for someone to collapse onto them after a hard day's work, and artworks in gold frames hang above them. But it's the back wall that captures Jane's attention. It is decked in floor-to-ceiling shelves of rich cherrywood, each crammed with books.

Jane can spot classics – Dickens, Austen, Hardy – mixed in with thrillers – Rankin, Cleeves, Highsmith. Poetry collections jostle with art books, novellas with memoir. She spots Natasha's own novel sitting alongside other new-looking books and assumes that these are the works Hugo has recently edited. She wonders if her own novels sit proudly on her old editor's shelf, or if they were discarded in the local charity shop.

While Jane and Daniel are drinking in the space, Natasha has not paused for thought. She strides to the bookcase and runs her finger along the shelves, stroking each spine as she skims the titles.

'Hugo was naturally dramatic,' she says to her friends, not turning around. 'He loved Edgar Allan Poe, Sherlock Holmes, that sort of thing. It would be *just* like him to— Ah-ha!'

She stops at a thin book bound in red leather. It looks unusually worn compared to the titles either side, like a favourite pair of comfortable trainers next to rows and rows of once-worn dress shoes. She is grinning when she turns around.

'Conan Doyle. *A Study in Scarlet*,' she says, wiggling her eyebrows.

Daniel looks at Jane, who takes from his expression that he too has absolutely no idea what is going on.

Sliding the book from the shelf, Natasha reaches her other hand into the gap. Her grin broadens as she twists something and pulls. Part of the bookcase swings forward.

'*Voilà!* I present to you, Hugo's hidden study!'

Natasha is looking back at them, grinning from ear to ear, delighted with the theatre of the moment, with her own cleverness, with the delight of a bookworm who has discovered a real-life hidden door.

But Jane isn't smiling because she can see inside the room. She can see the large, heavy desk in the centre of it. And for the second time in her short trip to London, she is staring at a dead body.

The smell hits them just after the sight – sweet and stale, like rotting meat left out too long on the kitchen counter. Like rotting meat, Jane realises with a lurch of her stomach, because that is exactly what Hugo has become. When movement feels possible, she walks through the bookcase aperture and into the concealed study. His eyes are open, tongue lolling, skin a sickly grey. Nonetheless, she touches his neck with a single finger: ice cold.

Unsurprisingly, Hugo's room is lined with books, a plush Persian rug covering most of the floor. A laptop sits open in the centre of his antique desk, more books stacked either side. The captain's chair behind it, facing directly towards the door, is occupied by its deceased owner.

The room is grand, yet in a way that is far less polished than the rest of the immaculate house. It's a private space, and Jane gets the sense that it is the only one really lived in, at least since Hugo's wife walked out of their home and his life. Lived in, died in.

A sob comes from the doorway and she turns to see Natasha there, splayed fingers over her mouth and eyes round. A white-faced Daniel puts an arm around her, squeezing her tight, and slips his phone from his pocket with his free hand.

'We need to call the police.'

'We will. But . . . let's just wait a moment,' says Jane.

He glances at his phone. 'Don't have any signal in here anyway. Be quick.'

Pulling her hands inside the sleeves of her cardigan so as to not leave any fingerprints, Jane moves around the room, trying to avoid looking at the body. Daniel, on the other hand, looks at nothing but.

Jane pokes at the remains of some burnt paper in the fire-place. It looks like a letter but she can only make out a few remaining words: . . . *a chance . . . deserves.* She rummages through desk drawers and finds nothing but the general detritus one may expect anywhere – miscellaneous cables, envelopes, discarded pens, paperclips, an old Tesco Clubcard, a lonely cufflink. When she prods the laptop, bringing the screen to life, it announces itself as password-protected. Finally, she plucks up the courage to search Hugo's pockets – a pen, a leather wallet.

'What I don't understand,' Natasha whispers, removing herself from Daniel's protection and stepping into the room, 'is the text message.' She picks up a framed photo from the desk, the view of a city from a hilltop. 'Weird. This is the Escarpa Viewpoint, near where I grew up.'

'That text you had from him reading *"Sorry"*?' says Daniel. 'An admission of guilt before . . . what? His suicide?'

'No.' Natasha shakes her head, finally looking up from the photo. 'Because these are the clothes he was wearing on Thursday night. And can't you smell it? He's been dead for days. He was *dead* when he sent me that text.'

Jane is awake, and she suspects her friends are too. Daniel's usual snoring from the sofa is absent, and Natasha keeps shifting around in bed next to her. Despite Jane's limbs feeling as heavy and lifeless as old rope and her eyes as dry as last night's martini, her mind won't stop ticking over. Hugo Strauss's dead body slumped in his captain's chair. Tick. Daisy in the basement. Tick. The furious voicemail from DI Hawberry. Tick, tick, tick.

After Daniel, finding phone signal in the kitchen, managed to call 999, it hadn't taken long for sirens to announce the arrival of the police and the rather redundant ambulance. All the paramedics in the world couldn't save Hugo Strauss. The pair of uniformed officers they had seen earlier – PCs Johnson and Blake – came first, both looking jittery and worried, presumably by their significant oversight of a dead body.

A tearful Natasha had taken the lead, explaining that she had simply come to borrow a book from her editor, let herself in with the spare key and gone straight to his study. The PCs had written this down, along with everyone's contact details, and assured them that the lead detective would soon be in touch if they couldn't wait at the scene any longer. In no rush to meet Hawberry again so soon, Jane assured them that they could not.

Still, even though they'd avoided being dragged down to the station, it was late by the time they reached the hotel. Jane was hungry, exhausted, and deeply sad. Natasha sniffing quietly, blinking wet eyes. Daniel kept one arm around her shoulders the entire time, bravely failing to mention the audible rumbling of his stomach.

It was in near silence that they had climbed into bed with an unspoken agreement to discuss everything in the morning. Jane still imagines she can detect the scent of death on herself, but knows it's impossible. Her skin is red and hot from prolonged scrubbing under a boiling shower.

Tomorrow is Sunday. Natasha needs to check out and Jane must go back to Cumbria if she wants to keep her job. With an unsettling pang in her chest, she remembers the chatter on social media about Natasha's link with death. What will they say when the news spreads that her editor, too, has bitten the dust? Some of the comments seem quite unhinged already.

There is no doubt that Natasha's long-fought-for career as an author is in real danger. Jane only hopes her friend's *life* isn't in danger too.

Chapter Seventeen

Sunday, 8.00 a.m.

Is there anything more joyful than a tidy kitchen? Lucy hums happily as she drops an egg into the pan of boiling water on the stove, smiling at her own reflection in the oven door.

She feels pretty in her purple dress patterned with black roses, her customary string of pearls and dark lipstick. Even though it's perfectly possible she won't speak to another living soul today, she always likes to look her best. Especially during times like these.

Lucy Tallow cannot abide the practice of coming to the table in one's pyjamas, hair unbrushed, and beginning the day in squalor. It is one of the many reasons she hates her flatmate, the slovenly swine. Lucy has tried and tried to educate 'Peony' (surely not her real name) on proper decorum, but it falls on deaf ears. Luckily, she is currently 'finding herself' in Ibiza, so Lucy can enjoy the place in sweet silence. It's allowed her to alphabetise the spices and rid the fridge of old kebab boxes.

Today, she is going to play a bit of The Quester's Heart and then spend some time reorganising her bookshelves without Peony's thumping music disturbing her peace.

She'd started the morning by reading up on Daisy's death online. The cause has been announced as cyanide, but it reads as though the police have no real suspects.

At the kitchen table, Lucy raises a teaspoon and taps politely at the eggshell, as though knocking to come in. The egg obliges, a thin line forming across the pointed end. She neatly decapitates it, and plunges in a finger of toast.

It had been pure chance that she'd caught sight of Jane walking down Charing Cross Road yesterday while out on an errand, but it had taken Lucy a good thirty minutes of following at a distance before she'd plucked up the courage to engineer their meeting. That conversation and this morning's news mean that the guilt that plagued her for the last few days has now abated, and trepidation has given way to a sense of dawning relief. No one has asked her a single question about Daisy's death so far, and it doesn't seem as though they are going to. And her own conscience? Well, the way Daisy moved through the world, something bad was always going to happen to her one day.

How do you like your eggs in the morning? She hums to herself. *I like mine with antique pearls, a clean house, and an enemy's untimely death.*

Her smile falters. Daisy *was* an enemy, but there is more to it than that. Guilt raises its head again, but she refuses to look at it.

Scooping out the yellow remains of the egg with a spoon, she inspects its perfection. She is very good at cooking eggs, a skill that most people have not mastered. Peony mostly eats bacon sandwiches and old pizza slices. She couldn't boil an egg if her inner child depended on it. When Lucy is successful, she won't need a flatmate.

She'll live in a beautiful townhouse, just like Hugo's.

Lucy pulls her laptop towards her and flips it open. She wouldn't usually do this at the breakfast table – her mother would be horrified – but she needs the distraction.

TheQuestersHeart.com loads, and Lucy's character appears on the screen. Purple hair, black dress, a glowing star to illustrate her position as a practitioner of level-six witchcraft. It takes her aback for a moment, that proof of her power, but she pushes it out of her mind. *You're being silly, Lucy. It's not real.*

Her character is nearing the end of her current quest, and for a good fifteen minutes she manages to lose herself in battling the Demon of the Cursed Wood, a few fellow questers popping up to help her in exchange for a small share of her loot.

When she triumphs, she lets out a breath of satisfaction and gets to her feet. She rinses her plate and cutlery before putting them into the dishwasher, which is stacked in pleasingly logical order in contrast to Peony's usual disaster pile. Her laptop dings and she dries her hands with embarrassing haste, skipping back to check it.

Hello :) Nice work on the Demon. He's hard to beat.

RedRuin66 is online, his goblin character marching along next to her witch.

Lucy can't help but smile as she types back.

You'd be wise not to underestimate me RedRuin. ;)

Taking the laptop and her coffee into the living room, Lucy lies back on the sofa. The smell of incense and Night Jasmine from the half-burnt black candles in the fireplace clashes with the tang of lemon-scented cleaning products. Her eyes take in the fireplace, the melted black wax, the ash of burnt herbs. She thanks the heavens once more that she has the place to herself.

But then again, maybe things wouldn't have gotten so out of hand if she hadn't been alone here.

I'd never underestimate you, Moonshade987. Intelligence oozes from every move you make.

Lucy glows with pleasure. Oozes! From her! He is right, of course, but it's good to have it officially recognised. A notification pops up that RedRuin66 has made a move in their mini-game, and she opens it to retaliate.

What are you doing on this fine day, my lady Witch?

Eating eggs and beating you.

Ha!

Yourself?

Losing to you probably. And scrolling the internet.

Lucy moves one of her elves diagonally across the board from orange to black, and his Warden takes it. For a few minutes they move around the board, occasionally taking a piece and reacting with emojis.

I don't know if you've seen anything about that man who died?

She stares blankly at RedRuin's message on the screen. His Elf Archer takes out another of her elves. A chill prickles her skin.

What man?

RedRuin66 is typing . . .

Lucy bites the skin around her thumbnail as she watches the text box, waiting for an answer.

You not going to fight back Moonshade?

She flicks another elf forward without thought.

What man?

It is taken immediately. Damn.

Just a guy in London, where you are.

He *can't* be talking about anyone related to her. It's just a coincidence. So many people die, world-over, every single day.

His Dragon Rider leaps one square to the left, momentarily distracting Lucy from the conversation. She frowns at the screen, cracks her knuckles. He's playing an odd game, and it occurs to her that this conversation might just be designed to unnerve her.

Especially after that girl the other day, he types. Seems weird.

She's scoured the news sites for information on Daisy's death. As yet, the police seem to be trying to keep a lid on any interesting details and it hasn't made any front pages. It is unlikely, in her opinion, that this man has heard of it, even with the ramping up of coverage this morning after the announcement of the cause of that death. He must be talking about someone else. If she moves her Warden to the right, she'll be close to cornering his Great Knight and winning the game. But is that his plan?

'RedRuin66 is typing . . .

Daisy Olsson, that was the girl who died.

She pauses, her fingers frozen on the keyboard.
Yes. The news said it was cyanide poisoning, she types. It had been there in black and white just that morning.
He is typing again.
On-screen, she is aware he has moved and it's her turn, but finds she cannot move, cannot breathe. It takes a huge effort to continue, moving a piece at random that leaves her own Great Knight open.

And then yesterday a guy, RedRuin66 continues. Hugo, that was his name. Hugo Strauss. You know him?

His Dragon Rider leaps forward to claim her Great Knight, and on-screen he erupts in a ball of flames.
Lucy Tallow slams her laptop shut.

Chapter Eighteen

Sunday, 9.30 a.m.

Their sojourn at the Savoy has come to an end, and at many hundreds of pounds a night, no one feels they can justify extending it. Besides, Jane needs to head back to Cumbria. If she misses the Monday morning meeting, Deborah will give her another official warning.

All in all, everyone around the café table is feeling rather depressed, even with a pile of *pains au chocolat* in front of them.

'We've still got a whole day,' says Daniel, morosely tearing a pastry in half. 'And tonight, everyone can stay at my house?'

'I don't know if your housemates would like that, Daniel,' Natasha says. 'Aren't there eight of you in six bedrooms as it is?' She sighs, turning to stare out of the window. 'I'll get a cheap hotel as I have my emergency meeting at Polar Bear tomorrow, then I'll head home too.'

'And you have work tomorrow, Daniel,' Jane says kindly. 'You can't risk your new job.' *Nor can I risk mine any further,* she thinks.

The silence lengthens as everyone miserably picks at the food.

'Look,' Jane says eventually, 'Daniel is right. We still have a whole day ahead of us. I know we're all tired, and the task feels quite . . . '

'Insurmountable?' Natasha offers.

'Impossible?' Daniel tries.

'Herculean?'

'As likely to be completed as the Sagrada Familia?'

'Actually,' Natasha says, turning to Daniel, 'that *is* progressing. It's scheduled to be completed sometime in the next ten years. Though it has been being built for well over a century. We, however, have one day left.'

'I was going to say that the task feels quite *difficult*,' Jane says with a chirpy verve that she does not feel in her soul. 'But it can be done!'

They look back at her sceptically.

'What's the point, Jane?' Natasha says, staring moodily into her coffee cup. 'I think it's pretty clear what happened. Hugo killed Daisy, ran for it, and when he got home, killed himself. There is no other explanation that fits.'

'We don't *know* that,' Daniel says, not sounding like he believes his own words. 'We don't even know the cause of his death.'

'If someone poisoned them both at the party, they *both* would have died there,' Natasha says with finality. 'But Daisy died immediately, and Hugo got all the way home and into his study. I suppose he could have had a heart attack or something, but even so, the coincidence is too great for them not to be connected.'

'Murder probably is quite stressful,' Jane concedes. 'If it was a heart attack, I think we can assume it is still linked to killing Daisy. But there might be another explanation. There is no motive that we know of, and Hugo *was* a lot bigger than Daisy. The poison could have taken longer to work on him?'

They stare back at her sceptically.

'I don't need to get the train until . . . ' Jane does some quick mental maths '. . . 5 o'clock this afternoon. It's only 10 a.m. now. That's . . . seven hours! Think what we can do in seven hours!' She feels the old optimism, which in her is never too far away, start to seep back into her bones. Grabbing a *pain au chocolat*, she tears it in two and stuffs one half into her mouth. Raising her coffee cup like a glass of champagne, she holds it aloft until her friends do the same. 'Let's get to the *truth*.'

Natasha smiles, and a grin creeps back onto Daniel's face.

'Now,' Jane continues, 'Hugo's death. I agree that Natasha's theory seems the most probable. But if that *isn't* the case . . .'

'Then we've got a murdered man all alone in a secret room, who sent a text message after he died, *and* a poisoned editorial assistant in an empty room.'

They lapse into silence again, but this time it doesn't feel slack and sad. It feels charged with thought, with energy, with – dare Jane think it? – excitement.

'If someone killed both Daisy and Hugo,' begins Natasha, 'there must be a connection between the two of them greater than the work association. One that we aren't seeing.'

Natasha and Daniel start firing off unconvincing theories, and Jane lets her mind and eyes wander. To their right, a young mother tries to persuade her precocious child to drink the Matcha latte she's bought him, while to their left, a couple argue in heated whispers.

'The connection *has* to be work-related,' Daniel is saying. 'Perhaps they saw something? Knew something? Something to do with one of Hugo's authors?' Natasha flinches, and Jane is reminded of the gossip online. 'I can do some poking around in the office tomorrow. Maybe Daisy screwed up something big – she made a lot of mistakes.'

'Something *is* bothering me about their working together,' Natasha says hesitantly. 'Daisy was an editorial assistant at one of the most respected publishers in the business, and yet she was *dreadful* at her job.' She pushes her hair behind her ears, eyes on the ceiling as if searching there for answers. 'You said it yourself, Daniel – she made mistakes. She was always late. She sent me the wrong contract. Scott said she didn't even like reading! So how did she *get* that job, and how was she *keeping* it?'

Jane watches the arguing couple next to her, drawn in by the way the woman, significantly older than the man, keeps touching his wrist in a proprietorial manner, the man pulling back whenever he can, eyes darting furtively towards the large window.

'An affair,' says Jane. The couple jump and look up at her guiltily. She turns hastily to her friends. 'We've established that Hugo's wife has left him, but we don't know why. Could Daisy and he have been sleeping together?'

'He was old enough to be her father!' Natasha says with disgust.

'It happens all the time,' Jane says with a shrug. 'Oldest story in the book. Powerful man sleeping with his assistant. It would have upset a lot of people too. Scott for one, *and* Hugo's wife.'

'Scott *helped* us by getting Hugo's address,' says Natasha with a frown. 'Though . . . he might have *wanted* the body found, I suppose? The suspense must be awful, and it steers us away from him as a suspect?'

Scott Wallace hadn't looked like he was doing well. Grief for an ex-girlfriend, or stress following a double homicide? Or, perhaps, he is just a slob?

'We can rule out Hugo's wife though,' Natasha adds. 'I researched her last night. She's in the US and was speaking at a conference at the time of the murder. It's even been filmed. And judging by what we saw in that house, she moved on a while ago.'

'Then there's the guy from the dating app,' says Daniel. 'Let's not forget *him*. A lot of creeps online.'

Jane nods along as Daniel excitedly lists the reasons why Daisy's mysterious suitor is suddenly his new prime suspect. Her friend's enthusiasm is one of his many winning qualities, but he does tend to make random leaps in his theorising. Only a minute before, he'd looked convinced of Hugo's guilt, and yesterday, Scott's.

He is right on many counts though. The mystery man was supposedly very keen on Daisy, though she had been less so on him. If he found out that she was sleeping with Hugo, could he have been driven insane by jealousy? Could he have hit out at them both, and vanished before anyone even learnt his name?

Jane realises that the group has fallen silent again. The arguing couple are now kissing. The child has poured his Matcha into his mother's handbag.

'There is the slight problem,' Natasha says, 'of having absolutely no idea who this man is though. We don't even know his *name*.'

Jane can see the brief flash of enthusiasm draining from her friends once more. This is too big, too twisty, too complex for them to untangle. But she thinks again of her mother at their old kitchen table, expertly slicing runner beans into a large bowl, a frown of concentration on her face. *Needles in haystacks are hard to find, Jane, my dear, unless you stand on them.*

That's what they need to do then. Throw themselves at this conundrum and hope something unexpected shows up to announce itself by sticking them in the ribs.

And you know what they say, her mother's voice continues, *sometimes it takes a village.*

Jane slams a palm down on the table, making everyone jump.

'Here's what we are going to do,' she says, her voice unwavering and eyes blazing. 'We are going to find out who could have got hold of cyanide. We are going to find the identity of Daisy's online admirer. We are going to find the connection between her and Hugo.'

'*How*?' says Natasha, looking panicked by Jane's sudden chutzpah.

'Many hands make light work,' she says with a smile, hearing her mother whisper it in her ear. With another brainwave, she pulls out her phone and dashes off a text to Scott Wallace.

'Er,' says Daniel. 'What?'

'We are going to ask for *help*. I think one Detective Inspector Ramos still owes us a favour or two. If the police have Daisy's phone, then he might be able to tell us if she'd been in contact with anyone unusual the night she died. Daniel, you know how to use those dating apps – you are going to try and track down our suspect from the information we have. Remember, Lizzy told us he is tall, handsome and works in finance. A guitar player and a gamer too, I think? Natasha, *you* are going to research uses for cyanide. *I* am going to look into Hugo's past and try and find a connection to Daisy.' Jane gets to her feet. 'Come on!'

'Where are you going?' Natasha says, looking downright alarmed now. 'You just said we were researching!'

'We're doing that on the move.' Jane pulls out her phone, smiles at Scott's reply, the requested information given without comment. 'We only have a few hours, remember?'

'Where are we moving to?' Daniel says, hitching his backpack onto his shoulder, nearly knocking out a waitress in the process.

'We are going to see if Daisy herself can give us any answers. Scott's just given me her home address.'

They have to find the connection that led to Daisy and Hugo being murdered within hours of each other. Was it love? Was it hate? Or was it, strange as it sounded, *books*?

Jane might be failing at writing her novel, but she is determined to find that needle. And she has until her train departs at 5 o'clock to do so.

Chapter Nineteen

Sunday, 11.10 a.m.

Daisy Olsson lived in a part of town called Hackney which, Jane is informed, is rather trendy. This becomes obvious the moment she steps out of Hoxton Station and sees a poodle wearing a beret.

Scott has given them nothing but the address, followed by a request to please leave him alone now, which is more than fair. Though, of course, his still being firmly on their suspect list means that Jane can't promise anything.

As they walk, she pulls her mobile phone from her bag again. The idea of calling in a favour from Detective Inspector Ramos seemed genius in the café, but as minutes tick by it feels more and more fanciful.

Ramos works in Cumbria. He is nothing to do with this case. On top of that, he has no real reason to pass classified information on to *them*. Though, it *is* true that they helped him catch a killer just months ago, not only securing justice for a murdered woman but also bringing the detective inspector some sorely needed praise from his boss. Jane had even seen him in the local news, awkwardly smiling in black and white next to the headline: DI CATCHES DANGEROUS KILLER BEFORE THEY STRIKE AGAIN.

It's worth a try.

The phone rings three times before it is answered.

'Hel—' A shuffling sound and the loud clatter of a receiver crashing to the floor makes Jane pull her own device away from her ear.

'Hello? Detective Inspector?'

'Crap. Sorry. Hello? Ramos speaking.'

The twang of his accent reminds Jane of home. She smiles, imagining the kind man with thinning hair and watery blue eyes, so many miles away.

'Ramos, it's Jane here. Jane Hepburn.'

Contrary to her fears, Ramos is delighted to hear from her. He talks happily about what has happened since they saw each other last – a bonus at work, he's lost three kilos, and acquired a goldfish.

'I've even read your books,' he announces, causing her to flush red. 'Well, not all of 'em mind. I'm on book four, *The Troubled Knife*. It's a corker. Anyway, enough about me. What are you up to? Not getting involved in anything you shouldn't be, are you?' He lets out a booming laugh and drops his phone again.

'Well . . . '

The laughter stops, and he sighs deeply down the line.

'. . . It was definitely cyanide poisoning that killed Hugo too,' Jane announces to her friends 20 minutes later. 'Ramos looked it up on the police database while we were talking.'

They have come to a stop in a small park filled with locals. Young women drinking a bottle of prosecco from plastic glasses, howling with laughter, despite it not yet being mid-day. A handful of extremely small, fluffy dogs sniffing at each other's private parts. A group of children playing football, an old man smoking a cigar, a woman doing press-ups. Something that Jane has noticed about London is how every shared space is full of *all* types of people. Even though it is so busy, so crowded, it seems that there is space for everyone in this city.

'I can't believe Ramos *told* you that,' Daniel says, jumping up from a bench. 'You must have charmed him, Jane.'

She blushes. 'I did nothing of the sort. We are trying to solve a crime, and he is a police officer. Plus, he *does* owe us.'

'Well,' Natasha says, raising her voice over Daniel's snickering, 'let's just be grateful for Ramos's indiscretion.' She grins at them both. 'And Jane's flirtation skills.'

Jane pushes on. 'He's going to speak to a contact in London and get back to us when he's seen the phone records. And then, after this, we're even. No more favours. Anyway, are we near Daisy's?'

'Oh, yes,' Daniel says. 'We've just been waiting until you were done flirting. Daisy's house is over there.' He points through the park towards the black iron railings that separate the grass from the road. 'Number 2, Queensbridge Road. Flat B. Let's go.'

They turn onto a wide road flanked with terraced houses of yellow London brick. If not for the car radio playing ear-splitting drum and bass at the traffic lights it would be quite peaceful. Oh, and the man shouting at a tree while he drinks Special Brew. And the seagull eating a dead rat over there.

'Do we have a plan?' Natasha asks as they make their way towards the gate.

'She didn't live alone, did she? Not on a publishing salary in this area,' Daniel says. 'I guess we see if anyone is in. If not . . . we have a poke around as best we can.'

The road is similar to Hugo's, but far less grand. Push bikes over Porsches, fag butts over fountains. Even so, the houses are tall and well kept, with large sash windows and shiny front doors. Most are divided into flats, evidenced by the multiple door buzzers.

Number 2 consists of two flats, and Daniel bravely strides up the steps to ring the bell of Flat B.

Butterflies panic in Jane's stomach. She wonders what DI Hawberry found here, if anything. A diary detailing an affair with Daisy's boss? A threatening note from ex-boyfriend Scott?

The moments tick by and Daniel presses the bell again, holding his finger down for thirty seconds while the sound buzzes obnoxiously loudly beyond the door.

'Nothing,' he eventually says, releasing his finger.

Jane peers up at the windows, half-expecting to see a face vanishing behind a curtain. But all is still.

To the right of the door are two large windows. She edges over and peers through the first.

The room is beautiful. It's large and bright, with wooden floors and verdant green plants in lacquered pots. Jane can see a television in one corner, brightly coloured cushions scattered on a big leather sofa, a discarded blanket on the floor. A coffee mug sits abandoned on a table. And books, hundreds and hundreds of books.

She shuffles over further, standing on tiptoes to see more. A gilt-framed mirror above a mantelpiece; framed photos jostling for place along it. Jane squints. She can just about make out Daisy in one of the pictures – long blonde hair, big smile, arm flung around another young woman, this one with dark curly hair that spirals around her face. The photo is faded though, and something feels off about it.

'Erm, can I help you?'

Jane topples into a nearby bush. There is a fair amount of crashing around while she manages to right herself, including putting her hand on an old banana skin that has turned to mush, and narrowly avoiding some dog faeces. When she finally resurfaces, it is to find her two friends and a stranger staring at her.

'Sorry,' she says with as much dignity as she can muster. 'I'm Jane. Jane Hepburn.'

'Right. Hello, Jane Hepburn. And . . . can I help you?'

The woman looks to be in her late twenties, black box braids pulled into a low ponytail and a suspicious frown on her face. A huge bunch of butter-yellow tulips rests against one shoulder and a ring of keys dangles from her other hand.

Jane's mind is blank. What would Sandra Baker do in such a situation? In book six, *Killing Time,* she was caught trying to break into a suspect's house. She said something brilliant, witty, disarming. What was it?

'Hello? Miss Hepburn?' The woman taps her foot impatiently.

'Er . . . ' says Jane.

Natasha steps in. 'We're so sorry to bother you. This must look rather strange. Do you happen to live in Flat B?'

'Flat A.'

'Ah, okay. Well, we were just trying to visit Flat B, but no one seems to be in. So we'll be off now.'

'Did you know her?' Daniel says, as Natasha and Jane prepare to make a hasty retreat. 'Daisy? I don't know if you heard . . . '

'Yeah, I heard. You friends of hers?' The neighbour's eyes scan them and soften. Maybe it's the banana mush. 'The police were round on Friday. Didn't know her well, but I know she was too young to die.'

'How long had she been here?' Jane asks.

'Oh, not long. The other woman, the older one, rented the place last year, but I barely saw her. The younger one, Daisy, moved in not long after. Nine months ago maybe? Lodger, I think. I only ever spoke to her about parcels and the like. Gorgeous though. Looked like a supermodel. Would come in late a lot and cause a racket.' She looks momentarily guilty. 'Not that I'm complaining, I wouldn't talk ill of the dead.'

'Did you see anyone . . . odd visiting her?'

'I do have a job, you know? And a life? I'm not just watching out the window to see what the bombshell upstairs gets up to.' She sighs, shifting the bunch of tulips to her other shoulder and pushing back her braids. 'There was a guy. He used to hang around outside and wait for her. Saw him a few times. Only noticed him because of these horrible tracksuits he would wear. Heard them bickering a few times, him yelling up at the window for her to let him in and her refusing. That's about it.'

'Thanks for your time,' Natasha says, and they turn to leave.

They are a few feet down the road when Daisy's neighbour calls out to them.

'Oh, and there was the *big* argument?'

Jane whips around.

'Heard her having a blazing row with someone. Six months or so back now.'

'What about?' Jane says, hurrying over to the doorstep again. 'Who with?

'Couldn't make out the words and didn't see who it was with. Just heard the shouting through the floorboards, you know? It wasn't the other one who lived there though, because she showed up halfway through.'

Jane nods slowly, filing the information away in her brain. Daisy was arguing with someone not long before her death. About what? And with whom? Scott? *Hugo?*

'Do you have *any* idea who it might have been?' pleads Natasha. 'Anything at all you can tell us?'

'Nope, sorry,' the woman says, putting her key in the lock and pushing open her front door. 'Only that it was definitely a woman.'

Chapter Twenty

Sunday, 2.30 p.m.

Scott Wallace doesn't really have any friends.

That's why it hurt so much when Daisy left him. It wasn't just the nice legs, though it was partly that. It was the way they had laughed together, and how he'd always have someone to text when he saw a funny-looking dog. She was unlike anyone else he met, especially at that publishing house. Daisy Olsson was wild. A little unhinged, if truth be told. And it made Scott feel *alive*.

Then she'd broken his heart.

She had always been private, never told him anything real about herself or her past or her dreams. Never let him into her heart, or even her home. No mother and a father who lived abroad, that's as much as he ever got out of her no matter how hard he pushed, begged, wheedled.

Then he'd messed it all up. He'd 'disrespected her boundaries' and gone digging behind her back – just to get to know her better, to *understand* her. But she didn't see it that way. Daisy tossed him aside like an old pizza box and never looked back, moving on to the dating apps to catch a bigger, better fish who'd cause her less trouble. Said he'd been a 'distraction' from her work anyway.

He didn't know why she cared, she hated that stupid job anyway. Assisting some man to speak to up-their-own-arses authors, booking him fancy restaurants to take indecently long lunches in. Hugo Strauss. The worst example of them all in Scott's book, and Daisy had complained about him constantly.

Scott leans forward on his sofa, fumbling around on the floor for a vape pen filled with watermelon-flavoured nicotine. Daisy got him onto the vaping.

He lies back, head on the armrest, and takes a drag of toxins into his lungs so long it makes his head spin.

Before Daisy, he'd only had friends online. Now he's back there, spending both his working day and his free time staring at a screen. A poor imitation of real companionship. Still, better than nothing, and less of a risk to the heart.

He'd told the police when they'd called this morning that he'd barely met Hugo, which wasn't strictly true. He'd met him last Thursday night. Tracks have been covered since then though, so he doesn't know why he feels so anxious. The email demanding Hugo meet him at the party has been deleted thanks to his IT privilege, and no one, as far as he knows, saw them together. But still.

The police are one thing, but the nosing around of that motherly woman and her cronies is concerning Scott. He couldn't really think of a reason not to give them Daisy's address, and it made him look helpful, but he won't be speaking to them again. Scott plans to extricate himself. Clear his conscience, maybe get a nice new girlfriend, a more interesting job. Start afresh.

There is one little issue holding him back though. That terrible heavy feeling of a secret waiting to be discovered.

He could go to the police. He could end all of it, just like that. But he isn't brave enough, and besides, he isn't even sure what he'd confess at this point.

He wants a Tango, but he'd have to get up and walk to the fridge for that, which is simply not possible, so instead he imagines the cool, fizzy liquid sliding down his throat, the sugar buzzing in his brain. Scott has work to do. Not for Polar Bear, but his occasional side gig in freelance coding. If it weren't for that, he would never be able to live alone in this city, even in a dive like this. But he doesn't want to work. He wants to talk to someone.

Clamping the sickly-sweet vape pen between his lips, he rolls onto his stomach and stretches out his hand for his laptop.

He knows he shouldn't, but he can't help it. He's lonely. *And besides,* the little voice whispers in the back of his mind, *you need to know. You need to find out. If you are ever going to move on, from Daisy, from Hugo, from death, from guilt, then you need to know. And if necessary, sever any loose ends.*

Chapter Twenty-One

Sunday, 3.45 p.m.

'This guy says he likes wearing adult nappies,' says Natasha, holding up her phone to display a dating profile. 'He says it's not medical, and: "It's not a fetish. It's a lifestyle."'

'I don't think that was Daisy's thing.'

The day has not been a satisfying one. After the flood of hope with Detective Inspector Ramos's help and the visit to Daisy's address, it has dripped slowly down the drain over the ensuing hours. It is now mid-afternoon, and Jane is ever-more aware of the minute hand on her watch approaching the time she needs to board the train home.

Having collected their bags from the hotel, they are now sitting outside the Royal George pub, just a minute's walk away from Kings Cross Station, where Jane's train departs at 5 o'clock.

The sun is still bright in the sky, though only a small slice of it reaches them due to the imposing buildings and leafy green trees. Still, Jane thinks, it feels good to have even the tiniest amount on her skin. When spirits are low, sunlight is a saving grace.

Daniel is flicking through men on the dating app with increasing despondency. He's set up a profile with a picture found online of a beautiful blonde woman with similar features to Daisy. However, finding a particular man online in one of the biggest cities in the world is proving difficult, especially when they have so little to go on.

The man they are looking for is tall, handsome, plays the guitar, games, and works in finance. So far, Daniel has struck up conversations with 16 potential subjects, whittling them out after they reveal their jobs (lawyer, plumber, acrobat, dog psychologist) or hobbies (paddle boarding, cooking, 'sitting down'). So far, only one man has matched all criteria, but when Daniel asked if he had spoken to a girl named Daisy he was nonplussed.

'That one could have been lying,' Natasha says for what feels like the 8,000th time.

Daniel groans and slams his phone face down on the table. 'Anything on the cyanide, Nat?'

In Agatha Christie novels, cyanide is widely available in the form of rat poison, but the piles of dead husbands during that era eventually put a stop to that. These days, unhappy wives have to respond to the much less effective use of the court system. Cyanide, it turns out, is both *extremely* dangerous and difficult to get hold of.

'Even *touching* the stuff can be fatal. It's still occasionally used in pest control, but it's not like you can just buy it down B&Q. Traditionally it was used in jewellery making and photography, but they've modernised. Now it's mostly used in laboratories and gold mining, to extract the ore. You can obviously get anything on the dark web though.'

'And can you do that, Daniel? Get on the dark web?' Jane asks, topping up everyone's wine with the last drops from the bottle.

'No. I've never done it and don't know how. I bet *Scott* could though.'

Jane has never heard of the dark web before today. She'd barely got her head around the run-of-the-mill *light* web. Apparently, there is a secret section of it, only accessible by ne'er-do-wells and tech nerds, where you can buy anything from a suitcase full of drugs to a professional assassin. Maybe *that's* how modern women get rid of their husbands?

Jane sips the wine, the end of a bottle of Picpoul, which had tasted fresh and zingy when first opened but is now warm and too acidic, pinching at her cheeks like an old librarian.

Tick tick tick. She looks at her watch again: 4.05. Her terrifying meeting with her boss at Baxter's Insurance is looming.

Natasha puts her phone down too, and Jane knows it's the unspoken acknowledgement – they have run out of time. They have failed. From the hanging baskets overhead full of happy pink petunias, a drop of water splats onto the table.

Natasha is staying for one more night to attend the important meeting with her publisher in the morning, but after that has vowed to head back to Bath. Jane does feel bad about leaving her friend at such an awful time, but it can't be helped.

'Can't tempt you, Jane-o?' Daniel says, nudging her. 'Just one more night for you too?'

Jane smiles sadly, tips the final drops of wine into her mouth and grabs the handles of her plastic bags, ready to announce her departure.

But then her phone rings.

It's not a number she recognises.

On her watch the minute hand ticks on, on, on towards 4.30.

Jane taps the green icon on her screen and raises it to her ear.

The call isn't pleasant.

'JANE HEPBURN.' Her friends flinch at the volume, and Jane can picture Detective Inspector Hawberry's severe grey ponytail, her deep scowl, her too-tight suit straining at the seams as she swells with rage on the other end. 'Why, *WHY*, were you in Hugo Strauss's *house*? How is it that *you* have found a *second body*? You are looking pretty bloody suspicious if you ask me! And you *should* be asking me, because I'm the bloody head of this bloody investigation in case you hadn't—'

Jane holds the phone further from her ear and mouths at her friends, *She sounds mad.* Daniel frowns, a deep crease forming between his startlingly blue eyes. Natasha nervously shreds a beer mat.

The tinny voice is still perfectly audible around the table.

'And where's his *phone*? If you took Hugo Strauss's mobile phone, Ms Hepburn, I'll throw you in jail faster than you can say Casa-bloody-blanca! I want to know why you were there, I want to know how you got in, I want to know how you found that body. And then I want you on a train out of this city and back to whatever backwater you came from.'

Daniel's frown deepens and he opens his mouth as though to protest.

'You are *not* helping, Miss Hepburn!' the disembodied voice booms from the phone. 'I don't care how bored you are with your little life, you are *not*—'

Daniel reaches over and plucks the phone from Jane's hand.

'Now look, Detective Inspector, that's enough. You cannot talk to my friend like that, just because you were too . . . *useless* to find Hugo Strauss's body. You should be thanking her. She's brilliant, she's brave, and she might just be your best bet in this investigation. So if you know what's— No! Now *you* let *me* finish. If you know what's good for you, you will treat her with some *respect*.'

Daniel ends the call and hands Jane back her phone. She takes it silently, stunned.

Natasha arches an eyebrow. She raises her glass.

'To the impressive Jane, and the equally impressive Daniel who will always have our backs.' Daniel blushes as he clinks his glass against hers. Jane remains speechless. No one has ever stood up for her like that, fought in her corner, not since she lost her mother, who once marched into school to complain to the head teacher about another child putting Jane's lunch down the toilet. But that hadn't helped, it only gave birth to the rhyme: *Jane's the name, her mum's insane, you can hear her shout through the windowpane.*

She's about to tell Daniel this when her phone rings again.

'Oh, let me answer, Jane,' he says, holding up his hand. 'If she wants more, I've got it.'

But no. A friend fighting her battle has given her strength to continue the war. With a deep breath in, she accepts the call.

'I won't be pushed around by you,' she says into the phone. 'I shan't be accused of murders that you know full well I didn't do, thank you very much, and I won't apologise for finding things out just because *you* haven't managed to!'

'Well, that's a little uncalled for, Hepburn,' says a rumbling familiar voice.

'Ramos!'

Blood rushing to her cheeks, Jane hurriedly explains the mix-up, which Ramos good-naturedly laughs off.

'Ah, yes, DI Hawberry. Her bark is worse than her bite, allegedly. Rumour has it she's on the verge of being sacked. This case might be her last chance, and stress doesn't bring out the best in some people. Now, if you've quite finished insulting me, on to what's important.'

'You seem to be in rather a good mood?' Jane says, suspicious of the detective's apparent willingness to help.

Daniel and Natasha lean across the table to hear the far more subdued tones of Detective Inspector Ramos through the speaker.

'Oh well, maybe I am. To be quite honest with you, I have a date later. It's with the journalist who interviewed me about the Carrie Marks case as a matter of fact. So I suppose I have you to thank for *that* too.'

'A date!' Daniel shouts. 'Tell us more!'

'I thought we were solving a murder here?'

'Yes, yes, go on, Ramos,' Jane says, and everyone leans closer still. The occasional London bus and black cab speeding past drown out some of his words, but the group catch most of what is said. Jane scribbles in her notebook at top speed. Natasha's eyes widen with wonder at all that Ramos is willing to tell them.

They say their goodbyes after 15 minutes and end the call.

'Well,' Daniel says at last. 'That journalist must be really pretty.'

The Met have had trouble finding out much about Daisy's life, partly owing to her lack of family in the area. However, they have gone through her phone and home laptop. While they have not so far found anything that points to a glaringly obvious killer, they have found multiple things of interest. She was indeed talking to a man on a dating app – he goes by the name of Kyle – and she had recently declined to meet him on the night of her murder, saying she was 'really busy right now', though she *had* mentioned the location of the party.

'Matched with any Kyles, Daniel?' Natasha whispers excitedly. He shakes his head as he scrolls back through the matches.

Ramos confirms that Daisy had multiple text messages from an ex-boyfriend, one Scott Wallace, which went from romantic to furious, pleading to 'downright unhinged'. Jane underlines *unhinged* three times in the notebook.

'Other than that,' Ramos said, 'they don't have a huge amount. Cause of death you know already.'

'Can you tell us *anything* else? Anything about Daisy?'

'Hmm, let's see. She was 23. No family known. Worked at Polar Bear publishing house. Hadn't ever been in trouble with the police before. That's about it.'

'Last numbers she called?'

'She didn't seem to make many calls. Mostly incoming ones from Scott Wallace, Deliveroo and people trying to sell Personal Injury claims. But there *was* one outgoing call on the night she died.'

'What time? Can you send us the number?'

'I don't have it in front of me, and I really shouldn't . . . well, okay, I'll double-check and give you a call tomorrow.'

Ramos sounded like he was having a grand time, and Jane remarked that there probably weren't many murders happening in the small Cumbrian town where he worked. A double homicide probably made a nice change from slapping the wrists of teenagers stealing Toffee Crisps from the corner shop.

'Actually,' he said, 'I've moved. I'm in the bigger one up in Windermere now. It's a bit of a promotion really, since our last case. A lot more going on there.'

Jane couldn't help smiling at 'our last case'. If only he was in London to help them further through *this* puzzle.

When the call ends, their investigation notebook looks a lot fuller, and everyone clamours to speak at once. Daniel allocates himself the task of tracking down every London-based Kyle working in the financial industries, and Natasha volunteers to take on the task of connecting 'unhinged' Scott Wallace to cyanide. It feels as though they are back on track, boosted by the Ramos's help.

Jane looks at the time on her phone: 4.30 p.m. If she runs, she just about has time to catch her train, to save her job, to do as Hawberry demands. Her heart feels sick.

4.32 p.m.

But looking at the excited faces of her friends across the table and the new leads scribbled in her notebook, Jane knows no one is going home today.

Chapter Twenty-Two

Monday, 8.06 a.m.

Marabella Rhodes believes in expensive bedding. It's one of her most deeply held beliefs, along with *serving orange juice without pulp is a criminal act*, and *flights should be booked on a laptop, not a phone*. She slides deeper into the bed, organic cotton sheets, £130 from Selfridges, softly caressing her skin.

Even so, to her they feel like sandpaper. Marabella can feel everywhere the fabric is touching her. Every part of her body hurts, from her toes to her heart. It's like she has flu.

She doesn't like telling people she is sick because it's such an ugly thing to be. Marabella does not want anyone picturing her, red-nosed and snotty, trembling under a blanket. Or worse, sitting hunch-backed on the toilet. But in this case, it's what she'll do. Tell people she has flu.

Marabella had been sitting in her office, feet on the desk and coffee in hand, when she'd received the phone call. The police had wanted to know why she'd been calling Hugo Strauss so much over the last few days, were they close? No, she'd said. No, not close, just old work friends. Colleagues really. Marabella was a practised liar.

When they'd told her Hugo was dead, she'd said it was a terrible shame. Then she'd answered her emails, called to shout at her assistant despite its being Sunday afternoon, called to shout at an editor despite its being Sunday afternoon, sweet-talked a crying author despite its being Sunday afternoon, and packed up to go home. It wasn't until she'd crawled into bed last night that she let herself fall apart.

The alarm, snoozed ten minutes earlier, begins to tweet at her again, the mechanical birdsong designed to wake one up in a soothing, natural manner.

'SHUT UP.'

The phone is buried deep in the bed, and she has to throw off the covers to find it, the tweeting becoming louder, more frantic, each minute. Stabbing at the off button, she sits, duvet-less, on her bed. At least she is awake. Multiple missed calls from Eric, now back from France and keen to see her. Is it too much to lie to him too? A new relationship lives or dies on honesty.

Marabella knows she can't really say she has flu. She has a business to run. A life to hold together, one she is very fond of. Looking around her beautiful Islington home, she gives herself a shake. She needs to get a grip, or she is going to lose everything.

Good shoes always make her feel more human. Organic coffee and a fairtrade banana, along with an almond croissant from an expensive bakery delivered by an exhausted-looking man on a motorbike. It's that sort of day. At the kitchen table, she bites into the flaky pastry, sugar coating her fingers, and flicks through old photos of Hugo Strauss. Here is one of him at a bar in Soho, drinking an Old Fashioned and laughing at something hilarious she'd just said. Hugo wasn't an easy laugher, and it always felt like a challenge. Making him roar like that, like he was doing here in Soho, it was the best feeling in the world.

She flicks to another: Hugo and her in Lisbon, wind in their hair, grinning madly. Too much. She couldn't think about that weekend. *Pull yourself together, Marabella.*

Opening her laptop instead, she brings up her emails. Despite putting in a stint on Sunday, there was still plenty she hadn't managed to get through after her brief holiday in France. There was a draft contract to look through before it went to the author, some half-hearted publication plan for a book that everyone already knew wasn't going to sell, and a hundred other calls on her attention.

Marabella comes back on the draft contract with outraged comments about royalty percentages and payment splits that she knows will be ignored – you've got to play the game. She replies that the marketing plan looked completely fine, but lacks originality. She responds to someone from Polar Bear Publishing about the emergency meeting with Natasha that day. She forwards two emails from editors wanting a lunch meeting to her assistant Abi. She files 18 submissions from writing hopefuls. She replies to three of her authors who are freaking out for various, self-indulgent reasons.

Agenting comes first, it always has. Only when she has wrestled this inbox into submission does she open her *other* email inbox: Sales@RareSignedBooks.com

First Daisy, now Hugo. The police are going to be on this full throttle, and they already have her number. They will be back.

With a sigh, Marabella opens the back-end page that controls RareSignedBooks.com. She scrolls to the settings and hovers the mouse over the command to 'suspend website'.

She'd always been able to replicate someone's signature. Used to sign things on behalf of her old boss, who was too lazy to do it herself. She enjoyed it, as one often enjoys things they are naturally good at, and made a habit of copying all the swirls and scribbles she saw in books stickered as 'Signed by the author'. Just for fun.

Agenting has always been her primary business, and she is a very effective literary agent. But it has taken years, decades in fact, to build her agency to the point where the money flows in in abundance. There were many lean years. And Marabella isn't a lean-living person.

That's why she'd turned her little hobby into another business. One that brought in a few extra pounds, kept her in single-origin, fair trade organic coffee beans and the good crisps. A business that, once she moved on from signing modern-day thrillers and started investing money in copies of the works of classic authors to add a simple swirl of a pen top, started to bring in thousands.

It hadn't started off as fraud. That 'signed' Stephen King she'd included in the haul for her niece's school bring and buy sale was there by mistake – it was only after it went for £300 that cogs started whirring in Marabella's mind. It had been . . . sort of an accident.

But since when was that an excuse?

Lots of things are *sort of an accident,* but they still have consequences. That coffee stain on the white rug, partially hidden by the side table, was an accident, but it still meant she'd needed to move all the furniture around. Her assistant double-booking her lunch the other week was an accident, but it still resulted in an important editor sitting alone in the Ivy for an hour. And, of course, Hugo. Hugo was an accident. But that doesn't make him any less dead.

Chapter Twenty-Three

Monday, 10.15 a.m.

Is there anything more dispiriting than a saggy mattress?

Jane turns onto her side and the bed protests so loudly one might think it was being sentenced to death. Maybe it is time it was.

Still, it is affordable. The guest house is, conveniently for Natasha, right by the office of Marabella Rhodes, and stepping through the doors last night felt like stepping back in time. Everything that could possibly be in floral print, *was* in floral print. The heavy curtains, the sofa, the carpet, the teacups, the hostess's blouse. Doilies dot surfaces, dusty vases host plastic flowers older than Jane herself, and the air smells strongly of lavender. A temptingly large Victoria sponge cake – Jane's favourite – sat under a glass dome on the sideboard.

Their room boasts two single beds – with floral duvet covers, of course – one little window which does not open, one cracked sink, an uncomfortable-looking chair in the corner and, thank the heavens, a small station for making tea. The bathroom, shared, is down the corridor.

Still safely under the covers, she sips Earl Grey and folds over the corner of her page. She's been reading the copy of *A Magpie's Lament* that she bought in Waterstones. It really is depressingly brilliant. Where does Lambert get his ideas? she wonders. Jane has looked upon multiple real-life bodies in the past year and she *still* has nothing to say.

Natasha has already left for her meeting with her agent a few doors down, and Daniel headed home the night before – he has work today and, besides, camping out in the Savoy is one thing, but Geraldine Trott's B&B is quite another. This leaves Jane to work on her non-existent novel and deep dive into the lives of the murder victims alone.

Leaning half out of the bed, she pulls her bag towards her, removes her laptop and pulls up the Word document of half-baked ideas for a new novel.

Priest finds body. God is the killer?

Dragons and cats. Coming-of-age story.

Butcher falls in love with vegan, what happens next?

Rubbish.

All of a sudden, Jane feels deeply alone. She wishes she'd tagged along with Natasha and sat outside until she was finished, or even was at the Baxter's Insurance offices – anything but being confronted with her own failures in black and white. In their investigation, they only seem to succeed in unearthing more and more questions rather than any answers. And as for her writing career? Well, one of the 'ideas' noted down is 'Scrambled Hearts': *Chef falls in love with egg supplier, but can he break out of his <u>own</u> shell?*

She opens a new Word document and stares at the glowing white of the blank page.

She'd been trying to come up with ideas between meetings at work, but it was difficult.

Tree Surgeon /detective solves high-altitude crimes had been scribbled down while she was listening to an update about the modern fridge-freezer customer's needs. *Game of Thrones meets Holby City* had been when she'd finished work for the day but had felt emotionally drained after a telling-off from Deborah about her minute-taking.

Jane has been feeling fed up and strung out. Exhausted and impatient. The thing is, after writing her series about PI Sandra Baker for so many years, she is scared she has nothing else to say. What she writes next needs to be bigger, better. *Perfect.*

Which has resulted in Jane being too scared to write anything at all.

Deciding that she isn't in the right mood, she exits the document and brings up Instagram to check on the Natasha conspiracy.

It's not good.

The rumblings of suspicion have grown over the weekend. Now, Natasha's name brings up countless posts about her connection to not one, not two, but *three* murder victims within a year. Jane clicks on a newly uploaded video.

'Don't trust this woman!' the boy on the screen shouts. 'She is a killer, or she is cursed. Either way, if you buy this book you are *directly supporting evil*. She—' Jane hits exit.

They *need* to find out who did this. There's nothing yet in her inbox from Deborah Templeton, but Jane's absence from this morning's meeting will have been noted. She should call, should come up with an excuse or a reason or pretend she's broken her leg, but she can't bring herself to.

Come and get me, Deborah, she thinks masochistically. *Do your worst. See if I care.*

Hugo next. So far, social media is more interested in his death than the mainstream press. Hawberry must be doing a good job of keeping a lid on things.

Jane clicks on one of the few articles available. *Eminent Publisher Found Dead in his Canonbury Town House.* Serious eyes, framed by the famous bushy eyebrows and beard of Mr Strauss, stare out at her. What secrets are hiding behind those eyes? Did this man have a hand in Daisy's death? Even in his own?

The thing with a public figure like Hugo is that he crops up on the internet a lot. A simple google of his name brings up link after link of book announcements, prize nominations, lectures, all mixed in with notifications about the other Hugo Strausses in the world. A German rower from the 1930s who won Olympic gold. A long-dead watercolour artist. A mini-scooter competitor.

An article about the Oxford University Dramatic Society, complete with photograph, shows the Hugo she's looking for at twenty-one, staring seriously into the lens. It's odd seeing him as a young man; without the beard he is almost unrecognisable. Jane scans along the faces in the photograph, all white and mostly male, until one makes her pause. Frowning, she zooms in. There is no doubt about it. That perfect quiff, flashy grin and chiselled face is undoubtably Lambert Graves.

'Well, I never,' she mutters to herself. 'They've known each other all this time.'

Leaving the photo, she starts to add other search terms alongside Hugo's name:

Hugo Strauss past. Hugo Strauss controversy. Hugo Strauss childhood.

It's when she types in *Hugo Strauss tragedy* that something interesting finally comes up. Frowning, she scans the list of links to news sites dotted down the page and clicks the top one.

DEVON WOMAN DEAD IN CAR ACCIDENT TRAGEDY

**The husband of Johanna Carney says he
'will never forgive, never forget'**

At 21:30 on 22 February, Johanna Carney was returning to her holiday rental in Seaton when she was hit by a silver Jaguar F-PACE. She was pronounced dead at the scene.

The driver of the vehicle was identified as 53-year-old Hugo Strauss, who was visiting Seaton on holiday.

'He seemed like a nice enough man,' said May Lapworth, the owner of the holiday cottage in which Mr Strauss was staying. 'I'd never rent to someone I felt was a danger. The roads around here are a death trap.'

'May has all sorts at that cottage,' said Dick Rathbourne, who lives next door. 'Irresponsible people from London who don't know the area, have loud parties and leave a mess. It was only a matter of time until one of them did something like this.'

Mrs Carney's husband, Michael, said of his late wife: 'Johanna was the light of my life. There won't be a day that passes when I won't think of her. There won't be a day that I won't miss her.'

Devon and Cornwall Police have refused to comment on the investigation at this time.

Jane sits open-mouthed in shock.

She types in Hugo's name alongside that of Johanna Carney and more headlines spring to life.

MAN ARRESTED IN FATAL COLLISION WITH CYCLIST

Driver Avoids Prison In Road Death Case

Jane continues to scroll, feeling sick and scared. Of what, she doesn't know. Perhaps that she has found out the truth, and that it is deeply, dreadfully sad.

Finally, she lies back in exhaustion, accidentally spilling tea onto the duvet.

The clock on the wall shows that it's almost 10.45 and Jane's stomach rumbles. She'll get some breakfast, *then* she'll get to work on her novel. Besides, after what she's just uncovered, she deserves a pastry or two.

Chapter Twenty-Four

Monday, 11:30 a.m.

Natasha is reeling.

This should have been a good day. As her agent had been away for the book launch, Natasha had hoped that when they met there would be a celebratory brunch of sorts. She had pictured sweet mimosas, expensive eggs, silver teapots, and a warm, contented feeling in her soul.

Instead, they have an emergency meeting with Polar Bear after their rather low-energy takeaway coffee and pastry. On top of that, Marabella is acting strangely. She explains to Natasha that she found her office had been broken into on her return from France, and though nothing important was taken, the intrusion has made her feel on edge. She asked about Hugo with tears in her eyes, and any words of congratulation about the publication were muted.

Natasha didn't raise her suspicion that Hugo took his own life after murdering his assistant. It is only a theory, and besides, Marabella doesn't seem in the mood for grisly speculation.

It isn't long before they get on to the most pressing subject.

'Now, we need to talk about the online buzz about you and these murders,' Marabella says, tapping her bank card on the reader and pocketing the receipt. 'That is going to be what Polar Bear want to discuss.'

'Oh . . . you've seen all that?'

Marabella gives her a pitying look.

'Let's walk and talk.'

Everyone has seen it, she explains as they weave through the pedestrians, sipping the expensive coffees on their way to the Polar Bear offices. 'Including the publishers and retailers.'

The reaction of the bookshops is split. Some, panicking about aligning themselves with an author viewed at best as 'cursed' and at worst a murderess, are dismantling window displays, pulling Natasha's books from the shelves and returning their stock. Others are leaning into the hype, trying to sell the book on its sinister association. Neither scenario is what Natasha had dreamt of.

'They *must* know it's all rot?' she whispers. 'They can't *believe* I'm actually . . . cursed, can they? And since *when* did people listen to nutters on the internet?'

'TikTok is the religion of the 2020s,' Marabella says, throwing up her hands. 'Which makes the people uploading these videos the new Messiahs.'

Natasha groans, and her agent puts an arm around her shoulders. 'It can be smoothed over, I'm sure of it. We're going to speak with the Managing Director, Raymond Stokes, get an idea of how he sees things progressing. We'll fix this.'

Natasha has been to the Polar Bear offices just once before, not long after the life-changing incident of the famous publishing house buying her manuscript. Hugo Strauss had taken her for lunch in a wood-panelled restaurant nearby, then introduced her to countless people who shook her hand and complimented her work. It had been a whirlwind, though whether it was pleasant or not she could not quite work out.

This time, however, she can definitely say is *not* pleasant. She stops dead outside the aggressive block of silver and glass, the well-known logo of a white bear guarding the entranceway.

'Come on,' Marabella says, firmly but kindly. 'We can take whatever they have to say.'

To Natasha's delight, it's a grinning Daniel who appears to greet them.

'It would usually be Hugo or his assistant welcoming you,' he tells them in the elevator. 'But as they are both . . . well, I volunteered.'

Marabella looks as though she's barely listening, staring straight ahead at her reflection in the mirrored wall. She is shorter than Daniel, almost Natasha's height, curvy, with poker-straight grey hair and eyes that are long and cat-like, outlined in kohl.

When the lift doors slide open on the seventh floor, Natasha feels as though she has left her stomach in the lobby. Her legs feel numb as she follows Daniel down the corridor, her head buzzy with white noise, as though it's full of bees. Is this the day that everything falls apart? Has the dream of being an author come to an end so soon? Perhaps they will burn all the copies of her book on a big bonfire, chanting *Cursed! Cursed! Curs—*

'Here we go,' says Daniel, pushing open the door of a meeting room.

'Please stay,' Natasha chokes out in a whisper.

A man leaps up from an armchair, stretching out his hand to shake hers.

'Hello there, Natasha! I'm Raymond. Raymond Stokes. And lovely to see you again, Marabella. Please, please, take a seat. Donald here will get us some coffee.'

Raymond Stokes has the air of a man for whom life had gone well. His voice is plummy and smooth, skin clear and tanned. His hair, still thick and dark despite middle age being in the rearview mirror, is slicked back on his head like fresh tarmac.

He clasps his hands and smiles at Natasha as they all take seats. Raymond's dark blue suit is creaseless and expensive-looking, his shirt as bright white as his teeth and open at the neck, perfectly fitting. Something about him makes Natasha's skin crawl.

She shares a hard sofa with Marabella, lets her eyes scan the room as her agent makes small talk. The walls are of frosted glass, apart from one which boasts posters of famous authors.

Perhaps some of them have sat in this very seat. Natasha does not know if any of them became embroiled in murder. Oscar Wilde? He was always up to something, wasn't he? And people still like him. Didn't Norman Mailer stab his wife?

'So, Natasha, Natasha, Natasha . . . ' Raymond Stokes is looking at her, shaking his head sadly. 'What a dreadful turn of events. Losing Hugo like this. And after what happened with your previous agent too! *Most* unfortunate.'

'And Daisy Olsson.'

'What? Oh, yes. The assistant too. Dreadful. Dreadful! And . . . I don't know if you've seen . . . what's being said online?'

'Spit it out, Raymond,' snaps Marabella, rolling her eyes and flicking her hair back over her shoulder.

The door creaks open and Daniel backs into the room, concentrating on the brimming cups of coffee in his hands.

'Is this oat milk?' Marabella asks as she takes hers. 'Oh, well, never mind.'

'Yes, yes,' Raymond is saying. 'It's just that, people are . . . so silly. They let their imaginations run away with them! So very silly.'

'Raymond . . . '

'Well,' he continues hurriedly with a nervous glance at Marabella, and Natasha notices that a perfectly oiled strand of his hair has come unstuck and is now protruding at an odd angle. 'The problem *is*, this isn't great for *sales*.' He says it with a practised smile on his face, like that of a doctor delivering a chlamydia diagnosis. 'We've *tried* to steady the ship, but we've already had a *few* retailers say they're walking the plank, so to speak.' After a beat of silence, he clarifies. 'They're pulling the book from the shelves.'

Natasha feels the walls closing in on her. She tries to control her breathing and keeps her eyes unfocused and dry. If she tunes in too much to what is being said, she will burst into tears.

'And that was before this morning,' Raymond Stokes continues. 'I don't know if you read the *Courier*?'

'What?' Natasha's head snaps up. 'What do you mean?' So far, she'd seen the gossip about her taking over social media platforms one by one. But that was okay. That was bearable. That was just online. But if the story has reached a *national newspaper*?

'Well, yes.' Raymond falters, taking a restorative sip of his coffee then looking pointedly up at Daniel who is lingering by the door. 'That will be all, Donald.'

A comforting hand squeezes Natasha's shoulder before she hears the door swing closed. Raymond leans over to pick up a newspaper from behind his armchair. He hesitates before evidently deciding that there are no words to soften this blow and putting it down on the coffee table silently.

AUTHOR LINKED TO THREE MURDERS – GUILTY? OR 'CURSED'?

Natasha Martez, the celebrated author of debut thriller *One Dark Minute*, published just last week, has become embroiled in something far darker than her fiction. The young Portuguese writer, currently living in Bath, appears to be the missing link between multiple murders in the publishing industry.

An arrest for the first murder – that of Martez's literary agent Carrie Marks – was made earlier this year following a confession caught on camera. The Cumbria police force have not suggested Natasha was involved in the crime, though she was present at the moment of arrest.

However, when Ms Martez's editor Hugo Strauss and his assistant Daisy Olsson both met an untimely end last week, eyebrows were raised.

One prominent book blogger commented, 'I just don't think this could possibly be a coincidence. This person, whether by her own doing or not, is dangerous, and people need to be careful about associating with her and her novel. I'm not saying she's a killer, but maybe she's into witchcraft? Or maybe she's—

Natasha doesn't unfold the paper to read the rest of the article. A tiny photograph of her face sits alongside it. She doesn't know when it was taken, but her eyes are half-closed and she looks a little shifty. Sitting back on the hard sofa, she closes her eyes and exhales.

'Well,' Marabella is saying, 'not good news. Obviously. But at least it's only small, and on page 24. No one reads past the first few, do they? And what are you doing about it, Raymond? Does Natasha have a new editor yet? Who is sorting this nonsense out?'

'Frankie Reid, a relatively new hire, will be taking over from Hugo. The thing is, though, we aren't really sure *how* to sort it out. Our publicity department is leaning on their contacts, but other than that . . . until the culprit is caught and it all blows over . . . '

'And if they are *not* caught?'

Natasha is letting the words wash over her. Two people are dead, she reminds herself. In the grand scheme of things, her book is unimportant. It's just that it doesn't feel that way. Not to her.

After what seems like hours of back and forth between Marabella and Raymond, the majority of which Natasha has blocked out, a gentle knock sounds on the door. It inches open, and Natasha feels a flood of relief as Daniel's familiar face appears in the crack.

'Mr Stokes, sorry. But the marketing team are waiting to come into this room. And there is also a little, er, *situation* in the art department. There are tears.'

'Fine.' Raymond Stokes takes a deep breath and transforms his face with a winning smile. The strand of ungelled hair has made its way back into place at some point during the discussion. He puts his hands on his thighs and makes eye contact with each of his guests in turn, the universal signal for *time's up*.

'Thank you for coming in.' Raymond gets to his feet, and Natasha notices how very small he is. 'Let's just . . . let's hope very much that the killer is caught, eh? And, Marabella . . . we need to catch up about Lambert Graves at some point.'

Natasha gets heavily to her feet.

'Yes. He's upset about Hugo.' Marabella stands too, brushing invisible crumbs from her jacket. 'He'll be keen to know who his new publisher will be. After all, he only moved to Polar Bear because of Hugo in the first place.'

'I'll be looking after Lambert myself for now. But time is ticking on. Do you know when he is sending in the new book? It's a few, er, *months* late now.'

Daniel is waiting by the open door, attempting to look helpful rather than like he is eavesdropping. He gives Natasha a wink. It makes her feel stronger.

'The new book?' Marabella is saying, collecting her handbag. 'He sent it in last week, I believe. I was on holiday, and then all this happened with Hugo, so I haven't had a chance to read it yet but I saw it drop into my inbox. Are you not in Hugo's emails?'

'Yes, we certainly are.' A deep crease has appeared between Raymond's eyebrows. 'And there's nothing there from Lambert. I'll check again, but if you could resend the book, that would be much appreciated.'

They are ushered out of the fishbowl room into the wider office. Beautiful young people stride purposefully around the open-plan space. A woman surely no older than twenty-two appears from what looks like a stationery cupboard, wiping red eyes.

Natasha reflects that every office has a crying cupboard, and she used to use it frequently back when she worked full-time at the university. Was the boredom and dissatisfaction of her work there better or worse than the tumultuous heartbreak of being a novelist?

As they wander towards the lift, Raymond and Marabella are having a low, muttered conversation that Natasha can't be bothered to try and listen to. The last few hours have made her feel sick, and separate, and sad. The way her dreams have been derailed. The way the world is turning on her, her face for all to see in a national newspaper. The way everyone mourns the eminent, successful Hugo Strauss, but forgets his lowly assistant. It's too much to bear.

At the lifts, Daniel presses the button and they all wait politely.

'Oh, my phone!' Marabella is patting down her pockets. 'I think I left it in the meeting room.'

'Douglas will get it,' Raymond says without looking at Daniel, and he obediently trots off, returning moments later, holding out a black iPhone.

'Thank you, Douglas,' says Marabella, giving him a rare, tired smile.

Raymond begins a protracted goodbye to Natasha, attempting to reassure her and making vague promises about *doing all we can*. But the words wash over her like seawater. Because when Daniel passed the phone to her agent, the photo on the lock-screen flashed up. It's a view that Natasha recognises at once, because it's a place she's visited many times. The Escarpa Viewpoint in Lisbon.

But also because she saw the exact same picture very recently. On Hugo Strauss's desk.

Chapter Twenty-Five

Monday, 14.30 p.m.

Jane Hepburn is used to being alone. But in London, alone seems to mean something quite different.

When she is alone in Cumbria, the nearest companions are often the sheep on the hill. There are five of them, and so she has named them after the Spice Girls.

In London, alone means that she is surrounded by hundreds of people at any one time, often having them physically bash into her, stand on her foot or, horror of horrors, *speak* to her. This morning she has had conversations with multiple people she previously did not know. All of whom, Jane suspects, were mad.

Still, she has learnt a lot about chem trails, time travel, and how the NHS is controlled by Russian spies. So it's not been a total waste.

Jane shifts guiltily in her seat, quailing under the stare of the waitress. She picks up her empty cup and pretends to sip it. The waitress rolls her eyes in an exasperated but not unkind manner and leaves her be.

She has been sitting in this café for two hours, the first of which she spent staring at a blank Word document hoping it would turn into a novel. Searching for inspiration, she'd started transcribing conversations happening around her. Sadly, she was very near the till, so these usually consisted of, 'A latte, please.' 'Dairy or oat milk?' 'Oat.' 'That'll be £4.50.'

When she had six pages of orders written down, she'd deleted the lot and started delving more deeply into the accident Hugo Strauss had in Devon all those years ago.

Jane writes down the facts of the case she has already, adding to the list with each new crumb of news she uncovers.

The victim's name was Johanna Carney. She was cycling back to the holiday house she was sharing with her family and friends, just outside the village of Seaton, at 9.35 p.m. one February evening when Hugo's car swung around the corner. Johanna hit the windscreen of a Jaguar driven at 60 m.p.h., was hurled over the top of the car and landed 80 feet away in the centre of the road. She was pronounced dead at the scene.

Hugo Strauss suffered whiplash.

He hadn't *technically* broken any laws. This being a small country road, the speed limit *was* 60 m.p.h., though it is deemed inadvisable to drive at this speed, especially in the dark. Strauss claimed that Johanna came out of nowhere and there was nothing he could do, and she, of course, was not alive to contradict him.

Hugo was found guilty of causing death by careless or inconsiderate driving, since his speed was foolish on a small, twisty road at night. He was sentenced to pay a hefty fine and banned from driving for twelve months.

'*Twelve months' driving ban*,' Jane gasped aloud when she read this. 'For *killing* a woman?'

No one could really prove Johanna's death was Hugo's fault. Maybe it wasn't. Even so, the story made Jane sick to her stomach. The more articles she read, Facebook posts about related memorials, and campaigns for road safety she unearthed, the sicker she felt.

Johanna's husband Michael was frequently quoted. As well as extolling the many virtues of his beautiful late wife in the press, he also championed a failed attempt at lowering speed limits on country roads, and campaigned against Hugo's light sentence. In the past few years, however, Michael Carney has gone quiet, and a Facebook post suggests he now lives in his late wife's birth country of Sweden.

Had Michael become sick of campaigning for justice *within* the law? Had he instead sworn vengeance of a more old-fashioned kind? And, if so, how did Daisy fit into all this? She would have been just 16 at the time of the accident.

Jane finds Michael's abandoned Facebook page and stares at his profile picture – still him and his wife on their wedding day.

Johanna looks just as tall as Jane, but willow-thin with the sort of lean, tanned limbs that she could only dream of. Blonde hair is tumbling from an updo, and she's looking at her new husband and laughing, radiant with joy. A fresh-faced Michael looks bewildered, as if he can't believe his luck.

The image provokes a pang of jealousy in Jane's gut. Her own romantic life has been limp and unsatisfactory, mostly lived vicariously through the pages of fiction.

She doesn't expect a great love to appear in her life. Sure, she did once picture herself in a long white dress (in her imaginings she was a lot more glamorous than in her mirror). But over the years, Jane has come to realise that she is just not the type of woman to spark such emotion. A man, or woman, has *never* looked at her like Michael is looking at his new bride, and she knows they never will.

Still . . . Sometimes it burns.

Johanna's wedding dress is simple and classy. A beauty like hers needs little adornment. It skims her body like water, stopping an inch above the ground to show a gold heel . . . There is something oddly recognisable about the woman. Maybe she just has the sort of face that Jane encounters in every model in existence. That embodiment of perfection.

She finds Johanna's Facebook page, still available but seemingly untouched for decades. In her profile photo she is laughing in the sunshine with a toddler and a curly-haired friend. Her ice-blue eyes are arresting, and it seems so odd, so sad, so desperately unfair, that Hugo Strauss ended this woman's time on earth so prematurely.

Jane shudders and closes Facebook. The waitress's eyes are boring into her. She checks her watch: 3 o'clock. A few hours until Daniel finishes work, and she still hasn't heard from Natasha.

Feeling defeated, she opens her email inbox and skims through one from Deborah Templeton, with HR ominously CC-ed into it, demanding her presence, in person, at a disciplinary meeting first thing tomorrow morning and reminding her she is on her third warning.

Jane's phone buzzes on the table, a welcome name flashing up on the screen.

'DI Ramos,' Jane says as she accepts the call, her heart leaping.

'Miss Hepburn,' rumbles the warm voice. It makes her smile, washing away a little of the lonely, sick sadness that has been creeping up on her all day. That voice feels like a steaming cup of chicken soup. Jane has always known that wallowing is allowed, but for a limited time only. Strengthened by Ramos's voice, she sits up straight, throws back her shoulders, and finds her inner PI Baker.

'How was the date?'

'Lousy, truth be told. She was a bit of a bore. Wasn't interested in my theory about the correlation between choice of murder weapon and favourite animal at *all*.'

'Oooh, that sounds fascinating!' Jane says with a grin. 'What goes with badger?'

'Easy – rope. Clearly, I should be taking *you* for a drink instead!'

Jane laughs, too loudly in the small café, her spirits buoyed. 'Anyway, what do you have for me, Ramos?'

'Straight to the point, I see. Well, I looked at Daisy's phone records again, as you requested. She only made the one call on the day she died, at 6.52 p.m. Don't know who to, but I'll send the number over in a text.'

6.52? That would be just half an hour before Jane found her lifeless body.

'Thank you, Detective Inspector. I mean it.' She wishes he was here. She wanted to hug him, walk along the Thames and pick his brains. 'Could I trouble you to take a look at the phone record of Hugo Strauss?'

He sighs deeply and Jane fancies she can feel his outbreath. 'You cannot. I mean it, Jane, I'm going to get in trouble if I keep poking around and I've already pulled in a favour from an old friend on the Met. True, I owed you. And, I admit, I like helping. Somehow you make policing fun again. But I can't give you anything more.'

Jane knows when to retreat. She says her goodbyes and sits staring at her screen, waiting. Sure enough, a minute later, a text arrives from him. It's brief. One eleven-digit number and a 'good luck'. Ramos, she reflects, is a man of his word.

It's with bated breath that she taps the phone number on-screen.

Call? Yes.

The ringing tone is loud in her ear. Daisy Olsson, a woman who rarely called anyone, dialled this number just before she died. Around the time that Hugo Strauss went missing. With a thrill, Jane realises that the answer to everything could hinge on this call.

Finally, the ringing cuts off and a gruff voice sounds down the line.

'Mike's Taxi. I taxi, you payi.'

Jane cancels the call.

So Daisy called for a *taxi*. Jane's disappointed but what was she expecting? Someone to answer with a chirpy, 'Hello, dastardly murderer here!'?

But if this man was one of the last people to speak to Daisy, he is important. Was she ordering a taxi home, even though the party had just begun? Was she planning to go and see someone – the man from the dating app, for example – leading Scott to lash out? Is Mike the taxi man also a friend or lover of hers?

The most likely explanation, Jane reflects, is that Daisy was trying to escape from Hugo, but he managed to get to her before she could disappear. She imagines him fleeing Cecil Court after he has poisoned his assistant, going home to take his own life. But *why*?

Jane stares out of the window, lost in thought. She can see Marabella Rhodes's office from here – a smart building of smooth white stone, pillars lining up along the ground floor like soldiers. An arch curves over the smart black door, and smaller ones frame each sash window. A shiny brass plaque sits to the left of the door.

All of a sudden, one of the passers-by catches her eye. Someone whose name is cropping up surprisingly frequently in this investigation. She leaps out of her seat, steps on a slice of cucumber, and slides inelegantly across the floor, just managing to steady herself against the shoulder of an angry woman with a chihuahua.

'Sorry! Sorry!' Jane shouts as she rights herself and runs for the door. 'Sorry!'

Jogging across the street, she sees again the blond quiff and gold-studded ears of Lambert Graves.

'Excuse me?' Jane shouts. 'Ex – excuse me? Mr Graves?'

Graves stops, which Jane is most grateful for because she is starting to get a stitch. He looks amused as she comes to a halt in front of him, breathing heavily and clutching at her side. She glances over her shoulder and can still see the café. Perhaps she should start doing some exercise if she needs to chase potential murderers so often.

'Ah, a fan, I presume?'

'No,' Jane says, finally standing up straight. Lambert's face falls. 'I mean . . . sorry, not *not* a fan. You are brilliant, of course.' He brightens. 'It's just that I saw you, the other night? At my friend's book launch? And I . . . I wanted to say hello.' Jane can feel the unwelcome sensation of a blush creeping up her neck. The decision to accost him was made so quickly, she didn't think about what she would say once she was in front of Lambert.

'Oh, I see,' he says with a frown, shaking his head. As he does, the golden studs in his left ear glitter in the sunlight and an overpowering smell of aftershave fills her nose. 'Terrible business. That poor girl. And now . . . well, you probably wouldn't have heard . . . '

'About Hugo Strauss?' Lambert raises his eyebrows in surprise, and Jane pictures again Hugo's body still sitting at his desk, the thick smell of death filling the room. 'He was my friend's editor too. Natasha Martez?'

'Oh, charming! How charming. Yes, little Natasha's book did look marvellous. We share an agent as well as an editor, don't you know? She left us all a message about Hugo last night, you see. I was actually just hoping to speak to Marabella about my latest work.' He gestures over at the white stone building.

Jane bristles at that 'little Natasha' but tries to smile through it. After all, she reasons, Natasha *is* pretty short. 'She's out, I'm afraid. With Natasha actually.'

Lambert makes a show of looking at his watch.

'Ah. Well, the meeting *was* supposed to be at 10.30, I suppose.' He looks up at Jane with a charming grin, teeth pearly white. 'Timekeeping has never really been my forte.'

He reminds Jane of a golden retriever, and she can see why he managed to get parts in films despite his lack of obvious talent.

'I tell you what, why don't you and Natasha join me for dinner later? I would love to get to know her . . . and yourself, of course. Didn't get a chance to talk at the party after . . . well, you know.'

Before Jane can open her mouth, he has whipped out his phone and is passing it to her.

'Add your number and I'll send you the details. Tonight works for me.' Because any other option feels incredibly rude, she finds herself typing in her name and mobile number.

'Lovely, lovely,' Lambert says, tucking it back in his jacket and looking again at his watch. 'Now you look out for my text!'

He cocks his hands into two finger guns and shoots at her, one after the other: *bang bang*.

The smell of aftershave is thick in her throat.

Back in the café, Jane takes her seat again. Luckily her laptop is where she left it, though when she sees again the damning email from work on the screen, she almost wishes someone had pinched it. There is something bothering her about Graves, but she can't put her finger on what. They could use this opportunity to ask him about Hugo – if Graves has known him since university, then he will know about the car accident. He was there on Thursday too, and hadn't that funny editor, Lucy Tallow, mentioned seeing them talking? Hadn't Edward mentioned it also, that very night? Besides, it's not every day one gets to have dinner with a bestselling author and ex-film star.

And, Jane thinks, a smile coming to her face, *I know the perfect taxi company to get us there.*

She minimises the terrifying work email, only to be confronted once again with the blank white document – the page awaiting the first words of her next book. The bigger, better, perfect book that she cannot write.

But maybe it doesn't have to be *perfect*? Not straight away anyway. What she needs is a detective figure who feels fresh and real and new. Jane thinks of the kind, warm voice of Detective Inspector Ramos, of the gentle way in which Natasha handled the weeping Lizzie Yardley, the way Daniel joked with Scott Wallace, getting him to open up. She thinks of Hugo Strauss, slumped on his chair in the secret study, of Daisy in the bookshop stock room. Two deaths, two rooms that no one else entered.

What was it Ramos said? *You make policing fun again.* She lets herself feel all of the emotions that have passed through her over the last few days, drawing them in deeply into her lungs and heart and mind.

And then, after many months of silence, Jane begins to type.

Chapter Twenty-Six

Monday, 6.12 p.m.

It is the mousing hour of 6 o'clock. It's when the people depart
the offices of Eagle's Wing Press, and the mice come out from
their hidey holes to take control of the place. Lucy Tallow is
often the only person in the building by the time the transition
is complete at 7 o'clock. Sometimes she likes to pretend that she
is Queen of the Mice.

Lucy isn't one for mess and dirt, but sadly she is doomed to
share a planet with people like her colleagues, many of whom
have the hygiene standards of beasts. At least her part of the
desk is clean, wiped down with disinfectant wipes three times
a day and liberally spritzed with Lavender & Sage to promote
clarity and spiritual calm.

'See ya, Lucy,' Marcus mumbles, bag slung over his shoulder
as he makes for the exit.

'Good evening, Marcus.'

6.15. It's late for him. He is usually one of the 5 o'clock on
the dot types. Lazy, like everyone else.

She sprays more Lavender & Sage to find that spiritual
calmness again. Live and let live.

It wasn't like this in her previous job at prestigious Polar
Bear Publishing. The offices there had been swish and mouse-
free, people caring so much about their jobs that they would
stay late to finish up projects before celebrating successes at the
local pub. *Don't think about it, Lucy.*

She could go home too, but work is a good distraction from
the mounting tsunami of guilt and panic that keeps threatening

to engulf her. She inhales deeply, drawing the scent of the essential oils deep into her soul. *Calm calm calm.*

The type-set files of a new fantasy novel are on her screen, and she forces her attention back to it.

A lot of editors dislike this final part of the process, but Lucy thrives on it. She likes the order of it, the tweaking of tiny moving parts towards perfection. She likes to see the pages laid out as they will be in the physical book, likes to spot an error that no one else has noticed.

Across the floor, she hears the dull thud of a door shutting. That will be Alice, always the second-last to leave. Sometimes she tries to outlast Lucy, but she always breaks. Lucy keeps very still for a full moment, listening intently. Nothing. She is totally alone.

Well, she thinks as she watches a mouse inspect Marcus's keyboard crumbs, *not* totally *alone.*

Saving her place, Lucy closes the document and brings up a web browser in Incognito mode. As she has done multiple times today already, she types in the name of Hugo Strauss.

Nothing new. She skims through the same articles that mention his death, lost among the many that laud his accomplishments. It's an odd feeling, her old boss being gone from the world.

In a new tab, she opens up TheQuestersHeart.com. RedRuin66 is showing as offline, but their chat is still open from Sunday, his last words visible at the bottom of the page.

Hugo. Hugo Strauss.

Why had he brought up Hugo? Was it just a coincidence, or does he know more than he is letting on? She wants to trust him. She doesn't have many friends, but she has been burnt before, in similar circumstances. With a sense of tingling unease, she opens their mini-game and moves her Warden across the screen to kill RedRuin's Dragon Rider with a shadow spell.

Your move RedRuin ;)

Coincidence, she tells herself with a forced smile. They do happen. Like when her dad gave her the pearl earrings the same Christmas her mum got her the pearl necklace, even though they hadn't spoken in ten months. *Just a coincidence.*

No one knows what she has done. Even if it is eating her alive, even if it is consuming her soul, she will have to push past it.

In a third tab, Lucy opens a folder on her computer called *Other.* There are three photographs in the folder, and nothing else. All emailed to herself so she could use the office printer.

She clicks on the first and feels a sick swooping in her stomach. The sparkling blue eyes of Daisy Olsson stare out of the screen, her perfect blonde hair falling around her face, the dimpled cheeks, high cheekbones and cushioned lips creating a face fit for a runway. Lucy deletes the image. Snuffs out Daisy Olsson with a single click.

The next brings up the face of Hugo Strauss. His bushy beard hiding the frequent smirk. Hugo was a bad man. A spiritually lacking man. Lucy lets out a long, slow breath. Her old boss can't hurt her now.

Working at Polar Bear Publishing had been a dream come true for Lucy, especially under the respected Mr Strauss. She was honoured to bring him his morning coffee, to take minutes in his meetings, arrange his train tickets. She was overjoyed when she was given the opportunity to write book cover copy for some of his authors, to feed into his edits, to offer an opinion on artwork. Sure, thrillers weren't really her thing, but still – she'd felt like she'd *made it.*

What she had not felt either honoured or overjoyed about, was covering up his affair.

Lucy had been working at the company for four months when she became suspicious of her boss, and six months when she was sure. Hugo was married to a pretty American woman called Jessie. Lucy spoke to her when she called, sent her flowers from Hugo on their anniversary, and even met her a few times when she came into the office. She had a rounded, red-dyed bob, a long body and a tiny head, like a pin you might put in a map.

Jessie was kind, always taking time to ask Lucy about her day and dropping a card on her desk at Christmas. Would Lucy have felt differently if Jessie had been monstrous? If she was unattractive, would Lucy have been more understanding? She likes to think not, but you can't always control your judgements.

But as it is, her judgement was this: her boss was a cheating scumbag.

The first clue was the lunch. It was Lucy's job to book Hugo's working lunch reservations and coordinate with the person he was meeting, so she was always clued up on where he was and who he was with. When it came to lunch partners, there were those he liked ('he's a top man, Lucy, book us somewhere expensive' and those he groaned about ('can't stand that woman so I'll need good food. Book us somewhere expensive'), which was only natural.

But there was one lunch guest he passed no comment on, instead just requesting a good table at Clos Maggiore. When Lucy googled the restaurant, she found that it is officially the most romantic in London.

That in itself meant little. But when he requested the same table for the same meeting just two weeks later, Lucy was confused. Unless he had urgent business with them, Hugo never met with people at this frequency. When she enquired, he snapped at her.

'Important stuff about Lambert Graves, Lucy. Just book the table.'

Book it she did, but she didn't forget it.

The second clue was the phone call.

It came one Wednesday evening, when Jessie called the office trying to 'catch Hugo before he left'.

'Sorry, Ms Strauss,' Lucy had said. 'You've missed him. Did you need to tell him you'll be late for dinner? I can call the restaurant?'

'Oh, no, he has plans with some old university friends over in Oxford tonight. Never mind, it wasn't important. I'll text him.'

But Lucy could have sworn that Hugo had said he was seeing his wife that evening. And why on earth would he have asked her to book a table for two in Mayfair if he was seeing a group of friends in Oxford?

The final clue was Lisbon. When he didn't arrive in the office one Monday morning, Lucy had assumed he was ill or stuck on the train, until he'd emailed to say that he was in Portugal and his flight had been cancelled. It was pure chance that Marabella Rhodes's assistant had called to chase up a payment that day, and pure chance that he had mentioned the fact his boss was out that day due to a cancelled flight. Stuck, he told her with some joy, in Lisbon.

With that final piece of the puzzle in place, the whole picture stared Lucy right in the face. Her boss, Hugo Strauss, was having an affair with the revered literary agent Marabella Rhodes. And Lucy had been *helping him*.

The next day when Hugo reappeared, humming happily, slightly tanned, she couldn't even look at him. When he asked for a coffee, she made it stronger than he liked it. When the post came, she put his Amazon parcel in the bin. She didn't tell him about the doughnuts left in the kitchen. Didn't spray his desk with Lavender & Sage. Didn't point out the toothpaste on his tie. But it wasn't *enough*.

And then Jessie called. She really *was* ringing to check dinner plans with Hugo this time, and Lucy barely registered what she was doing when she told her a time half an hour earlier than Hugo planned to arrive. Time enough for a quick conversation.

Lucy's voice was steady when she imparted the news. *Your husband is having an affair. I'm sorry. You didn't hear it from me.*

Jessie had promised not to tell her husband how she'd found out. Maybe she kept her promise and Hugo guessed, or maybe it all came out in a flaming row. It doesn't make any difference to Lucy. All she knows is that three weeks later she was called into her boss's office and told it would be best if she left. She would not be required to work her notice. His face was cold and hard, the strain of separation already showing in the darkness under his eyes and stain on his shirt collar.

Legally, Lucy could have fought against the dismissal. But in reality? When a highly respected, successful man tells a young female assistant to pack her bags in silence, they do. Lucy traded her job for her morals, and she felt content with that. Sometimes. Other times? She burns with rage.

She sighs, spinning around slowly on her desk chair, waving her arms in the air. The lights are motion-sensor, so one of the drawbacks to being the last in the office is that she has to do this every 10 minutes. A pity the mice don't set it off, she thinks, watching the one sitting on Marcus's desk gathering up the crumbs from his Pret baguette.

In the end, the universe proffered her an olive branch of sorts with this assistant position at Eagles's Wing Press. It's a world away from where she was and with even worse pay. Every morning Lucy forces the memory of the snazzy offices and famous author names from her mind along with the tears from her eyes. Still, this is better than nothing, and with the rotten reference Hugo gave her, 'nothing' was her only other option.

She knows she did the right thing in telling Jessie. That the universe will make it all okay in the end is something she *has* to believe – even though the trauma and injustice of it all still keeps her up at night.

On the screen, she hovers the cursor over the final icon in the *Other* folder. Even the thought of the face in that photograph brings bile into her throat and a swirling mist of panic to her mind.

Too late now, she thinks, trying to still her heart. *Too late for Daisy, for Hugo . . . and, I'm afraid, for you too.*

A chime from the computer makes her jump. On TheQuestersHeart.com the message icon is flashing, and she opens up the chat.

Hello, my wonderful witch.

His Sword Carrier slides forward, from orange square to black.

Good Sir. Terribly sorry about your Dragon Rider.

Lucy's Warden continues its journey forward another two squares.

She'll be upset if RedRuin66 lets her down too. She's been let down so many times. Her mother leaving their family for the neighbour. Hugo. The last person she made friends with on TheQuestersHeart – they were the one, really, who started this whole murder mess. And Daisy Olsson of course. Her betrayal was almost the worst.

No bother, Moonshade. The path to victory is rarely smooth.

A mouse runs past Lucy's feet and she pulls them up onto her chair. She'd told Daisy about losing her job. Of course she had, Daisy was her best friend. Her *only* friend. But she didn't expect Daisy to jump into her grave, emailing Hugo directly to offer her services as an assistant, ready to start immediately. Lucy was deeply hurt. She'd said as much in their flaming row six months back, but Daisy hadn't cared a bean. In fact, they had barely spoken since that day.

Taking the Dragon Rider has given her an injection of confidence, and she clicks back onto her email, decisively opening the final one she'd sent herself a week earlier.

The lights in the office click off once again. In the darkness, Lucy takes one look over her shoulder to double-check she is entirely alone, breathes in deeply, and clicks on the final photo.

His expression is happy. Dirty-blond hair in loose curls around his face, clashing terribly with the neon yellow cap on his head that almost matches the yellow of his tracksuit. The swooping sensation is back in Lucy's stomach. On the mouse, her hand has started to tremble, her breath coming fast in her chest. What is she doing? She needs to stop this, but she can't. It's in motion and she is too small, too insignificant, to halt it.

Ding.

Your turn. Or are you stumped?

Lucy edges her Warden forward another square. RedRuin66 moves his Sword Carrier to safety.

You're not taking me down today, Witch.

The beginning of the end had started right here, on Questers. She had befriended a man on here months ago. They'd stayed up late, playing and chatting into the early hours, telling each other about their lives. Lucy had fallen in love, or fancied she had. Fallen hard. When she had finally plucked up the courage to ask him to meet, he'd gone silent. She felt her heart had been broken, found herself checking TheQuestersHeart for messages 20 times a day. But when he reappeared, she would have done anything not to have received that message about his real identity. The memory makes her body curl with mortification.

She frowns at the screen.

RedRuin, though nice to chat to, could be anyone. She isn't as naive as she once was. Lucy needs to know who he is and what he knows. She slides her Warden forward once more and takes out his Elf Archer with a shadow gather spell. Thinking through the steps of her conversation, she starts to type.

Read anything else interesting in the news?

If RedRuin is who he says he is, just a German Questers enthusiast spending a year in London who also likes fly fishing and candle making, that's great. But if he isn't, if he knows too much, then he must be stopped. She doesn't have a choice.

RedRuin66 is typing . . .

There wasn't much else about the Hugo man. Unless you know more?

Is she going to do this? She has to.

How about you meet me? And I'll tell you everything.

Chapter Twenty-Seven

Monday, 6.18 p.m.

Jane stands on the pavement outside her new B&B, awkwardly tugging at the hem of the freshly laundered red dress she wore to the party on Thursday night, a sweaty bottle of Blossom Hill white wine clutched in her other hand. Next to her, Natasha is buried in her mobile phone – Jane dreads to think how bad it's got online now. Daniel, dashing despite the wrinkled shirt and too-short trousers he wore to work, looks repeatedly up and down the road for an approaching car.

'We're going to be super late,' he grumbles. 'Honestly, Jane, Hampstead is *miles* away.'

'I'm sure Lambert won't mind.'

'We should have got the Tube,' Daniel says, and Jane takes from his mood that he must be hungry.

Natasha sighs, slipping her phone into her pocket. 'Then,' she says, 'we would have missed the chance to interview the man who was maybe the last person to speak to Daisy before she died.'

Jane had updated first Natasha then Daniel on her progress as they came out of the Polar Bear offices. She'd relayed everything about Lambert Graves's invitation to dinner, Hugo's car accident and the death of Johanna Carney, all down to the last number Daisy Olsson called before she died – Mike's Taxi. Natasha, who had been glum and red-eyed when they met, had gone from confused to impressed, and Daniel had punched the air with excitement.

The feeling of despair Jane had felt in the coffee shop feels far away now. Sure, more questions had been unearthed, but questions were leads, and leads were good. Her mood was further heightened by having finally made a promising start on a new story – though she wasn't quite ready to tell her friends about *that*.

'Oh, I almost forgot to tell you!' Natasha says. 'I saw something weird earlier too. Nothing like what Jane's found, but still suspicious.'

'Go on,' Daniel says, bouncing on the balls of his feet and peering into the darkness for their taxi.

'Well, Marabella's screen background . . . It was a photo of the Escarpa Viewpoint. I'd recognise it anywhere. Used to drink wine up there as a teenager.'

'And that's suspicious because?' Daniel says impatiently.

'Because it is the exact same photo that we saw framed on Hugo's desk. It's not a common place for out-of-towners to go, and sort of a weird photo to have in a frame in pride of place.'

'Almost,' Jane says slowly, 'as though it's a place you associate with someone you love.'

'Exactly! It got me thinking . . . '

'He's here!' Daniel yells, and Jane looks up to see an old Citroën Picasso turning onto the road. A triangular sign is perched on its roof, proclaiming *Mike's Taxi*. With a dubious crunching sound, the car pulls up to the kerb and the window rolls down.

'Mike's Taxi!' the driver shouts. 'I taxi, you payi!'

After dusting what she hopes are crisp crumbs from the seat fabric, Jane drops into the front seat, Natasha and Daniel into the back.

The man who they establish to be the one and only Mike is in a much better mood than he was on the phone. In fact, he is positively radiant. As they make their way through the city, Mike tells them long stories about his children's school ('total dump but they've got some nice hydrangeas out front'), his wife's new haircut ('she looks jus' like Margot Robbie, if

Margot Robbie was eight stone 'eavier and lost a few teeth') and his day so far ('slept like a log with concussion, my love!').

Mike is a squat, toad-like man, sitting so low in his seat that Jane fears he can't entirely see where he is going. Her sense of unease is only exacerbated by the nail-biting speed he prefers to travel at, and his rather last-minute approach to corners.

It isn't until they slam to a stop at some traffic lights that Jane manages to wrest control of the conversation.

'You have many regulars, Mike?' she asks, wiping her sweating palms discreetly on the seat.

'Oh, yeah, I got my regulars. They pay the bills!'

'I got your number from a friend of mine. Daisy Olsson?' Jane tries, feigning nonchalance while she studies Mike's side profile. He frowns but isn't startled by the name. The light turns green and the car lurches forward, swerving around to the left. In the back seat, Jane hears Daniel slam into the window.

'Daisy, Daisy, Daisy,' Mike says to himself, tapping the steering wheel. 'Remind me?'

'I think you actually gave her a lift the other night? On Thursday? From Cecil Court near Covent Garden?'

'Oh, Daaaiiiissy! Yeah, I know the lass.'

'You spoke to her then? On Thursday?' Jane is gripping the edges of her seat in anticipation. They know Daisy called him, but she certainly didn't get in any taxi. *Why?* What, or who, stopped her from escaping to safety?

'Ah, yes, I did talk to her then! She calls me now and again for her boss, ya see? Grumpy bugger he is. Never cracks a smile. Hugo whatsit.'

Jane spins in her seat to give her friends a meaningful eyebrow raise. Of *course*! Daisy booked the taxi for *Hugo*. She was his assistant after all.

The driver swerves around a corner and Jane slams into her own window. A muffled 'Ow!' that sounds a lot like Natasha comes from the back.

'Oopsie!' Mike says cheerfully. 'Almost missed that one.'

'Did Daisy sound . . . her normal self? When you spoke to her on Thursday?'

'Oh, yeah, I'd say so. Hugo was a bit off though. He's never that friendly, like I said. But he looked proper Moby Dick that night.'

The car slams to a halt. Jane flies forward, the seatbelt cutting painfully into her skin. A fox with a mangy tail trots happily across the road in front of the car. Mike puts it back into first gear and zooms off again as fast as the 1.2l engine of his Citroën Picasso will allow.

'Moby Dick?' gasps Natasha from the back seat, rubbing a red seatbelt-shaped mark on her neck.

'Sick! Sick as a dog! Sweating and groaning. Probably ate a bad oyster or something. Typical of these fancy sorts. I was just happy he didn't empty his dinner all over my car.'

'So Hugo left the party early because he was ill,' Jane shouts over the whine of the engine accelerating. 'And you took him back to Canonbury?'

'Yeah,' Mike says, swinging left onto a main road. 'That's right. Why you asking anyway?' He turns to look at her. For the first time a shadow of suspicion crosses his face.

'No reason!' Jane squeaks as they career along at 20 m.p.h. over the speed limit with Mike's eyes looking anywhere but at the road. 'I was at that party on Thursday and I just remember her calling you,' she invents wildly. The bottle of Blossom Hill rolls violently in the footwell, and Mike turns his eyes back to the road.

As the car slows and turns into a side road, everyone lets out a long-held breath.

Hampstead is leafier than anywhere else Jane has seen in London. Huge, ancient trees tower behind artfully crumbling stone walls. Ivy climbs up brickwork, wisteria festoons doorways. As they drive, the houses become larger and more concealed.

'Should be somewhere round 'ere,' Mike says, peering up at a gothic-style building that looks like an old schoolhouse. 'You alright to get out and have a wander?'

Gratefully, Jane, Natasha and Daniel climb out of the car, Daniel rubbing a red mark on his forehead and Natasha looking slightly sick. Mike gives them a cheery wave out of the window, completes a frantic six-point turn and speeds off down the road, taking out three dustbins.

Thanks to his F1 skill, they are only five minutes late.

'So Hugo left the party because he was *ill*,' Jane says, watching Mike's Picasso disappear around a corner. 'You know what this means?'

'Yeah,' moans Daniel. 'Mike must have driven him *to* the party as well.'

'No,' Jane says patiently, waiting for her friends to grasp the importance of this new information. 'It means that Hugo *was poisoned in Cecil Court as well*. Not in his home! I don't know why he took so much longer to die than Daisy, maybe he only ingested a tiny amount? But he was *already dying* on the way to Canonbury. Hugo didn't take his own life because of killing Daisy, and no one broke into his house to kill him there.'

Natasha gasps, finally understanding. 'Hugo is innocent. *He* is a victim, just as much as Daisy is!'

They stare at each other, open-mouthed. 'It still doesn't explain the text message,' Jane says, racking her brains. 'The one he supposedly sent you two days after he was killed.'

'We're already late,' Daniel says, looking uneasy. 'Come on.'

'The house is called Aurum Manor,' she says to Daniel, who is peering at the nameplate of a mansion partially hidden by ivy. 'No number.'

'Aurum,' Natasha mutters, walking further down the road, looking at each house in turn. 'Interesting. Means gold in Latin.'

Jane catches Daniel rolling his eyes and tries to hide her smile. Natasha's well of knowledge is bottomless.

'His wife is a jewellery designer, isn't she?' Jane asks. 'Maybe it's related to that?'

'Not really a designer,' Daniel chips in. 'More of a hobby for her, I think, but Lambert mentions it in interviews all the time. He's always wearing pieces she's made too.'

A moment later, Natasha lets out a loud 'Ha!' from around the corner.

'Subtle,' she is saying as Jane hurries over. 'Very subtle. Gold Manor.'

It surprises Jane that her new novel pops into her mind then – could this house feature in it? It's a shock to feel the creative juices stirring in her again, to have them filter into her real life while she collects fragments of story.

She is standing in front of a pair of gates, large and gold enough to guard Heaven. Behind them, a gravel driveway curves gently towards a huge red-brick house with an arched front door of dark oak. A handsome turret with lead-latticed windowpanes stretches proudly up on one side, ivy creeping over the brickwork as if in an to attempt to hide the whole property from view. Numerous windows – tall, narrow and gothic-looking – blink back at them like a many-eyed spider.

Aside from the gaudy golden gates, the house is stunning and is presumably worth multiple millions of pounds. Jane feels a tingle run down her spine. Could the man who lives here throw light on these murders? *Is he,* and the thought startles her as it bursts into her brain, *even involved somehow? After all, why has he invited them here, really? Does he know they are investigating and wants to see what they know?*

Does he want to stop them?

Daniel reaches out and pushes the gate, which swings open with a loud *creak*.

You're being paranoid, Jane.

'Unlocked,' he whispers. 'Shall we?'

With a brave wink, he opens the gate further and steps through to a crunch of gravel underfoot. Jane is rooted to the spot, worry that Lambert has lured them here to hurt them paralysing her.

A voice calling out of the shadows in the day's fading light causes them all to jump.

'Hello?'

It unsticks Jane's feet, and she steps into the driveway. An incongruously shabby Volvo Estate is parked up, previously hidden by the hedge, next to a shiny Mercedes. The boot of the Volvo has been flung open and a woman is looking up at them, seemingly pausing in her efforts to force what looks like one last box into a packed car. She returns to her labour and, with a whoop of success, slams the boot shut.

'Oh,' Jane stutters. 'Sorry, the gate was open? And we just . . . we are here to see Mr Graves?'

The woman stares at them with curiosity, hands on hips, unbrushed mousy brown hair curling outwards around her small, round face like a halo. She has a smudge of dirt on her button nose. She looks curious rather than cross, her full lips quirking into a questioning smile that puts Jane at ease.

'Well, if the eminent *Mr Graves* requires your presence,' the mystery woman says with a laugh, 'who am I to hold you up!' She chucks an M&S bag full of books on the passenger seat and walks over to them, wiping her palms on her jeans.

'Vicky. Vicky Graves.'

She holds out a hand for Jane to shake.

If Jane had stopped to consider what a woman with a passion for jewellery and Lambert Graves might look like, it wouldn't be this. Vicky is dressed demurely in blue jeans and a now-dirty white top, without a scrap of make-up or so much as a single earring. A naturally striking woman, but one who has chosen to avoid the trappings of the beauty industry, instead giving off a pleasingly unpolished and practical air.

Vicky is staring at her expectantly so Jane snaps herself back to the present. 'Um, sorry?'

'I said, how do you know my dearest, soon-to-be ex-husband?'

'Oh, well, I just met him in the street. But Natasha here shares a literary agent with him. And an editor. Or *shared* an editor anyway.'

Vicky's face falls, deep lines forming to either side of her mouth and across her forehead. She has, Jane thinks, a most expressive face. Her lips are plump and a natural rosy pink; her eyes – large and a little protruding – darken at the mention of the dead man.

'Ah, yes. I heard what happened to Hugo.'

'I actually found his body,' Jane blurts out, feeling inexplicably nervous under the woman's shrewd gaze. Vicky's eyebrows raise.

'Ah,' she says. 'I see.'

After an awkward pause, she glances around her for any items she may have missed. Scooping up a fallen paperback novel, a bra so old it'd turned grey and a lone Croc sandal, she throws them into the passenger's footwell of her car.

'Well, nice to meet you all.'

Vicky Graves stalks around to the driver's door of the car, holding up a hand in farewell, and they continue on towards the front door.

What an interesting woman, Jane thinks. Not who she would expect to be the wife of the extravagant Mr Graves. She, practical, down to earth, even a little dowdy. He, dramatic, loud, flamboyant. Perhaps that is what drew them together. Or it is what has torn them apart.

'Come on,' mutters Natasha. 'We're pretty late now.'

Closing the gap between them and the house, raises a fist and knocks.

'On second thoughts,' a voice says from behind them. Vicky Graves appears at Jane's side, pulling a key from her pocket. 'It's late and I'm starving. If you don't mind, I think I'll join you.'

Chapter Twenty-Eight

Lambert Graves is very proud of his house. It is extremely shiny. Probably the shiniest house in London, if you don't count Buckingham Palace. He is always keen to invite people into his world and show them just how rich and tasteful he is. Who else would have thought of having gold-plated banisters? And the chandelier in the dining room is *twice* as big as the one that was there when he moved in.

It was all dull stuff back then. The first interior designer he'd hired had bored him rigid with it. 'Original features' this, 'heritage paint colours' that. *Rip it out!* Lambert had said. *Who needs old rubbish?*

She'd cried when he insisted on smashing off some stupid ceiling rose. It may well have been from the 1800s, but it got in the way of his projector. What's a cinema room without a projector? She'd quit when he'd told her *that* was 'the modern-day ceiling rose'.

Still, it's not quite the same with Vicky gone. True, she'd rolled her eyes at some of his design choices. She's more of a white paint and a nice pot plant kind of woman. Rickety old bookshelves and a tartan armchair, that's her ticket. Maybe that's why it didn't work out between them. But they'd lasted a good 18 years in marital— if not exactly *bliss*, then at least contentment. Something he'd taken care to remind her of every day since she'd announced her desire for a divorce 10 months previously.

She still hasn't fully moved out. Going in dribs and drabs, box by box, though she has now moved from the guest room to another address altogether, which he admits was a bit of a blow.

The truth is, he *needs* Vicky. He simply can't survive without her, no matter how hard he tries. And, by Jove, has he tried! He's ended up doing all *sorts* of unethical things in her absence, and it's about time she stopped this nonsense and came back home.

From the window of their bedroom, Lambert watches his wife try and force a box of books into her car. She's having trouble, but he isn't going to help. No sir-ee. Leave her to stew a bit on how hard things are without a man at her side before rushing out there.

With a smile, he inspects his hair in the screen of his phone, checking his trademark quiff is still perfect. He'll go out in five minutes for maximum effect.

A thunk sounds through the window and Lambert looks up to see Vicky wiping her hands on her jeans, the car boot closed and the box inside. Damn it. She always was the more practical one.

Stalking away from the window, he storms down the stairs, stopping to check his appearance in a gilt mirror on the landing. Guests will be arriving any moment, and Vicky, or lack of Vicky, isn't going to stop him doing what he does best: putting on a show.

The dining room looks glorious by candlelight. Especially when there are 35 candles, all alight with twinkling little flames. He relights two that have gone out and straightens the four place settings on the large round table.

'Fontaine!' he shouts through the door. 'I hope those cocktails are ready!'

A tired voice floats along the corridor to reach him. *'Oui, Monsieur Graves.'*

Having staff is a luxury Lambert revels in. He himself can't cook a bean, and having a French chef-slash-butler adds a certain *je ne sais quoi.* He hates to think what would happen if there really were to be a divorce from Vicky. Would he have to cut back? Hire a chef from Birmingham for half the pay and have them put on an accent?

In the dining room, Lambert is just pondering whether one of the napkin swans looks a bit sinister, when a loud knocking sets the front door shuddering.

He dashes towards it, ready to fling it open, but to his surprise it flings right back at him, almost hitting him in the face.

'Vicky! And guests! Hello!' They look a little taken aback by his warm welcome. People often find his flamboyant personality surprising. And who doesn't like a surprise? 'Welcome, my darlings, welcome! Please do come in.'

He is thrown slightly off kilter by Vicky's little trick in joining his guests, as she knew he would be. He frowns at her as she passes and she gives him a half-wink. The minx.

Lambert closes the door behind them all and sweeps his arm around the entranceway as though to say, *Well, here it is!*

'Darling! I didn't know you were joining us for dinner?'

'It's still my house too, Lambert. I don't need your permission to be in it.'

'Of course! It's always, *always* a pleasure to have you by my side, as you know.'

He grins at her – people can't resist his smile. It's what made him money back in the eighties. That and his grandfather's hedge fund. Vicky rolls her eyes and he steps back to let them in before she can say anything more.

Lambert has always thought of his wife as a little like a koala bear – she seems harmless, but has a vicious bite, and, when it comes to him, has always known where to hook a sharp claw. It's partly why he loves her, even if she hates his guts.

In the entrance hall, the tall lady he'd met in the street – Joan something – gives him a weak smile.

'Nice to meet you again, Lambert?' Her voice rises nervously. 'This is Daniel Thurston, a publicity assistant at Polar Bear Publishing, and, of course, Natasha Martez.'

'Marvellous! Marvellous. You work at Polar Bear, eh, Danny? Keeping you busy, I hope. Do I have you to thank for the *rave* reviews on my latest book?'

'Um, I mostly just post things out in Jiffy bags.'

'And Natasha! Natasha, Natasha, Na – tash – a. The young upstart coming for my crown.' He winks theatrically and laughs like a shopping centre Santa Claus. 'Ha-ha-ha! Well, it *is* marvellous to see you.'

The beat of silence reminds Lambert he's missed someone out.

'And . . . Joan! Of course! Wonderful Joan. Old friends, old friends.'

'Jane. It's Jane Hepburn.'

'Of course, of course. Well, let's not just *stand* here gabbling away! Let's GET YOU A COCKTAIL.'

Phew, Lambert thinks, ushering his guests towards the dining room just as Fontaine scuttles out to his cue. This is going to be hard work. It's supposed to be a party, and they've got all the joy of a parking ticket.

Still, Vicky hasn't agreed to have dinner with him for ages. And he can entertain everyone perfectly well himself – he does love to tell the story of The Kangaroo Incident. The one about getting that award in Belgium is hilarious too. He doesn't really need anyone else to say much at all in order to throw a good dinner party. After dinner, he'll give them the grand tour; people *love* the grand tour.

And even if they *are* total bores, he thinks, casting a look over his shoulder at his guests, this evening could still prove incredibly . . . *useful*.

Chapter Twenty-Nine

Monday, 8.05 p.m.

There really are a lot of candles, thinks Jane. It's like sitting in a fireplace. A drop of sweat falls from the tip of Daniel's nose, landing on his meringue.

The main course of Chicken Fricassée has just been removed from the table and replaced with an extravagant-looking Eton Mess. The starter had been a single scallop, served in the shell with some sauce on top. Daniel had blanched at the sight of it, so Natasha had speared it with her fork when Lambert wasn't looking and eaten it herself. At the time, Jane had been impressed by Natasha's stealth, but she is starting to suspect she could dance naked in the cream and her host wouldn't pause for breath. Vicky Graves barely acknowledges her husband, focusing instead on her food and, in between courses, staring out of the window.

Could such a self-absorbed man be a killer? It's a question Jane has been wrestling with ever since they arrived. *Why does he keep cropping up in this case? Why was he at that book launch? Why has he invited us here?*

Had his old friend Hugo injured his fragile ego perhaps, by insulting his latest work with cruel edits? Had beautiful young Daisy turned down his advances? He seems too, well, foolish to have successfully got hold of an illegal substance, but then again, he was once an actor.

'. . . And then,' Lambert says with his Santa Claus chuckle, 'the kangaroo only got *into* the filing cabinet! The bouncy chap was throwing paper *everywhere*. Making a *proper* mess, I can tell you. His tail whacking things off the shelf—' He mimes the motion, almost hitting the poor Frenchman in the stomach as he pours the wine. 'But then I came up behind him and jumped on his back, like *this*. And wrestled him to the ground, like *this*.' After wrestling an imaginary kangaroo to the table, Lambert leans back in his chair to take a swig of his wine. 'Lucky I was there, that's the truth of it. Didn't take me too long to get him back in his cage after that. Free entry to London Zoo for the Rest. Of. My. Life.'

He punctuates each of his final words by banging his glass on the tabletop like the quite literal speaker of the house.

'That really is amazing, Lambert,' Natasha says politely while Daniel rolls his eyes so hard he can probably see his own skull.

Up close, Jane can tell how Lambert Graves is clinging to the beauty of his youth. A faint line by his ears tells of a facelift, and his hair seems a little *too* blond for a man of his age. Still, whatever the methods, she can't deny his film-star grin and sparkling eyes are impressive.

'Oh, it was nothing really,' he says with a wave of his hand. 'Well, not *nothing*, of course. The zookeeper said it was an act of bravery such as he had never seen before. But nothing, really.'

'Oh, *do* stop being such an incurable *bore*, Lambert,' Vicky says, dropping her spoon in her empty bowl. 'Though I suppose if you are incurable, you *can't* stop. How tragic.'

Lambert opens his mouth to retort, but she cuts across him.

'Now, let's hear about our guests, shall we?' She pushes her empty bowl out of the way and leans forward on her elbows. 'Daniel, tell us about your work at Polar Bear Publishing. Do you think all the authors – ' she side-eyes her husband ' – are absolutely *dreadful*.'

Lambert chuckles with a jovial *ho ho ho*, knocking back his wine and waving to the butler for more without turning in his seat. 'My wife, ladies and gentleman. Wit as sharp as her talons. But, yes, do tell us, Danny.'

'I haven't really met many authors yet,' Daniel admits. 'I've not been there long.'

'Ah, well, it'll come, it'll come, my boy! I've only been with them . . . what? . . . 10 months or so myself.'

'Yes,' Vicky breaks in. 'Dear old Hugo Strauss tempted my husband away from his last publisher with a very generous offer that he simply could *not* refuse.' She smiles sweetly at her husband. 'And who could blame Hugo? *A Magpie's Lament* is a masterpiece, don't you think?'

Lambert falters momentarily, then recovers himself and flashes his pearly teeth at them.

'I suppose it's not for *me* to say,' he says with a laugh. 'But anyway, Danny, you're at a good place, I'd say.'

Jane tries to catch Daniel's eye across the table, but he is looking down at his plate, poking at his Eton Mess. Now that Lambert is showing interest in something outside of himself, they need to get him speaking about the right things – he was talking to Hugo on the night of the murder after all. This is their chance, finally, to ask him about that, about Daisy, about *murder*. Jane looks over at Natasha instead, and the ghost of a smile crosses her friend's face. Jane understands she means, *Trust Daniel*.

'Well,' Daniel says. 'Perhaps. But two murders since Thursday has tainted it all a little. Certainly gave everyone a lot to talk about by the coffee machine.'

The table stills, and Lambert puts down his knife and fork. He tweaks his napkin swan.

'Of course. You will have felt the loss of Hugo Strauss and his assistant just as m—'

'Daisy.'

'Sorry?'

The candlelight gives Daniel's frown more gravitas. 'His assistant. Her name was Daisy Olsson.'

'Well, yes. You will have felt the loss of Hugo and *Daisy* as deeply as Natasha and I did. Hugo was my editor. A sacred relationship. A . . . friend too.'

Vicky shifts in her seat, the lines of her face shifting in the candlelight.

'You didn't see anything that night?' Natasha asks. 'Anything odd? Did you speak to either of them?'

'Well . . . well, I didn't see anything *suspicious*, if that's what you're asking. I spoke to Hugo about this and that, but not the girl. Say, would anyone like some more wine? Your glass is nearly empty, Miss Hepburn.'

'No, thank you,' Jane begins, 'I'm feeling a little tip—'

'Fontaine! Miss Hepburn's glass!' Lambert clicks his fingers and the butler steps from the shadows with a deep scowl on his face. *If Lambert ends up murdered,* thinks Jane, *there will be a plethora of suspects.*

'Don't feel too sorry for the man,' Lambert says to her, seeing her apologetic glance towards the butler. 'He has tomorrow night off for some dance class nearby, don't you, old chap?'

'*Oui,*' Fontaine says tightly as he refills Jane's glass and retreats again.

'Dancing. Not my thing, but the world needs all sorts! What was I saying?'

Across the table, Natasha leans forward to scoop up some more strawberries, burning herself on a candle and yanking back her hand.

Jane decides to try something else.

'Just that it is so tragic to witness a life cut short. I . . . think I heard something, a while back. About Hugo.' Jane feels sweat forming between her shoulder blades and isn't sure if it's the stress of the moment or the heat from 35 candles. 'And some sort of . . . accident?'

'An *accident* you say?' Lambert says, cocking his head as if to dislodge a memory. 'Oh, I don't kn—'

'A *car* accident?'

He frowns, his suddenly serious face turning sinister in the flickering shadows. He slowly shakes his head, the gold adorning one ear throwing shards of refracted light around the room. 'Ah. That. Not something one likes to discuss.'

Vicky gets to her feet. 'I'll make us some coffee.' Jane wonders how Vicky feels about her husband working with an old friend who walked free from killing a woman, simply because the publishers offered him more money.

'Tell us about it?' Natasha asks breathlessly.

Lambert's eyes flick to the door of the dining room, then he sighs and sits back in his seat, throwing his face into shadow.

'Dreadful business. Dreadful.' He pauses before continuing. 'She doesn't like thinking about it,' he says in a stage whisper, gesturing at the door his wife departed through. 'Well, it happened years ago now, of course. Six, I think. In this little nowhere town in Devon.' Lambert swirls the wine around his glass, apparently savouring the tense atmosphere.

'It really *wasn't* Hugo's fault. He was driving back to the holiday cottage when she just . . . appeared! On a little push bike, in the dark! Smack-bang on the bonnet. Died instantly. Nothing he could do. Turned his life quite upside down. He barely drank after that.'

'Barely *drank* again?' Natasha asks, her voice low. The flickering candles and their discussion of a sudden, violent death give the room the atmosphere of a séance. Jane half-expects the ghost of Hugo Strauss to rise up from the strawberries.

'Well, yes. Not many people knew that. Awkward questions, you know. Would always carry a glass of something at events for appearance's sake. I believe he did feel a little guilty about the drinking part.'

'He was drunk?'

'No! No, no, no. Not *drunk*. Not Hugo. He'd had one or two, in the local pub. It's not like being in the city, you know. Not like London. If you ever want to go to the pub in the country, you *have* to drive. Anyway, they breathalysed him and he *wasn't* over the limit.' Lambert leans forward again, his face coming back into the light. He gives them a jovial smile. 'Bang *on* the limit, the lucky bugger, but not over. Mind you, if the police hadn't taken so long to turn up, who knows?' He chuckles, as though Hugo was a rascal schoolboy who'd got away with a terrific prank.

'He got a slap on the wrist, but it was clearly an accident. He did rather blame himself though. The wife blamed him too, of course.'

'Is that why she left him?' asks Jane, remembering the empty half of Hugo's wardrobe, the flowerless vases, the empty dressing table.

'What? Oh, Hugo's wife. No, not back then she didn't. It probably left a mark though. She went about six months ago now, back to Florida. Poor chap. First that, now this. All going wrong for him.'

'His . . . murder, you mean?'

'Yes, yes, that. Beastly of her to leave him, upping sticks like that. She'll regret it! They aways do.' He frowns at the door again, and Jane suspects he is thinking of his own wife, her car outside stuffed with boxes. 'Or, well, perhaps not now. Because he's dead.'

'So Hugo's wife is definitely in Florida then?' Natasha asks casually.

'Yes, yes. She's a Yank, only moved here when she married him. Maybe she missed the sun, and she was working out there a lot anyway.' He shrugs, and Jane mentally scores a second line through the ex-Mrs Strauss on her list. 'Dreadful business,' Lambert says again, then slams his palms flat on the table. 'Right!' He leaps to his feet, making poor Fontaine flinch. 'Who wants *the grand tour of Aurum Manor?*'

Jane couldn't care less about the colour of Lambert Graves's bedroom walls. But PI Baker would never pass up an opportunity to have a nose around a suspect's home.

This might just be her chance to find out what the Graveses are hiding. Maybe it's just their marital troubles causing tension to fill the room, or maybe it's something much darker. But one thing is for sure – there is more here than meets the eye.

All that glitters, Jane's mother whispers in the back of her mind, *is not gold.*

Chapter Thirty

Monday, 9.00 p.m.

Jane is dead on her feet. She feels as though she's traipsed around *six* manor houses and can no longer find the enthusiasm to make appropriate noises of appreciation when confronted with framed film posters featuring a grinning Lambert Graves, walls displaying his literary awards and obscenely large armchairs upholstered in gold velvet. She is still clutching her now cold coffee – too strong and bitter for her taste.

After handing out coffee, Vicky has wandered off with Fontaine, presumably not wildly interested in a tour of the house she is in the process of moving out of. Closing her eyes, Jane lustfully thinks of the soft white sheets of the Savoy, the comfortable bed, the silver teapot. That's what she wants: a cup of good English Breakfast tea, and to go to bed. Even the saggy mattress in her B&B would be a sweet release.

'Now you'll love this bit,' Lambert says, pulling a key from his pocket, eyes twinkling. 'Really special. That's why I keep it locked.

'*Here*,' he says, opening the door with a flourish, 'is my wife's workshop. Where she makes *these* delightful geegaws.' He waggles his bejewelled fingers at them.

A cabinet on one wall holds a display of twinkling rings. There's a large pink armchair next to it that Jane longs to sink into. Along another wall is a work bench, interesting-looking tools strewn across it.

'She's a genius really,' Lambert says wistfully. 'A genius. Studied languages in Scandinavia, you know? And a master's in

Literature from Oxford. An amazing woman. Well!' he rallies. 'Let's carry on!'

He slams the door, locks it and continues. The group trudge up the stairs after their host.

'Terrible shame it's grown too dark to show you the garden properly,' Lambert says, stopping at a window on the landing and peering out. Daniel yawns widely. 'You see over there, that's the pool. Don't use it myself, but can be jolly fun for parties.'

It hasn't been possible to slip away during the tour, and Jane is starting to worry she won't ever get a chance to poke around. She takes a few steps away from the group, muttering *headache* with a hand to her temple. Lambert doesn't seem to notice, so she takes a few more steps.

Glancing back at her friends, she sees Lambert put an arm around Daniel's shoulders, pulling him closer and pointing out at the lawn. Surely they have seen nearly everything by now? This could be her last chance.

Tiptoeing around a corner, Jane finds herself in a dark corridor. They'd been here earlier, but she can't quite remember which door leads to which room. Was the games room on this floor or the one above? It's the study she'd like to find – they'd been afforded a glimpse of it half an hour ago – but with the wine and the gathering darkness and the size of the place, it's all become a blur. Even so, she is quite sure it's close by.

Plumping for the first door on the left, Jane grabs the handle and turns it with the care of a mother bird tending her eggs. Bathroom. She tries the next room – bingo. Stepping inside, she breathes out into the silence.

Heart in her throat, Jane moves further into the room, moonlight illuminating her surroundings.

Suddenly, Lambert Graves leers at her from the shadows.

Jane lets out a strangled yelp, jumping backwards and banging into the desk, knocking papers to the floor. She starts to stutter her apologies, before realising he isn't moving. Jane laughs weakly in relief as she realises her mistake.

He is around thirty years younger in the picture, wearing a black cloak and holding a skull. Rather incongruously given his prop, he is giving the viewer his trademark toothy grin. The poster is for a film adaptation of *Hamlet* which, if Jane remembers rightly, was panned by the critics due to Lambert's performance, and for the racy scene between him and Ophelia that she was sure hadn't come up during her GCSEs.

Lining the walls that don't feature the poster are shelves – some empty, a few still crammed with books. Copies of Lambert's own novels, including editions in French, Spanish and Dutch, stand proudly in a line. The bare sections make Jane think of the boxes in the driveway. Vicky's books must have been in here too.

They are an odd couple, but the invisible string that attaches people who have lived side by side for years is still present. *Will they really split, or is it a temporary blip?* Jane wonders. *And is that anything to do with Lambert's relationship with Hugo? Does Vicky, perhaps, suspect her husband of something worse than vanity, worse than greed?*

In front of the window stands a huge oak desk. It's strewn with bits of paper, notebooks, pens and dirty mugs, a laptop sitting in the only cleared space. Jane puts down her cold coffee and opens it, but it's password-protected, so instead she pulls the desk drawers out one by one: all empty.

A clock chimes the half-hour. She needs to get back to the group. Jane crouches to pick up the papers she'd knocked from the desk, a mixture of printed pages and handwritten scribbles. As she places them back on the desktop, a name jumps out at her.

The light is dim, but she leans closer to read the cramped writing.

At the bottom of a page of thick, linen paper, in looping blue ink: *Hugo*. Jane edges the paper out from the pile.

All of a sudden, the door swings open and a light clicks on. Jane leaps back from the desk.

Vicky Graves is standing in the doorway, looking at her quizzically.

'Miss Hepburn?'

'Mrs Graves! Oh, I'm so sorry. I was looking for the bathroom. I got a little lost? And then . . . and then . . . well, I saw this, er, this amazing poster? And I couldn't help myself, I had to take a closer look.' She gestures frantically at Lambert dressed as a grinning Hamlet.

'I see.'

'So sorry. Rude of me. I'll be going n—'

'That's when we met, you know?' Vicky steps into the room, looking up at the poster of her husband. 'On that production. I used to be a dramaturg. They would hire me for Shakespearean productions, to help the actors understand the text, the history, the verse rhythms.'

'What a wonderful job.' Much more her than Baxter's White Goods Insurance.

'Depends on the actor,' Vicky says with a wry smile. 'Some are dreadful, and stupid to boot. But Lambert— I know he can be a bit . . . ' she makes a gesture with her hand that somehow sums up the man's presence '. . . but he wasn't quite as obnoxious back in those days. Our differences worked well together for a time.'

She sighs, shaking her head gently as though she's forgotten Jane is even there. 'Those were good days. But he has always been . . . impetuous. Some things, you just can't stand by and tolerate.' With a start, she turns away from the poster. 'Anyway, you should probably be getting back before they send out a search party.'

Jane grabs her coffee cup and hurries from the room, hearing the door click shut behind her. At the end of the corridor, she turns to see that Vicky Graves has not followed her. Jane's relieved, not fancying her snooping being announced to their host.

If *only* she'd had a chance to read the whole letter rather than just the last few lines. The part she did read is explosive, though she isn't yet sure exactly what it could mean.

. . . life's work, my friend. I have not decided my next step, but I fear I cannot stay silent if this is the case. Let us talk in person soon.

Yours in hope,

Hugo

'Well,' Lambert's voice is saying as Jane finds the stairs, 'that's about it! I hope you enjoyed the tour?'

She rejoins her friends, answering their quizzical looks with a shake of her head.

'We did, thank you, Mr Graves,' Natasha says. 'Though I must say, it's quite worn me out. I think we'll be heading back now if that's quite alright?'

'Of course! Oh, but our friend Ms Hepburn hasn't finished her coffee! We could retire to the drawing room and—'

Daniel takes the cup of cold, potent coffee from her hand and knocks it back.

'Ah, well, home it is,' Lambert says with a smile. 'I'll show you out.'

It's not until half an hour later, Jane's eyes closed and her head resting against the cool glass of the Tube compartment's window, that the realisation hits her. She sits bolt upright, eyes wide and heart thumping.

All of a sudden, she knows exactly why Daisy Olsson died.

Chapter Thirty-One

Monday, 10.49 p.m.

Geraldine's Guest House closes the front door at 11 p.m. This means that Natasha and Jane, bodies heavy with exhaustion, have to jog from the Underground station to avoid having to spend the night curled up under old copies of the *Daily News* in a doorway.

They arrive, panting, to find Geraldine at the door, tapping one foot and dangling the keys from her little finger.

'You made it then?' she says, sounding disappointed.

'Yes,' Jane gasps on an out breath, clutching at the stitch in her side.

'I'm not staying up, you know,' Geraldine says, still frowning. She is already wrapped in a dressing gown – pink, floral and comically ancient – and mauve slippers. 'Can't spend the night serving you drinks and the like. You'll have to sort yourselves out and lock up.'

'Oh, we don't need anything, Geraldine,' Natasha says, their host still blocking the doorway like a bristling Jack Russell. 'Straight to bed for us.'

'And what about your *guest*, Miss Hepburn?' she says, ignoring Natasha and looking right at Jane, who stares back, non-plussed. 'I'd kick her out, I would. If it wasn't for the fact she says she's *police*.'

Geraldine's living room feels like the inside of a tea cosy. It would be comforting, if not for being suffocatingly hot and smelling strongly of wet wool.

The door creaks open to reveal DI Hawberry standing, hands clasped behind her back, looking at a picture of a horse galloping through a field of daisies. She spins round at the sound of their entry, scowling at Jane.

Natasha, not having been summoned to the meeting, has been shooed up to bed by Geraldine. Yawning widely, she did not put up a fight. Jane wishes more than anything she could do the same. *But Sandra Baker would use this to do some digging,* she reminds herself. *Buck up, Jane, she's just a normal woman, like you.*

'Hello, Ms Hepburn, nice of you to join me,' says the detective with a grimace that is perhaps supposed to be a smile. 'Take a seat.'

Jane sinks into the sofa as Geraldine shuffles in with a tray.

'Pot of tea, Detective Inspector. And some biscuits, just in case,' she says, much politer than she had been to her paying guests. She turns to Jane as she places the house keys reverently on the coffee table. 'Now you'll have to lock up, Miss Hepburn. It's a big responsibility, most unorthodox. But in the circumstances . . . can you manage it?'

Despite being slightly offended at being spoken to like a toddler, Jane nods, her throat dry and constricted.

Once Geraldine has shuffled out again, the silence in the room feels extremely heavy, oppressive like the heat and the smell. Jane gulps.

'Would you like some tea, Detective Inspector?'

'No,' Hawberry snaps. 'Well, okay, yes. One sugar.' She takes a seat on the arm of the opposite sofa.

The DI is in the same ill-fitting blue suit as she was wearing on Thursday night. She is tapping one foot impatiently, glaring around the room while Jane pours the tea.

'And one sugar,' she says cheerfully, dropping in a cube. 'Now. How can I help you?'

'You are meddling where you don't belong, Miss Hepburn. In my case!' Hawberry slaps the arm of the sofa. 'You found the first body, *fine*. Someone has to. But then, hey presto, you find another! Sneaking around in a suspect's home, in his *secret room* for that matter. And you just *happen* to stumble on a corpse?'

Detective Hawberry's eyes are bulging in her pinched face, her cheeks growing redder as she rants. Jane fears she is only just getting started. She is pleased, at least, that they are in private – though she wouldn't put it past Geraldine to be listening at the door.

'I barely have any time as it is, and then I get here to speak to you this evening only to find you are gallivanting around town, not answering your phone, despite my officers having told you to stay easily contactable!'

'Why don't you have a sip of your tea, Detective Inspector? You might feel a little better.'

Hawberry looks, if possible, even angrier at this very sensible suggestion. The moment hangs in the balance while her mouth works silently until, as though giving up, she raises her cup to her lips, gulps down the tea, and puts it back on the tray.

She then sags in front of Jane's eyes. It makes her think again of the mattress waiting for her upstairs. Hawberry closes her eyes and exhales a long, steadying breath. Next she does something so surprising that Jane almost drops her own cup. She starts to cry.

Jane isn't great with tears. Not being someone who has ever had a glut of friends, she hasn't spent much time perfecting the consoling pat on the back or there theres or cheer up, chuck. Her preferred method of comfort is to offer a cup of tea. But Hawberry already has tea. In fact, the tea seems to be the problem.

DI Hawberry howls, head thrown back and tears streaming down her cheeks.

'Your tea Detective! Drink your tea!'

Jane pushes the cup back towards her companion, who is by now hiccuping and snorting, and she drops onto the seat of the sofa. Eventually, Hawberry picks it up again and takes another shaky sip. Like a switch has been flicked, the tears are turned off as quickly as they started.

'I'm . . . I'm sorry, Miss Hepburn. What must you think of me!'

A strand of greying hair has come loose from her ponytail, and the ghost of mascara lingers under her eyes. Hawberry sniffs deeply, wiping her nose on her cuff. The eczema on the back of her hand looks raw.

'I think you are a woman who is very stressed, trying to catch a killer who is very clever.'

Then Jane has a brainwave. She gets up and goes to the sideboard where Geraldine's Victoria sponge cake sits under a glass dome. Cutting two slices, she puts them on plates. 'Now,' she says kindly, setting a slice down in front of the detective and retaking her own seat. 'Eat your cake, drink your tea, and tell me all about it.'

It is past midnight by the time DI Hawberry has stopped talking. Their crumb-filled plates and empty teacups have been replaced by two glasses of sherry that Jane dug out from the sideboard. It's sweet, viscous, a little warm and leaves a taste of raisins and caramel lingering in her mouth. It grows on Jane the more she drinks, and as she tops up their glasses, she mentally crosses her fingers, hoping it doesn't turn out to be priceless.

Hawberry has undone the buttons on her too-tight suit and removed the tie from her straw-like hair. It bounces around her face now, making her look younger and more relaxed, if a little scarecrow-like.

'So if I can't solve this case,' she says, raising her glass to her lips, 'then that's it. I'm screwed. It's basically my last chance. Oh, God, that's delicious, isn't it? Who knew *sherry* was nice? Thought it was for old biddies and vicars. And the Spanish, I suppose.'

Over the last hour, Hawberry has confessed to Jane that she has made multiple blunders at work over the past four years, resulting in warnings and official reprimands. On the discovery of Daisy Olsson's death, she was told in no uncertain terms that if she messes up this investigation, she's out on her ear.

Rosalind Hawberry wasn't always bad at her job. In fact, she flew up through the ranks at record speed, an impressive arrest record making her a formidable opponent to the ne'er-do-wells of Inner London. That was, until her husband Jonathan was diagnosed with liver disease, and she became, as well as a full-time detective in the Metropolitan Police, his carer at home. She cannot afford much paid help, and so she struggles to make it work the best she can. The result? A constant nagging feeling of failure both at home and in the station.

'Don't your bosses have any compassion?' says Jane, shaking her head.

'They do not. But, hey, you can't blame them. Killers need catching, no matter how difficult my home life is. Jonathan's sister has come to stay for the week while I'm working on the Olsson and Strauss murders. To give me more of a shot. But even so, my head's all over the place.'

Jane thinks back to the final days of caring for her mother before she died. The nights of interrupted sleep, the snarky emails she received from Deborah Templeton about missed meetings, the ever-present heaviness in her mind and the exhaustion that sadness brings to your bones. She imagines trying to catch killers at the same time, and Rosalind Hawberry's behaviour makes a little more sense.

'Sorry I bit your head off,' Hawberry says, not meeting her eye. 'But really, you *shouldn't* be meddling in a live police investigation. How *did* you find Hugo Strauss? And none of that guff about borrowing a book that my brain-dead colleagues bought, please.'

Jane swirls the liquid in her glass, considering her next words. In her very first novel, *Rush of Blood*, PI Baker sits opposite a grizzled detective in a situation not dissimilar to this – the sherry was whisky and the room was a back office instead of an elderly woman's living room, but still. Can Jane pull off what her alter ego does with such ease?

'How about this?' Taking another small sip before meeting Hawberry's eye, she chooses her words with care. 'I help you, and when we solve the case, my friends and I disappear. You get the credit.'

Yes, that's exactly how Baker would have put it. Then she'd knock back her drink and slam the glass down on the table.

Jane follows suit and ends up missing what Hawberry replies as she bends double, coughing violently.

'Sorry – cough – went – cough – down the – cough – wrong way.'

'I said, what's the catch? What's in it for you?'

Hawberry is looking as sceptical as Jane's mother had looked the time they went to a psychic. The old woman had told them she could see an accident in the recent past, and recovery would happen. It wasn't much of a stretch – Jane was on crutches at the time. 'I've seen your little TikTok appearance from a few months back,' Hawberry continues. 'Are you chasing fame?'

'Not at all.'

'Then what's in it for you? Why are you trying to solve this case?'

'I . . .' Jane begins, wondering how to answer. What *is* in it for her? Her work situation, the real one that pays the bills, is becoming ever-more perilous the longer she stays in the capital. She has started writing again but it's a long way from anything concrete. There is neither glory nor gold for her in solving this. 'Well, I *want* to.'

Jane shrugs, and Hawberry's frown deepens.

'And the scandal is hurting my friend Natasha. It ruined her book launch, which isn't a big deal in the grand scheme of things. But now the internet thinks she is involved in several deaths and as a result her book is being pulled from shelves. I want this solved and put to bed before it can do anymore harm. I . . . I haven't had many friends before, Detective.'

'That's it?'

'And I want justice for Hugo and Daisy, of course.'

'And?'

'And the truth. I want the truth.'

'*And?*'

'And, well, I suppose it is rather *fun*.'

The women, sitting side by side as if they are old friends, are now a good way through the sherry bottle.

Jane has had her notebook out, talking Hawberry through their investigation so far. The detective's eyebrows have disappeared into her hairline, and she keeps shaking her head in disbelief.

'What do you *mean*, you "spoke to a confidential source" to obtain confirmation of cause of death?'

'I can't tell you that, I'm afraid,' Jane says, mindful of not getting Ramos into trouble.

Hawberry has remained mostly silent throughout Jane's explanation, occasionally scribbling something in her own notebook. Jane approves. She likes a woman with a notebook.

'So let's get this straight,' the detective says with a sigh. 'The assistant at the bookshop told you that Daisy had both an ex-boyfriend and an online admirer in the picture. You've identified one of them, Scott Wallace. We've spoken to him, of course, but have you found out anything about the other man?'

'Very little. But he isn't our focus anymore. Not after I realised that Daisy Olsson was never supposed to die.'

It had been Daniel's impetuous move while standing on Lambert's stairs that had made everything finally click into place for her. The way he'd taken the cup of cold coffee from

Jane's hand and slugged down the dregs, so they could leave the house as quickly as possible.

They had asked themselves over and over again: *why would anyone want to kill this young woman?* Sure, she has an ex-boyfriend who hasn't moved on, an online suitor who is a little over-keen. But none of it seemed *enough*.

Hugo on the other hand? As a prominent man in his sixties, there was a far greater chance he had picked up enemies along the way, discovered secrets, broken hearts, made mistakes. He'd even got behind the wheel of his car after drinking and killed an innocent woman. *Hugo* was the intended victim, and Daisy had simply been caught in the crossfire. Jane is sure of it.

'I don't quite understand,' Hawberry says slowly, ruffling her messy grey hair.

'Think,' Jane says, taking another slug of her sherry, even though her head is starting to spin like a rotisserie chicken. '*Think*. Hugo asked Daisy to call him a taxi, right? Mike the taxi driver said that when he picked up his fare, Hugo was feeling ill.'

Hawberry flicks back in her notebook, nodding as she reads what Mike told Jane. '"Sick as a dog",' she reads aloud. 'So?'

'*So* we can assume that Hugo fell suddenly ill at the party, and asked Daisy to call him a taxi even though he was supposed to be giving a speech. Too ill even to say goodbye.'

Jane speaks slowly, making sure Hawberry is following her train of thought despite the late hour. 'Lambert said Hugo didn't drink after the car accident in Devon, but he always carried a glass at parties to stop people pressuring him.'

Hawberry nods again. 'My Aunt Nina does that. She says it stops Uncle Tommy trying to push her off the wagon all the time. No one likes Uncle Tommy much.'

'Exactly! Hugo wouldn't want to go into *why* he doesn't drink at work events – having killed a woman while close to the drink-driving limit is hardly light conversation – so he held a glass all night and *never took a sip.*'

'Then how did he ingest the poison?'

'Perhaps it splashed onto his skin? My friend Natasha has been looking into cyanide poisoning and it's so toxic than even contact with it can kill. I was covered in wine after that party, what with all of those raucous people crammed into the alley.'

Hawberry gasps, the picture clearing in her mind before Jane has finished explaining. 'If that's the case, it would have taken much longer for the cyanide to take deadly effect on him, but it's still fatal, and he would have felt ill rather quickly. Then . . . then he asks his assistant to call him a taxi,' she says, the words coming slowly as the action plays out in her head. 'When Mike arrives . . .'

'. . . Hugo hands Daisy his undrunk glass and vanishes!' Jane is bouncing in her seat in excitement.

She can picture it now: Daisy confusing their glasses and unknowingly knocking back the poisoned drink. Perhaps taking it to the stock room to enjoy with her vape now that her boss has gone home.

'Hmm,' says Hawberry, chewing the end of her pen. 'It's possible. *Possible*. Though we still don't know who actually put poison in the glass.'

She hasn't shut any of Jane's theories down, but she hasn't applauded them with the gusto Jane, frankly, expected either. Jane has the satisfaction of being able to share one or two things that the police hadn't found out, though, one of them being Natasha's suspicion that Hugo was having an affair with the literary agent Marabella Rhodes. Hawberry, however, is giving very little back.

'The woman Hugo killed, have you spoken to her husband?' Jane asks.

The DI nods.

'I have, he's a no-go. Lives in Sweden and has a solid alibi.'

Jane is sceptical. 'Honestly, Rosalind,' she chances the first name and rushes on in case she is chastised, 'Hugo killed the man's wife and walked away scot-free! Are you *sure* her widower couldn't have done it?'

'I'm sure. And it's Detective Inspector Hawberry to you.' She sighs and drops her voice. 'Look, I shouldn't be sharing information with you but, take it from me, Michael Carney is out of the picture. He's head teacher of some fancy international school now, and was definitely not in the country on Thursday.'

She glances down at her notes again. 'I'll look into this affair between Hugo and what's-her-name, though.' A shadow of a smile appears. 'Thanks.'

'And the letter I saw on Lambert Graves's desk? It almost felt as though Hugo was threatening him? And Lambert *was* there at the party that night.'

'You saw two lines,' says the DI, waving away the information. 'It could mean anything. Hugo was his editor, it's hardly odd for them to be talking. Though curious to communicate by letter in this day and age.'

'Perhaps one of them didn't want the conversation to be traced? Or perhaps Hugo was just old-fashioned like that.'

They sip their drinks, both lost in thought.

Hawberry leans forward to pluck Jane's notebook from her hand and flicks back through the pages.

She tips the last drops of her sherry into her mouth and shudders, then looks back at Jane's page. 'What's this?' She taps at some writing at the bottom of the page.

SORRY

Jane had almost forgotten about the text message Natasha had received from Hugo in the early hours of Saturday morning, so much has happened since.

'Well, *he* didn't send it,' Hawberry confirms when Jane explains. 'He died Thursday night. Dead men don't text.'

I can barely get a living one to, thinks Jane.

'And quite aside from that,' Hawberry continues, 'there wasn't a phone on the body at all.' Jane remembers searching Hugo's pockets – of course! How hadn't she realised there was no phone? 'We're getting a court order to access his records regardless, but it's been a weekend, and it hasn't been the biggest priority. Should have them tomorrow though. You know, I half-believed *you'd* taken it,' she says with a shrug. 'You didn't?'

Jane thinks back to that study. Natasha standing by the door with her hands over her mouth. Daniel, white-faced, trying to call the police.

There was no phone signal in the study, but there *was* one in the kitchen. Hugo must have tried to send an apology to Natasha for leaving the party, but the message only *sent* when someone removed his phone from the room. Someone who broke in at 3 a.m. on Saturday, saw Hugo Strauss's body, removed his phone and then left without doing anything else.

Tiredness comes crashing back over Jane. The bad night's sleep, the trekking across London and back, writing, dinner with Lambert, drinks with Hawberry. Revelations and realisations and clues and riddles. It all weighs down on her like a pile of bricks, forcing her deep underwater.

She yawns widely and Hawberry gets to her feet, giving the impression her bones are creaking.

'Who do *you* think it is?' Jane says rather desperately. 'Who did it?'

'I don't know, Jane, or they'd be in cuffs.'

'But who do you *suspect*?'

'If I had to say right now, it's Scott Wallace. There is so much that man is hiding, and it's always the ex-boyfriend. He could have taken down Hugo out of jealousy . . . I don't know. But everything you've told me tonight has been very helpful. I'll certainly be acting upon it.' She gives Jane another of her rare smiles. 'Don't put yourself in danger, Miss Hepburn. Don't put your *friends* in danger. I'd best be getting back. Jane – thank you. Let's keep in touch.'

The detective lets herself out. It takes a few moments before Jane realises that, though she has shared all she knows, Hawberry has barely given her anything in exchange.

Chapter Thirty-Two

When Scott Wallace psychoanalyses himself, which he has a habit of doing, he might relate his obsession with Daisy Olsson to his own unsatisfactory childhood. It was his love of comics and computers, and dislike of reading, that his mother, an English teacher, had so frowned upon. *Pick up a book, boy!* She'd said it over and over again, batting the latest adventures of Superman out of his hand. *Are you stupid?*

It was pure irony that he'd ended up working in a publishing company, albeit in the IT department. When he met Daisy – beautiful, funny, impetuous – and she'd told him how she couldn't care less about reading either, he'd felt a rare spark of joy. They were both out of place, both weirdos, both more partial to *Mario Kart* than McCarthy. It felt like approval, and he basked in it.

Scott continues his walk around Burgess Park, scuffing his shiny yellow trainers in the dusty earth as he goes. He got up to go to work but ended up walking right past the Tube station and taking refuge here. His 'safe space' Daisy would have said. He would say his fortress.

The thing with Daisy was that there was always a wall inside her he couldn't scale – and he didn't handle it well. She spoke about *boundaries* and *trust*, but he heard *secrets* and *lies* and responded with *who the hell are you, Daisy Olsson?* She hadn't let him meet her friends or family, nor even allowed him inside her home.

It's lonely being on the other side of someone's wall, and after so *many* years being a bit lonely, he couldn't take it. *Can I really be blamed for going a little too far?* he thinks. *For doing what I did?*

Scott marches on, finding himself at the gate now, pushing it open with a creak that shudders down his spine. He didn't realise where he was going at first, but it's crystallising in his mind now. His feet, in those mocking yellow trainers, knew before his head did.

Scott blames his job for what has happened. He rolls the thought around in his mind and finds, with satisfaction, that he can make that stick. Sort of. Scott's clever, or is when it comes to computing anyway, but he's stuck answering IT requests for idiots who know all about punctuation but nothing about programming. It's unchallenging, low-paid, and sending him mad. Surely, that would test anyone's moral compass. Surely anyone would get a little carried away, let their imagination run away with them.

The *guilt* though. To his irritation, it stabs at him again. Pausing just outside the park, he pulls out his phone to check. Nothing new.

Not entirely his job to blame then, but books. He blames *books*. Yes, that's it. Books are why he works in that awful place, full of toffs and snobs like that cringey Hugo Strauss Daisy had hated so much. Books are why he never bonded with his mother. Books are why he got mixed up with them all. Books are probably what gave *her* those wild plans and ideas. You don't get that with nice safe computers, all sensible noughts and ones.

Bloody books.

He leans against the iron railings and closes his eyes, thinking back to a time when his 'safe space' wasn't this expanse of inner-city green but hidden under his duvet, torch in one hand and comic in the other. *Hellboy* was his favourite. He used to skip over the dialogue and get lost in the illustrations of forgotten gods, malevolent witches, grotesque faeries. If only life were still that simple. If only hiding under a duvet really kept horror from your door.

But something he did learn from comics and computer games is this: once you are in too deep, the only way out is through.

Scott has until 5 p.m. until he meets *her*. Then he'll know for sure what it is he has done. And what he has to do next.

Until then? Leaning against the park railings, he looks down again at his phone. His finger hovers over the icon of the offending app. In a way it was fun, pretending to be the man his mother wanted him to be, the man Daisy probably wanted him to be deep down. Awful too, of course, but satisfyingly so. Like the throb of a burn the day after the fire.

And with that, he touches the flame. Pressing down on the little red square with the flickering tongue of fire, he opens the dating app and reads through the only conversation there. He imbibes every line, feels every knife to his heart all over again. Enough. He deletes the app from his phone, removing *Kyle* from the world forever.

Now to address the other issue. His time playing Kyle didn't trouble him, not really. It was natural to have wanted to see what Daisy was doing after their break-up, to see the sort of things she said to new men. It wasn't hard to get her talking – after all, he knew her. He crept into her heart once, it wasn't difficult to follow the same path with a different face. The plan was to ask her to meet up, then reveal it was him all along, therefore proving how right he was for her.

But he can admit now, that is where it should have stopped. He shouldn't have climbed over the wall into the private spaces she didn't want him to see. Shouldn't have caused havoc there that ended in not one, but *two* deaths.

Pushing himself up off the railings, Scott Wallace makes a decision.

He has spent a lifetime hiding – under duvets, in storerooms, behind online personas. Sneaking around is what has caused all of this. Hellboy wouldn't hide, wouldn't sneak. He would act.

Time for Scott to do just that.

Chapter Thirty-Three

Tuesday, 10.30 a.m.

Jane Hepburn has a particular view of what a beach should be, which she thinks is absolutely fair enough.

This pebbly monstrosity on the edge of the Thames is not a beach. Jane had left the guest house in a rush, fleeing the sounds of Geraldine's fury about her failure to remember to lock the front door. Jane is hoping to check out before the landlady notices the sherry levels.

As she waits for Natasha – who, as she is not in Geraldine's firing line, is taking her sweet time – she remembers sitting on the dunes in Burnham-on-Sea as a child, the air fresh with salt and an undercurrent of chips. The sand had been heaped in mountains, tufts of coarse grass sticking out of it like scraps of hair on a man who isn't ready to let go of his youth. It was always windy, the grains of sand getting into her eyes and hair, but she'd been happy there, sitting by her mother, eating an ice cream whatever the weather. There was usually a gang of assorted children bonding over sandcastles and planning secret holiday escapades, but Jane would stay by her mother's side, reading a novel featuring the Famous Five. Back then, she'd always taken reading about adventures over living them.

What about now? Jane imagines her mother asking, but alarmingly, Jane can't quite find her voice. It's been nearly a year since she lost her, which feels like no time at all. But then again, it's been a year in which so much has changed that it could have been a whole lifetime.

This morning, Jane logged into her email account to attempt to make contact with Michael Carney via his school website – it hadn't taken long to check the names of head teachers at international schools in Sweden. Just as she'd sent her enquiry, another email from Deborah Templeton landed in her inbox. Today's disciplinary meeting had started at 9 a.m. sharp and Jane had neither shown up nor explained her absence.

> The situation has been escalated. Please confirm your attendance at a second disciplinary meeting tomorrow, Wednesday, at 9 a.m. At this point, Jane, I must ask you – do you want this job or not?

She closes her eyes, feeling the sun on her face, and allows herself to be transported back to the sand dunes. She's seven years old, already taller and broader than every other girl and most of the boys in her class. Her only friend, Bridgit, recently called her a *Heffalump*. Jane hadn't known what it meant, so she'd had to ask her mother, who'd given her a sad smile and told her not to worry.

You know what they say, she hears her mother saying. Jane smiles in relief at the perfect memory of her presence. *When one door opens . . . Get on with that new book, Jane.*

'Jane?'

Natasha is hurrying towards her along the embankment, smiling broadly. Her hair bounces gently as she moves, her ears poking out either side like handles on a vase, two takeaway coffees in her hands. The sight fills Jane's heart, pushing away the heavy grief for her mother, worry about her job at Baxter's and the confusing intricacies of her brand-new novel.

Natasha plops down beside her and hands over a flat white.

'Geraldine isn't happy with you.'

'I said sorry about the door!'

'It's something about sherry?'

'Oh, dear.'

'Never mind that old bag. We'll buy her a new bottle. Now, tell me again what you learnt from Hawberry.'

Jane went over the conversation she'd had the night before, again realising that she had learnt very little.

'Something we *do* know now,' Natasha says with satisfaction, 'is that Hugo is *innocent*. What Mike said about him feeling ill in the taxi proves he was poisoned at the party, and didn't poison *himself* when he got home.'

'The phone thing too. I think he tried to text you from his office, but it didn't send until someone removed the phone from the room. Hawberry said it wasn't on the body. Someone broke into his house before we did and took it. Why? And *who*?'

The two women sit in silence, watching the muddy brown water of the Thames drift gently past them. The sun is bright, but the air has a chill that causes Jane to wrap her arms around her knees.

'I spoke to Daniel on the way here,' Natasha says eventually. 'Told him all about your theory on Daisy's death being accidental. He likes it. He is now convinced Lambert Graves is the guilty party.'

'He was convinced it was Scott Wallace yesterday.'

'Yeah, well. You know Daniel. He is always certain, and always certain to change his mind. But I must say, that letter you found *does* feel suspicious.'

'Hawberry suspects Scott, Daniel suspects Lambert, I sort of suspect Michael Carney, no matter what the police say . . . we are all in a muddle. How about you?'

'I don't know,' Natasha says slowly, staring out at the water.

Jane sighs, pulling out her phone and seeing a number one on her email icon.

'I think there is something we are missing,' Natasha continues. 'Perhaps some*one* we are missing. I know you think Daisy's death was accidental, but I'd still like to know more about that big argument she was heard having in her flat. We have no women on our suspects list though.'

'Well, let's focus on what we *can* do,' Jane says, getting to her feet with a grin. She holds out her hand to Natasha, pulling her up.

'Which is this: Michael Carney has agreed to speak to us at midday.'

PI Sandra Baker always says that, if you want privacy, a loud place is better than a quiet one. With this in mind, they secrete themselves in a booth in a chain café. Jane sips a mint tea – too much coffee makes her paranoid and, with a murderer on the loose, she doesn't need any more of that – and connects her laptop to the wi-fi.

'He should be joining the call in five minutes,' she says, checking her watch. 'Are you ready? Anything we need to ask?'

'Let's just be sensitive,' Natasha tells her . 'He *did* lose his wife after all. I'm sure he doesn't want it dragged up again. Really, we just need to double-check his alibi.'

Natasha is flicking through photos on her phone as she speaks, and Jane fears the online gossip has got worse. But when her friend holds up the screen for her, it's Michael she sees, standing frozen outside a large house.

'Look at where he lives! Stunning. How has he got that on a teacher's salary?'

'His wife was a supermodel or something, wasn't she? She must have left him a fair amount. And there was probably life insurance too. Where's that picture from?'

'A magazine article about international schooling.'

Jane gives an impressed whistle and navigates to Johanna's abandoned Facebook profile once again, staring at the beautiful woman laughing with her curly-haired friend and toddler in the sunshine. Every inch a supermodel. She clicks on Michael's profile, where he is still grinning wildly on his wedding day.

'Er, hello?'

Natasha slams down her phone and they snap their attention to the laptop screen. A man is peering out at them, a kind smile on his face.

Michael Carney has aged far more than he should have done in the six years since his wife's death. Along with the expression of unbridled joy, the handsome face has all but gone, and Jane thinks now of a sad old walrus she saw at the zoo in Leeds, with its large drooping eyes and forlorn expression. It is all the more jarring given they have just been looking at photographs of him in better days.

His saving grace is the full head of hair, a slightly lighter blond than the greying stubble blossoming over his face, and the earthy hazel of his eyes.

'Jane Hepburn, isn't it?' he says. 'And . . . ?'

'Oh, this is Natasha,' says Jane. 'And hello. Thank you for talking to us.'

'Always happy to make time to talk to parents considering Elwood Academy,' he says with an artificial jollity that doesn't reach the eyes.

Natasha kicks her under the table. Jane didn't actually *say* they were parents, but now he has assumed it, she won't disabuse him of the fact.

'Well, thank you,' she says with the assumed authority of someone who can afford private school fees. 'We, er, didn't see you at the open evening last Thursday. Were you unable to make it?'

'No, no, I was there,' he says slowly, a frown causing his forehead to furrow like a field. 'Didn't you see me? I was at the table right in the centre of the room. I made a speech. I had back-to-back appointments, though, so I'm sorry if we didn't get a chance to chat one-to-one. What is your child's name?'

'Um, Sarah,' Jane invents wildly. 'Back-to-back appointments, you say? Well, you must be very busy. We won't kee—'

'Sarah Hepburn . . . she's not related to Jonathan in Year Four, is she?'

'Yes!' Jane shouts. 'Sarah is . . . Jonathan's little sister. That's . . . that's it.' Sweat is forming between her shoulder blades and she can feel Natasha's eyes boring into her.

On a napkin her friend scribbles: *What are you doing?* and pushes it across the table. Jane wishes she could answer.

Michael's frown deepens.

'I didn't know Jonathan had a sister.' His eyes flick between them.

'He, er, didn't know he had one. Until recently. It's very complicated.'

'Families often are,' Natasha says, finally coming in to bat. 'Don't you think, Mr Carney? Are you married yourself?'

'Well,' he responds awkwardly, clearly thrown off by the question, 'I was. My wife is no longer with us, I'm afraid.'

'Oh, I'm so sorry,' Natasha says, bringing her hand to her mouth. Her acting is rather impressive. 'You must miss her terribly. Would you tell us about her? How did you meet?'

Michael stares quizzically back at them, eyes darting and mouth slightly ajar. Suddenly, he sits back in his chair, his expression stony.

'Who are you?' he barks.

They do not reply. Natasha's hand resting on Jane's suddenly feels clammy.

'Do you', Michael fires at them, 'or do you not, have a child called Sarah Hepburn?'

Jane slowly shakes her head.

'I met Jonathan's parents last year and I don't recognise either of you. And families may well be "complicated", but that stretches the meaning of the word a bit far. So, are you journalists?'

'N-No,' Natasha stutters. 'Not press. We're very sorry, Mr Carney. We are more like . . . '

'Private detectives,' Jane says. 'And . . . authors.'

'*Authors?*'

'Look,' she says, throwing caution to the wind and leaning closer to the screen. 'We didn't mean to mislead you. We're sorry about that. But we are investigating some murders, here in London. And one of the victims was— '

'Hugo Strauss,' he spits. 'I know. Do you really think the police haven't already spoken to me? Checked out my alibi? Well, they did, and it's solid. I had meetings with about 30 parents that evening and made a speech that was in the local press. Not to mention the fact that I'm in *Sweden*.'

'Understood,' whispers Jane, who has never been so keen to end a conversation as she is right now.

'And in answer to your question,' he says, eyes flicking to Natasha, 'I met my wife in London, 28 years ago. She was doing a photoshoot in Covent Garden, but she got lost. Couldn't find the right street.' His voice softens, the rough edges sanded away by nostalgia. 'I was the lucky bugger she stopped and asked for directions.'

He explains how he had walked Johanna to where she needed to go, purposely taking a longer route so he could spend more time with her. He was 20 minutes late for work himself, but couldn't have cared less – not only had he plucked up the courage to ask a Swedish supermodel to dinner, but she had said yes.

'She thought I was funny,' he says in a small voice. 'Didn't care that I was just an ordinary-looking bloke. I went to stay with her in Sweden and never left. Life got better and better for us . . . that was, until the accident.'

The Michael Carney in the wedding photo is far from ordinary-looking. He might not quite match the exceptional good looks of his wife, but his face is chiselled and symmetrical, his smile wide and pleasing. He has the same thick blond hair today, even if it looks less cared for. Michael would still be very attractive, thinks Jane, if not for the sadness corroding him from the inside out.

'Would you tell us about what happened?' Natasha says in a low, kind voice. Michael sighs, and nods.

The Carney family had rented a Devon holiday cottage with some old friends just outside Seaton for a weekend trip. Johanna had cycled to the nearest shop to pick up some more wine for them to share by the fire. She was cycling home when Hugo Strauss's car came flying around the corner and stole her future.

'Johanna was sensible,' Michael says, face hardened, tears gone. 'He must have appeared from nowhere, going 60 miles an hour in the dark. Straight from the *pub*. She didn't have a chance.'

'You blame him then?' Jane asks. She can't think of a more subtle way to ask.

'Yeah,' Michael replies bluntly. 'Of course I blame him. He killed my wife, and for that he was punished with a brief driving ban and a fine that wouldn't touch the sides of his plutocratic lifestyle.' He sits forward, eyes blazing and hands clenched into fists. 'You know the legal drink-driving limit in Sweden? Zero. If you have had *even half a pint* you cannot get behind the wheel of a car. I campaigned to get the rules changed to this in England, but no one's interested.'

Michael sighs and sits back in his chair, anger dissipating as quickly as it came. He stares forlornly into the camera.

'I understand why some people might suspect me now that Hugo Strauss has been found dead,' he says at last. 'I'm not sad the man is dead but I had nothing to do with it, and was nearly a thousand miles away at the time. Besides, I'm trying to move on with my life. Maybe you should do the same.'

Outside in the sunlight, the two women stand and stare out over the Thames in silence.

'I was so sure,' Jane says after a few minutes, 'that the accident was the key.'

'Just because one awful thing has happened, doesn't mean it's related to another awful thing,' Natasha says wisely. 'There are a lot of awful things in this world.'

'So,' Jane says, head in hands, 'it's not Michael Carney, and we know Hugo himself is not the killer. I still suspect Scott Wallace is hiding something though, and that letter on Lambert's desk was mighty suspicious too . . .'

'Hugo's affair with Marabella is interesting as well, though I can't really believe she'd have anything to do with it, and she was in France.'

'She's a powerful woman. Someone could have acted on her behalf while she was out of the country creating a watertight alibi?' Jane doesn't believe it, even as she says it. 'And there is always the chance Hugo tried to end their affair and she struck back at him? It's said that poison is a woman's weapon after all.'

'We're taking our eyes off Scott, and the mysterious man from the dating app, because we think Daisy's death was an accident. But that might not even be true,' Natasha says, sounding hopeless. 'Oh, I'm going back to the B&B for a lie down, my head hurts. Coming?'

'No,' Jane says, giving her friend a sad smile. 'I'm going to walk a little while longer. Sometimes things happen when you walk. Pieces fall into place.'

They part ways and Jane strolls aimlessly beside the river. So many suspects, so many scraps of information, so many stories of individual grief, so *few* answers. There is something she is missing. Something that is staring her right in the face.

Chapter Thirty-Four

Tuesday, 12 p.m.

As Jane walks, mulling over her morning, clues from the case start to become confused with something else – her new novel. The storyline is revolving around in her brain, and soon, she finds herself itching to sit down and dive back into it. The protagonist – a bumbling detective with an undistinguished past, passion for Chocolate Hobnobs and an unfortunate nose – is taking shape in her mind. The conversation with Michael Carney bubbles underneath.

She is on the South Bank now, the ever-revolving white circle of the London Eye coming into view. Part of Jane wants to hop right back on the train to Cumbria and put this whole thing behind her. She could sit down at her little desk and crack on with the novel, order a takeaway from Mr Nicey Spicy and eat it on her too-small sofa with her laptop on her knees. She could be at her next disciplinary to beg her case and save her job. But what about Daisy? About Hugo? About *Natasha*?

It's been five days now since Jane arrived in Kings Cross Station, intending to pop into her friend's book launch, raise a glass, and head back home. Five days since she crept down the basement stairs in the Willow Tree Books stock room and found the lifeless body of Daisy Olsson.

And what exactly has she learnt in that time? Sometimes it feels like a whole lot of nothing.

An old woman scuttles past her, thick round glasses magnifying pale blue eyes that remind her of Ramos. A teenager blares music from a speaker sticking out of his pocket, bringing club sounds to every pavement he slouches along. The huge white wheel spins lazily in the near-distance and she stares at it as if hypnotised.

Jane gives herself a shake. Enough moping. There is a time and a place for it, and then she must pull herself together. She is in London! One of the greatest cities in the world! There might be a case to solve, she might have a book to write, an agent to secure, a friend to help and a job to save, but the sun is bouncing off the water and she has her health – isn't she also allowed a little enjoyment?

The world is your oyster, Jane, she hears her mother whisper. *So make hay while the sun shines.*

Yes, she thinks, watching the huge revolving Ferris wheel. *Yes, I shall.*

In the queue for the London Eye, Jane pulls out her copy of *A Magpie's Lament,* opening it at Chapter 14. The more she reads, the more confused she becomes. The prose is beautiful, the characters subtle and believable. The love and understanding the protagonist has for their friends is real and complex. She can't make it square with the brash, boastful man she met the night before, charming as he was. But then again, she supposes that is what writing fiction is all about, embodying someone else.

She becomes lost in the story as she waits, the sun turning the tip of her nose pink and her back damp.

'Jane?'

She jumps, slamming the book shut in surprise. The voice is familiar, but she can't place it. She is almost at the front of the queue now, but spins around, searching the crowd behind.

Waving at her, pushing his way past a group of Spanish tourists taking pictures of themselves by the wheel, is a young man in a camouflage-patterned tracksuit, a neon yellow hat on top of his dirty-blond curls. The grey bags taking up residence under Scott Wallace's eyes have darkened to the colour of gunmetal. He isn't smiling.

'Scott?' Jane remembers DI Hawberry's words last night. *It's Scott Wallace. There is so much that man is hiding.* 'What are you doing here?'

And how does he know I'm here?

'I'm supposed to be at work,' Scott says, looking nervously over his shoulder. 'But . . . well, I haven't gone in, have I? Got up to go, just didn't do it. Walked around all morning, then ended up here. You said you were staying nearby and I hoped . . . when I saw you . . . feels like . . . I dunno, fate?'

Up close, Scott looks dreadful. His skin is ash-white, his eyes bloodshot, and he is jiggling from foot to foot. *Drugs?* thinks Jane. *Or guilt?*

'I need to talk to someone,' he says in a low voice, edging closer. 'And not that detective with the stick up her arse. I think I need to talk to *you*.'

Jane's heart is thumping. She is alarmed by both his presence and his appearance. She thinks once more of that school guinea pig and remembers, all of a sudden, that it bit her finger once. Made it bleed. Her mind is terrifyingly blank.

'Madam?'

Jane turns to see that she is at the front of the queue. The bored-looking woman behind the ticket counter clicks her fingers.

'I'm sorry, er, can you wait just a moment?'

'No, I can't *wait a moment*. You wanna go up or not?'

'Oh, look,' Jane says. 'You can see the Houses of Parliament!'

'Yeah,' Scott replies. 'And there's a dog down there doing a poo.'

The wheel takes 45 minutes to complete a revolution, and Jane and Scott are only a quarter of the way around. Jane is fascinated by the way people keep shrinking as they climb higher, though is slightly distracted by the potential murderer next to her.

'That's the Polar Bear Publishing offices. The massive building with all the glass,' says Scott. Jane peers down the river at the building with the midday sun bouncing off its numerous windows. 'Should be in there right now, answering stupid IT questions from thicko book people.'

'Excuse me,' she says. 'I happen to be a thicko book person myself.'

'Sorry. Are you any good with computers?'

'Well, no.'

'And over there are the Magic Box offices.' He points to a square building near Blackfriars station with rectangular windows and a grassy roof terrace. 'Maybe I'll try and get a job there next.'

'So, Scott.' Jane continues to look out over London as she speaks. 'Tell me. What's going on? Why didn't you go to work today? Why do you look like you haven't slept in weeks? And what exactly do you want to talk about so badly that you have paid £45 to join my trip on the London Eye?'

'Mad price, innit?'

'Completely mad. But I'd queued for quite a while by the time I found that out.' Jane sees the camouflaged shoulders slump in his reflection. 'Come on, Scott, spit it out.'

Is she about to hear a confession to murder? High in the air, trapped in a toughened glass pod alone with him, Jane feels that she should be afraid. But she isn't. There is the fact that she is so on display for one thing – though a murder in this glass capsule would be quite cinematic – and for another? This young man seems vulnerable.

'That policewoman. Hawberry. You met her?' Jane nods. 'I reckon she thinks I did it. Killed Daisy and Hugo. But I didn't. I'd *never* hurt Daisy. But . . . but I think I know who did.'

Jane reaches into her handbag, fumbling around until she finds her packet of Extra-Strong mints, the next best thing to tea. She puts one in her mouth to calm herself and offers the packet to Scott. They stare back out over London as they rise higher and higher into the air, and he finally begins to talk.

Scott Wallace first met Daisy at work when her computer wouldn't turn on. He came up to her desk to explain that it wasn't plugged in at the wall, and fell head over heels in love.

'Looked through her emails remotely and found she was subscribed to this newsletter from a band called the Sharp Points. So next time I was up on her floor, I wore one of their T-shirts, struck up a conversation and asked her out.'

'Highly unethical,' says Jane, watching a man the size of a woodlouse propose to his girlfriend on Westminster Bridge. 'But not murder.'

'That's nothing. After she dumped me, I invented a whole persona on a dating app to try and make her fall in love with me again.'

Jane rests her head against the glass in sudden understanding. 'He wasn't called *Kyle* by any chance, was he?' What a waste of their time.

'Yeah!' says Scott with surprise. 'You know about that? Wow. Anyway, I felt kind of weird about it. Like, I know it was a dick move. But I didn't like to see how fast she was moving on. I had to convince her to think again – we were right together! You see, for a book person, Daisy wasn't half bad. She was funny, energetic, a bit wild.' Jane took offence to Scott's continued character assassination of 'book people', but decided to let it go in the face of the other revelations. 'Hell, she didn't even *like* books. She was perfect.'

He gets distracted eulogising about the dates they had been on until Jane stops him, pointing out that they are now at the top of the wheel – halfway through his allotted time.

Jane doesn't like Scott Wallace. She hadn't liked the school guinea pig he reminds her of either, and that aftershave is highly off-putting in this enclosed space.

'Okay, okay, I'll get to the point. It started . . . oh, I don't know, about two months ago. On a game called The Quester's Heart.'

Jane isn't sure what she'd been expecting when they stepped into the pod together, but it wasn't this story. The whooshing feeling she has only known a few times in her life blows through her, the feeling that tells her, *here we go*. Or maybe it's the fact that their pod is now on its way down.

'Daisy always had this barrier up, see? I loved her, and I just wanted to get close to her, to understand her, but she wouldn't let me.

'You had only been dating about three months by that point?'

'Three months is long enough to know! But it drove me mad, all the stuff she kept to herself. I wasn't even allowed in her flat. She used to say that the other woman who lived there wouldn't like it, but I wasn't buying that. I'd turn up at the door but she'd just come straight outside.'

Jane remembers what the downstairs neighbour had said. *He used to hang around outside . . . him yelling up at the window for her to let him in and her refusing.*

'Anyway, one day she was at mine and I was playing this game Questers online, and Daisy was like, *Oh, my friend loves that! She's always on it*. Well, this was the first time I'd heard her mention a friend! She was some purple witch thing, used to boast about being a level six.

'Daisy said they'd fallen out and wouldn't tell me why. Shut the conversation down when I pushed. But I couldn't get it out of my head that this was someone else who knew her. And they'd had some mysterious argument . . . I couldn't help myself – I went looking for her in the game.'

'There must be hundreds of players on there?' Even Jane has heard of The Questers Heart, though knows little about it.

'Level-six players though? Not many. And those that play as a purple witch? Actually, only four. I looked in the directory. Soon found her.'

'Right.'

Jane isn't sure what to make of this. On the one hand, his trampling of Daisy's boundaries and borderline unhinged behaviour in tracking down her ex-friend is concerning, but on the other – who is she to talk? She hardly covered herself in glory on that call with Michael Carney.

'We started chatting on Questers,' Scott continues, pacing around their pod now, his camouflage tracksuit giving the impression that he is stalking invisible prey. 'I wanted to ask about Daisy, see? That was the idea. But it wasn't easy, and anyway . . . I started to like the witch girl. We got on. And soon I started to feel bad about lying to her, see?

'When she asked to meet up, like on a date, I just couldn't do it anymore. She was my friend by then and it felt like I was betraying her *and* Daisy. So, I told her.'

'You told her?'

'Told her who I was, that I was going out with Daisy, that I was sorry and the rest.'

Jane feels a burn of humiliation on this woman's behalf. The sting of rejection at being turned down for a date, then the ferocity of the pain that would come from being told you were being played by your enemy's boyfriend, like vinegar on the wound.

'She lost it,' confirms Scott. 'And now I just can't get it out of my head that it was her!'

He drops to a crouch, his head in his hands. 'That she . . . that *she* killed Hugo and Daisy. And it was *my* fault.'

'I don't follow?' Jane says. The ground is drawing closer towards them, people growing taller, birds and rubbish and signs coming into clearer focus. She isn't sure what to make of this story or the man who told it. It's duplicitous, under-handed, unethical. However, guilt for what he thinks he may have caused radiates from him.

'She thought Daisy had been in on it and it was . . . some big *joke*. That we'd been laughing at her the whole time. She said . . . she said, *I hope you die. I hope you all die.*'

'But what about *Hugo*?' Jane says in confusion. 'Why would she kill him?'

'Well, he kind of started it all. *He* is why they fell out.'

The link, Jane thinks, *at last!* Their pod is approaching ground level now. In the back of her mind, there is a trace of annoyance that she hasn't been able to pay proper 360° attention to her surroundings on the way around. But beyond that, a feeling of relief. Because she can sense that things are finally, suddenly, about to come together.

'She told me everything on Questers, before she knew who I was. She was Hugo's assistant, and she exposed his affair with the literary agent. Told his wife. Hugo sacked her, then Daisy swooped in and took the assistant's job. They had this massive fight about it and didn't speak again. Lucy felt betrayed – kind of cheated, I guess?'

'Lucy? Lucy *who*?'

He pulls out his phone and types in the name, holding it up for Jane to see the photograph. At the sight, she feels her stomach drop through the floor of the pod.

'Lucy Tallow. She's an editorial assistant at Eagle's Wing.'

The small woman from Natasha's book launch – dark bob with purple streak, pearls strung across her throat, copious black eyeliner – stares up at her. The woman who had 'bumped into' Jane in Waterstones, full of questions about the investigation.

'And the thing is . . . ' Scott says quietly just as their pod locks into place and the door swings open. 'The thing is, if it *was* Lucy . . . then I'm next.'

Chapter Thirty-Five

Tuesday, 13.10 p.m.

Marabella Rhodes is lying face down on her office floor.

She turns her head to rest her cheek against the wood and spots an earring she lost three months ago under the filing cabinet. A beautiful, twinkling sapphire. It says a lot about her current situation that she doesn't care a bean.

The inspector with the bad hair and cheap suit has just left, and Marabella feels drained of blood. *It has come to my attention,* she'd said, *that you and Mr Strauss were a little more than friends.*

Marabella had known it was coming. After all, the cat was let out of the bag by that meddling little assistant Hugo used to have, Lucy. *She'd* be lucky ever to see a submission from Marabella's agency in her entire career.

Jessie Strauss turning up on her doorstep had been a real low point in Marabella's life. Actually telling her she could *have* the man if she wanted him badly enough to steal him. Oh, it was shaming, *awful.* But not quite as awful as Hugo, running up the stairs behind his wife, swearing that Marabella meant *nothing* to him, nothing at all. She was *nobody.*

No one calls Marabella Rhodes a *nobody.*

She'd wanted to be angry with him. She *was* angry. But mostly, in that moment, she was broken.

Marabella has never married. Her career has always been her chief focus. But when she and Hugo had had a few too many drinks at a work event and ended up in bed together, her world changed. After a lifetime of carefully protecting her heart, she laid it out on the block for him to butcher.

And now where is she? Lying on the floor of her office after having been basically accused of murder.

The door creaks open, but she can't find it in herself to move a muscle.

'Um, Marabella?'

'Hi, Abi.'

Her assistant steps over her body, then crouches down. She is tiny, even shorter than Marabella, which is one of the reasons she likes her.

'Got you a chicken Caesar salad.'

Marabella smiles despite herself. Abi has correctly intuited that today is one when her faltering vegetarianism can get in the bin.

'Come on now.' Abi helps her into a sitting position and props her against a wall. 'Got you a coffee too. Full fat cow's milk.'

It's pushed into her hand. The warmth feels good and she takes a sip, allowing it to revitalise her.

'How . . . how were the police?' Abi murmurs. 'Is everything okay?'

Since starting her side business, Marabella has had a lot of assistants. None of the others got even a whiff of it. But two months into her job here, Abigail Ellis had already intuited that something wasn't quite right, and had gone digging for more. It turned out that her last boss – Marabella's professional nemesis, the late, great Carrie Marks – had been a bit of a crook, leading Abi to indulge her naturally suspicious nature.

Far from turning Marabella in to the police, though, she'd offered to pitch in with the admin in the autographed books business, in exchange for a small pay rise and the new job title of Junior Agent. She even still fetched Marabella her coffee. Abi, in the end, had been a Godsend.

'It was *humiliating*,' Marabella finally manages to spit out. 'Truly. First she painted me as some sort of . . . *tart*, then as some sort of . . . *criminal*.'

'Hmm,' Abi says, plopping down to sit cross-legged opposite her. 'But did she know anything about the, you know, criminal activity?'

'No,' Marabella says grudgingly. 'Nothing.'

Abi breathes out in relief. It would be her neck on the block too if it all came out.

'But it's time for that to end, Abi. For good. With the break-in, and now the police sniffing around . . . it's just too risky. And besides, we don't need it.'

'Of course not, we're the best literary agency there is,' Abi says, and Marabella is grateful to have this tiny woman of low moral calibre and high ambition by her side. 'We'll sign more authors, grow. I can help. You make me a full agent and I'll start—'

'We'll see. Now you'd better go home and destroy those signed books you took to your flat. I'm going to clean up my computer. Then I'm going to fight for my author. We still have time to turn around this situation for Natasha Martez, I just need to find the way.'

When Abi has left, Marabella stares at the photo on her phone lock-screen of the Escarpa Viewpoint, a souvenir of a perfect weekend she and Hugo had shared. With a steely resolve, she changes it to one of her on the night she won Agent of the Year. Time to reconnect with the woman she always planned to be.

Chapter Thirty-Six

Tuesday, 2.15 p.m.

When Jane was 14, too tall and uncertain of her place in the world, she'd forgotten to return a stack of books to the library. She had just discovered Miss Marple, and had become lost in mystery and murder, a fictional world where an unassuming woman, underestimated by all those around her, can pip everyone to the post.

She'd realised the books were due back only 20 minutes before the library closed, but made it there. Just.

Not since then, she reflects as she weaves through tourists and businessmen, has she moved through the world with such, purpose, determination and conviction.

The Eagle's Wing office is 30 minutes by foot from the London Eye. Jane covers it in 20. Standing outside, she looks up at the building – grubby, square and soulless – a list of the businesses housed inside displayed on a small white sign by the door.

Standing across the street, Jane catches her breath, feeling the thin line of sweat cooling on her spine. *Lucy Tallow*. She'd met the strange young woman on the night of the murder. She'd been friendly, chatting away like she hadn't a care in the world. Could she really have gone on to kill two people just moments later?

But the memory of the scared look on Scott's face tells Jane that, yes – Lucy very well could have done. A woman scorned – a tale as old as time. Lucy had been betrayed by her best friend, by her boss, by the man she believed she loved. She'd lost it all, finding herself alone and jobless, only managing to land a poorly paid position in this inauspicious new home. She'd wished them all dead, *sworn revenge upon them.*

Has everything else just been a distraction until now? Charismatic Lambert, creepy Scott (who was also the mystery suitor from Daisy's dating app), grieving Michael Carney? All of them red herrings?

The ramshackle office of Eagle's Wing is a far cry from Polar Bear Press, where sleek modernity blends perfectly with publishing tradition. Instead, one window is covered in cardboard, and no one has washed off the graffiti scrawled across the brickwork that reads, simply, *poo.*

Inside, a man in a suit is slumped on an ageing sofa, head resting on one hand while the other scrolls languidly on his phone. A woman marches across the dimly lit lobby, a stack of books in her arms, the click of her heels echoing like gunshots. Jane has never been here before – when she signed with Eagle's Wing many years ago, she met her editor in a nearby café. She can see now why authors weren't welcomed eagerly to the offices.

At the reception desk, Jane asks for Lucy Tallow with as much authority as possible.

'Do you have an appointment?' the receptionist says, not looking up from her screen, her springy brown curls bouncing as she types.

'Um, no . . . but please tell her an author is downstairs and that it is *vital* she comes down. Tell her . . . tell her *Daisy* is here to see her.'

Jane sinks down onto the sofa next to the besuited man staring at his iPhone, and waits. She watches the receptionist speak into the phone, glancing up at Jane as she does so. Five minutes pass, each of which feels like an eternity, before the door of the elevator opens with a jolly *ding.*

Lucy Tallow looks exactly as Jane remembers. Small, pale, her black and purple bob neat and shiny, the same string of pearls around her throat.

Her eyes scan the lobby nervously and Jane wonders if part of her is expecting to see the ghost of the woman she killed just three days previously.

Finally, as Jane gets to her feet, the eyes latch onto her. Lucy frowns, and then a flicker of confused recognition passes across her features.

'Jane, wasn't it?' Lucy says as she reaches her. 'Or is it . . . Daisy?'

'I'm sorry, I just really needed to speak to you.'

'I'm at work, I'm afraid. But if you want to submit a manuscript, you will have to do so via your literary—'

'It's not that.' Jane looks around them. The man is still on the sofa, the receptionist is watching them with open curiosity, a pair of laughing women are emerging from the lift. 'We shouldn't talk here. You won't *want* to talk here.'

Lucy Tallow assesses her visitor, considers these words. Finally, she gives a curt nod.

'I can give you ten minutes before I have to be back at my desk. Come on.'

Jane follows Lucy through some double doors off the lobby and down a corridor in silence. She assumes she is being escorted to a meeting room and is taken aback when Lucy pushes open some double doors to what looks like the post room, an eighties power ballad blasting from an old boom box in the corner.

Lucy nods to a man stamping piles of Jiffy bags, who calls out in a jolly tone that the kettle's just boiled, and pushes open another door.

'In here, come on.'

They are in a small kitchen, spotless and tidy aside from the stack of mugs by the sink waiting their turn to be washed.

'Post-room kitchen. I come here sometimes . . . when I need to escape from upstairs. Darren doesn't mind.'

Assuming he is the man they just passed, Jane pulls out a plastic chair and takes a seat. Lucy washes two already clean mugs thoroughly and comes to the table with tea and a small plate of digestive biscuits. An encouraging sign.

Even so, Lucy is jittery, barely meeting her eye. Could it really be that the car accident from six years ago has nothing at all to do with Hugo's death? That *Lucy* is the sole answer?

'Miss Tallow,' Jane begins. 'I need to speak to you about Hugo Strauss and Daisy Olsson. And I know you don't have much time.'

Like milk souring on the spot, the pearly pallor of Lucy's skin turns grey. Her mug, halfway to her lips, stalls in midair, and she returns it to the table.

'Who are you?'

'I'm Jane. Jane Hepburn. We met the oth—'

'No, I mean, who *are* you? What are you doing here?'

'Well, I *am* an author. But I'm also looking into the murders of editorial staff at Polar Bear Publishing.'

Lucy wrinkles her perfect little nose, her polite veneer cracking at the edges now. 'A crime-solving author? How novel. Pun not intended.'

'Hugo sacked you when you exposed his affair.'

'Requested I leave,' she corrects Jane with a sad smile. 'It would have been illegal to sack me. Stupidly, I did as he asked. I didn't understand, at the time, that I had any other choice.'

'And Daisy?' Jane continues. 'You were friends and had a falling out?'

It's hearsay rather than confirmed fact, but if Lucy is indeed the killer it's safe to suppose that they *did* fall out over something or other. People don't just go around killing their friends willy-nilly.

'I met Daisy at an event in a bookstore. We became friends. Or so I *thought*.' Lucy dips a biscuit in her tea and nibbles at the edge of it. 'She wasn't just a friend. She was my best friend. My only friend really. We spent so much time together. We even got matching purple in our hair.' She strokes a finger down the brightly coloured streak in her bob. 'Hers faded, but mine was permanent. Maybe there is something fittingly . . . poetic in that.

'Anyway, I was Hugo's assistant, as you know, and it all went south when I told his poor wife about his infidelity. He was sleeping with that literary agent, Marabella Rhodes? It was the right thing to do.'

Jane nods to convey she sympathises. Lucy seems naïve and well behaved, sweet even. Could she really be the cold-blooded mastermind behind two murders?

But Jane can imagine her mother's shrewd glare over a cup of tea. *You know better than to judge a book by its cover*, she says. *There might be a wolf under that sheep's clothing.*

'Daisy and I went out for drinks the same day I was asked to leave,' Lucy continues. 'We spent *hours* lambasting Hugo. Going over what a scum bag he was. And a few days later . . . you know what? Daisy is his new assistant!' She lets out a shrill giggle that couldn't contain less humour if she tried and shoves the rest of the biscuit into her mouth, crumbs cascading down her dress.

'She'd learnt a lot about the job from me, a lot about Hugo. She called me and said that she'd gone in there and presented herself as being perfect for the role and ready to start straight away. He snapped her up. You see, Hugo can't do anything for himself. Can't even use a printer.'

The door of the tiny kitchen swings open and Darren pokes his head around it.

'You alright in here, ladies? I'm gonna be on my break in a few minutes so will need to come in and use the microwave. Gotta a fish curry that'll blow your socks off.'

'Of course,' Lucy says with a smile. 'We won't be long.'

He nods and the door swings closed. Time is ticking.

'After everything Hugo did?' Lucy continues, leaning forward and lowering her voice, speaking quickly now. 'Not just cheating on his wife, but sacking me for calling him out? Daisy just . . . used me. She did sound a *bit* guilty, but either way . . . we had an absolutely flaming row and didn't speak again. I . . . I don't have many friends, Miss Hepburn. And I learnt a lesson there about making the right sort.'

Lucy meets Jane's eyes defiantly. Her intense stare, that perfect black bob and the mess of crumbs beneath it, all combine to give her an unhinged look that makes Jane physically recoil. *That must have been the argument Daisy's downstairs neighbour heard.*

'So you killed them – that night at Willow Tree Books?'

The radio in the post room switches off, music dying. Lucy is staring at Jane, as though weighing something up. Her eyes start to fill with tears that she manages to keep from falling, and Jane feels her façade crack. This woman, she thinks, is very sad. Very lonely. Jane can always recognise loneliness.

'She tried to speak to me,' Lucy says quietly. 'That night. But I walked away. You're right, I was angry, but I'm not a violent person, Jane. I'm *not*. And Daisy? She was . . . my friend. Once. Anything I did do . . . I didn't mean . . . '

The door swings open, making both women jump and Jane slop her tea across the Formica.

'Sorry, ladies, time's up,' Darren says. 'Unless you mind me listening in on your gossip, o' course.'

'No, no, Darren, we'll get out of your hair,' Lucy says, jumping to her feet and smoothing down her hair. 'Enjoy the curry. Jane, I need to get back to work, you can find the exit, I presume?'

'Lucy . . . wait!'

But she has disappeared from the kitchen before Jane can even get to her feet, and when she is back in the corridor, the editor is nowhere to be seen.

Outside on the street, Jane steps into an alleyway and leans against the cool stone facing of a building, breathing hard. She needs to find somewhere to sit and think about this woman who brings everyone together. Who had grudges against both victims, wished them and another man dead, who swears she is not violent but has done *something*. Had she intended for only Hugo to die, and now the accidental death of her old friend Daisy, caught in the cross-fire, is tearing her up with guilt?

Anything I did do, she'd started to say, *I didn't mean . . .*

Yes, Jane needs time and space and quietness in which to consider if she's just shared tea and biscuits with a killer.

Chapter Thirty-Seven

Tuesday, 4.08 p.m.

Jane stations herself outside the Sherlock Holmes at a rickety wooden table on the cobblestones, recently vacated by a Canadian couple and their guidebook.

The area around the pub isn't quiet by Cumbrian standards, but it's still a relief from the hordes of people pushing past each other on the Strand. The city is taking its toll and Jane feels exhausted in mind and body. She sips at a refreshing glass of Diet Coke, the bubbles fizzing on her tongue like gossip.

At the next table, a young couple sit with half-pints of lager. The woman is beautiful as most young women are, but in a way Jane never felt. Her strawberry-blonde hair is shoulder-length and freckles dance across her nose. She laughs, taking the hand of the man she is with and leaning forward to kiss his fingers. Jane looks away.

It's been years since she has had a romantic partner, or even been on a real date. Her ex-boyfriend Stefan had chewed her up and spat her out. Nothing came of her flirtation with Edward Carter. It's okay though, she thinks to herself, sitting up straight. Mustn't mope. Some people are just not built for love. Love is for the beautiful, like the laughing girl with strawberry-blonde hair. It's not for plain Janes. Not for her.

Jane's phone buzzes and she feels her heart leap to see a text message from Detective Inspector Ramos.

Just checking that you haven't found any more bodies Sergeant Hepburn? X

Odd, thinks Jane, staring at that X at the end of the message. Maybe he did it by mistake, like when she texted the dentist *goodnight xxx*. Still, she taps out a reply to say she hasn't, but she *has* found more suspects and feels on the verge of a breakthrough. With a smile, she adds that, though she appreciates the new rank of sergeant he has bestowed on her, he should know she has ambitions for his DI badge in the coming weeks. If only Ramos was officially working this case. Hawberry may have warmed towards her slightly, but Jane still isn't sure if she can be fully trusted to share things.

Feeling a little better, Jane pulls out her notebook and scribbles down what she's learnt today. Lucy Tallow clearly felt deeply betrayed by both her old boss and her friend. On top of that, Scott compounded the betrayal and added a hearty drop of humiliation into the mix. A motive for murder? Most definitely.

Ms Tallow comes across as a woman with strong morals, someone who cannot stand cheating and lying and disloyalty. Does that fit with murder? Some people, Jane knows, have a strange sense of moral righteousness. When she was young, she'd had a vegan aunt who was convinced the death penalty was the perfect response to bicycle theft.

Someone took Hugo's phone from his body in his study. Did Lucy break in to check her victim was indeed dead, swiping his phone in case . . . what? To check he hadn't told anyone of his suspicions while he still could?

That didn't feel right.

Jane puts down her pen with a sigh and resumes watching the happy couple from the corner of her eye. A bowl of chips has arrived for them, and the man is feeding them to his girlfriend. A little far, that. Jane may pine for a hand to hold or a shoulder to cry on, but she can manage eating by herself, thank you very much.

Stefan had cheated on her with his new assistant. A tale as old as time. And what of Hugo and his wife? What of the curly-haired Vicky Graves, piling books into the back of her car? Romantic love for Jane is maybe overdue, but it's also overrated. And maybe she is over *it*.

Jane checks her watch. 4.15. Natasha should be here soon, and Daniel said he'd join as soon as he could escape work, but time still seems to have slowed right down now she has so much to tell them.

Turning to the equally dissatisfying part of her life, Jane opens her email with a heavy feeling of dread in her stomach. Sure enough, an email awaits from Baxter's HR department.

Dear Ms Hepburn,

I am writing to address your absence from the disciplinary meeting today, which was attended by myself as your HR representative and Deborah Templeton, your manager. As you know, your attendance was necessary in order to discuss your conduct and continued unauthorised absence. This leads me to the conclusion that you are lacking dedication to your role at Baxter's Insurance Company.

As per procedure, the meeting has now been rescheduled for tomorrow at 10 a.m. in the HR meeting room. Please be advised that this meeting is mandatory, and should you fail to attend again without good reason your employment will be terminated.

Please do inform me whether or not you intend to attend the meeting at your earliest convenience.

Have a lovely evening :)

Stacy Fischer, HR Manager

Not quite the time for a smiley face, thinks Jane. With a sigh, she starts to word an apologetic response, but is saved from

the task when the phone buzzes in her hand. She's so surprised that she drops it and knocks her glass of Coke flying
into the air and down onto the cobbles, where it shatters. The
cosy couple whips around to stare as Jane flaps about, picking
up chunks of glass as her face starts to burn red. *Sorry,* she
mouths at them. *Sorry,* she mouths to the other tables looking at her. *Sorry,* she finds herself mouthing to the glittering
shards at her feet.

Dumping the glass on the table, she picks up her phone and
answers it before even looking at the screen.

'One gin and tonic, please, Baker!' Daniel trills, his happiness
evident. 'I'll be 15 minutes.'

'Already! You haven't snuck out of work, have you?'

'No, no. We have flexible hours. I'm allowed to leave by
4.30.'

'But it's only . . . '

'I'm flexible about what 4.30 means. See you soon.'

It feels much nicer to be sitting at the table with Daniel by
her side, and Jane relishes his excitement as she tells him all
about the conversation with Michael Carney, her ride on the
London Eye with Scott Wallace ('Not a euphemism, Daniel!')
and her informative tea in the post-room kitchen with Lucy
Tallow.

'That Lucy sounds odd,' he says, polishing off his drink with
a loud slurp through the straw. 'Cuckoo.'

'She's just lonely,' Jane says a little defensively. Lonely, like
Scott Wallace, like Hugo Strauss, like Jane herself. But is she
lonely still? Daniel pushes his floppy brown hair back from his
eyes and polishes off his gin and tonic. Maybe not.

'Natasha's nearly here,' he says, squinting at his phone in the
sun. 'I'm going to get us more drinks and a bowl of chips.'

By the time Daniel returns, expertly balancing three gin and
tonics in slim glasses, straws bouncing jauntily with each step,

Natasha has arrived. Her eyes display some evidence of tears, but the firm set of her jaw when she asks Jane about her day says that she does not want to talk about her book.

'So the office,' Daniel says, pulling out a chair, 'is buzzing about our friend Lambert Graves.' He slurps at his drink loudly and lets out a deep sigh. 'It's chaos.'

'What's happening?'

'His new book,' Daniel says with his trademark grin. 'It's vanished.'

They make their way through the bowl of steaming hot chips as he tells them everything.

Two weeks before his death, Hugo had informed everyone that Lambert Graves had finally delivered his highly anticipated new novel, albeit four months late. However, Hugo had never shared it with anyone else, and Daisy was the only other person with access to his emails.

The IT team has now granted the CEO access to Hugo's email account as he 'very sadly won't be returning to work'.

'But there is no sign of it in there. Nothing,' Daniel says, sitting back in his chair and reaching again for the bowl only to find it empty.

'How could it have just vanished?' says Natasha, deep parallel lines forming between her eyebrows. 'Unless Hugo was *lying* about it being delivered in the first place. But why would he do that?'

'Won't Lambert's agent have it?' Jane asks.

'Well, that's the *really* puzzling thing,' Daniel says, leaning back in his chair and putting his hands behind his head, clearly enjoying being centre-stage. 'Raymond gets on the phone to Marabella Rhodes and asks *her* to send over the book. She then says that *she* can't find it either!'

'What the . . .' Jane shakes her head in confusion. 'And what does *Lambert* say?'

'They can't get hold of him,' Daniel says with a shrug.

'But the real question is,' Natasha says, leaning forward with her hands on the table, 'can this be connected to the murders?'

The timing is certainly intriguing – a manuscript delivered months late and vanishing into thin air around the time of the deaths? But there are too many theories, too many suspects, and Jane's head is whirling. A missing manuscript, a betrayed editor, a jilted lover . . .

'It's all very odd,' Daniel is saying, 'because according to his agent, Lambert is usually a consummate professional. Always delivers on time, always answers emails. But he has just . . . changed since moving to Polar Bear Publishing 10 months ago.'

'He's going through a hard time personally,' Natasha says with a shrug. 'With Vicky leaving him. That situation seemed . . . odd. She was packing up boxes and seemed intent on ending her marriage, but still stuck around for dinner?'

Yes, thinks Jane, remembering the car parked up outside the looming mansion, Lambert opening the doorway, heavy gold rings on his fingers and studs in his earlobe.

Daniel and Natasha are bickering about the likelihood of this new mystery being connected to the murders. Daniel is convinced it means something but Natasha is sure it doesn't, that Lambert's behaviour can be explained purely by the turmoil of separation.

'What's more important,' she is saying, 'is this business with Lucy threatening the two victims! We should be worried about Scott.'

'Yeah, we *should* be worried about Scott,' Daniel retorts, 'as there's a good chance he is the killer and trying to shift blame onto Lucy! It's him or Lambert, mark my words.'

'Women are just as capable of being killers, Daniel!'

'This isn't a feminist issue, Nat!'

Jane tunes out of the conversation completely, bringing her mother's face to her mind.

All the glitters, she repeats, *is not gold.* She looks down at her watch, the quick movement of the second hand. *Tick tick tick.* How long do they have to catch the killer before any evidence vanishes entirely? Before Scott, if what he said was right, is harmed too? What happened to Lambert's manuscript? Why isn't he answering his phone? Something occurs to Jane then and she feels sick dread in her stomach. Is *he* safe? *Tick tick tick.* She pictures her mother's face, the infuriatingly raised eyebrow. *I need more,* Jane thinks.

Some people, she hears her mother whisper, *aren't meant to captain the ship, so they ride on the coattails of others.*

Jane can still hear Natasha and Daniel arguing, their voices growing louder in frustration.

'Come *off* it, Daniel! Hugo lied about Lambert delivering his book because it was so late. Hugo had a boss too, you know? Maybe he was going to get in trouble? You are forgetting that Hugo literally *killed* a woman six years ago. I think that's a *little* more important than a late manuscript.'

'It's not *late* – it's *missing*! What if this, all of this, comes down to *books*?'

Jane remembers the letter she'd seen on Lambert's desk. '. . . *life's work, my friend. I have not decided my next step, but I fear I cannot stay silent . . .* '

Jane thinks again of Vicky Graves, packing boxes of books into her car. She remembers Lambert's study, the shelves almost empty now. The books must mostly have been his wife's. A strange man. Not at all who she imagined while reading *The Magpie's Lament*, such a beautiful work. Almost Shakespearean . . .

'All that glitters,' Jane whispers, 'is not gold.'

'What?' Daniel and Natasha say together.

'Didn't it strike you as odd,' she says, 'that there were so few books in Aurum Manor? They all seem to have been taken by Lambert's wife.'

Natasha's frown deepens. 'I guess. But why does that matter?'

'*He* has no books. *She* has hundreds. *He* loves the limelight. *She* is a scholar of literature. *She* leaves him. *He* delivers no book.'

'And?' A strand of Daniel's dark hair falls in front of his brilliant blue eyes, and he blows it away impatiently, still rocking on the back legs of his chair. Natasha leans further forward still, her frown deepening. 'What are you saying, Jane?'

'What if things aren't completely as they appear? What if Lambert Graves didn't write his own books? What if his *wife* did?'

Chapter Thirty-Eight

Tuesday, 4.45 p.m.

The thing with gold, thinks Lambert Graves as he raises his blowtorch, is that it's always perfect. Even if you mess it up.

Not like words.

Take this ring, for example. It's a smallish hoop, and that's about all that is necessary for it to be a successful ring. He'll just do a bit of smelting here and there – and *voilà*! Done. Beautiful. He wipes the sweat from his brow.

He can do a lot more than that though, Lambert thinks to himself, lovingly gazing at a glass cabinet displaying his latest work. Delicate bracelets with vaguely religious iconography and nifty pillbox rings shine back at him, all inspired by jewellery from the Middle Ages and manufactured using ancient techniques. Vicky had found the inspiration in her old books, but Lambert had brought it all to life.

He's even *sold* one or two pieces. Acting, modelling writing . . . Lambert has tried a lot of different paths, found most of them rocky in their own way. This, he reflects, is really the only thing he's ever been any good at. Apart from being drop-dead gorgeous, that is.

The thing with fashion is that nothing's right, and nothing's wrong. No director shouting at you to, 'Look sadder!' No pesky editor on the phone night and day.

Not that being an author has been a bad life. Jolly good fun, most of it. Especially all of those lovely awards, the boozy parties and big cheques. He just needs to find a way to stop the publisher from being so damn' pernickety about all the *words*.

Lambert stands up straight, wiping his brow again. His eyes dart guiltily towards his phone, the screen showing the stacked up missed calls and text messages from Marabella and Raymond Stokes. He turns it face down and decides to make a spicy Margarita instead. He can use the Mezcal he brought back from Mexico last year, the one with the worms in the bottom of the bottle.

He has always been one to exaggerate. Not *lie*. He's not a *liar*. He just bends the truth a bit, to make it better. Like when he failed his degree and so printed out a certificate on some fancy paper to show his parents. A little bit of a stretch of the truth, but everyone's happier! They got something to put in a frame, he got a first-class degree and no bollocking.

The writing *exaggeration* was just a particularly successful manoeuvre and therefore ran a little bit out of control. He can see that now. But really, it was hardly his fault, and no one was hurt. At least at the start.

He'd told everyone at the Eton reunion he was going to be a writer because his *Hamlet* production had just been panned in the national press, and Donald Easton – the swotty swine – was boasting about a poem he got in the *New York Times Book Review*. It was rubbish, some nonsense about a fish that was supposed to represent loneliness or other such tosh.

But when Lambert had given it a go by writing an action-thriller, well, it had been *hard*. He'd spent three whole days on it and got a pretty good car chase down on paper, but couldn't quite work out who was chasing whom or why. His brain was tied in knots, and when he found out he'd need to write another *95,000 words,* he threw in the towel.

But then there was Vicky. She'd been the consultant on the set of *Hamlet*, employed to teach him about Shakespearean pronunciation and the like. He found most of it crushingly dull, but the woman's eyes were mesmerising.

Oh, Vicky. Lambert's heart gives a pang at the thought. If she was still here, she'd probably be tapping away on her keyboard, and he'd shout: 'Spicy margarita, Señorita?' And she'd tell him to leave her alone, but not really mean it. In the evening, they'd watch that television show about hoarders she liked, the one where weirdos never throw away their pizza boxes and have hamsters living in their shoes.

Removing his thick gloves and face mask, Lambert turns off the equipment and locks up the workshop, his heart weighing heavier by the second. The phone feels hot in his pocket, as though it's glowing with the angry words of a thousand emails and voicemails and text messages.

He mixes himself a drink, heavy on the worm juice and light on the lime, and retires to the study – Vicky's study really – to collapse into an armchair. The shelves are mostly empty now that she has spent the last few weeks clearing out. So is the fridge, so is his heart, and so – very often at the moment – is his glass.

If he can't think of a way to fix the mess he's landed himself in, he'll lose everything. He'll be fine for money of course, probably always will be, but he won't be able to show his face in London. Will have to leave his beloved house. Lambert pulls at a thread on his t-shirt, twisting it around his little finger tighter and tighter under it cuts off the blood supply and the tip pulses red.

'Fontaine!' he calls weakly, hoping the butler is nearby. 'Fontaine!'

Eventually, Lambert hears slow footsteps coming from a back room, and his butler's sulky face appears in the doorway.

'*Oui, monsieur?*'

'Ah, there you are. Make me another of these, will you?' He waves his empty margarita glass with his best charming smile. 'Thanks.' He doesn't like the desperation in his own voice.

Lambert had been on numerous marvellous dates with the shy but whip-smart young dramaturg when the subject of writing first came up. He'd told her about his abandoned attempt at a novel and the awful chaps from school who were still expecting him to produce something. She'd told *him* about her passion for words but abhorrence of the limelight keeping her from doing anything about it, other than her behind-the-scenes advisory role. And so, a beautiful partnership was born, in more ways than one.

He got an agent, got a book deal, got to tell smug Donald Easton he'd made the top ten bestsellers list, and Vicky got to spend her days in a beautiful house writing whatever she wanted.

The arrangement had worked for both of them for years. She didn't like the publicity, whereas he thrived on it. She liked spending hours tapping away on the computer, he loathed it. They both enjoyed the money it brought in.

But now? She's left him. Sick of his ego, she says. Sick of the house, and the drinking, and the sound of his voice. Sick of being taken for granted. Sick of him taking credit for her work. It's time, she says, to put *herself* out there. It was his accepting the new contract with Hugo at Polar Bear Publishing, without her go-ahead, that was the final nail in the coffin for both their marriage and their business arrangement.

Vicky had sworn to keep their secret about his, *their*, novels, purely to keep herself out of the papers, but refused to write another word in his name. Lambert isn't proud of how he'd reacted to that statement. There was a little bit of a 'Well, see if I ****** care!' and a fair amount of 'Go to Hell!' and a sprinkling of 'Just watch me!' If Vicky *has* been watching, she won't have been too impressed.

Lambert tried his best. He really did. Hunched over a laptop until the early hours, he painstakingly typed out 45,000 words of car chases and love affairs and toilet humour gags, and he was pretty proud of the result. But Hugo? Well, Hugo was less enamoured. Clever man, that Hugo Strauss. Clever enough to work out exactly what had been going on all these years as soon as he read that first post-separation manuscript.

But now Hugo is gone, and so is anyone who read that disastrous draft. Marabella hadn't got around to it, said she would when she got back from holiday. And Lambert's taken care of that. So he might be back to square one, but at least his secret is still safe.

His phone buzzes – Raymond Stokes's name is flashing up on the screen again – and he throws it across the room just as Fontaine enters it, cocktail in hand. He raises an eyebrow but doesn't say a word.

Lambert wouldn't mind getting rid of Fontaine really. Dreadfully smug, and he can tell the butler despises him. He'd liked Vicky, but since she's left, he's let distaste stream from his pores like sweat, filling the manor's every room. Far too well paid too. However, Lambert fears there is a chance, a tiny sliver of a chance, that his butler has figured out about the writing *exaggeration*, so when he asks for a pay rise, he always gets it. No questions asked.

'Not writing today, *sir*?' Fontaine says, setting the glass down on the side table and stepping back in one swift movement, as though he can't bear to be too close. He has a way of moving that gives Lambert the creeps sometimes. Fluid, affected. Like a shark.

Is there something knowing in the question? Something mocking? Lambert suddenly feels too aware of the second cocktail in front of him.

'Yes!' he says, getting to his feet. 'Yes, I think I will get on with it. I'm a little behind, to be honest with you. But I should . . . yes, I should finish it today.'

'Finish the whole book?' Fontaine says, raising his eyebrow again in a way that says *I see you*.

'It's not the *whole* book,' snaps Lambert, striding to the desk. 'It's the *end*. Because I've been working on it for a long time, as you well know.' He snaps open the laptop like he's cocking a gun – *let's go*. 'It's true I'm celebrating too soon though,' he says, gesturing to the cocktail while typing in his password. 'So please take that away.'

Fontaine whips away the glass, a smile playing around his mouth that makes Lambert shudder, and retreats from the room without another word.

Opening up a blank Word document, Lambert types CHAPTER ONE. After staring at it for a while, he deletes it and retypes in sentence case. Chapter One. Then he underlines it, and makes it bold, then unbold, then bold again. Perfect.

The minutes tick by, and he can hear his phone buzzing again in the corner of the room. It was so much easier when Vicky would handle this bit. If only there was another way for the novel to just . . . appear.

And he has it! Like a light dawning in the darkest of woods, hope and understanding come to him.

Opening a new page on his internet browser, he types into the search bar ChatGPT. His watch, a gold Omega Vicky bought him for his fiftieth, says it's nearly 5. If he is going to finish the entire novel today, he needs to get cracking. A creaking sound just outside the door makes him start and guiltily slam the laptop shut.

The opulent hallway is empty, but he suspects the sneaking lizard of a butler to have slipped out of sight just in time.

'Fontaine,' Lambert calls as he smooths his ponytail in the mirror, tweaking his gold cufflinks. 'Are you there?'

The man slides back into view and Lambert pastes a fake smile on his face.

'Don't worry about dinner tonight, I'll get a takeaway. You take yourself out for dinner on me before your dance thing. I can finish this, er, novel while ordering in some food only *half* as fine as yours.'

Fontaine smiles, lowering his head in a sign of subservience that somehow speaks only of the power he wields. Lambert will show him. He'll show him, and Marabella, and Vicky, and Hugo. He made it into a Hollywood movie despite everyone saying he had the talent of a slug, and he can manage this. He gives his beautiful home an appreciative look, and glances again at his watch. There is still time to save this. He will do *anything* to save this.

Chapter Thirty-Nine

Tuesday, 5.30 p.m.

'It's plagiarism!'

'No, it's fraud.'

'It's immoral.'

'But it's not,' Jane stresses, leaning forward on the rickety table outside the Sherlock Holmes, '*murder.*'

They've spent the last half an hour bickering about Lambert Graves. He may well be a scum bag, a liar, a no-good fraudster and a terrible host, but what is that to them? Really?

'Announce it on the internet, Jane!' says Daniel. Natasha, to Jane's surprise, nods firmly in agreement. 'Expose him!'

She is tempted. Since all that business at Killer Lines earlier this year, Jane's social media channels have gained a steady following, despite her barely having posted herself. The thought of Lambert Graves's unmerited success makes her seethe with anger. It's as though all of the years of struggle, of late nights typing, rejections, poor sales and okay sales and poor sales again, of plot holes and character development, of humiliating author events with no one present, of small wins that feel like huge trophies and large fails that feel like death – it's as if all of those moments are happening to her simultaneously. And they are happening while surrounded by towering piles of novels by Lambert Graves, all branded with accolades such as 'Number One Bestselling Author', 'Booker Prize Winner', 'International Sensation'.

Jane remembers how much the publication of her first novel meant to her. Seeing her words appear in print, bound in a jacket featuring the retreating figure of Private Investigator Sandra Baker, a blurb daring a reader to take it to the till. It had felt huge, triumphant, exhausting, because these were *her* words, her characters, her love, her creation.

What was there to be gained from doing nothing but sitting back and taking the praise? Money, she supposes. Money and glory. Glory Lambert Graves does not deserve. Glory that is a slap in the face to every other writer out there who tries and fails, tries and fails, tries and tries and tries.

But it is not, as she has already said, murder.

'If we're right, Lambert deserves what's coming to him,' she says, speaking slowly as the thoughts form. 'His world is crumbling without our help. We need to focus.'

'Lambert *could* have killed Hugo and Daisy after they guessed his secret,' Natasha says. 'And somehow deleted the manuscript from their computers . . .'

'The phone!' Daniel says, so loudly that the people on the other tables turn. 'Hugo's phone,' he whispers. 'Listen, Hugo *did* tell everyone Lambert had delivered *something* – what if he tried to write something himself, and it was so bad it made what had been happening with the other books for years *obvious*? Hugo confronts him, so Lambert kills him, then takes his phone to delete the manuscript from his email.'

'That letter,' Jane muses, 'from Hugo, on Lambert's desk. It said something about his "life's work", then, *I have not decided my next step, but I fear I cannot stay silent if this is the case. Let us talk in person soon.*'

'That's confirmation! Hugo was going to expose him!' Daniel says triumphantly.

'Not *confirmation*,' Natasha says firmly. 'But definitely suspicious.'

'We need to prove it,' says Jane. 'But how? *Think.*'

They fall silent, and, unbidden, the latest email from Baxter's Insurance pops into Jane's mind again. If she isn't going to lose her job, she needs to get to the train station right now, or at the very least contact her boss to explain. Ironic really, that Lambert has all this success when he has no talent, only confidence. Always something Jane has been sorely lacking.

She pulls out her phone and resolves the situation as succinctly as possible.

A *wham* announces Daniel's chair flying back and landing against the cobbles. He is on his feet, blue eyes glinting, a wide grin bringing his face to life.

'I've got it,' he says. 'But we need to get going.'

'Where? What?!' Natasha says, getting to her feet in a panic.

'We're going dancing.'

They can only find one likely dance class in Hampstead on a Tuesday evening. They make it to the front doors of the church hall just in time. Jane is breathing hard, her lungs expanding painfully as though they are wrapped in barbed wire. Her face, she can feel, is the shade of a London bus.

'We could have taken a taxi,' she gasps, as Natasha goes inside to purchase their entry tickets.

'I've told you, Jane,' Daniel says in exasperation, 'taxis take longer and cost a fortune.' He looks as fresh as ever, but you can't resent youth, Jane reminds herself. Or you can, but you can't let it *show*. He pushes open the door to the reception area where Natasha is speaking to a striking woman behind a desk, bleached-blonde hair piled into a precarious bun atop her head.

A smell of sweat and body lotion combined makes Jane shudder. She has been to a dance class once before after her mother suggested it might be a good place to meet a man. It had been swing dance, and her partner had tried to throw her between his legs but only succeeded in hurling her smack, bang on the floor. Her head had hit the wood with a loud *crack* and she'd blacked out. When she came to, it was just in time to hear her partner complaining to the instructor, 'It wasn't my fault, she's far too big!'

It's not a memory that fills her with excitement for the coming hour. Still, did Sherlock Holmes give in when faced with Irene Adler? Did Indiana Jones turn back at the sight of snakes? No. Nor will she, Jane Hepburn of Appleton, turn back from her own nemesis. Rhythm.

'I've told you, love, it's full,' the woman is saying to Natasha in a bored voice. 'We've got ballet tomorrow if you're interested.'

Jane battles the relieved smile threatening to take over her face. 'We'll just have to wait outside,' she whispers to Daniel.

'Jane, this class lasts *three hours*,' Natasha says, hands clutching at her hair in frustration. 'You haven't forgotten about Scott Wallace, have you? If we are wrong about Lambert, then it's Lucy who is the number one suspect. The same Lucy who threatened three people, two of whom are now dead. We don't have *time* to stand around!'

Lambert or Lucy. Lambert or Lucy. Both of them seem suspect to Jane, but they lack *concrete* evidence for either.

The outside door bursts open, hitting her painfully in the face.

'Oh, God, bab, I'm sorry!' a man shouts in a thick Birmingham accent. 'Are you okay?'

She is bent double, hands covering her pulsing nose to stem the flow of blood. The man passes her a tissue, and she straightens up with it clutched to her face.

Lambert's butler, wearing very tight trousers and an open-necked silk shirt, lurches back in surprise.

'Monsieur Fontaine,' Natasha says, 'we're sorry to disturb your evening off. It's just rather important that we speak to you.'

'But I'm . . . late,' he says weakly, gesturing to the meeting room.

'We're full anyway, Gary,' the woman on reception shouts, seemingly entirely uninterested in Jane's bloody face. 'You know you 'ave to be on the dot.'

'Well then!' Natasha says brightly. 'You should be free to have a super-quick chat.'

The receptionist shoos them into a storeroom showing traces of the various other events that take place in the hall: bunting looped around a coffee machine, yoga mats fighting with cake stands, hi-vis bibs piled on a half-deflated tyrannosaurus, a sharp knife protruding dangerously from a child's bucket.

Monsieur Fontaine perches on the edge of the half-hidden desk and looks at them expectantly while Jane squeezes past some hand-painted Bake Sale signs to a dirty sink and wipes her face on a wet tea towel, so filthy only God Himself knows its original colour.

'Well? What has my *charmant* boss been up to now?' Fontaine says with a sigh. The Birmingham accent appears to have vanished.

'We need to ask you about the books,' Jane says. 'Lambert Graves's books. And who wrote them.'

'Doesn't the name on the cover give you a clue?'

'It's not always . . . accurate.'

'Sometimes,' Natasha adds, 'someone writes on another's behalf. Or perhaps they . . . help?'

After a moment of silence, Fontaine laughs. It is a wheezing sound, like a car out of petrol, or as though his lungs are full of dust. It's sinister in the small, cluttered room and sends a chill down Jane's spine.

'Oh, go on then. I'll tell you what I know. Can't *wait* to see that yampy old fraud brought down!'

Everyone finds a place amongst the clutter and listens intently as Fontaine tells his story. He readily confirms their suspicions about Vicky Graves writing the books that made her husband rich and famous.

'Vicky were fine wi' it at first,' he says, still perched on the desk with his foot swirling in the air to the faint sounds of the music coming from the other room. 'Mrs Graves has always been a bit of a pushover, truth be told. But something changed end of last year. They were rowing, and she partly moved out.'

Jane can't help but notice that, as Fontaine talks, his accent is wavering somewhere between Birmingham and Paris.

'And Lambert's editor Hugo found out?'

'Yes, I reckon so. I read a few pages of his attempt when he were out at dinner one night . . . utter drivel. Any editor worth his salt would clock what was going on by page three.' Fontaine laughs again, the wheezing sound of old bellows filling the cramped space.

'You're not really French, are you, Monsieur Fontaine?' Natasha asks.

'French? No, o' course I'm not French,' he scoffs, another wheezy laugh breaking through. 'From Wolverhampton, me. But that pretentious loser wanted a French chef, and I wanted a pay check. Real name's Gary Staines.' He holds out his hand for Natasha to shake.

In this investigation, Jane wonders, is anyone who they seem? What would her mother say? *It's all smoke and mirrors, Jane.* 'God knows what will happen when it all gets out. Because it will, you know. He seems to know it too these last few days. Wouldn't be surprised if he disappears for a while, though he'll miss the stupid jewellery room. All that stuff is his work by the way, not Vicky's. People just assumed the jewellery was her and, since he took the writing, I guess it seemed sensible to go along with it. Always going on, he is, about making those ugly rings of his, and his "new smelting crucible" and "traditional techniques for gold extraction" and "new line of —"'

'Sorry,' Natasha interrupts. 'What do you mean, his *traditional techniques for gold extraction*?'

'What? Oh, I don't know, do I?' Fontaine says, looking longingly at the door as though remembering he doesn't *have* to spend his night off in this dusty storeroom. 'He is very into being "authentic", whatever that means. Always trying out bonkers new ways to—'

'Okay, thank you, Mr Fontaine,' Natasha cuts in. 'Er, Staines. We won't take up any more of your time.'

He looks taken aback by this sudden dismissal, and positively alarmed when Natasha grabs him by the arm and unceremoniously shoves out of the door.

Slamming it shut, she turns to her friends, eyes wide with urgency.

'Do you remember what I told you the other day? About cyanide?'

'Um, that it smells like almonds?' Daniel tries. 'Or was that Jane?'

'About the places it might be found? Its *uses*?' Natasha isn't looking at them now, but is tapping away on her phone. 'Yes!'

'What? What is it?' Jane says in panic. The room, small and cramped and filled with things, feels like it's closing in on them, like an answer is buried in there, just out of sight.

'It didn't occur to me at the time because it's *such* an old-fashioned technique. Certainly not *legal*.'

'Quit talking in riddles,' says Daniel in frustration. 'And tell us!'

'One of the chemicals used in *the traditional extraction of gold*,' Natasha says, finally looking up from her phone, 'is cyanide.'

The sky is starting to darken, but the heat of the day hasn't left the air. Jane is half-walking, half-running through the

Hampstead streets which are buzzing with people searching for a bite to eat, a glass of wine, perhaps a fake Frenchman who can salsa.

'Wouldn't Marabella Rhodes have read the manuscript?' says Daniel, edging past a group of students outside the cinema. 'She's Lambert's agent?'

'Not . . . if . . . ' Natasha says through laboured breaths '. . . he sent . . . oh, can you two slow *down!*' She stops dead and waits for her friends to return to her. They set off again at a more leisurely pace. 'Not if he sent it while she was on holiday. Marabella is religious about not working when she is in her French house, and she was there in the weeks leading up to Hugo's death.'

'Her office!' Jane shouts, another piece of the puzzle rearranging itself in her mind. 'Marabella's office was broken into, remember?'

'Of course!' Natasha shouts.

'What's that got to do with it?' Daniel says, face twisted in confusion.

'Well, Lambert would have sent it to both his agent and his editor,' Natasha explains. 'Marabella might not have read it, but it would have been in her inbox waiting for her.'

'And,' Jane picks up, 'after Hugo's reaction, Lambert must have known that he could never allow her to read it. So he broke in and deleted the email from her computer, then stole Hugo's phone to delete the evidence there too.'

'And Daisy?' Daniel asks sadly. 'She would know things that no one else did. She was a loose end to be tied up.'

Up ahead they can see the station, and it occurs to Jane that she has no idea where they are hurrying to, no idea what they are supposed to do now that they know. Because it seems clear that they *do* know the killer's identity. She stops and turns to her friends.

'The whole life Lambert built for himself was at stake. His reputation, his wealth, his future. Lambert Graves was caught out in a lie spanning 26 years. He buried the evidence, and killed Hugo and Daisy for good measure.'

The three stare at each other, wide-eyed and serious. People jostle past them on their way from the station, arriving home from work or seeking an evening out. None of them consumed by thoughts of murder, none of them with deadly information at their fingertips.

'We need to get to Aurum Manor,' says Daniel. 'Now!'

'No,' says Jane. She wants to – oh, how she wants to! But she remembers Hawberry's words and the deal they made. *Don't put yourself in danger Miss Hepburn. Don't put your friends in danger.* 'No,' she says again, taking a seat on a metal bench. 'We need to slow down, go back to our hotel, and call DI Hawberry.'

'Jane,' Natasha whispers, 'think what *Baker* would do. The police won't get it. They won't understand how serious what Lambert has done is, or how much ridicule he faces. They won't understand how someone might kill over who wrote some *books*. *We* need to go there. Now. Record a confession, find evidence before it's too late. Fon— I mean, *Staines* said he might disappear!'

'Hugo was an adulterous dirtbag who'd killed a woman,' says Daniel. 'But he still didn't deserve to die like that. And Daisy?' His voice cracks on her name. 'Daisy didn't deserve any of this. We can't trust Fontaine. He might have called Lambert already and told him what we know. We need to *move*.'

Actions speak louder than words, Jane hears her mother whisper.

'Oh, bugger it.' She gets to her feet. 'Let's go.'

Chapter Forty

Tuesday, 7.12 p.m.

Locking her front door, Lucy pauses to take stock of a situation that has, she admits, become wildly out of hand.

For the fifth time, she checks the items are present in her tote bag. Everything she needs to end this, tonight. Satisfied, she sets off into the fading light of a September evening, scared but determined.

Her flatmate will be back tomorrow and the place will soon be full of chaos and noise and mess, everything Lucy hates. But she'll welcome it, because this time alone has allowed her to give too much space to her thoughts and resentments, even to act on them. Yes, when Peony is back, she'll start afresh. Maybe she'll even try and be her friend. Adopt a whole new aesthetic. Get into day raves and magic mushrooms.

First, Scott Wallace.

The bus pulls up just as Lucy reaches the stop – surely a sign the universe is sending her that she is on the right path. Life is full of these little signs, if you look out for them. The day she was fired by Hugo, her phone hadn't charged overnight and she'd stepped in a puddle on the way to work, a clear signal to have stayed in bed.

But this is the modern world, and you do not have the luxury of always tuning in to the universe's helpful signals. Not if you want to become an Editorial Director by thirty.

The humiliation of the day she was told to pack up her desk at Polar Bear still smarts. Lucy Tallow, the hardest-working person in that whole office, slinking out with her box of books and Quester's Heart merchandise like a common criminal. Her lifelong dream had been to work at that company.

But it was the ruin of her friendship with Daisy that she couldn't forgive. The best friend she'd ever had. Daisy had looked a little shamefaced when she'd told her about taking the job, but Lucy had felt like her world was imploding. She'd hated Daisy then, but she'd hated Hugo even more.

The bus stops and a group of teenagers get on, laughing and shouting, waving cans of energy drink. Some spills and Lucy pushes herself further against the window as though it might protect her from the rest of the world.

Just three more stops before she is there.

Despite everything, she is excited to meet Scott in person. If she closes her eyes, she can almost pretend that this last week hasn't happened. That she asked him on Questers if he wanted to meet, and he said yes, and now that is what is happening. That there were no confessions, no deaths, no steps taken down paths from which there are no return.

Lucy smooths her dress anxiously as the bus approaches Peckham. Not so far from her own place really. Think of the fun they could have had, had this taken a different track. She raises a hand to her necklace and revolves each pearl slowly on the string.

One more stop.

It makes her think of her dad, this necklace. He'd given it to her after the divorce, and she'd treasured it because it matched the earrings her mother gave her the same year. It felt like a sign, to her, from the universe, that the family would soon be back together. That they were all *meant to be*. But she is an adult now, and she can see she was wrong. Because her dad, like Hugo, was a cheat, and her mother deserved better, no matter what the universe thought.

Inverton Road, the woman's voice announces on the speaker, and Lucy wonders, not for the first time, how long it took her to record the name of every bus stop in London.

Her legs feel weak as she stands.

'Excuse me,' she mutters to the group of teenage boys, and one of them mocks her high-pitched voice.

'*Excuse me excuse me excuse me.*' On the pavement now, the air is chillier than expected. Lucy checks the contents of her bag again. She is ready. With a deep breath, she smooths down her hair and sets out to rectify the sorry mess she's created.

Chapter Forty-One

Tuesday, 7.50 p.m.

The golden gates of Aurum Manor swing open at a gentle push.

'How did we not see it before?' Jane whispers. 'This whole place is a love letter to money. Not to art. Not to *books*.'

Carefully, they make their way down the driveway, the gravel crunching underfoot so loudly Jane expects the birds to startle. The windows of the house are dark and quiet.

Lambert could be out, though his Mercedes is still in the driveway. In her pocket, she touches the cold metal of the kitchen knife she'd taken from the dance centre's storeroom to try and calm her battle-drum heartbeat. Something feels wrong.

Daniel raps on the door, but there is no answer.

'He could be out to dinner maybe?' Natasha says.

But Jane remembers something Daniel said earlier. *They can't get hold of him.* She knocks hard on the door, forgetting for a moment that this man is a killer. Daniel rushes to peer through the nearest window. No movement, no sound.

Something white by Jane's feet grabs her attention, and she looks down to see a piece of notepaper. Bending to pick it up, she notices the Sellotape attached, telling her it's fallen from the door.

'*I'm sorry,*' Jane reads aloud. '*Forgive me. Goodbye.*'

Daniel looks at her, slack-jawed. 'Does he . . . does he mean . . .?'

'We need to get in there!' Jane hammers on the wood, images of Hugo in his study spinning through her mind. She was scared of finding Lambert living and breathing behind this door but is far more scared of finding him not. Whoever he is, whatever he has done, too many people have died this week.

Natasha is overturning plant pots looking for hidden door keys, and Jane frantically tries the door handle. To her surprise, it flies open. They freeze on the threshold, the open chasm of the dark hallway looming ahead of them.

'Where do we even start?' Daniel whispers frantically. 'This house will take hours to search!'

'If he really is taking his own life,' Jane says decisively, 'he'll be where the poison is. The jewellery room.'

She leads the way through the dark, silent hall, her heart thumping loudly in her chest. They pass the sweeping staircase and framed film posters of Lambert Graves looking down over them, go past the dining room now devoid of candlelight. Eventually, they come to the door of Lambert's jewellery room.

What will they find through there? A man ready to fight to protect his secret? Or a man who has died to escape the consequences of his own actions? She has seen too many dead bodies over the last year. Her mother, her literary agent, Daisy Olsson, Hugo Strauss. She has no wish to find another tonight. She hears Hawberry's words again. *Don't put your friends in danger.*

They look at each other with wide eyes. Daniel shrugs and shakes his head, every fibre of his being signalling, *I don't know! Don't ask me!*

Natasha puts her hand gently on Jane's arm and gives her a nod. It says, *We are here with you.* It says, *I'm not scared.* It says, *Let's do this.*

Jane raises a hand and knocks.

'Why have you knocked?!' hisses Natasha, swatting her arm.

'Because it's polite!'

'He's a cornered murderer who is potentially about to off himself! Don't give him any warning!'

'Stop bickering,' Daniel says, pushing by. He twists the handle, and almost to Jane's surprise, the door swings open

'What the—?'

Lambert Graves sits up on the sofa in the corner, a laptop tumbling to the floor. 'You! What are you—? How did you—?'

'Mr Graves,' Natasha says softly, 'we are sorry to interrupt you like this. We mean no harm.'

'It's just,' Jane picks up, stepping into the room, 'that we came to talk to you about . . . About your books. And Hugo. And Daisy. And, um, we saw your note?'

Lambert's eyes flick between the three of them, confusion writ large on his face. 'My books?' he says weakly. 'My *note?*'

Jane can't help but notice that Lambert Graves is not dead. Nor does he look as though he is preparing to be. In fact – she takes in the debris surrounding him; empty coffee mugs, screwed-up paper, crisp packets, the laptop – he looks like he is *writing.*

'We think you've got yourself caught up in some trouble,' Daniel says, bravely stepping forward. 'So why don't you tell us exactly what is going on?' Lambert stares blankly at him, slack-jawed. 'I'll make some tea, shall I?'

Lambert rubs his eyes and hauls his body into an upright position. His exceptionally handsome face looks tired, age starting to take its toll.

'Oh, okay,' he says at last. 'But make it a margarita, will you?'

Natasha is sitting cross-legged on the floor, Daniel happily next to their murder suspect on the sofa. He sips the cocktail in his hand and winces. Jane feels as though she needs to keep some semblance of authority here, so remains on her feet and occasionally strides back and forth across the room in a manner she'd seen in a film once.

'Let's get this straight,' she says in exasperation. 'You don't know anything about any *suicidal note*?'

'Well, I put a note on the front door, sure. But it didn't say anything about suicide, dear girl!' He chuckles, rolling his eyes at Daniel as though they are old chums. 'Although, I suppose if you read it a certain way . . . '

Jane gives up on her pacing and sits down on a footstool. It's a little too low, her knees pushing up past her hips, and she regrets her choice. She tries to rearrange herself subtly and falls to the floor.

'What did you *mean* for it to say?' Natasha says kindly. She is so good at this, thinks Jane. She has a calming presence and the patience of a primary school teacher. Daniel too. People naturally like him and his charisma disarms them. In comparison, Jane feels prickly and tactless.

Lambert Graves twists around his index finger a thread protruding from his t-shirt, looking worried. He's gone from ageing murderer to little boy who's accidentally spilt some milk.

'Just, well . . . Vicky was coming tomorrow to grab some final things, you see? I just wanted her to know I'd left. And that I was sorry. Maybe a little *dramatic* . . . but that is sort of my signature style.'

'And you think that's enough?' Jane snaps. The 'famous author' is infuriating. She wants to shake him, to hit him, to pour his stupid drink over his perfectly coiffed hair. 'You think "*sorry*" is enough to make up for what you did?'

'Jane,' Natasha says quietly, giving her a warning look. She knows that look. It's one her mother used to give her when young Jane would rile her up. *Don't poke the bear,* her mother would say. Don't antagonise the murderer, Natasha is saying. Jane bites her tongue. But *really*? Sorry isn't good enough. Sorry is nothing. Sorry doesn't bring back Hugo or Daisy.

Lambert ignores her, turning instead to Daniel. 'I've had a few cocktails, truth be told. Now I think about it, that note *could* seem a little ominous, couldn't it?'

'You think?' Jane snaps.

'What were you going to do next?' Daniel asks. 'If you weren't planning to, you know . . . '

'Disappear, my dear boy! Just until it blows over. I have a house in Florida with a comfortable bed, a decent-sized pool and a fine view over a beach that hosts a weekly volleyball match.' He winks.

Jane stands up from the footstool, which uses a lot more core muscle than she anticipated. She can't bear to look at this pumped-up, over-privileged cockatoo anymore. Pretending to examine the work bench – complete with blowtorch, hammer, pliers and numerous other tools she can't name – she half-listens to him go on about the merits of Miami.

They'd caught Lambert just in time. With satisfaction, she realises that if they had gone to the police rather than acted themselves, they probably would have been too late.

'Mr Graves,' Natasha says gently, 'I don't think this is the kind of thing that just blows over.'

'Don't be so pessimistic!' he says with a chuckle. 'Look, I know I did wrong, but I said I was sorry! I know I won't be able to show my face in London for a little while but surely after a—'

'For the last time,' Jane says, spinning on her heel. 'You can't just say *sorry*. You *killed* two people, Mr Graves! I don't know if Daisy was an accident, or if you meant it. I suppose she was just . . . just *collateral damage* to you. You've built your life on lies, and you've killed to cover it up. You cannot *sorry* your way out of this.'

Lambert jumps to his feet. His suit, an expensive bright blue check, is crumpled, a smear of what looks like butter on one lapel. Dark circles linger under his eyes, which, despite that one face lift a few years ago, is starting to show his 57 years. However, it's his expression that is most striking. Thick eyebrows furrowed in anger, mouth open as he searches for the right words, blue eyes darting between the three onlookers.

Despite the seriousness of the moment, Jane reassesses the man in front of him. Rather than the glossy golden retriever of yesterday, this is a cockatoo ready to take flight to avoid the cage.

'Hugo *knew* you didn't write your own books. You poisoned him to keep your secret, not realising Daisy was going to take his glass – or maybe you *wanted* her gone in case she'd seen the manuscript too. You snuck into Hugo's study and took his phone so you could delete the email containing your *attempt* at writing your own book.'

'Now wait just one . . . '

'You broke into the office of Marabella Rhodes,' Jane continues, speaking louder to cover his spluttering self-defence, 'and deleted the manuscript from *her* email before she could read it. You are a *liar,* Lambert Graves. You are a *fraud.* And you are a *killer.*'

Lambert's mouth opens and closes like a fairground fish, a deep purple stain making its way up his neck, all the charm leached from his famous face. Jane takes half a step back, afraid suddenly that this man is going to hit her, to hurt her. Her friends are watching in silence, but even though there are three of them, are they a match for someone who has already taken lives to hide his secrets?

Don't put your friends in danger.

Emotion fills Lambert's face. His hands ball into fists. Jane becomes very aware of the size of those hands, the strength of them, of her and her friends' isolation on the home territory of a desperate murderer. In her pocket, she grips the kitchen knife from the storeroom. It feels small and insignificant against such an opponent.

And then Lambert lurches towards her.

Chapter Forty-Two

Tuesday, 8.20 p.m.

In Chapter 62 of Jane Hepburn's second book, *Murder at Dawn*, her protagonist Sandra Baker is attacked when confronting a killer. Jane described how time sped up as Baker disarmed her attacker with an expertly placed karate chop to the throat and a tequila bottle over the head. She'd anticipated each step as though it was dialled down to point five speed, moved each limb with the grace and precision of a panther.

Jane is horrified to find that doesn't happen to her.

As the hands of Lambert Graves come towards her, Jane fumbles the kitchen knife from her pocket. The tip of the blade snags on her cardigan, her foot catches on the edge of the rug, and she is about to fall flat on her back when Lambert reaches her. He pulls her into a bone-crushing hug.

'I didn't *kill* anyone!' he cries, arms tightly around her. 'I wouldn't! How can you think . . . ?' A sob shudders through his body that shakes Jane's bones. She can feel the cold metal of his rings against her cheek, and pats his back awkwardly.

'I haven't behaved well, I know it!' Lambert laments. 'But a *killer*? Me?'

Despite herself, Jane's shoulders untense, but her stomach drops too. She'd been so sure of a confession.

'Then why were you running?' Daniel asks, throwing his head back against the sofa and closing his eyes. 'What was that note saying *sorry* about?'

'Because of the writing deception? My time as an author is up, dear boy. You . . . you were right about that.' Lambert pulls away from Jane and wipes his nose on his sleeve, leaving a trail of mucus behind. His golden hair has become dishevelled, and his chiselled jaw is quivering. He is still handsome, but the façade is finally crumbling. If only he had been able to access *this* version of himself in *Hamlet*, he might have made it as an actor. He collapses back on the sofa, sobs subsiding but sniffing deeply and wiping at his eyes.

Natasha puts her head in her hands, and Jane turns back to the work bench, her pulse still pounding. A small pile of jewellery sits there, hastily gathered for his flight perhaps. The jewellery that connects him to the poison. That, along with the lying, the letter, the threat that his whole life was about to crumble, had meant she'd been sure he was the killer. Where did she go wrong?

She realises that the time has come to call Detective Inspector Hawberry and tell her exactly what they know. But she is also aware that, as soon as she does, the police will descend on Aurum Manor and take Lambert in for official questioning. They will be cut out again. There are more answers they need to find while they have the chance. She looks at her watch, its gold more scratched and tarnished than the pieces in the case in front of her, but more beautiful because of it.

She can hear Lambert take a deep breath, but can't bring herself to turn back to look at him. She knows the secrets he is about to divulge, and she doesn't care. Doesn't care that he is a liar. Who isn't? Scott Wallace hiding behind his keyboard personas. Lambert Graves behind his wife. Daisy Olsson betraying Lucy to secure her friend's job. All of these wolves dressed in wool.

And Jane? *No,* she hears her mother whisper. *You are a writer, no matter what the book deals or the sales or the fancy agents and editors say. You write, therefore you are a writer. Hold on to that.* Jane smiles to herself, realising only later that it wasn't really her mother's voice in her head. It was her own.

What would her mother actually have said? *Sometimes, Jane, a sheep is just a sheep.*

As Lambert tearfully confesses what they already know, that he has never written a word and his wife is the brains behind the books, Jane studies some gaudy ear studs she recognises as pieces Lambert himself sometimes wears.

'I did break into Marabella's,' he is saying. 'I confess! I did that. You've got me. I couldn't have her reading it after everything that Hugo said on Thursday night.'

'And Hugo's phone?'

Lambert turns pale and looks down at the floor. 'Yes,' he whispers. 'Yes . . . I did take that. I went to his house the day after the party. He'd confronted me there then vanished, and . . . I just wanted to talk to him! Just talk. The front door was ajar, so I went in. Found the study door wide open, and old Hugo . . . Look, I know I should have called the police. But what if they'd thought it was me? So, I used his finger to unlock his phone and took it with me so I could delete the email and check if he'd told anyone else. I shut up the house and waited for someone else to find him. I'm not proud of it.'

A question that's been niggling at Jane comes into her mind.

'Why did you invite us for dinner, Lambert?'

He looks confused. 'Well, I'm a natural host! A good one too! I *like* welcoming people into my home. And I must confess . . . I was keen to speak to someone else who knew Hugo. I've been driving myself a little mad, wondering if he had told anyone about my "writing" before he died.'

He looks so miserable, so broken, that Jane feels herself soften very slightly. The grinning Hamlet is a world away.

'So what's going on here?' Natasha asks eventually. She gestures around the room – the abandoned coffee cups, the open laptop, the heaped jewellery. 'Why haven't you left yet?'

'Well, I thought I'd have one last shot, you know? One last roll of the dice here where I'm happiest. I'm using this interesting tool, just a little helping hand. AI, you might have heard of it? Basically does it all for you!'

'You're going to hand in an AI-written novel!'

Natasha whirls back to face him. She's not a physically intimidating woman, but her voice is full of fury.

Lambert sighs again, shielding his eyes dramatically.

'Oh, I tried, I tried. It seemed like the perfect solution. I thought if I could get a draft down this evening and send it in to Raymond Stokes, everything would be okay! Stay in the house, collect the cheque, tell Vicky I'd done it all without her help, win her back . . . bish-bash-bosh, everyone's a winner.'

Everyone? Jane thinks to herself, turning determinedly back to the jewellery. Yes, if *everyone* is just this one man in particular. She supposes she can't expect someone who can't string a sentence together on the page to have a brilliant grasp of word definition.

'I've been at it for hours,' he moans. 'But it's no good. It doesn't sound one bit like Vicky's stuff. I started packing up. Miami, here I come.'

Natasha takes the laptop from the floor and brings the screen to life. A snort makes Jane jump, and she turns to see Natasha shaking with laughter. Lambert groans ever louder.

'Is it *that* bad?' he asks. 'I had hoped, with some tweaking?'

Natasha clears her throat and begins to read aloud. '"*The man of elevated height perambulates around the chamber, ruminating on the events that have occurred. He observes the sky through the window, which is dark grey in colour. The man of elevated height and brown eyes feels melancholy, and understands that he must commit the crime of murder in order to proceed.*"'

'Wow,' says Daniel. 'Stunning stuff.'

He starts to laugh, and Jane feels her own heart lighten, even the shadow of a giggle make its way up her throat. Before long, she, Daniel and Natasha are roaring with laughter, even Lambert Graves giving a rueful grin.

It's dreadfully late, and Jane has found accusing the wrong man of murder rather exhausting. But at least she has her friends. And at least she is a better writer than both a robot and Lambert Graves.

'But the cyanide!' Natasha says as the laughter subsides. She is still on the floor, lying on her back now, eyes screwed shut in concentration. 'You use it, don't you? In your jewellery making? That's what Fontaine meant by "traditional methods"?'

'Er, I . . . well,' Lambert stutters, but clearly decides there is little point in lying at this juncture. 'Well, yes, I do. Though Fontaine shouldn't be . . . my private business. It's the traditional way to extract gold from the ore, you see? Fascinating process. I'm not *technically* supposed to have it, so I'd rather you didn't shout about it . . . '

Jane really needs to call DI Hawberry. She checks her phone only to find she has no signal, which prompts a rush of relief, followed by a stab of guilt. She turns to see Natasha waving Lambert onwards, tired of his prevarication.

'It's called cyanidation, you see? I heard about it and thought I'd give it a go. Only tried it a few times as it was jolly hard. And it's not easy to get hold of the stuff, like I say. Luckily, I have a guy who can find . . . most substances. You find these useful guys, you see, if you've worked in the movies.'

Lambert has perked up post-confession, and he begins to explain a complex process of crushing and cyaniding, refining and smelting, that makes Jane's head spin. She turns back to the pile of jewellery. She has never really owned any herself. Never had anyone to give it to her, and it does seem such an extravagance to buy for oneself. She has her father's watch, her only memory of a man she never knew.

If the day comes, she vows, *that I get a new book deal, I'll buy myself something gold.*

Lambert seems as though he may be able to talk about gold extraction and jewellery making for the rest of time, so Jane is relieved when Daniel interrupts.

'Is there anyone else who could have got hold of it? The cyanide? Does anyone go in your workshop?'

'Not without me present. I always lock this place up, and it wouldn't be an easy fortress to breach, let me tell you! Even my darling wife doesn't have the key.'

But the substance that took two lives being present in Lambert's workshop *cannot* be a coincidence.

A bracelet? Jane wonders. Or would I prefer a ring? Yes, maybe a lovely golden ring.

One in particular catches her eye. It reminds her of something, though she can't immediately tell what. It must be the one on Lambert's own finger.

'Mr Graves?' she says, not turning around. He appears at her side, quite jolly now despite his certain ruin. She holds the ring up to the light. 'This is an interesting piece.'

'Oh, the pillbox rings have taken your fancy, have they! *Gorgeous* items, if I do say so myself. Popular in Europe during the Middle Ages.' Natasha and Daniel join them, looking curious. 'You see,' Lambert says, gently taking it from Jane's fingers, 'this stone hides a secret. It opens, just like this.' With a flick of his finger, the front of the ring hinges back, like a locket, to reveal a small depression in the mount beneath. 'They used to call them poison rings,' he says, gazing at his creation with adoration. 'Because you can store the deadly powder inside, and so easily tip it into someone's drink. Beautiful things, dastardly tricky to make. I only recently mastered it.'

Jane's mouth is dry, her head whirring, palms sweating. Pieces are busily rearranging themselves, falling into place yet again, but the picture makes no sense whatsoever. Or does it?

'And have you,' she manages to say despite her mouth feeling as dry as a tomb, '*sold* any of these creations?'

'Just the one,' Lambert says cheerfully, placing the ring back into the cabinet. 'To our old friend Hugo's assistant actually.'

Everyone looks at each other, eyes wide.

What?

'Can't remember the girl's name,' Lambert continues, not noticing the reaction he has sparked in the room. 'But she would have been very pretty, if not for this big purple streak in her hair.'

Chapter Forty-Three

Marabella Rhodes is punishing herself. With a deep breath, she folds the rest of the KitKat back into the wrapper and puts it in her desk drawer. She doesn't deserve it. That'll teach her.

With Abi's help, she has spent the afternoon dropping the rest of the 'signed copies' off at different charity shops around the city. She couldn't quite bring herself to dispose of them entirely, and if some poor sod browsing Barnado's on a Sunday ends up making a fortune from a scribble in *Heart of Darkness*, good for them. Half the people who buy these things have more money than sense, and at least she is doing her bit for wealth distribution in London. Stick a feather in her hat and call her Robin Hood.

She doesn't regret starting it, and she doesn't regret hanging up her pen. There was already an undercurrent of noise about fake copies on the bookdealing messenger boards, and when things go on too long, you get caught. Just look at Hugo. If their affair had been the brief fling they'd both sworn it would be at the start, he would have hung on to his marriage. Maybe even his life. Oh, Hugo.

She looks up at the clock. Gone 9. She should be relaxing, try-ing to wind down her mind before bed, but she knows she won't be able to sleep anyway and would rather catch up on work.

She loves her job. Seeing people through from discovery to their book launch and beyond is a pleasure like no other. Better than sex, better even than money. She loves discovering new writers and championing them, loves meeting editors and then sending them a new author's work that she just *knows* they will adore. Loves, at the end of the day, books. Her first love, with clever, funny, treacherous Hugo as her second.

She'd somewhat forgotten that love lately.

Turning back to her laptop, she scrolls absent-mindedly through the emails. Multiple panicked messages from Raymond Stokes. She doesn't know what *she* is expected to do about Lambert not answering the bloody phone. One from Abi bravely requesting a promotion after her 'hard work today'. Marabella doesn't even mind the implied threat, she almost respects it. She'll make her a full agent in the morning. Another from Eric, who she can't avoid forever but finds herself wanting to. Finds herself realising he was just a distraction from her broken heart.

She's feeling down, flat, squashed, lousy. She'd loved Hugo, even though he'd turned on her in the end to try and save his marriage, and misses him now he is gone. All that's left now are her authors.

Pushing back the chair, absolutely beautiful and imported from Ghana at an extortionate cost, cripplingly uncomfortable, she gets to her feet and stretches her arms above her head.

In the kitchen, she turns on the expensive silver coffee machine that had been an extravagance she'd allowed herself after selling a 'signed' copy of *The Grapes of Wrath* last year. Many items in her home are connected to her signed editions, each one a small celebration of a great work of literature, someone's foolishness and her own creativity. She pours oat milk into the jug and starts to froth it into a warm foam, the steamer making a piercing wailing sound against the metal. With her other hand, she grinds the beans. Ethiopian, delivered this morning and frightfully expensive. Maybe she'll have to start cutting back on things like this if she's surviving on legitimate business alone from now on.

It was all getting too much anyway, since the death of her rival, Carrie Marks. Many of Carrie's clients came knocking.

A few, like Natasha, she scooped up straight away. There is always space for someone new. There needs to be, to keep the joy and mystery and sense of possibility alive.

Marabella shouldn't be drinking more coffee at this hour. She should run a hot bath, pour a cool glass of wine and read a book. But her blood is up, and she hates to dampen the excitement in her work that has been missing for so long.

Padding back into her home office in her socks, Marabella sips her coffee, revelling in the silence of her home. When Hugo was here, there was noise, shoes in the wrong place, another laptop jostling for space, and guilt. Always that undercurrent of guilt and unspoken thoughts of his wife. Maybe one day she'll fill this place with new, guilt-free sounds – laughter, and chatter, the comforting shuffle of a partner's slippers as they go to make tea. The joyful sounds of a happy home. But for tonight, she will appreciate the silence.

The desk lamp illuminates the Ghanaian chair, and that makes her feel guilty too. She'd promised herself that she would love the chair. That it was worth the money because of how much work she'd do when she had it. But no one is here to see her, so she plucks up her laptop with one hand and sits instead on the old sofa against the opposite wall. The coffee is strong, and hot, and chocolatey. The sofa is deep, and worn, and comfortable.

Emails are still coming in, despite the hour. It's not a surprise, her job doesn't really have boundaries like most people's. Authors are a notoriously anxious breed, prone to be up late worrying about something or thinking of ideas they need to tell her about at once, even though they usually seem insane in the morning. Still, she has to calmly reply that they should fulfil their contracted thriller before they give too much time to, say, the 'time-travelling hamsters' or the '*Game of Thrones* meets *Neighbours*' or '*Ru Paul's Drag Race* but a romance and set in space'.

She scrolls back and finds one that came in a few hours ago from a name she doesn't recognise. It's a submission from someone new. That's no surprise either; she gets hundreds of these every week. Mostly, she filters them through Abi, but as it's late and she's in want of distraction, she opens it.

It's from someone called Jane Hepburn, formerly a client of Carrie Marks apparently, though Marabella has never heard of her. She sips again at her coffee and looks at her watch. She really should call it a night. Her bed has fresh white sheets on, and she could climb into it and read a real book, by an author who knows what they are doing. With a sigh that tells of her expectation, she opens the document. Three chapters of a crime novel that she can whizz through in ten minutes or so and send a polite templated turndown. She looks at her watch again.

She remembers her vow of just moments ago. That, with forgery in her past, she is going to throw herself back at this job, throw herself into the unexpected. She can give it ten minutes.

Leaning over to her desk, she gropes about for her glasses, just managing to hook them up and drag them towards her. With them perched on her nose, she settles back on the sofa and returns to the screen.

The First Murder by Jane Hepburn. She begins to read.

Chapter Forty-Four

Tuesday, 9.10 p.m.

'He's not answering!' Jane shouts, and stabs the call button again. 'Come on, Scott, come *on*.'

Lambert Graves watches them from the doorway with a bemused look on his face as Jance paces up and down his drive, phone to her ear.

'Let's calm down,' Natasha says. 'Scott knows that he might be in danger. He wouldn't let Lucy into his house.'

'He might be in a pub or anywhere busy,' Jane says frantically. 'She might slip something into his drink when he isn't looking! We need to find *one* of them!'

All of a sudden, her phone buzzes with a text message.

'Oh!' Jane is flooded with relief when she sees Scott's name flash up on the screen. 'Oh, thank God. It's him.'

Hey Hepburn. Cn't tlk now. Am clring things up with Lucy.

'They are together.' Jane feels faint. 'They are together *right now*.'

Where?

They wait in agitation for the reply to come.

Burgess Park. It's all gd. Speak tomorrow.

'Burgess Park!' she shouts, despite having no idea where that is. 'We need to go! Now!'

'Oh, that's a bus jobby,' Lambert says from the doorway, still looking baffled. 'Takes a while. Hold on.' He dips inside, then returns with a bunch of keys. 'Let's go.'

Lambert Graves might only understand half of what is going on, but he also understands his role in the mission is simply to drive fast.

'Did you see that FI film I was in?' he shouts over the sound of the wind. 'I did some training for that one. Much more fun than the Shakespeare training, I'll tell you that!' He swerves dangerously around a BMW and zips through an orange light. 'Be there in a jiffy!'

It takes just 20 minutes for them to reach Burgess Park. Daniel looks green in the face, and everyone's hair is in comical disarray, apart from Lambert's seemingly solid quiff.

He pulls up to the park railings with a screeching of brakes and burning of rubber, the grin on his face looking a lot more natural than any they'd seen to date.

'This solving crimes lark is rather fun. Maybe I could join you next time?'

'Um, yeah, maybe,' Jane says, helping her friends from the back seat. 'Look, thanks a lot, Lambert. If we don't contact you in 20 minutes, call the police.'

He gives then a thumbs up and speeds away, still at top speed despite the only thing he has to get back to being an empty house and a ruined career.

'Let's go.'

Jane pushes open the gate with a creak and they enter the park. It's large and mostly in darkness, though one path is illuminated by yellow overhead lighting. They cannot see a soul.

'Should we split up to search?' Natasha asks.

'No!' Daniel says at once. 'Haven't you ever seen a horror film? We stick together.'

They creep through the darkness, eyes scanning the expanse of green for any sign of a person. Jane is painfully aware that it's been over 20 minutes since they heard from Scott, and that cyanide takes just seconds to kill.

'There!' Daniel is pointing to a flickering light in the midst of some bushes. Jane squints; she can just make out two silhouettes.

They run towards the spot, the scene coming into sharper detail the closer they get. Scott and Lucy, sitting on the ground with an odd collection of things in between them – three lit candles, a bunch of lavender and what looks like a pile of sage.

Lucy is staring up at them, black-ringed eyes round with fear, while Scott simply looks confused. Both, Jane is relieved to confirm, are alive, but the sight of the can in Scott's hand sends terror through her.

'Don't drink that, Scott!'

'Um, what in hell?' He gets to his feet and comes over to Jane, who is bent double, breathing hard.

'Put the can down!' Daniel says striding forward, hand outstretched.

With a confused frown, Scott takes a swig.

When everyone is sure of the fact that Scott isn't going to drop down dead, they agree to take a seat on the grass, still eyeing Lucy warily. For her part, she remains silent, eyes downcast and brimming with tears.

The purple streak is just about visible in the darkness, her pearl necklace and silver moon stud gleaming, the dark purple lipstick making her look like she's devoured a plate of plums.

'Okay,' Scott says, swigging again from his Tango, 'it looks like we might need to clear a few things up.'

Jane's eyes dart between Lucy and him. The last she heard, Lucy had wished fervently for Scott's death, and now here they are, sitting side by side in a park. This is the woman to whom their investigation has led them.

Scott reaches across and takes Lucy's hand, squeezes it. She looks at him gratefully and Scott blushes. Really? Jane can't find a date in all of London or Cumbria, but the potential murderer gets one just like that?

'That's right,' Lucy says, finally meeting Jane's eyes. 'That's why we met tonight, to clear things up. Now you're here, we might as well tell *you* the whole truth too. There is no getting away from it.'

Lucy sighs deeply, staring down into the flames. The grass is damp on Jane's knees and the night air has picked up a chill, but it's Lucy's sudden low chuckle that sends a shiver through her.

'I know, Miss Hepburn, that Scott's told you a few things already. You know that he and I had connected online, resulting in a . . . negative reaction from me when the truth came out about who he really was.'

'I felt sick with guilt about lying to her, you know?' Scott says. 'Really sick. Thing is,' he looks at Lucy and she squeezes his hand in support, not taking her eyes from the flames, 'I didn't know her at first. I just wanted to find out more about Daisy. To understand why they fell out maybe. But the more we spoke, the more I liked her. Really liked her. Then, when Daisy died . . . well, I was worried Lucy was *involved*. After . . . after everything she'd said.'

The flickering candles illuminate a tear tracking slowly down Lucy's cheek.

'And I was,' she whispers, 'I *was*.'

'Lucy, stop it,' he says in a voice gentler than Jane expects from him. 'I freaked. I needed to *know*, so I went back into the game the very next day. Felt bad about it, about lying again, you know? But I *had* to find out. If Lucy had . . . well, it would be partly my fault. I was the like, final betrayal for her. The one that set her off. When my boss told me I had to get into Hugo's emails because he'd passed away as well, I was even more scared.'

'I understand,' Lucy says gently. 'I forgive you.'

'I see,' says Jane, not seeing at all. Lucy, by her own admission, was involved in the murders, but *she* forgave *Scott*?

'What did you do, Lucy?' Natasha asks gently. 'You said you had something to do with the murders?'

Lucy looks up, tears streaming now. Her eyes are round and glistening, fear etched across her face.

'Don't judge me,' she whispers. 'Please . . . I deeply regret what I did.'

'Don't worry, just tell them,' Scott says.

She probably should worry, thinks Jane. *If she killed two people.* She edges forward on her knees, eager for the final scraps of the truth at last.

'I . . .' Lucy begins before faltering and taking a deep breath. 'I . . . I *cursed them.*'

Jane sits back. 'Um, what?'

'I was so upset, you see? Furious. When I found out the man I'd been speaking to was Daisy's boyfriend, I just felt so foolish! So I cursed them all. Scott, Daisy, and Hugo too for good measure – it was *his* fault Daisy and I fell out after all, and even though I got a new job, I never really forgave him. I have these books. Wicca books? You just need a photo of the person you are putting the curse on, certain herbs, six black candles, the right words and crystals – lapis lazuli and morion are recommended . . .'

She continues to detail the exact steps of her spell while Jane tries not to groan in disbelieving frustration.

'Lucy,' she finally breaks in, 'you did *not* murder Hugo and Daisy with a magic spell. I promise you.'

'That's what I've been telling her!' Scott says, throwing up his hands. 'Lucy, it was a coincidence. It was nothing to do with you! Otherwise I'd be dead too, right?'

She looks around the circle, desperate to believe them.

'She's been driving herself wild with guilt,' he continues.

'After the first death, when I heard it was Daisy . . . I was so upset,' Lucy whispers. 'To think I'd done that. Then I managed to convince myself it was a coincidence. I'd cursed *three* people, right? Not one. It was nothing to do with me. But then, when Hugo . . . ' She dissolves into tears and Scott puts an arm around her shoulders.

'So what's all this?' Daniel asks, gesturing to the objects in the centre of the circle.

'I was cleansing Scott from previous enchantments,' Lucy says in a whisper. 'Just in case.'

He gives them an embarrassed smile and a shrug that clearly says, *well, what was I to do?*

'Wait,' Jane says, putting up a hand. Time is ticking on and they are further than ever from the truth. 'Lucy, there is more. We need to know about your trip to Lambert Graves's house.'

Lucy tilts her head to the side in apparent confusion. 'What? I've never been to his house.'

She is a good actress. 'You went there,' Jane says firmly, 'and bought a ring. He told us. Hugo's assistant he said, and mentioned your hair.'

Lucy continues to look confused.

'A pillbox ring,' Natasha breaks in, and pulls up a photograph of the ring from Lambert's house. 'Like this.'

'Oh, like Daisy's?' Scott says. Jane turns to him in surprise. 'Yeah, she had one like that. Saw it on her the night . . . the night it all happened.'

'What did he say about the hair?' Lucy asks. 'You know Daisy used to have a streak too, right? I told you, we had it done together, back when we were friends. My hair's dark so it had to be bleached in, but hers wasn't permanent. It'd faded by the time we'd stopped speaking.'

'*Daisy's ring?*' Jane whispers, and suddenly, she remembers. The glint of gold on Daisy's finger in the dimly lit basement. *That* was where she had seen it before.

'Don't know how she afforded it,' Scott says, still oblivious to how important this information is. 'Looked pricey. She said it was something to do with her mother? I kind of assumed it was handed down.'

'Her mum was some sort of model, I think,' Lucy adds with the air of someone desperately trying to be helpful. 'Maybe she got it as a gift from a designer or something?'

'Oh!' Jane sits bolt upright, grabbing Daniel's arm. 'Oh, I *see* now! I see! How could we have been so *stupid*?'

'What?!' Natasha leans forward to stare around him at Jane, her brow furrowed in confusion.

'Daisy was *dreadful* at her job,' Jane says, thinking aloud. All the pieces of the puzzle slotting into place at *last*. 'She didn't even *like* books – you told us that, Scott, remember?'

'So?' he says, bafflement writ large on his face.

'So those publishing assistant jobs are hard to get! Hundreds of applicants – even *more* than hundreds. Daniel, you said she'd be late every day. She didn't care. How did Daisy, a woman with no experience, no passion and no work ethic, get that plum job? And how did she *keep* it? And why would she even *want* it?'

'Long hours, terrible pay,' Daniel confirms, nodding in agreement. 'I don't know why someone would want to do it if they didn't even like books.'

'Well, like I said,' Lucy breaks in with a frown, 'I think she used my sacking and everything I'd told her—'

'But that doesn't make *sense*. You can't just walk into that office, demand to speak to an important publisher and request a job, even if there *is* one going,' Jane says, head in her hands now as she laments her own blindness to the facts.

'Yeah, true,' Daniel says, nodding even harder. 'Believe me, I tried. I had to jump through thousands of hoops to get my job, and I can still barely afford to eat.'

'So . . . what?' Natasha asks. 'You think it's something to do with the ring? You think Lambert Graves put in a word for her?'

'No,' Jane says, feeling light-headed, both buoyant and sad. 'I think it's because of Daisy's *mother*. Didn't you hear what Lucy just said? Daisy was the daughter of a *model*.'

'Oh!' shouts Natasha. 'What? No! How did we not make the connection! So stupid!' She hits the grass with a small, closed fist, making the candle wobble dangerously. Lucy and Scott watch them with bewildered looks on their faces.

Jane closes her eyes and thinks back to when she was flicking through Michael Carney's photographs online. Not just him and his late wife, the woman killed by Hugo Strauss all those years ago, but a toddler too. A little girl.

'*Michael and Johanna's daughter*,' Natasha says, her mind clearly following the same track as Jane's.

The daughter who never forgave the man who killed her mother. Who asked him for a job knowing he couldn't say no. Who pretended she had forgiven him in order to get close enough to poison him.

And in doing so, accidentally poisoned herself.

'The killer we've been looking for is Daisy Olsson?' Daniel whispers, awe-struck. 'The victim? The *victim* is the killer?'

'You mean, she took that job just to get close to Hugo?' Lucy whispers. 'Wow. I wonder if she was ever really my friend at all.' She shakes her head sadly. 'When did the lying start?'

Jane has experienced this before. The moment that a truth is laid bare. She can feel it in the air, the possibility, the excitement, but the fear and sadness too. Jane didn't know Daisy Olsson, but she feels like she knows her in death. Beautiful, funny, full of vitality. Disorganised, chaotic, questionable taste in men. Jane has been campaigning for her killer to be caught for days now, and this discovery gives her a heavy, sad feeling.

Perhaps sometimes, just like in the moment before fully waking, ignorance really is bliss. And if that is the case, why is she still here? She knows enough. But there is something more, something just out of reach. What is it?

Mentally she flicks back over all she has seen during the last few days. Each of the photos of Johanna Carney – with her husband, the little girl, her curly-haired friend. In her mind she rifles through evidence on Lambert's desk, sees the flash of a burgundy-coloured passport – no longer, she realises the colour for those from Britain, but of *Sweden*. She replays the words of the letter she'd seen there, a piece that still isn't fitting.

. . . life's work, my friend. I have not decided my next step, but I fear I cannot stay silent if this is the case. Let us talk in person soon.

But Lambert is innocent? And all of a sudden it's obvious. Because of course, that wasn't really the desk of Lambert Graves at all.

'Lucy,' Jane says, her voice quavering as she addresses the person who knew Daisy best. 'Who did Daisy live with?'

'Um, some older woman?' Lucy says with a frown. 'She's not there all the time though. I think she's called Vicky.'

Chapter Forty-Five

Tuesday, 11 p.m.

Vicky Graves stares at a framed photograph while she stirs her camomile tea, as she does every evening. It's been months since she started moving out of the glittering prison that is Aurum Manor and this flat might only accommodate a fraction of her things, but it still feels more like home than that place ever did.

Lambert and she did have fun together over the years. They led a nice life – she writing in her little study, the pressure slightly alleviated by her carefully preserved anonymity; he obsessing over hideous jewellery in the workshop and handling the publicity. They'd meet in the lounge for a cocktail or two, take a stroll around the grounds or eat pasta at the local Italian. The man was larger than life, and shockingly handsome of course, and she had loved him once. Vicky has always loved people who are too much. People who can fill her quiet world.

Johanna Carney was just like that, or Olsson as she had been back when they met. At her funeral, her pathetic husband had gone on about how Johanna was 'too good for this world'. Rubbish! She was what *made* the world good. Vicky knew it from the moment they met at Stockholm University, at twenty-one years old. Johanna was beautiful, yes, but she was also funny and clever.

Her friend made dark jokes that set most people gasping, but not Vicky – she'd cackle with delight. Johanna had an appalling diet, consisting mainly of pizza and cheese Singles, loved hot baths and cold wine, loved clothes, loved reading, loved *life*. Always had something new to say about a book or a film that would make Vicky broaden her mind an inch at a time. Johanna was *special*.

Vicky only studied in Stockholm for a term, but they stayed best friends for decades. She treasured the trips she would take to Sweden to spend time with her best friend. She remembered telling her when she met Lambert; remembered Johanna introducing her to the starry-eyed Brit, Michael, who was so clearly head over heels in love with her. Remembered the day she was maid of honour at their wedding; was made godmother to little Daisy when the day came.

Vicky has just two regrets: suggesting that weekend in Devon on one of Michael and Johanna's rare trips to the UK, then saying yes when Lambert proposed inviting his pal Hugo and his wife to 'make it a real party'.

Of all the 'yeses' she'd ever said – yes, I'll take that study abroad programme, yes, I'll marry you, yes, I'll write that book, yes yes yes yes yes – *that* was the most fateful, loaded yes she'd ever uttered. Vicky will never forgive herself for that.

Dumping the teabag in the sink, she shuffles through to the living room. This house feels a world away from the mansion she shared with her husband. The walls are freshly painted cream, the original Victorian floorboards sanded, oiled and adorned with an old Persian rug. Bookshelves fill the alcoves to either side of the fireplace, brimming with everything from *Harry Potter* to *Ulysses*. Vicky isn't a discriminatory reader. House plants occupy the corners, and wooden shutters painted a jolly red flank the large sash windows. The room feels tasteful, homely, and it smells of cigarette smoke and expensive candles, just the way she likes it. Still, it is rather quiet, living here all alone.

They'd all been there the night everything happened. Michael and Johanna, Lambert and herself, Hugo and his wife Jessie, and Daisy of course, only sixteen and sulking in her room staring at a screen. They'd rented a holiday cottage together as a treat, the adults planning to play board games, cook nice food, get a little drunk. Johanna had volunteered to cycle to the shop for more wine when they ran dry, even though it was dark. She didn't mind, she said. She'd be quickest.

Hugo had stayed behind at the pub they'd been in for lunch, chatting up some woman. He'd always been a real cad. Jessie was starting to get angry he wasn't back yet, was calling and calling him.

The sirens pulled them all outside. Pure curiosity at first. And there she was. Funny, clever, kind, opinionated Johanna lying still as old bones on the tarmac, and Hugo standing there in his stupid tweed jacket, speaking to a policeman, white as a ghost behind his beard.

Michael hurried Daisy inside, but the girl had seen. They'd all seen.

And women don't forget.

The doorbell rings, causing Vicky to start and spill her tea. She takes her time wiping up the spill, pulls her dressing gown tighter around herself and ambles to the door. There is no one she is in a hurry to speak to these days.

Vicky Graves undoes the three locks that keep her safe at night and pulls open the heavy door to reveal a lone woman she vaguely recognises. She is unusually tall and broad, chestnut hair pulled back into a messy ponytail.

'Hello?'

'Um, hi? Vicky? It's Jane. Jane Hepburn.'

Chapter Forty-Six

Tuesday, 11.05 p.m.

When Jane Hepburn loses her keys, she always checks the
fridge. She also checks under the sofa, in the biscuit tin, and
in her sock drawer. When she, invariably, finds them in the
pocket of the last jacket she wore, she always gives herself
a kick. Things are so frequently right in front of you. If you
interrogate all you know, the answer will be right there, where
it belongs.

Just like her keys.

It is true that romantic love is not the only sort powerful
enough to drive a murder, she knows this. But nor is the love of
one's own reputation, or the love of a child for their parents. If
there is one thing Jane has learnt this year, it is the importance
of another kind of love: friendship.

If someone took Daniel or Natasha away from her, what
would she do? Would she silently weep and take to her bed?
Would she immediately exact a brutal revenge? Or would she
stew on it? Let it eat her up and poison her blood until she was
consumed by it before, finally, one day, lashing out?

Vicky Graves is in pyjamas. Jane had never thought wearing
pyjamas could be construed as a power move, but it turns out
it can.

Her curly brown hair looks even more wild and unbrushed
than it had the last time they met, and she stifles a yawn as she
stares at Jane standing on her front step. She says nothing.

'We met,' Jane continues, 'at your husband's house earlier
this week?'

"

PI Sandra Baker never loses her keys, and would never have been so short-sighted in this investigation. Jane has let important background players slip her notice – Daisy's landlord, Johanna Carney's daughter, the curly-haired friend in those old photographs. Still, she cannot yet fully see the connection Vicky Graves has to all of this, but it is past time to find out.

'Ex-husband.' Vicky frowns, running a hand through her tangled hair. 'What is it you want?' The frown deepens, the significance of the situation perhaps dawning on her. 'I was about to go to bed. How do you have my address?'

'I don't think this is a doorstep conversation,' Jane says with a kind smile. She pushes her shoulders back, forcing herself to stand up straight and embody PI Baker. Baker wouldn't be asking, she'd be *telling*. 'I *need* to come in.'

Panic creeps into Vicky's face: the rounding of the eyes like widening ripples on water, the slight parting of the lips.

'This is all rather odd,' she says at last. 'I . . . can't think of what to say.'

'That's unusual,' Jane says, tilting her head to the side the same way Baker did when she apprehended the killer in *A Desperate Death*. 'You are *so good with words*.'

The subtext of the sentence hangs in the air between them like the lights of a firework long after the bang. Vicky nods and steps back, allowing Jane through the front door. In the corridor, she pauses.

'Give me just a moment, it's a frightful mess.' She smiles and dashes into what Jane presumes is the living room. She can hear frantic movement, the opening and closing of cupboards and the shuffle of slippered feet on the rug. A crash and a swear word. Eventually, Vicky flings open the door and invites her in.

Jane doesn't know how to feel in the presence of this woman. Part of her is impressed. She is the secret novelist of twelve works of outstanding fiction, busily working away behind the smokescreen of her husband for years. But she is also, quite possibly, a murderous criminal mastermind.

Vicky's job, her reason for being, is to create complex stories that entangle and trick, hide and reveal. Surely all great novelists, deep down, are capable of planning the perfect murder?

Does Jane have a reason for being? Are her stories good enough to claim *that* as her reason, if good enough means anything much at all? And by that measure, is she as capable as this smiling, pyjama-clad woman of planning a murder? Perhaps not. But Jane is, she realises with a burst of pride, at least capable of *solving* one.

'I'm a little surprised to see you here,' Vicky says, perching on the arm of a tan leather chair with a bemused smile.

Jane sits down on the faded sofa, sinking deep into the seat. She is too low down and feels silly, like a child waiting for a shopping mall Santa.

'May I ask again,' Vicky continues, inspecting her ragged nails rather than looking at her guest, 'how exactly you got my address? I assume my *husband* sent you?' She says the word *husband* as though it is absurd, as one might say *alien*, or *wizard*. The way Jane's mother would raise her eyebrow and say, 'The biscuits disappeared by *magic*, did they?'

Vicky gets to her feet before Jane can answer and starts to pace back and forth across the living room. The floorboards caw like a crow each time she passes a certain spot and the sound sends a needle through Jane each time.

'I'm here because . . . well, I know. I know everything. About the books, about the—'

'It's not going to work,' Vicky interrupts as she continues pacing, arms folded across the chest of her tartan pyjamas, and Jane feels instinctively that she should let her speak. 'I've told him, I'm not doing it anymore, if that's what he's sent you about. I'm going to be my *own person*.'

Vicky stops and stares out of the window.

'It all got so out of hand, the writing. But when he . . . well, I couldn't continue after that.'

Jane isn't entirely sure what Vicky is talking about. It's time to direct this conversation herself. Wishing she had her friends by her side, she shifts on the sofa and clears her throat.

'We didn't get your address from Lambert.' Vicky turns back to her in surprise. 'We got it from Scott Wallace. The ex-boyfriend of Daisy Olsson. Because, as you well know, this was also her address.'

Vicky's face turns grey, lips hardening into thin, angry lines, her eyebrows furrowed.

'I don't know what you are talking about,' she snaps. 'Daisy who? I'd like it if you left now.'

'Daisy Olsson. Or should I say Carney? The daughter of your best friend. The woman Hugo Strauss killed six years ago – Johanna. Ringing any bells?'

'How dare . . . I don't know what . . . '

'The young woman,' Jane speaks over her, and although she doesn't raise her voice, her certainty in the face of Vicky's blustering silences the other woman, 'who you took in and sent to kill Hugo Strauss, resulting not only in his death, but *hers too*. Your hands may be clean of blood, Mrs Graves, but your conscience can't be.'

Vicky's mouth opens and closes as though she hopes words might eventually appear in it, arms still folded across her chest. Jane is expecting an explosion. Of tears, of fury, or violence, she doesn't know.

Finally, after a full minute has ticked by, Vicky gently perches herself back on the arm of the chair.

'I know who you are,' she says, meeting Jane's eye. Her voice is as light and airy as a Victoria sponge, as though they are discussing the approach of autumn or the selection of biscuits in the corner shop. 'Some failed novelist. I looked you up after we met. You've got a silly detective series.' She shakes her head in derision, and Jane feels shame burn in her gut. Lambert's words at dinner surface in her mind: *My wife, ladies and gentleman. Wit as sharp as her talons.* 'That other woman you were with is just starting out, probably thinks she's some sort of hotshot. But she's already cancelled, correct? Ha! It takes a lot to survive in this game, you know. A lot. Quite an achievement to kill a career so *very* quickly though.'

Anger elbows Jane's shame aside. How dare this woman talk about her friend like this?

'And that *boy* was just some dogsbody from Polar Bear Books.' She shrugs as though Daniel is as far beneath her notice as chewing gum on the pavement. 'Where are your friends now, Miss Hepburn? Or were they not really friends, hmm? Sent you off on your own for your big Poirot moment, have they? You should focus on your own sorry life rather than meddling in the lives of others.'

'We aren't meddling in lives,' Jane manages to say with quiet dignity. 'We are meddling in death.'

'Go on,' Vicky says with resignation, throwing back her head to look up at the ceiling rose. 'Tell me your little theory then. I have things to be getting on with.'

Jane has a sickening realisation that she has played this all wrong and wishes beyond measure that her friends – and they *are* friends – were here with her now. Why had they decided Jane would get more from Vicky by going in alone, while they called for backup from DI Hawberry?

Did they expect Vicky to crack with grief, with sorrow, with regret? Instead, standing before Jane is this sneering, cruel woman with a hard face and confrontational air. Still, Jane is almost a foot taller. If it comes to it, she can overpower her. If this unexpected killer thinks she can make Jane leave – and give herself a chance to escape – with this onslaught of words, she is wrong. Jane Hepburn isn't someone who runs away.

'You were best friends with Johanna Carney. Is that correct?'

Vicky doesn't answer but instead goes to look out of the window again. Jane lets the silence hang until Vicky turns back to her with a deep, resigned sigh.

'Forgive me,' she says with a tight smile. 'I should have offered you tea.'

'Um, no, it's quite alright.'

'No, no, I won't hear of it. Besides, I can never manage to talk about . . . talk about Johanna without at least a cup of tea in my hand.' She shakes her head, curls bouncing as she moves.

Vicky disappears, leaving Jane sitting alone in the silent room, the clock on the mantelpiece ticking loudly as a bomb. Through the open door, Jane can hear the kettle starting to boil and the clinking of mugs. It reminds her of Vicky's frantic 'cleaning' of the room when she arrived and, with a guilty look at the open door, Jane gets to her feet. She moves around the room, peering under ornaments and behind the sofa. Across from her is a small bureau, and she steps over to it, wincing at the creak of the floorboard. Slowly, quietly, she slides open a drawer to find nothing but pens, Post-its and screwed up receipts.

The next one reveals stacks of half-used notepads. The third and final drawer, something else. Jane reaches in and removes the first framed photograph. Vicky Graves, at least a decade younger and a stone lighter, smiling broadly next to a breathtaking woman she recognises as Johanna Carney. It's the photo Jane saw through the window on Sunday, only she'd assumed it was of Daisy.

The next photo shows a group of six – Vicky and Lambert, Johanna and Michael, Hugo and Jessie – sitting around the dinner table at Aurum Manor, glassy-eyed and happy. Jane is marvelling at the way Johannah's smile lights up her face, the way her eyes dance in the colour between blue and green, just the way that Daisy's had, when a voice makes her jump.

'Beautiful, wasn't she?'

Jane puts down the photos guiltily. Vicky is smiling at her sadly, holding two cups of steaming tea. She places Jane's down on the coffee table and Jane returns to her seat. Vicky goes to the bureau and picks up the photo.

Jane reaches forward to collect the yellow mug from the table, old and stained with the watermarks of decades of conversations. The tea is scalding hot.

Chapter Forty-Seven

Tuesday, 11.20 p.m.

'Hugo and Lambert were friends from Oxford,' Vicky says. 'Idiots, the pair of them. Always were. Rich men who thought the world and everything in it was theirs for the taking. I met Johanna at university too, when I was studying in Stockholm. Met through Book Club and stayed best friends for decades. I'd go there a few times a year, and she came here when she could – though once she had a child it was mostly I who travelled. That weekend in Devon . . . it was a one-off that we all got together like that.'

She is lost in the photograph, staring at it with misty eyes.

'Until the accident,' Jane whispers.

'Accident? Is that what you call it?' She stands the frame lovingly on the bureau, but picks it up again at once, unable perhaps to let go of the past so easily. 'Going that fast on a dark country lane, after drinking too? Murder, I call it.'

'The court found him— '

'I'm aware what the court said,' snaps Vicky. 'But there is a gulf an ocean wide between what is wrong and what is illegal.'

Jane nods, picking up her steaming mug. She remembers the way her ex-boyfriend Stefan betrayed and belittled her. The way a bus driver had once laughed at her when she'd tried to pay with a library card. The way, when her mother died, none of the neighbours came to call. Yes, there is a gulf. The mug warms her hands as she sits in silence, watching Vicky Graves with interest. Vicky's gaze softens, and she goes again to perch on the arm of the chair, tea in hand.

'So, after Hugo was let off, what then? You told Lambert to move publishers and sign with Hugo? To get close to him?'

Vicky twists her mouth in disgust at the mention of her husband's name.

'No, I did not,' she spits, each word like a bullet. 'Years went by. Years of mourning a friend I would never be able to replace, but also years of trying to move forward. Trying to heal. We cut that man, that . . . *murderer* out of our lives, of course.

'And then *he* comes home one day, my *darling* husband. Good news! he says. Good news! Polar Bear Publishing, *the* Polar Bear, are trying to poach us!

'Well, Lambert was *delighted*. The prestige! They'd offered a stinking great sum of money to take us from Magic Box with *A Magpie's Lament* and whatever "he" wrote next. And then he just . . . let it slip. The editor, he says, Hugo Strauss, promises to take our books to the next level.

'God, was I in shock! I hadn't heard that name in years. Tried my damn' hardest to forget it, though obviously I never could. And here was Lambert, my husband, happy to cash the cheque and *work with him?* On *my* books?' Vicky is shaking with rage now. She gulps at her tea, her stubby hands tiny on the large mug. Jane recognises a faded Swedish flag just visible on the porcelain.

'Over my dead body, I tell him. How could he even *think* about it? And these were *my words* after all! My words! We had a flaming row and the subject was dropped. Until two weeks later when Lambert revealed he'd agreed it, with or without my approval.'

Vicky shrugs, smiling bitterly at Jane.

'His name *is* on the cover of all the books, after all. He thought I'd calm down. The past is in the past, it was an accident, Hugo had been punished enough, blah blah blah. But no. I packed my bags and called a lawyer. Finally saw the old dosser for what he was. An empty locket, shiny on the outside, but devoid of what should be inside – integrity, intelligence, loyalty.'

'And Daisy?' The clock is ticking and Jane wonders how the others are getting on with tracking down Hawberry. It occurs to her that this woman is a murderer who doesn't seem to feel regretful. In fact, she is being extremely open so far. And that is worrying. Because what kind of person confesses so readily to a crime and then lets the listener walk free? Jane puts her mug back down on the table and slides an Extra-Strong mint into her mouth to calm her nerves. 'Where does she come into this?'

'Daisy.' Vicky shakes her head, curls bouncing again. 'So like her mother. The night of the row with Lambert, I called Michael. He stayed in Sweden after Johanna died and we had fallen out of touch over the years, but I felt sure *he* would understand. Only, he wasn't in. And the person who answered the phone . . . oh, her voice! It was like going back in time. We switched to a video-call and she was *beautiful*. Just like Johanna back when we met. She was only a kid the last time I'd seen her.'

'Did you do it *then*? Persuade her to kill Hugo?'

Jane's mouth is dry with anticipation and dread. She is so full of confusion over what she feels for this woman. Respect? Horror?

Vicky chuckles, smiling as though she was being asked to relive a trip to the park with a toddler.

'No, no. We just talked. About Johanna mostly. I told her about Lambert and why I was calling. She told me that her dad would never talk about her mum. We bonded over that. She was sick of living in his house, but had no job, no direction, and a lot of anger. It only occurred to me after I hung up that we could be good for each other.

'A week later I rented this place and offered her a plane ticket to London and the other room, at no charge.' Vicky shrugs and raises her mug to her lips. 'We had fun together. It was almost like being back in Stockholm with Jojo.'

Jane dropped out of the Criminology course she took at university after just one term, drinking games and freshers' balls not agreeing with her. She never had a friend like Vicky, and lets herself indulge, for a moment, in lust for that life. Walking across campus, laughing arm-in- arm with someone.

'Daisy changed her surname by deed poll to her mother's when she got here. A sort of *stuff you* to her father, I think. But it suited us well. I encouraged her to renew her British passport in her new name, and she used that to get the job. Poof! Daisy Carney was gone. It really was as easy as that.'

Vicky chuckles, and Jane recoils. Vicky might be referring to an identity, but given that Daisy's life really was snuffed out in an instant, no matter what her name, the choice of words turns Jane cold.

'The idea of killing Hugo came up one night just a week into her living here, but we didn't mean it, not then. Daisy and I were drinking wine and talking about Jojo. She barely knew her mum, and I have a thousand stories about her. Lambert called and I ignored it. He called a lot during that period while I was between homes.

'I remember saying something like, *I'll never forgive him for this, just like I'll never forgive the man who took Jojo from us.* And Daisy said that at least Lambert was getting his comeuppance. Me leaving him . . . the end of his career when the truth comes out about him barely being able to write a greetings card. But Hugo – he never got that treatment. No real punishment. No consequences . . .'

Vicky trails off, staring at the clock on the mantelpiece as if it could turn back time. Jane can imagine how the idea evolved over a bottle of wine. Perhaps the next day one of them gingerly brought up the subject again, laughed it off. And again, and again, until one day the laughing stopped.

'Daisy was extremely likeable. Just like her mother, she had that incredible charm. She went to an event Hugo was throwing for one of his authors, just to get a look at the man, and ended up making friends with his assistant.

'She seemed to really like Lucy, but *I* saw it for the opportunity it was. We found out through her he was having an affair! Ha! Hardly a shock, was it? A man like that. I convinced Daisy to tell her friend it was her *duty* to speak to his wife, and she did it. Stupid of her. She got the sack, of course.' Vicky frowns down at the photo in her hand, as if wondering how she came to be holding it. 'Silly girl.'

'Then you wrote to Hugo?' Jane asks.

Vicky looks over in surprise as though she has forgotten Jane's presence.

'What? Oh, yes, you know about that, do you? I requested he give Daisy a chance at a job, said that it was the *least* he could do. He agreed, of course. What sort of heartless bastard would say no?' Vicky smiles sadly. 'Well, he *was* a heartless bastard, so it wasn't a sure thing.'

'There were scraps of the letter in his fireplace. It didn't mean anything to me at the time, but looking back . . . '

'We only ever communicated by letter. I thought that best, and he always was a man who enjoyed pretentious, old-fashioned things. I thought it would soften him up.' She nods at Jane's still-steaming mug of tea on the table. 'Drink up, it will make this conversation feel a bit less strange.'

Jane picks up her mug and cradles it in both hands. The letter she'd found in Aurum manner had been to Vicky, not Lambert. 'Did you know your plan then?'

'No, no. At that point it was all still a bit of a game. Get Daisy close to him and see what happened. We'd already helped to expose his affair and end his marriage. Maybe she could ruin his career? Doing anything too drastic would just get *her* fired, so she did little things to upset the apple cart. It was fun for a few months, but minor annoyances started to lose their charm after a while.

'It was I who suggested it, not Daisy. I want you to know that. Lambert left me some rambling voicemail one day. I had it playing while I was making my breakfast. Scrambled eggs with feta, a sprinkling of sumac,' she adds unnecessarily. 'I just heard the word in a sea of nonsense about his new jewellery-making process. Cyanide. He was using *cyanide*.'

Jane shivers despite the room being warm. To watch Vicky smiling down at the photograph of her friend, dressed in cosy tartan pyjamas and fluffy slippers and talking so freely about poison, was disturbingly incongruous.

'Well, it was all easy from there. Lambert makes these rings – poison rings they're called. It felt rather poetic in a way. I gave Daisy the money and Lambert's number. She called, full of praise, and asked to come and buy one. They aren't really for sale, his trinkets, but he is easy to flatter and said yes in the end.'

'Lambert didn't recognise her as Johanna's daughter?'

'Oh, they'd only met twice before, and not for years. Once when she was a small child, and then the weekend Johanna was killed. It was years ago, and she spent most of the time being a sulky teenager in her room. Besides, that Daisy was all grown up.'

'She stole the poison?'

'I called Lambert when she was in there and said it was *urgent* we talk. He wouldn't usually have left anyone in his gallery like that, but by then I had half-moved out and was threatening divorce – he wouldn't have missed the chance to speak to me for all the world. I kept him on the phone and out of that room long enough for Daisy to find the little drawer of powder and add a spoonful to the ring she was trying on.

'Putting it in Hugo's morning coffee was too risky, it could be traced back to her. But the launch party was going to be a big affair, everyone was going. Anyone who was there could have done it. I thought that best.'

It's unclear when all the love drained from Vicky Graves. Was it the day her friend was hit by Hugo's car? Or was it many, many months after that? Years even? Slowly dripping from her and being replaced with a bitter, cold hatred that only she, and perhaps Daisy, would mistake for love. It is scary, Jane thinks, to know that you could be one dreadful day away from losing your humanity.

'It all went wrong, of course.' Vicky looks over at her with a chilling smile. 'Well, not *all*. Hugo died. That was what we wanted. But I don't understand how Daisy died too. I really don't.'

'Hugo didn't drink alcohol,' Jane says in a whisper. 'Not since the acc— not since Johannah Carney's death. It wasn't something many people knew.'

'No, no we didn't know that. What a kicker.'

'We think some of the poisoned drink got onto his skin,' Jane continues. 'So it still killed him, just a little slower. Daisy must have drunk from his glass by mistake. I think he handed it to her and she mixed the drinks up.'

'Silly,' Vicky says with a sigh. 'Impetuous. Just like her mother.' The two of them sit in silence for a period, both thinking of beautiful, dead women and the way they met their ends. 'Well!' Vicky says finally, coming to. She gets to her feet and returns the framed photo to the bureau before turning to frown at Jane in displeasure. 'Something wrong with your tea, Miss Hepburn? Perhaps it's cold by now, what with all this talking. Shall I make you another?'

'No, no. It's quite alright. I'm not thirsty.'

'I was always told it was rude,' Vicky says with a rictus smile, 'not to drink something the host has made you.'

'Really, I'm quite . . . I think I should be g—'

Vicky Graves is on her in an instant.

Chapter Forty-Eight

Tuesday, 11.59 p.m.

Private Investigator Sandra Baker is often fighting for her life. She had to fight for it in book one, *Rush of Blood*, while the killer she was hunting tried to drown her in the river Avon. She fought for it in book six, *Killing Time*, when she'd chased a suspect down a dark alley and was hit with a leg of lamb. In book five, *A Desperate Death*, she'd fought for it on a bridge, wrestling with the killer over a steep drop. In *Death of Last Hope*, PI Baker's final outing, she'd lost the fight.

Jane Hepburn has never had to fight for her life. She has never felt the cool, sharp fear of it, the sudden desperation of knowing your time is up and the realisation that there was so, *so* much more you should have done. Strangely, it's her fictional lead character she thinks of in the moment, and how her fifth novel had been so perfectly titled. In so many ways, death really is desperate.

Vicky Graves is much smaller than Jane, but she is also angry, has the element of surprise on her side, and the only gym Jane knows is that guy from accounts. With her tartan-clad knees either side of Jane's body, Vicky closes one hand around her throat and grabs the mug of tea with the other. Jane is pushed back against the sofa cushions, too stunned to do more than blink. The pain in her throat is immediate, and the panic of air loss not far behind. Vicky rams the mug, brimming with untouched tea, towards her face.

This is when Jane remembers she has arms. She hits out at the mug, missing it by an inch. With the other hand she smacks

Vicky around the head, but not hard enough to deter the attack. Jane may be desperate, but Vicky is too. If Jane walks out of here with the truth, her life is over just as it is beginning anew.

'I have . . . no . . . choice,' Vicky pants, still trying to get the mug to Jane's mouth. 'You can't leave here, Miss Hepburn. You know that.'

The pressure on Jane's windpipe feels like a vice. The strength of her flailing arms is weakening, her vision starting to swim. The image of the wild, curly-haired woman in red tartan swims in front of her. She purses her lips ever tighter and tries to turn her face away.

'Hugo had . . . to die. And Daisy . . . made her own . . . mistakes. I won't go . . . to jail. It's MY TURN!' Vicky roars these last words, and Jane feels both the knees around her body and the hand around her throat grip even tighter, even harder, even more desperately. 'These men . . . they do nothing! Michael the *coward* did *nothing* to avenge Johanna! My *useless* husband, nothing but take, take, take! The *liar* Hugo Strauss, cheating on his wife, killing my friend!!'

Black spots appear before Jane's eyes, and she feels the last remnants of strength seep from her body. Her arm, pathetically hitting at Vicky's shoulder, flops to her side. She can still see the blurry shape of the woman on top of her, the yellow of the mug at her lips. And there is nothing, now, that Jane can do to stop it.

'I am going to be a novelist,' Vicky whispers. 'In my own name, Miss Hepburn. You understand that need, don't you? I was too easily beaten before to do that. Too cowed by Lambert with his posh voice and family money, saying someone like *me* would never be published. But now I am not. I'm going to do it. For myself, and Daisy, and Jojo. I'm going to write about *her*. And I can't let you ruin that.'

Jane feels the cool porcelain of the mug press hard against her mouth.

'Open up now,' a voice croons. 'Open up.'

The mug tips, and Jane feels the liquid, still warm, dribble down her chin. Her mouth is closed, but she can feel her ability to keep it so weakening. The bookcases, the large sash windows, the tasteful cream walls and jolly red shutters are all fading from view. The tea, laced, as Jane had started to suspect during Vicky's confession, with cyanide is dripping down her chin. She feels, or maybe only imagines, it burn against her skin. Even if Vicky doesn't get her mouth open, which seems inevitable, how much longer does she have now the poison is sinking into her pores? How many hours to cling desperately to life?

The title of her *seventh* book comes back into her hazy mind now: *Death of Last Hope*. That is coming, she thinks. That has come.

Jane can faintly hear a *bang* and is absently surprised that death starts with one, like a party. The pressure on her throat eases, as does the bony feel of sharp knees against her thighs. She imagines boarding the boat to cross the River Styx, the other side scattered with smiling faces. Johanna Carney, Daisy Olsson, Hugo Strauss. Her old literary agent, Carrie Marks. Her mother, arms outstretched. *You're never promised tomorrow, Jane,* she says in all her wisdom. *Death always comes too soon or too late.*

And then Jane feels a new, sharp, excruciating pain in her lungs as she inhales a burst of air, and is suddenly bent double, a hacking cough tearing at her chest.

Sounds come back into the room: shouting, shuffling, a crash. Jane blinks, vision clearing. She blinks again.

Vicky Graves is face down on the floor, Rosalind Hawberry on her back and pulling handcuffs from her pocket. Natasha is sitting next to Jane on the sofa, stroking her back and saying something she can't yet make out. Daniel appears in the doorway with a glass of water he presses to Jane's lips. This time, she drinks gratefully.

'You're under arrest, Ms Graves,' DI Hawberry is saying, 'for aiding and abetting the murder of Hugo Strauss, for your part in the death of Daisy Olsson, and for the attempted murder of Jane Hepburn. You do not have to say anything . . . '

Jane's throat hurts, her head hurts, her lungs hurt. But there is something else too. A sickness in her stomach, a pounding in her head. Is her breathing short because of her bruised windpipe, or because of the poison on her skin? She looks up at Natasha and tries to speak, but her throat feels blocked.

'What is it, Jane? What are you trying to say?'

Hospital, she tries again. *Help.*

Then, a few things happen all at once.

Wriggling under the weight of DI Hawberry, Vicky Graves lunges forward and grabs the mug of tea lying on the carpet, mostly empty but not completely. Jane's breathing, briefly relieved, starts to feel tight again and she slams a hand to her chest.

Vicky brings up the mug and pours the last dregs of tea into her mouth. She slams it down and locks eyes with Jane as she says, 'I'm sorry, Ms Hepburn. "Thy drugs are quick."'

Chapter Forty-Nine

Wednesday, 12.15 a.m.

There is something about being on the verge of death that really puts things into perspective.

In the ambulance, an oxygen mask is fitted over Jane's face while the paramedics check her vitals and thoroughly clean the skin touched by the poisoned tea. She is rushed through to the Emergency Room on a trolley, doctors barking incomprehensible updates as she glides through the busy scene.

Once sequestered in a private room, a nurse pushes a needle into a vein in Jane's right arm, hooking her up to an IV drip containing Hydroxocobalamin, a chemical which will bind with the cyanide in her bloodstream. Another nurse simultaneously pierces a vein on her left arm, connecting her to a second IV drip containing Sodium Thiosulfate which will work to convert the cyanide into a less toxic substance.

A third nurse removes her clothes and washes, again, any skin that the poison may have touched. A doctor checks her heart rate, her blood-oxygen levels, her blood's PH levels, her breathing.

Outside in the waiting room, Daniel and Natasha pace, not looking at each other or speaking but only hoping and praying to gods they don't really believe in that their friend will make it.

Down the hallway, in another room with another doctor, another team of nurses, Victoria Graves is pronounced dead from acute cyanide poisoning. She died before even reaching the hospital, her respiratory system shutting down in the ambulance after she had knowingly drunk a cup of tea to which she'd added a spoonful of poison as though it were sugar.

Jane Hepburn doesn't know any of this, of course, because she is drifting in and out of consciousness throughout. But she does know, when she fully awakes to see her friends smiling down at her, that she is very lucky, very loved, and that no longer having a job at Baxter's Insurance doesn't matter one jot.

It's two days after Jane confronted Vicky Graves, two days after she was poisoned and Vicky gulped down the mug of tea to avoid the looming consequences of her actions. Jane has been in hospital ever since, being monitored by the doctors, resting, and finishing *A Magpie's Lament*. Sure, the author might have tried to murder her, but it is still a good book.

When the door of her room creaks open, she folds down the page and looks up to see Natasha and Daniel peering in at her.

'You still getting out today, Baker?' Daniel says, flopping down on the chair next to the bed with a soft smile instead of his usual trademark grin. His floppy chocolate-brown hair forms a scruffy halo around his beautiful face. He leans across and hugs her, lying almost flat against her bed-bound body.

'Hopefully,' she says, her voice still low and croaky from where Vicky Graves bruised her throat. 'Once the doctor has been round to check me over one last time.

'Has your work been okay about it all?'

'Oh, didn't I tell you?' she says with a smile. 'There was so much going on. I quit. Just before we tracked down Fontaine and everything got rather out of hand.' Daniel whoops and does a celebratory jig while Natasha perches on the end of the bed and gives her a gentle hug. Jane doesn't tell them about the other email she sent in that wild moment of confidence – that of the first three chapters of her new novel to Marabella Rhodes.

'Brave Baker,' Daniel says with a grin. 'Stupid maybe, but brave.'

'Never mind that now,' Jane says, waving it away. 'How is . . . everyone else?'

Natasha perches on the end of the bed and gives a small, sad shrug. 'DI Hawberry got a pat on the back from her boss, despite not having anyone to arrest. At least they can put the case to bed. Apparently, they were just starting to connect the dots between Daisy's identities – her bank account only went back nine months and they couldn't find anything about her from before that time. Hawberry said they had border control searching through records of people who matched Daisy's description entering the country nine months ago.'

'Michael Carney didn't know anything apparently,' Daniel adds. 'I mean, he knew his daughter moved in with Vicky, but he thought it might be good for her. He had no idea that she was plotting murder, or even that she was working with Hugo. Didn't even know his daughter was dead, poor guy. Apparently, it wasn't unusual not to hear from her for a week or so. Seems mad to me that the police didn't connect it all sooner though.'

Jane shakes her head. 'Daisy was half-British, so she would have had dual citizenship. She legally changed her name and the only ID they found was the British passport saying Olsson. It was all above board on the surface. Would only have come to light when they started digging deeper.' She remembers again that flash of red in the Graveses' study. 'I remember seeing a passport on Vicky's desk. Must have been Daisy's Swedish one – she must have taken it from the apartment to keep it away from the police.'

They sit in silence for a beat, each mentally tracing the steps of the investigation.

'And . . . Vicky's funeral?' Jane says at last, her voice cracking on the name.

'Next week,' Daniel says shortly. He turns to look out of the window, face hard. Clearly, he isn't ready to forgive the woman, even in death.

Jane has had a lot of time to think since nearly dying, but she still isn't sure what to make of the people she has met over the last week. Was Daisy Olsson, née Carney, a heartless murderer or just an angry, motherless woman steered down the wrong path to her death? Someone used as a tool in a plot that broke her in the process. If she had lived, would she have got away with the crime? Would it have haunted her, or would she have found her conscience clear and justice done? It was impossible, of course, to know.

Vicky Graves was used as a tool in another way. Her overbearing husband taking her work and rightful glory, pressing her down into something smaller and more insignificant as the years passed until finally, too compact to shrink any further, she pushed back. A woman whose best friend was taken from her by a careless man behind the wheel of a car, and who was lonely ever since. A woman who had had enough of the men around her taking what was hers, and in striking back didn't care how many of them she struck down. A woman who, at the very end, couldn't let any more be taken from her, so took her own life instead.

Lambert, a fraud and a chancer. Scott, a misfit who found hiding behind personas easier than occupying his own skin, but also a deeply lonely man. Lucy Tallow, lonely too, so starved for closeness that she is willing to overlook any number of failures in order to get even an approximation of it. Jane makes a mental note to call her when she is out of hospital.

And what has Jane learnt about herself? Maybe just that life can be short, that life can be cruel, but also that it can be full of people who will be by your bedside when you wake up after being strangled and poisoned with cyanide by a small, curly-haired maniac.

That despite everything – her lack of a job and her failed writing and being too tall and too broad and too plain and too clumsy – she is no longer lonely, and that is such a beautiful gift.

'I grabbed this from the lobby,' Natasha says, pulling a copy of the *Daily News* from her bag and spreading it out on Jane's knees. The handsome face of Lambert Graves stares up at them, his golden hair pushed back in its perfect quiff. In the photograph, he is looking over his shoulder, his usually twinkling eyes narrowed in a shifty manner.

GRAVE CONSEQUENCES

Celebrated Author Lambert Graves Exposed as Fraud Following Wife's Death

Jane skims the article, Daniel and Natasha gathering around the bed. It is generously sprinkled with 'allegedlys', but the journalist has uncovered the meat of the story.

Following the suicide of Victoria Graves, 52, who is allegedly linked to the murders of both Daisy Olsson and Hugo Strauss (see page 3), Lambert Graves has been exposed as a fraud. His ex-butler Mr Gary Staines says, 'Lambert can't write to save his damned life. The man can barely hold a pen. He is as intellectual as a grapefruit.'

It is alleged that the late wife of Mr Graves, Victoria, was the true author of the works sold under his name, totalling 12 bestselling novels including one Booker Prize winner. Since the couple's separation earlier this year, the *Daily News* can exclusively disclose that Lambert Graves has failed to deliver the novel contracted to his new publisher, Polar Bear. According to Mr Staines, Graves has . . .

Daniel chuckles and Jane leans back on her pillow, smiling, while Natasha picks up the paper to read the rest of the article. Consequences do have a way of finding people, however hard they try to hide from them.

'This is good news for you, Nat, I suppose?' Daniel says when he has composed himself. 'Now this has been cleared up, maybe your book will go back on the shelves? The whole cursed author thing should die down?'

'Oh, it already has,' she says, looking up from the newspaper with a smile. 'Marabella called me this morning saying that booksellers are actually even *more* keen on the book now than they were in the beginning. Willow Tree Books has made it their book of the month. It's getting window displays, the reviews that were held back are going to run. Even TikTok has taken a turn.'

In the back of her mind, Jane hears her mother's comforting voice. *Into each life some rain must fall, but you know what they say: rain makes the flowers grow.* On her bedside table, her phone pings with a text message. It's from Detective Inspector Ramos, and her heart gives a little leap of joy at the thought of his comforting presence.

> Hope you're holding up, Sergeant. Heard Hawberry got a thumbs up for your hard work. How about I buy you a drink to celebrate when you make it back up North? X

That X again, sitting there innocently. What on earth could he mean by it? Tiredness is washing over her and the thought of the long journey back to Cumbria feels daunting. She'll sleep on the train, she imagines, head against the window, mouth slightly open in an unflattering manner.

Jane is about to put away her phone when she notices a small, red number over the envelope icon, informing her of one new email. Probably junk, or her P45 from Baxter's Insurance.

Even so, she opens it, her eyes widening word by word.

Daniel and Natasha are busy chattering about the details revealed in the newspaper article. It's Natasha who finally notices Jane's silence as she lies stock still, staring at her phone screen.

'Jane?' she says tentatively. 'Everything okay?'

'Um, yes?' Jane says, her voice cracking and coming out sounding like a budgerigar's cheep.

Jane Hepburn glances up at the worried looks of her friends, feeling a smile spread over her exhausted face. A plain face, she's always thought, on a nothing special woman. But after all, who decides who is special, after all?

'Yes,' she says, leaning her head back on her pillow and closing her eyes. 'Things are very much going to be okay.'

From: Marabella@RhodesLitAgency.com
To: JaneHepburn_007@hotmail.co.uk

Dear Ms Hepburn,

Thank you for sending over the outline of your new novel, *The First Murder*, along with the opening chapters. Although I would not usually take on a client from such a short sample, I have read your previous work and this, along with your new outline, is enough to convince me of your obvious talent.

I believe that the idea for the new series you have put forward has potential to be *far* bigger than the PI Sandra Baker series, and I'm excited about where this could lead.

This being the case, I am delighted to offer you representation as your literary agent going forward and have attached an agency agreement for you to look over. I am excited to work with you not only on this book, but on all of your future writing.

Best wishes,

Marabella Rhodes
Rhodes Literary Agency

Acknowledgements

Writing this book was difficult. Being an author may be the best job in the world but the 'book two curse' definitely paid me a visit with *A Killer Plot*. Still, I got to the end, I redrafted, I panicked, I redrafted some more, and eventually we got there. Many people made this experience bearable and they deserve recognition for it.

As always, thanks to my agent Hannah Todd, who is fun and fierce and deserves all of the success coming to her. Thanks, too, to the rest of the team at Janklow & Nesbit, especially to Mina Yakinya for everything she does to keep the wheel turning, and Janet Covindassamy for bringing Jane to Japan.

To Melissa Cox, my editor and friend, who is insightful and clever – thank you for helping untangle this book and beat it into shape. Alongside her, thanks to the magnificent Morgan Hamilton in the US, who worked with us on the edits and was instrumental in shaping this book.

To the whole Bonnier team (Leonie Lock, Melissa Kelly, Kelly Samler, Kasim Mohammed, Beth Whitelaw, Eleanor Stammeijer, Alex Kirby, Alex May and Evie Kettlewell), the PRH team, and the Canadian team – publishing a book takes a small army, and I'm grateful for the care and hard work at every stage.

To my parents, Annie and Simon, for their unwavering love and support, as always. To my brothers Rich, Luke and Patrick; to my sisters-in-law Anaïs and Ro; to my nieces and nephews; and to my new parents-in-laws, Marcia and Tony. My family seems to just get bigger and bigger over time, which is a joy and a privilege.

To wonderful friends, who I won't list but hopefully know who they are. Special thanks to the publishing gals who listen to me whine about this side of the process, give advice and tell me how brilliant I am (compliments are apparently my fuel).

To my husband, Rob. We got engaged while I was writing this and married while I was editing it. Thank you for listening to me panic about writing this book, encouraging me when I thought I couldn't do it, bringing me tea, bigging me up when I'm too awkward to do it myself, and grasping every tiny excuse for a celebration milestone. Mostly thanks for being a great partner who is always up for an adventure of one sort or another.

Finally, thank you to any readers who found Jane Hepburn in *A Novel Murder* and followed her here. She's not done yet.